The Historical Nights' Entertainment: First Series

Rafael Sabatini

PREFACE

In approaching "The Historical Nights' Entertainment" I set myself the task of reconstructing, in the fullest possible detail and with all the colour available from surviving records, a group of more or less famous events. I would select for my purpose those which were in themselves bizarre and resulting from the interplay of human passions, and whilst relating each of these events in the form of a story, I would compel that story scrupulously to follow the actual, recorded facts without owing anything to fiction, and I would draw upon my imagination, if at all, merely as one might employ colour to fill in the outlines which history leaves grey, taking care that my colour should be as true to nature as possible. For dialogue I would depend upon such scraps of actual speech as were chronicled in each case, amplifying it by translating into terms of speech the paraphrases of contemporary chroniclers.

Such was the task I set myself. I am aware that it has been attempted once or twice already, beginning, perhaps, with the "Crimes Celebres" of Alexandre Dumas. I am not aware that the attempt has ever succeeded. This is not to say that I claim success in the essays that follow. How nearly I may have approached success -judged by the standard I had set myself - how far I may have fallen short, my readers will discern. I am conscious, however, of having in the main dutifully resisted the temptation to take the easier road, to break away from restricting fact for the sake of achieving a more intriguing narrative. In one instance, however, I have quite deliberately failed, and in some others I have permitted myself certain speculations to resolve mysteries of which no explanation has been discovered. Of these it is necessary that I should make a full confession.

My deliberate failure is "The Night of Nuptials. " I discovered an allusion to the case of Charles the Bold and Sapphira Danvelt in Macaulay's "History of England" - quoted from an old number of the "Spectator" - whilst I was working upon the case of Lady Alice Lisle. There a similar episode is mentioned as being related of Colonel Kirke, but discredited because known for a story that has a trick of springing up to attach itself to unscrupulous captains. I set out to track it to its source, and having found its first appearance to be in connection with Charles the Bold's German captain Rhynsault, I attempted to reconstruct the event as it might have happened, setting it at least in surroundings of solid fact.

My most flagrant speculation occurs in "The Night of Hate. " But in defence of it I can honestly say that it is at least no more flagrant than the speculations on this subject that have become enshrined in history as facts. In other words, I claim for my reconstruction of the circumstances attending the mysterious death of Giovanni Borgia, Duke of Gandia, that it no more lacks historical authority than do any other of the explanatory narratives adopted by history to assign the guilt to Gandia's brother, Cesare Borgia.

In the "Cambridge Modern History" our most authoritative writers on this epoch have definitely pronounced that there is no evidence acceptable to historians to support the view current for four centuries that Cesare Borgia was the murderer.

Elsewhere I have dealt with this at length. Here let it suffice to say that it was not until nine months after the deed that the name of Cesare Borgia was first associated with it; that public opinion had in the mean time assigned the guilt to a half-dozen others in succession; that no motive for the crime is discoverable in the case of Cesare; that the motives advanced will not bear examination, and that they bear on the face of them the stamp of having been put forward hastily to support an accusation unscrupulously political in purpose; that the first men accused by the popular voice were the Cardinal Vice-Chancellor Ascanio Sforza and his nephew Giovanni Sforza, Tyrant of Pesaro; and, finally, that in Matarazzo's "Chronicles of Perugia" there is a fairly detailed account of how the murder was perpetrated by the latter.

Matarazzo, I confess, is worthy of no more credit than any other of the contemporary reporters of common gossip. But at least he is worthy of no less. And it is undeniable that in Sforza's case a strong motive for the murder was not lacking.

My narrative in "The Night of Hate" is admittedly a purely theoretical account of the crime. But it is closely based upon all the known facts of incidence and of character; and if there is nothing in the surviving records that will absolutely support it, neither is there anything that can absolutely refute it.

In "The Night of Masquerade" I am guilty of quite arbitrarily discovering a reason to explain the mystery of Baron Bjelke's sudden change from the devoted friend and servant of Gustavus III of Sweden into his most bitter enemy. That speculation is quite indefensible, although affording a possible explanation of that mystery. In the case of "The Night of Kirk o' Field, " on the other hand, I do not think any apology is necessary for my reconstruction of the precise manner in which Darnley met his death. The event has long been looked upon as one of the mysteries of history - the mystery lying in the fact that whilst the house at Kirk o' Field was destroyed by an explosion, Darnley's body was found at some distance away, together with that of his page, bearing every evidence of death by strangulation. The explanation I adopt seems to me to owe little to speculation.

In the story of Antonio Perez - "The Night of Betrayal" - I have permitted myself fewer liberties with actual facts than might appear. I have closely followed his own "Relacion, " which, whilst admittedly a piece of special pleading, must remain the most authoritative document of the events with which it deals. All that I have done has been to reverse the values as Perez presents them, throwing the personal elements into higher relief than the political ones, and laying particular stress upon the matter of his relations with the Princess of Eboli. "The Night of Betrayal" is presented in the form of a story within a story. Of the containing story let me say that whilst to some extent it is fictitious, it is by no means entirely so. There is enough to justify most of it in the "Relaciori" itself.

The exceptions mentioned being made, I hope it may be found that I have adhered rigorously to my purpose of owing nothing to invention in my attempt to flesh and clothe these few bones of history.

I should add, perhaps, that where authorities differ as to motives, where there is a conflict of evidence as to the facts themselves, or where the facts admit of more than one interpretation, I have permitted myself to be selective, and confined myself to a point of view adopted at the outset.

R. S.

LONDON, August, 1917

CONTENTS

I. THE NIGHT OF HOLYROOD

The Murder of David Rizzio

The tragedy of my Lord Darnley's life lay in the fact that he was a man born out of his proper station - a clown destined to kingship by the accident of birth and fortune. By the blood royal flowing in his veins, he could, failing others, have claimed succession to both the English and the Scottish thrones, whilst by his marriage with Mary Stuart he made a definite attempt to possess himself of that of Scotland.

The Queen of Scots, enamoured for a season of the clean-limbed grace and almost feminine beauty ("ladyfaced, " Melville had called him once) of this "long lad of nineteen" who came a-wooing her, had soon discovered, in matrimony, his vain, debauched, shiftless, and cowardly nature. She had married him in July of 1565, and by Michaelmas she had come to know him for just a lovely husk of a man, empty of heart or brain; and the knowledge transmuted affection into contempt.

Her natural brother, the Earl of Murray, had opposed the marriage, chiefly upon the grounds that Darnley was a Catholic, and with Argyll, Chatellerault, Glencairn, and a host of other Protestant lords, had risen in arms against his sovereign and her consort. But Mary had chased her rebel brother and his fellows over the border into England, and by this very action, taken for the sake of her worthless husband, she sowed the first seeds of discord between herself and him. It happened that stout service had been rendered her in this affair by the arrogant border ruffian, the Earl of Bothwell. Partly to reward him, partly because of the confidence with which he inspired her, she bestowed upon him the office of Lieutenant-General of the East, Middle, and West Marches - an office which Darnley had sought for his father, Lennox. That was the first and last concerted action of the royal couple. Estrangement grew thereafter between them, and, in a measure, as it grew so did Darnley's kingship, hardly established as yet - for the Queen had still to redeem her pre-nuptial promise to confer upon him the crown matrimonial - begin to dwindle.

At first it had been "the King and Queen, " or "His Majesty and Hers"; but by Christmas - five months after the wedding - Darnley was known simply as "the Queen's husband, " and in all documents the Queen's name now took precedence of his, whilst coins bearing their two heads, and the legend "Hen. et Maria, " were called in and substituted by a new coinage relegating him to the second place.

Deeply affronted, and seeking anywhere but in himself and his own shortcomings the cause of the Queen's now manifest hostility, he presently conceived that he had found it in the influence exerted upon her by the Seigneur Davie - that Piedmontese, David Rizzio, who had come to the Scottish Court some four years ago as a starveling minstrel in the train of Monsieur de Morette, the ambassador of Savoy.

It was Rizzio's skill upon the rebec that had first attracted Mary's attention. Later he had become her secretary for French affairs and the young Queen, reared amid the elegancies of the Court of France, grew attached to him as to a fellow-exile in the uncouth and turbulent land over which a harsh destiny ordained that she should rule. Using his opportunities and his subtle Italian intelligence, he had advanced so rapidly that soon there was no man in Scotland who stood higher with the Queen. When Maitland of Lethington was dismissed under suspicion of favouring the exiled Protestant lords, the Seigneur Davie succeeded him as her secretary; and now that Morton was under the same suspicion, it was openly said that the Seigneur Davie would be made chancellor in his stead.

Thus the Seigneur Davie was become the most powerful man in Scotland, and it is not to be dreamt that a dour, stiff-necked nobility would suffer it without demur. They intrigued against him, putting it abroad, amongst other things, that this foreign upstart was an emissary, of the Pope's, scheming to overthrow the Protestant religion in Scotland. But in the duel that followed their blunt Scotch wits were no match for his Italian subtlety. Intrigue as they might his power remained unshaken. And then, at last it began to be whispered that he owed his high favour with the beautiful young Queen to other than his secretarial abilities, so that Bedford wrote to Cecil:

"What countenance the Queen shows David I will not write, for the honour due to the person of a queen. "

This bruit found credit - indeed, there have been ever since those who have believed it - and, as it spread, it reached the ears of

Darnley. Because it afforded him an explanation of the Queen's hostility, since he was without the introspection that would have discovered the true explanation in his own shortcomings, he flung it as so much fuel upon the seething fires of his rancour, and became the most implacable of those who sought the ruin of Rizzio.

He sent for Ruthven, the friend of Murray and the exiled lords - exiled, remember, on Darnley's own account - and offered to procure the reinstatement of those outlaws if they would avenge his honour and make him King of Scots in something more than name.

Ruthven, sick of a mortal illness, having risen from a bed of pain to come in answer to that summons, listened dourly to the frothing speeches of that silly, lovely boy.

"No doubt you'll be right about yon fellow Davie, " he agreed sombrely, and purposely he added things that must have outraged Darnley's every feeling as king and as husband. Then he stated the terms on which Darnley might count upon his aid.

"Early next month Parliament is to meet over the business of a Bill of Attainder against Murray and his friends, declaring them by their rebellion to have forfeited life, land, and goods. Ye can see the power with her o' this foreign fiddler, that it drives her so to attaint her own brother. Murray has ever hated Davie, knowing too much of what lies 'twixt the Queen and him to her dishonour, and Master Davie thinks so to make an end of Murray and his hatred. "

Darnley clenched teeth and hands, tortured by the craftily administered poison.

"What then? What is to do? " he cried,

Ruthven told him bluntly.

"That Bill must never pass. Parliament must never meet to pass it. You are Her Grace's husband and King of Scots. "

"In name! " sneered Darnley bitterly.

"The name will serve, " said Ruthven. "In that name ye'll sign me a bond of formal remission to Murray and his friends for all their actions and quarrels, permitting their safe return to Scotland, and charging the lieges to convoy them safely. Do that and leave the rest to us. "

If Darnley hesitated at all, it was not because he perceived the irony of the situation - that he himself, in secret opposition to the Queen, should sign the pardon of those who had rebelled against her precisely because she had taken him to husband. He hesitated because indecision was inherent in his nature.

"And then? " he asked at last.

Ruthven's blood-injected eyes considered him stonily out of a livid, gleaming face.

"Then, whether you reign with her or without her, reign you shall as King o' Scots. I pledge myself to that, and I pledge those others, so that we have the bond. "

Darnley sat down to sign the death warrant of the Seigneur Davie.

It was the night of Saturday, the 9th of March,

A fire of pine logs burned fragrantly on the hearth of the small closet adjoining the Queen's chamber, suffusing it with a sense of comfort, the greater by contrast with the cheerlessness out of doors, where an easterly wind swept down from Arthur's Seat and moaned its dismal way over a snowclad world.

The lovely, golden-headed young queen supped with a little company of intimates: her natural sister, the Countess of Argyll, the Commendator of Holyrood, Beaton, the Master of the Household, Arthur Erskine, the Captain of the Guard, and one other - that, David Rizzio, who from an errant minstrel had risen to this perilous eminence, a man of a swarthy, ill-favoured countenance redeemed by the intelligence that glowed in his dark eyes, and of a body so slight and fragile as to seem almost misshapen. His age was not above thirty, yet indifferent health, early privation, and misfortune had so set their mark upon him that he had all the appearance of a man of fifty. He was dressed with sombre magnificence, and a jewel of great price smouldered upon the middle finger of one of his slender, delicate hands.

Supper was at an end. The Queen lounged on a long seat over against the tapestried wall. The Countess of Argyll, in a tall chair on the Queen's left, sat with elbows on the table watching the Seigneur Davie's fine fingers as they plucked softly at the strings of a long-necked lute. The talk, which, intimate and untrammelled, had lately been of the child of which Her Majesty was to be delivered some three months hence, was flagging now, and it was to fill the gap that Rizzio had taken up the lute.

His harsh countenance was transfigured as he caressed the strings, his soul absorbed in the theme of his inspiration. Very softly - indeed, no more than tentatively as yet - he was beginning one of those wistful airs in which his spirit survives in Scotland to this day, when suddenly the expectant hush was broken by a clash of curtain-rings. The tapestries that masked the door had been swept aside, and on the threshold, unheralded, stood the tall, stripling figure of the young King.

Darnley's appearance abruptly scattered the Italian's inspiration. The melody broke off sharply on the single loud note of a string too rudely plucked.

That and the silence that followed it irked them all, conveying a sense that here something had been broken which never could be made whole again.

Darnley shuffled forward. His handsome face was pale save for the two burning spots upon his cheekbones, and his eyes glittered feveredly. He had been drinking, so much was clear; and that he should seek the Queen thus, who so seldom sought her sober, angered those intimates who had come to share her well-founded dislike of him. King though he might be in name, into such contempt was he fallen that not one of them rose in deference, whilst Mary herself watched his approach with hostile, mistrusting eyes.

"What is it, my lord? " she asked him coldly, as he flung himself down on the settle beside her.

He leered at her, put an arm about her waist, pulled her to him, and kissed her oafishly.

None stirred. All eyes were upon them, and all faces blank. After all, he was the King and she his wife. And then upon the silence, ominous as the very steps of doom, came a ponderous, clanking tread from the ante-room beyond. Again the curtains were thrust aside, and the Countess of Argyll uttered a gasp of sudden fear at the grim spectre she beheld there. It was a figure armed as for a tourney, in gleaming steel from head to foot, girt with a sword, the right hand resting upon the hilt of the heavy dagger in the girdle. The helmet's vizor was raised, revealing the ghastly face of Ruthven - so ghastly that it must have seemed the face of a dead man but for the blazing life in the eyes that scanned the company. Those questing eyes went round the table, settled upon Rizzio, and seemed horribly to smile.

Startled, disquieted by this apparition, the Queen half rose, Darnley's hindering arm still flung about her waist.

"What's this? " she cried, her voice sharp.

And then, as if she guessed intuitively what it might portend, she considered her husband with pale-faced contempt.

"Judas! " she called him, flung away from his detaining arm, and stood forth to confront that man in steel. "What seek ye here, my lord - and in this guise? " was her angry challenge.

Ruthven's burning eyes fell away before her glance. He clanked forward a step or two, flung out a mailed arm, and with a hand that shook pointed to the Seigneur Davie, who stood blankly watching him.

"I seek yon man, " he said gruffly. "Let him come forth. "

"He is here by my will, " she told him, her anger mounting. "And so are not you - for which you shall be made to answer. "

Then to Darnley, who sat hunched on the settle:

"What does this mean, sir? " she demanded.

"Why - how should I know? Why - why, nothing, " he faltered foolishly.

"Pray God that you are right, " said she, "for your own sake. And you, " she continued, addressing Ruthven again and waving a hand in imperious dismissal, "be you gone, and wait until I send for you, which I promise you shall be right soon. "

If she divined some of the evil of their purpose, if any fear assailed her, yet she betrayed nothing of it. She was finely tempered steel.

But Ruthven, sullen and menacing, stood his ground.

"Let yon man come forth, " he repeated. "He has been here ower lang. "

"Over long? " she echoed, betrayed by her quick resentment.

"Aye, ower lang for the good o' Scotland and your husband, " was the brutal answer.

Erskine, of her guards, leapt to his feet.

"Will you begone, sir? " he cried; and after him came Beaton and the Commendator, both echoing the captain's threatening question.

A smile overspread Ruthven's livid face. The heavy dagger flashed from his belt.

"My affair is not with any o' ye, but if ye thrust yersels too close upon my notice - "

The Queen stepped clear of the table to intervene, lest violence should be done here in her presence. Rizzio, who had risen, stood now beside her, watching all with a white, startled face. And then, before more could be said, the curtains were torn away and half a score of men, whose approach had passed unnoticed, poured into the room. First came Morton, the Chancellor, who was to be dispossessed of the great seal in Rizzio's favour. After him followed the brutal Lindsay of the Byres, Kerr of Faudonside, black-browed Brunston, red-headed Douglas, and a half-dozen others.

Confusion ensued; the three men of the Queen's household were instantly surrounded and overpowered. In the brief, sharp struggle the table was overturned, and all would have been in darkness but that as the table went over the Countess of Argyll had snatched up the candle-branch, and stood now holding it aloft to light that extraordinary scene. Rizzio, to whom the sight of Morton had been as the removal of his last illusion, flung himself upon his knees before the Queen. Frail and feeble of body, and never a man of his hands, he was hopelessly unequal to the occasion.

"Justice, madame! " he cried. "Faites justice! Sauvez ma vie! "

Fearlessly, she stepped between him and the advancing horde of murderers, making of her body a buckler for his protection. White of face, with heaving bosom and eyes like two glowing sapphires, she confronted them.

"Back, on your lives! " she bade them.

But they were lost to all sense of reverence, even to all sense of decency, in their blind rage against this foreign upstart who had trampled their Scottish vanity in the dust. George Douglas, without regard for her condition either as queen or woman - and a woman almost upon the threshold of motherhood - clapped a pistol to her breast and roughly bade her stand aside.

Undaunted, she looked at him with eyes that froze his trigger-finger, whilst behind her Rizzio grovelled in his terror, clutching her petticoat. Thus, until suddenly she was seized about the waist and half dragged, half-lifted aside by Darnley, who at the same time spurned Rizzio forward with his foot.

The murderers swooped down upon their prey. Kerr of Faudonside flung a noose about his body, and drew it tight with a jerk that pulled the secretary from his knees. Then he and Morton took the rope between them, and so dragged their victim across the room towards the door. He struggled blindly as he went, vainly clutching first at an overset chair, then at a leg of the table, and screeching piteously the while to the Queen to save him. And Mary, trembling with passion, herself struggling in the arms of Darnley, flung an angry warning after them.

"If Davie's blood be spilt, it shall be dear blood to some of you! Remember that, sirs! "

But they were beyond control by now, hounds unleashed upon the quarry of their hate. Out of her presence Morton and Douglas dragged him, the rest of the baying pack going after them. They dragged him, screeching still, across the ante-chamber to the head of the great stairs, and there they fell on him all together, and so wildly that they wounded one another in their fury to rend him into pieces. The tattered body, gushing blood from six-and-fifty wounds, was hurled from top to bottom of the stairs, with a gold-hilted dagger - Darnley's, in token of his participation in the deed - still sticking in his breast.

Ruthven stood forward from the group, his reeking poniard clutched in his right hand, a grin distorting his ghastly, vulturine face. Then he stalked back alone into the royal presence, dragging his feet a little, like a man who is weary.

He found the room much as he had left it, save that the Queen had sunk back to her seat on the settle, and Darnley was now standing over her, whilst her people were still hemmed about by his own men. Without a "by your leave, " he flung himself into a chair and called hoarsely for a cup of wine.

Mary's white face frowned at him across the room.

"You shall yet drink the wine that I shall pour you for this night's work, my lord, and for this insolence! Who gave you leave to sit before me? "

He waved a hand as if to dismiss the matter. It may have seemed to him frivolous to dwell upon such a trifle amid so much.

"It's no' frae lack o' respect, Your Grace, " he growled, "but frae lack o' strength. I am ill, and I should ha' been abed but for what was here to do. "

"Ah! " She looked at him with cold repugnance. "What have you done with Davie? "

He shrugged, yet his eyes quailed before her own.

"He'll be out yonder, " he answered, grimly evasive; and he took the wine one of his followers proffered him.

"Go see, " she bade the Countess.

And the Countess, setting the candle-branch upon the buffet, went out, none attempting to hinder her.

Then, with narrowed eyes, the Queen watched Ruthven while he drank.

"It will be for the sake of Murray and his friends that you do this, " she said slowly. "Tell me, my lord, what great kindness is there between Murray and you that, to save him from forfeiture, you run the risk of being forfeited with him? "

"What I have done, " he said, "I have done for others, and under a bond that shall hold me scatheless. "

"Under a bond? " said she, and now she looked up at Darnley, standing ever at her side. "And was the bond yours, my lord? "

"Mme? " He started back. "I know naught of it. "

But as he moved she saw something else. She leaned forward, pointing to the empty sheath at his girdle.

"Where is your dagger, my lord? " she asked him sharply.

"My dagger? Ha! How should I know? "

"But I shall know! " she threatened, as if she were not virtually a prisoner in the hands of these violent men who had invaded her palace and dragged Rizzio from her side. "I shall not rest until I know! "

The Countess came in, white to the lips, bearing in her eyes something of the horror she had beheld.

"What is it? " Mary asked her, her voice suddenly hushed and faltering.

"Madame-he is dead! Murdered! " she announced.

The Queen looked at her, her face of marble. Then her voice came hushed and tense:

"Are - you sure? "

"Myself I saw his body, madame. "

There was a long pause. A low moan escaped the Queen, and her lovely eyes were filled with tears; slowly these coursed down her cheeks. Something compelling in her grief hushed every voice, and the craven husband at her side shivered as her glance fell upon him once more.

"And is it so? " she said at length, considering him. She dried her eyes. "Then farewell tears; I must study revenge. " She rose as if with labour, and standing, clung a moment to the table's edge. A moment she looked at Ruthven, who sat glooming there, dagger in one hand and empty wine-cup in the other; then her glance passed on, and came to rest balefully on Darnley's face. "You have had your will, my lord, " she said, "but consider well what I now say. Consider and remember. I shall never rest until I give you as sore a heart as I have presently. "

That said she staggered forward. The Countess hastened to her, and leaning upon her arm, Mary passed through the little door of the closet into her chamber.

That night the common bell was rung, and Edinburgh roused in alarm. Bothwell, Huntly, Atholl, and others who were at Holyrood when Rizzio was murdered, finding it impossible to go to the Queen's assistance, and fearing to share the secretary's fate - for the palace was a-swarm with the murderers' men-at-arms - had escaped by one of the windows. The alarm they spread in Edinburgh brought the provost and townsmen in arms to the palace by torchlight, demanding to see the Queen, and refusing to depart until Darnley had shown himself and assured them that all was well with the Queen and with himself. And what time Darnley gave them this reassurance from a window of her room, Mary herself stood pale and taut amid the brutal horde that on this alarm had violated the privacy of her chamber, while the ruffianly Red Douglas flashed his dagger before her eyes, swearing that if she made a sound they would cut her into collops.

When at last they withdrew and left her to herself, they left her no illusions as to her true condition. She was a prisoner in her own palace. The ante-rooms and courts were thronged with the soldiers of Morton and Ruthven, the palace itself was hemmed about, and none might come or go save at the good pleasure of the murderers.

At last Darnley grasped the authority he had coveted. He dictated forthwith a proclamation which was read next morning at Edinburgh Market Cross - commanding that the nobles who had assembled in Edinburgh to compose the Parliament that was to pass the Bill of Attainder should quit the city within three hours, under pain of treason and forfeiture.

And meanwhile, with poor Rizzio's last cry of "justice! " still ringing in her ears, Mary sat alone in her chamber, studying revenge as she had promised. So that life be spared her, justice, she vowed, should be done - punishment not only for that barbarous deed, but for the very manner of the doing of it, for all the insult to which she had been subjected, for the monstrous violence done her feelings and her very person, for the present detention and peril of which she was full conscious.

Her anger was the more intense because she never permitted it to diffuse itself over the several offenders. Ruthven, who had insulted her so grossly; Douglas, who had offered her personal violence; the Laird of Faudonside, Morton, and all the others who held her now a helpless prisoner, she hew for no more than the instruments of Darnley. It was against Darnley that all her rage was concentrated. She recalled in those bitter hours all that she had suffered at his vile hands, and swore that at whatever cost to herself he should yield a full atonement.

He sought her in the morning emboldened by the sovereign power he was usurping confident that now that he showed himself master of the situation she would not repine over what was done beyond recall, but would submit to the inevitable, be reconciled with him, and grant him, perforce - supported as he now was by the rebellious lords - the crown matrimonial and the full kingly power he coveted.

But her reception of him broke that confidence into shards.

"You have done me such a Wrong, " she told him in a voice of cold hatred, that neither the recollection of our early friendship, nor all the hope you can give me of the future, could ever make me forget it. Jamais! Jamais je n'oublierai! " she added, and upon that she dismissed him so imperiously that he went at once.

She sought a way to deal with him, groped blindly for it, being as yet but half informed of what was taking place; and whilst she groped,

12

the thing she sought was suddenly thrust into her land. Mary Beaton, one of the few attendants left her, brought her word later that day that the Earl of Murray, with Rothes and some other of the exiled lords, was in the palace. The news brought revelation. It flooded with light the tragic happening of the night before, showed her how Darnley was building himself a party in the state. It did more than that. She recalled the erstwhile mutual hatred and mistrust of Murray and Darnley, and saw how it might serve her in this emergency.

Instantly she summoned Murray to her presence with the message that she welcomed his return. Yet, despite that message, he hardly expected - considering what lay between them - the reception that awaited him at her hands.

She rose to receive him, her lovely eyes suffused, with tears. She embraced him, kissed him, and then, nestling to him, as if for comfort, her cheek against his bearded face, she allowed her tears to flow unchecked.

"I am punished, " she sobbed - "oh, I am punished! Had I kept you at home, Murray, you would never have suffered men to entreat me as I have been entreated. "

Holding her to hint, he could but pat her shoulder, soothing her, utterly taken aback, and deeply moved, too, by this display of an affection for him that he had never hitherto suspected in her.

"Ah, mon Dieu, Jamie, how welcome you are to one in my sorrow! " she continued. "It is the fault of others that you have been so long out of the country. I but require of you that you be a good subject to me, and you shall never find me other to you than you deserve. "

And he, shaken to the depths of his selfish soul by her tears, her clinging caresses, and her protestations of affection, answered with an oath and a sob that no better or more loyal and devoted subject than himself could all Scotland yield her.

"And, as for this killing of Davie, " he ended vehemently, "I swear by my soul's salvation that I have had no part in it, nor any knowledge of it until my return! "

"I know - I know! " she moaned. "Should I make you welcome, else? Be my friend, Jamie; be my friend! "

He swore it readily, for he was very greedy of power, and saw the door of his return to it opening wider than he could have hoped. Then he spoke of Darnley, begging her to receive him, and hear what he might have to say, protesting that the King swore that he had not desired the murder, and that the lords had carried the matter out of his hands and much beyond all that he had intended.

Because it suited her deep purpose, Mary consented, feigning to be persuaded. She had realized that before she could deal with Darnley, and the rebel lords who held her a prisoner, she must first win free from Holyrood.

Darnley came. He was sullen now, mindful of his recent treatment, and in fear - notwithstanding Murray's reassurance - of further similar rebuffs. She announced herself ready to hear what he might have to say, and she listened attentively while he spoke, her elbow on the carved arm of her chair, her chin in her hand. When he had done, she sat long in thought, gazing out through the window at the grey March sky. At length she turned and looked at him.

"Do you pretend, my lord, to regret for what has passed? " she challenged him.

"You tempt me to hypocrisy, " he said. "Yet I will be frank as at an Easter shrift. Since that fellow Davie fell into credit and familiarity with Your Majesty, you no longer treated me nor entertained me after your wonted fashion, nor would you ever bear me company save this Davie were the third. Can I pretend, then, to regret that one who deprived me of what I prized most highly upon earth should have been removed? I cannot. Yet I can and do proclaim my innocence of any part or share in the deed that has removed him. "

She lowered her eyes an instant, then raised them again to meet his own.

"You had commerce with these traitor lords, " she reminded him. "It is by your decree that they are returned from exile. What was your aim in this? "

"To win back the things of which this fellow Davie had robbed me, a share in the ruling and the crown matrimonial that was my right, yet which you denied me. That and no more. I had not intended that Davie should be slain. I had not measured the depth of their hatred of that upstart knave. You see that I am frank with you. "

"Aye, and I believe you, " she lied slowly, considering him as she spoke. And he drew a breath of relief, suspecting nothing of her deep guile. "And do you know why I believe you? Because you are a fool. "

"Madame! " he cried.

She rose, magnificently contemptuous.

"Must I prove it? You say that the crown matrimonial which I denied you is to be conferred on you by these lawless men? Believing that, you signed their pardon and recall from exile. Ha! You do not see, my lord, that you are no more than their tool, their cat's-paw. You do not see that they use you but for their ends, and that when they have done with you, they will serve you as they served poor Davie? No, you see none of that, which is why I call you a fool, that need a woman's wit to open wide your eyes. "

She was so vehement that she forced upon his dull wits some of the convictions she pretended were her own. Yet, resisting those convictions, he cried out that she was at fault.

"At fault? " She laughed. "Let my memory inform your judgment. When these lords, with Murray at their head, protested against our marriage, in what terms did they frame their protest? They complained that I had set over them without consulting them one who had no title to it, whether by lineal descent of blood, by nature, or by consent of the Estates. Consider that! They added, remember - I repeat to you the very words they wrote and published - that while they deemed it their duty to endure under me, they deemed it intolerable to suffer under you. "

She was flushed, and her eyes gleamed with excitement. She clutched his sleeve, and brought her face close to his own, looked deep and compellingly into his eyes as she continued:

"Such was their proclamation, and they took arms against me to enforce it, to pull you down from the place to which I had raised you out of the dust. Yet you can forget it, and in your purblind folly turn to these very men to right the wrongs you fancy I have done you. Do you think that men, holding you in such esteem as that, can keep any sort of faith with you? Do you think these are the men who are likely to fortify and maintain your title to the crown? Ask yourself, and answer for yourself. "

He was white to the lips. As much by her vehement pretence of sincerity as by the apparently irrefragable logic of her arguments, she forced conviction upon him. This brought a loathly fear in its train, and the gates of his heart stood ever wide to fear. He stepped aside to a chair, and sank into it, looking at her with dilating eyes - a fool confronted with the likely fruits of his folly.

"Then - then - why did they proffer me their help? How can they achieve their ends this way? "

"How? Do you still ask? Do you not see what a blind tool you have been in their crafty hands? In name at least you are king, and your signature is binding upon my subjects. Have you not brought them back from exile by one royal decree, whilst by another you have dispersed the Parliament that was assembled to attaint them of treason? "

She stepped close up to him, and bending, over him as he sat there, crushed by realization, she lowered her voice.

"Pray God, my lord, that all their purpose with you is not yet complete, else in their hands I do not think your life is to be valued at an apple-paring. You go the ways poor Davie went. "

He sank his handsome head to his hands, and covered his face. A while he sat huddled there, she watching him with gleaming, crafty eyes. At length he rallied. He looked up, tossing back the auburn hair from his white brow, still fighting, though weakly, against persuasion. "It is not possible, " he, cried. "They could not! They could not! "

She laughed, betwixt bitterness and sadness.

"Trust to that, " she bade him. "Yet look well at matters as they are already. I am a prisoner here in these men's hands. They will not let me go until their full purpose is accomplished - perhaps, " she added wistfully, "perhaps not even then. "

"Ah, not that! " he cried out.

"Even that, " she answered firmly. "But, " and again she grew vehement, "is it less so with you? Are you less a prisoner than I? D'ye think you will be suffered to come and go at will? " She saw the increase of fear in him, and then she struck boldly, setting all upon the gamble of a guess. "I am kept here until I shall have been brought to such a state that I will add my signature to your own and so pardon one and all for what is done. "

His sudden start, the sudden quickening of his glance told her how shrewdly she had struck home. Fearlessly, then, sure of herself, she continued. "To that end they use you. When you shall have served it you will but cumber them. When they shall have used you to procure their security from me, then they will deal with you as they have ever sought to deal with you - so that you trouble them no more. Ali, at last you understand! "

He came to his feet, his brow gleaming with sweat, his slender hands nervously interlocked.

"Oh, God! " he cried in a stifled voice.

"Aye, you are in a trap, my lord. Yourself you've sprung it. "

And now you behold him broken by the terror she had so cunningly evoked. He flung himself upon his knees before her, and with upturned face and hands that caught and clawed at her own, he implored her pardon for the wrong that in his folly he had done her in taking sides with her enemies.

She dissembled under a mask of gentleness the loathing that his cowardice aroused in her.

"My enemies? " she echoed wistfully. "Say rather your own enemies. It was their enmity to you that drove them into exile. In your rashness you have recalled them, whilst at the same time you have so bound my hands that I cannot now help you if I would. "

17

"You can, Mary, " he cried, "or else no one can. Withhold the pardon they will presently be seeking of you. Refuse to sign any remission of their deed. "

"And leave them to force you to sign it, and so destroy us both, " she answered.

He ranted then, invoking the saints of heaven, and imploring her in their name - she who was so wise and strong - to discover some way out of this tangle in which his madness had enmeshed them.

"What way is there short of flight? " she asked him. "And how are we to fly who are imprisoned here you as well as myself? Alas, Darnley, I fear our lives will end by paying the price of your folly. "

Thus she played upon his terrors, so that he would not be dismissed until she had promised that she would consider and seek some means of saving him, enjoining him meanwhile to keep strict watch upon himself and see that he betrayed nothing of his thoughts.

She left him to the chastening of a sleepless night, then sent for him betimes on Monday morning, and bade him repair to the lords and tell them that realizing herself a prisoner in their hands she was disposed to make terms with them. She would grant them pardon for what was done if on their side they undertook to be loyal henceforth and allowed her to resume her liberty.

The message startled him. But the smile with which she followed it was reassuring.

"There is something else you are to do, " she said, "if we are to turn the tables on these traitorous gentlemen. Listen. " And she added matter that begat fresh hope in Darnley's despairing soul.

He kissed her hands, lowly now and obedient as a hound that had been whipped to heel, and went below to bear her message to the lords.

Morton and Ruthven heard him out, but betrayed no eagerness to seize the opportunity.

"All this is but words that we hear, " growled Ruthven, who lay stretched upon a couch, grimly suffering from the disease that was, slowly eating up his life.

"She is guileful as the serpent, " Morton added, "being bred up in the Court of France. She will make you follow her will and desire, but she will not so lead us. We hold her fast, and we do not let her go without some good security of what shall follow. "

"What security will satisfy you? " quoth Darnley.

Murray and Lindsay came in as he was speaking, and Morton told them of the message that Darnley had brought. Murray moved heavily across to a window-seat, and sat down. He cleared a windowpane with his hand, and looked out upon the wintry landscape as if the matter had no interest for him. But Lindsay echoed what the other twain had said already.

"We want a deal more than promises that need not be kept, " he said.

Darnley looked from one to the other of them, seeing in their uncompromising attitude a confirmation of what the Queen had told him, and noting, too - as at another time he might not have noted - their utter lack of deference to himself, their King.

"Sirs, " he said, "I vow you wrong Her Majesty. I will stake my life upon her honour. "

"Why, so you may, " sneered Ruthven, "but you'll not stake ours. "

"Take what security you please, and I will subscribe it. "

"Aye, but will the Queen? " wondered Morton.

"She will. I have her word for it. "

It took them the whole of that day to consider the terms of the articles that would satisfy them. Towards evening the document was ready, and Morton and Ruthven representing all, accompanied by Murray, and introduced by Darnley, came to the chamber to which Her Majesty was confined by the guard they had set upon her.

She sat as if in state awaiting them, very lovely and very tearful, knowing that woman's greatest strength is in her weakness, that tears would serve her best by presenting her as if broken to their will.

In outward submission they knelt before her to make the pretence of suing for the pardon which they extorted by force of arms and duress. When each in his turn had made the brief pleading oration he had prepared, she dried her eyes and controlled herself by obvious effort.

"My lords, " she said, in a voice that quivered and broke on every other word, "when have ye ever found me blood-thirsty, or greedy of your lands or goods that you must use me so, and take such means with me? Ye have set my authority at naught, and wrought sedition in this realm. Yet I forgive you all, that by this clemency I may move you to a better love and loyalty. I desire that all that is passed may be buried in oblivion, so that you swear to me that in the future you will stand my friends and serve me faithfully, who am but a weak woman, and sorely need stout men to be my friends. "

For a moment her utterance was checked by sobs. Then she controlled herself again by an effort so piteous to behold that even the flinty-hearted Ruthven was moved to some compassion.

"Forgive this weakness in me, who am very weak, for very soon I am to be brought to bed as you well know, and I am in no case to offer resistance to any. I have no more to say, my lords. Since you promise on your side that you will put all disloyalty behind you, I pledge myself to remit and pardon all those that were banished for their share in the late rising, and likewise to pardon those that were concerned in the killing of Seigneur Davie. All this shall be as if it had never been. I pray you, my lords, make your own security in what sort you best please, and I will subscribe it. "

Morton proffered her the document they had prepared. She conned it slowly, what time they watched her, pausing ever and anon to brush aside the tears that blurred her vision. At last she nodded her lovely golden head.

"It is very well, " she said. "All is here as I would have it be between us. " And she turned to Darnley. "Give me pen and ink, my lord. "

Darnley dipped a quill and handed it to her. She set the parchment on the little pulpit at her side. Then, as she bent to sign, the pen fluttered from her fingers, and with a deep, shuddering sigh she sank back in her chair, her eyes closed, her face piteously white.

"The Queen is faint! " cried Murray, springing forward.

But she rallied instantly, smiling upon them wanly.

"It is naught; it is past, " she said. But even as she spoke she put a hand to her brow. "I am something dizzy. My condition - " She faltered on a trembling note of appeal that increased their compassion, and aroused in them a shame of their own harshness. "Leave this security with me. I will subscribe it in the morning - indeed, as soon as I am sufficiently recovered. "

They rose from their knees at her bidding, and Morton in the name of all professed himself full satisfied, and deplored the affliction they had caused her, for which in the future they should make her their amends.

"I thank you, " she answered simply. "You have leave to go. "

They departed well satisfied; and, counting the matter at an end, they quitted the palace and rode to their various lodgings in Edinburgh town, Murray going with Morton.

Anon to Maitland of Lethington, who had remained behind, came one of the Queen's women to summon him to her presence. He found her disposing herself for bed, and was received by her with tearful upbraidings.

"Sir, " she said, "one of the conditions upon which I consented to the will of their lordships was that an immediate term should be set to the insulting state of imprisonment in which I am kept here. Yet men-at-arms still guard the very door of my chamber, and my very attendants are hindered in their comings and goings. Do you call this keeping faith with me? Have I not granted all the requests of the lords? "

Lethington, perceiving the justice of what she urged, withdrew shamed and confused at once to remedy the matter by removing the guards from the passage and the stairs and elsewhere, leaving none but those who paced outside the palace.

It was a rashness he was bitterly to repent him on the morrow, when it was discovered that in the night Mary had not only escaped, but had taken Darnley with her. Accompanied by him and a few attendants, she had executed the plan in which earlier that day she had secured her scared husband's cooperation. At midnight they had made their way along the now unguarded corridors, and descended to the vaults of the palace, whence a secret passage communicated with the chapel. Through this and across the graveyard where lay the newly buried body of the Siegneur Davie - almost across the very grave itself which stood near the chapel door they had won to the horses waiting by Darnley's orders in the open. And they had ridden so hard that by five o'clock of that Tuesday morning they were in Dunbar.

In vain did the alarmed lords send a message after her to demand her signature of the security upon which she had duped them into counting prematurely.

Within a week they were in full flight before the army at the head of which the prisoner who had slipped through their hands was returning to destroy them. Too late did they perceive the arts by which she had fooled them, and seduced the shallow Darnley to betray them.

II. THE NIGHT OF KIRK O' FIELD

The Murder of Darnley

Perhaps one of the greatest mistakes of a lifetime in which mistakes were plentiful was the hesitancy of the Queen of Scots in executing upon her husband Darnley the prompt vengeance she had sworn for the murder of David Rizzio.

When Rizzio was slain, and she herself held captive by the murderers in her Palace of Holyrood, whilst Darnley ruled as king, she had simulated belief in her husband's innocence that she might use him for her vengeful ends.

She had played so craftily upon his cowardly nature as to convince him that Morton, Ruthven, and the other traitor lords with whom he had leagued himself were at heart his own implacable enemies; that they pretended friendship for him to make a tool of him, and that when he had served their turn they would destroy him.

In his consequent terror he had betrayed his associates, assisting her to trick them by a promise to sign an act of oblivion for what was done. Trusting to this the lords had relaxed their vigilance, whereupon, accompanied by Darnley, she had escaped by night from Holyrood.

Hope tempering at first the rage and chagrin in the hearts of the lords she had duped, they had sent a messenger to her at Dunbar to request of her the fulfilment of her promise to sign the document of their security.

But Mary put off the messenger, and whilst the army she had summoned was hastily assembling, she used her craft to divide the rebels against themselves.

To her natural brother, the Earl of Murray, to Argyll, and to all those who had been exiled for their rebellion at the time of her marriage - and who knew not where they stood in the present turn of events, since one of the objects of the murder had been to procure their reinstatement - she sent an offer of complete pardon, on condition that they should at once dissociate themselves from those concerned in the death of the Seigneur Davie.

These terms they accepted thankfully, as well they might. Thereupon, finding themselves abandoned by all men - even by Darnley in whose service they had engaged in the murder - Morton, Ruthven, and their associates scattered and fled.

By the end of that month of March, Morton, Ruthven, Lindsay of the Byres, George Douglas, and some sixty others were denounced as rebels with forfeiture of life and goods, while one Thomas Scott, who had been in command of the guards that had kept Her Majesty prisoner at Holyrood, was hanged, drawn, and quartered at the Market Cross.

News of this reached the fugitives to increase their desperate rage. But what drove the iron into the soul of the arch-murderer Ruthven was Darnley's solemn public declaration denying all knowledge of or complicity in Rizzio's assassination; nor did it soothe his fury to know that all Scotland rang with contemptuous laughter at that impudent and cowardly perjury. From his sick-bed at Newcastle, whereon some six weeks later he was to breathe his last, the forsaken wretch replied to it by sending the Queen the bond to which he had demanded Darnley's signature before embarking upon the business.

It was a damning document. There above the plain signature and seal of the King was the admission, not merely of complicity, but that the thing was done by his express will and command, that the responsibility was his own, and that he would hold the doers scatheless from all consequences.

Mary could scarcely have hoped to be able to confront her worthless husband with so complete a proof of his duplicity and baseness. She sent for him, confounded him with the sight of that appalling bond, made an end to the amity which for her own ends she had pretended, and drove him out of her presence with a fury before which he dared not linger.

You see him, then, crushed under his load of mortification, realizing at last how he had been duped on every hand, first by the lords for their own purpose, and then by the Queen for hers. Her contempt of him was now so manifest that it spread to all who served him - for she made it plain that who showed him friendship earned her deep displeasure - so that he was forced to withdraw from a Court where his life was become impossible. For a while he wandered up and down a land where every door was shut in his face, where every man of whatsoever party, traitor or true, despised him alike. In the end, he took himself off to his father, Lennox, and at Glasgow he sought what amusement he could with his dogs and his hawks, and such odd vulgar rustic love-affairs as came his way.

It was in allowing him thus to go his ways, in leaving her vengeance - indeed, her justice - but half accomplished, that lay the greatest of the Queen's mistakes. Better for her had she taken with Darnley the direct way that was her right. Better for her, if acting strongly then, she had banished or hanged him for his part in the treason that had inspired the murder of Rizzio. Unfortunately, a factor that served to quicken her abhorrence of him served also to set a curb of caution upon the satisfaction of it.

This factor that came so inopportunely into her life was her regard for the arrogant, unscrupulous Earl of Bothwell. Her hand was stayed by fear that men should say that for Bothwell's sake she had rid herself of a husband become troublesome. That Bothwell had been her friend in the hour when she had needed friends, and knew not whom she might trust; that by his masterfulness he seemed a man upon whom a woman might lean with confidence, may account for the beginnings of the extraordinary influence he came so swiftly to exercise over her, and the passion he awakened in her to such a degree that she was unable to dissemble it.

Her regard for him, the more flagrant by contrast with her contempt for Darnley, is betrayed in the will she made before her confinement in the following June. Whilst to Darnley she bequeathed nothing but the red-enamelled diamond ring with which he had married her - "It was with this that I was married, " she wrote almost contemptuously. "I leave it to the King who gave it me" - she appointed Bothwell to the tutelage of her child in the event of her not surviving it, and to the government of the realm.

The King came to visit her during her convalescence, and was scowled upon by Murray and Argyll, who were at Holyrood, and most of all by Bothwell, whose arrogance by now was such that he was become the best-hated man in Scotland. The Queen received him very coldly, whilst using Bothwell more than cordially in his very presence, so that he departed again in a deeper humiliation than before.

Then before the end of July there was her sudden visit to Bothwell at Alloa, which gave rise to so much scandal. Hearing of it, Darnley followed in a vain attempt to assert his rights as king and husband, only to be flouted and dismissed with the conviction that his life was no longer safe in Scotland, and that he had best cross the Border. Yet, to his undoing, detained perhaps by the overweening pride that is usually part of a fool's equipment, he did not act upon that wise resolve. He returned instead to his hawking and his hunting, and was seldom seen at Court thereafter.

Even when in the following October, Mary lay at the point of death at Jedburgh, Darnley came but to stay a day, and left her again without any assurance that she would recover. But then the facts of her illness, and how it had been contracted, were not such as to encourage kindness in him, even had he been inclined to kindness.

Bothwell had taken three wounds in a Border affray some weeks before, and Mary, hearing of this and that he lay in grievous case at Hermitage, had ridden thither in her fond solicitude - a distance of thirty miles - and back again in the same day, thus contracting a chill which had brought her to the very gates of death.

Darnley had not only heard of this, but he had found Bothwell at Jedburgh, whither he had been borne in a litter, when in his turn he had heard of how it was with Mary; and Bothwell had treated him with more than the contempt which all men now showed him, but which from none could wound him so deeply as from this man whom rumour accounted Mary's lover.

Matters between husband and wife were thus come to a pass in which they could not continue, as all men saw, and as she herself confessed at Craigrnillar, whither she repaired, still weak in body, towards the end of November.

Over a great fire that blazed in a vast chamber of the castle she sat sick at heart and shivering, for all that her wasted body was swathed in a long cloak of deepest purple reversed with ermine. Her face was thin and of a transparent pallor, her eyes great pools of wistfulness amid the shadows which her illness had set about them.

"I do wish I could be dead! " she sighed.

Bothwell's eyes narrowed. He was leaning on the back of her tall chair, a long, virile figure with a hawk-nosed, bearded face that was sternly handsome. He thrust back the crisp dark hair that clustered about his brow, and fetched a sigh.

"It was never my own death I wished when a man stood in my road to aught I craved, " he said, lowering his voice, for Maitland of Lethington - now restored to his secretaryship - was writing at a table across the room, and my Lord of Argyll was leaning over him.

She looked up at him suddenly, her eyes startled.

"What devil's counsel do you whisper? " she asked him. And when he would have answered, she raised a hand. "No, " she said. "Not that way. "

"There is another, " said Bothwell coolly. He moved, came round, and stood squarely upon the hearth, his back to the fire, confronting her, nor did he further trouble to lower his voice. "We have considered it already. "

"What have you considered? "

Her voice was strained; fear and excitement blended in her face.

"How the shackles that fetter you might be broken. Be not alarmed. It was the virtuous Murray himself propounded it to Argyll and Lethington - for the good of Scotland and yourself. " A sneer flitted across his tanned face. "Let them speak for themselves. " He raised his voice and called to them across the room.

They came at once, and the four made an odd group as they stood there in the firelit gloom of that November day - the lovely young Queen, so frail and wistful in her high-backed chair; the stalwart, arrogant Bothwell, magnificent in a doublet of peach-coloured velvet that tapered to a golden girdle; Argyll, portly and sober in a rich suit of black; and Maitland of Lethington, lean and crafty of face, in a long furred gown that flapped about his bony shanks.

It was to Lethington that Bothwell addressed himself.

"Her Grace is in a mood to hear how the Gordian knot of her marriage might be unravelled, " said he, grimly ironic.

Lethington raised his eyebrows, licked his thin lips, and rubbed his bony hands one in the other.

"Unravelled? " he echoed with wondering stress. "Unravelled? Ha! " His dark eyes flashed round at them. "Better adopt Alexander's plan, and cut it. 'Twill be more complete, and - and final. "

"No, no! " she cried. "I will not have you shed his blood. "

"He himself was none so tender where another was concerned, " Bothwell reminded her - as if the memory of Rizzio were dear to him.

"What he may have done does not weigh upon my conscience, " was her answer.

"He might, " put in Argyll, "be convicted of treason for having consented to Your Grace's retention in ward at Holyrood after Rizzio's murder. "

She considered an instant, then shook her head.

"It is too late. It should have been done long since. Now men will say that it is but a pretext to be rid of him. " She looked up at Bothwell, who remained standing immediately before her, between her and the fire. "You said that my Lord of Murray had discussed this matter. Was it in such terms as these? "

Bothwell laughed silently at the thought of the sly Murray rendering himself a party to anything so direct and desperate. It was Lethington who answered her.

"My Lord Murray was for a divorce. That would set Your Grace free, and it might be obtained, he said, by tearing up the Pope's bull of dispensation that permitted the marriage. Yet, madame, although Lord Murray would himself go no further, I have no cause to doubt that were other means concerted, he would be content to look through his fingers. "

Her mind, however, did not seem to follow his speech beyond the matter of the divorce. A faint flush of eagerness stirred in her pale cheeks.

"Ah, yes! " she cried. "I, too, have thought of that - of this divorce. And God knows I do not want for grounds. And it could be obtained, you say, by tearing up this papal bull? "

"The marriage could be proclaimed void thereafter, " Argyll explained.

She looked past Bothwell into the fire, and took her chin in her hand.

"Yes, " she said slowly, musingly, and again, "yes. That were a way. That is the way. " And then suddenly she looked up, and they saw doubt and dread in her eyes. "But in that case - what of my son? "

"Aye! " said Lethington grimly. He shrugged his narrow shoulders, parted his hands, and brought them together again. "That's the obstacle, as we perceived. It would imperil his succession. "

"It would make a bastard of him, you mean? " she cried, demanding the full expansion of their thoughts.

"Indeed it would do no less, " the secretary assented.

"So that, " said Bothwell, softly, "we come back to Alexander's method. What the fingers may not unravel, the knife can sever. "

She shivered, and drew her furred cloak the more closely about her.

Lethington leaned forward. He spoke in kindly, soothing accents.

"Let us guide this matter among us, madame, " he murmured, "and we'll find means to rid Your Grace of this young fool, without hurt to your honour or prejudice to your son. And the Earl of Murray will look the other way, provided you pardon Morton and his friends for the killing they did in Darnley's service. "

She looked from one to the other of them, scanning each face in turn. Then her eyes returned to a contemplation of the flaming logs, and she spoke very softly.

"Do nothing by which a spot might be laid on my honour or conscience, " she said, with an odd deliberateness that seemed to insist upon the strictly literal meaning of her words. "Rather I pray you let the matter rest until God remedy it. "

Lethington looked at the other two, the other two looked at him. He rubbed his hands softly.

"Trust to us, madame, " he answered. "We will so guide the matter that Your Grace shall see nothing but what is good and approved by Parliament. "

She committed herself to no reply, and so they were content to take their answer from her silence. They went in quest of Huntly and Sir James Balfour, and the five of them entered into a bond for the destruction of him whom they named "the young fool and proud tiranne, " to be engaged in when Mary should have pardoned Morton and his fellow-conspirators.

It was not until Christmas Eve that she signed this pardon of some seventy fugitives, proscribed for their participation in the Rizzio murder, towards whom she had hitherto shown herself so implacable.

The world saw in this no more than a deed of clemency and charity befitting the solemn festival of good-will. But the five who had entered into that bond at Craigmillar Castle beheld in it more accurately the fulfilment of her part of the suggested bargain, the price she paid in advance to be rid of Darnley, the sign of her full agreement that the knot which might not be unravelled should be cut.

On that same day Her Grace went with Bothwell to Lord Drummond's, where they abode for the best part of a week, and thence they went on together to Tullibardine, the rash and open intimacy between them giving nourishment to scandal.

At the same time Darnley quitted Stirling, where he had lately been living in miserable conditions, ignored by the nobles, and even stinted in his necessary expenses, deprived of his ordinary servants, and his silver replaced by pewter. The miserable youth reached Glasgow deadly sick. He had been taken ill on the way, and the inevitable rumour was spread that he had been poisoned. Later, when it became known that his once lovely countenance was now blotched and disfigured, it was realized that his illness was no more than the inevitable result of the debauched life he led.

Conceiving himself on the point of death, Darnley wrote piteously to the Queen; but she ignored his letters until she learnt that his condition was improving, when at last (on January 29th) she went to visit him at Glasgow. It may well be that she nourished some hope that nature would resolve the matter for her, and remove the need for such desperate measures as had been concerted. But seeing him likely to recover, two things became necessary, to bring him to the place that was suitable for the fulfilment of her designs, and to simulate reconciliation with him, and even renewed and tender affection, so that none might hereafter charge her with complicity in what should follow.

I hope that in this I do her memory no injustice. It is thus that I read the sequel, nor can I read it in any other way.

She found him abed, with a piece of taffeta over his face to hide its disfigurement, and she was so moved - as it seemed - by his condition, that she fell on her knees beside him, and wept in the presence of her attendants and his own; confessing penitence if anything she had done in the past could have contributed to their estrangement. Thus reconciliation followed, and she used him tenderly, grew solicitous concerning him, and vowed that as soon as he could be moved, he must be taken to surroundings more salubrious and more befitting the dignity of his station.

Gladly then he agreed to return with her to Holyrood.

"Not to Holyrood, " she said. "At least, not until your health is mended, lest you should carry thither infection dangerous to your little son. "

"Whither then? " he asked her, and when she mentioned Craigmillar, he started up in bed, so that the taffeta slipped from his face, and it was with difficulty that she dissembled the loathing with which the sight of its pustules inspired her.

"Craigmillar! " he cried. "Then what I was told is true. "

"What were you told? " quoth she, staring at him, brows knit, her face blank.

A rumour had filtered through to him of the Craigmillar bond. He had been told that a letter drawn up there had been presented to her

31

for her signature, which she had refused. Thus much he told her, adding that he could not believe that she would do him any hurt; and yet why did she desire to bear him to Craigmillar?

"You have been told lies, " she answered him. "I saw no such letter; I subscribed none, nor was ever asked to subscribe any, " which indeed was literally true. "To this I swear. As for your going to Craigmillar, you shall go whithersoever you please, yourself. "

He sank back on his pillows, and his trembling subsided.

"I believe thee, Mary. I believe thou'ld never do me any harm, " he repeated, "and if any other would, " he added on a bombastic note, "they shall buy it dear, unless they take me sleeping. But I'll never to Craigmillar. "

"I have said you shall go where you please, " she assured him again.

He considered.

"There is the house at Kirk o' Field. It has a fine garden, and is in a position that is deemed the healthiest about Edinburgh. I need good air; good air and baths have been prescribed me to cleanse me of this plague. Kirk o' Field will serve, if it be your pleasure. "

She gave a ready consent, dispatched messengers ahead to prepare the house, and to take from Holyrood certain furnishings that should improve the interior, and render it as fitting as possible a dwelling for a king.

Some days later they set out, his misgivings quieted by the tenderness which she now showed him - particularly when witnesses were at hand.

It was a tenderness that grew steadily during those twelve days in which he lay in convalescence in the house at Kirk o' Field; she was playful and coquettish with him as a maid with her lover, so that nothing was talked of but the completeness of this reconciliation, and the hope that it would lead to a peace within the realm that would be a benefit to all. Yet many there were who marvelled at it, wondering whether the waywardness and caprice of woman could account for so sudden a change from hatred to affection.

Darnley was lodged on the upper floor, in a room comfortably furnished from the palace. It was hung with six pieces of tapestry, and the floor was partly covered by an Eastern carpet. It contained, besides the handsome bed - which once had belonged to the Queen's mother - a couple of high chairs in purple velvet, a little table with a green velvet cover, and some cushions in red. By the side of the bed stood the specially prepared bath that was part of the cure which Darnley was undergoing. It had for its incongruous lid a door that had been lifted from its hinges.

Immediately underneath was a room that had been prepared for the Queen, with a little bed of yellow and green damask, and a furred coverlet. The windows looked out upon the close, and the door opened upon the passage leading to the garden.

Here the Queen slept on several of those nights of early February, for indeed she was more often at Kirk o' Field than at Holy-rood, and when she was not bearing Darnley company in his chamber, and beguiling the tedium of his illness, she was to be seen walking in the garden with Lady Reres, and from his bed he could hear her sometimes singing as she sauntered there.

Never since the ephemeral season of their courtship had she been on such fond terms with him, and all his fears of hostile designs entertained against him by her immediate followers were stilled at last. Yet not for long. Into his fool's paradise came Lord Robert of Holyrood, with a warning that flung him into a sweat of panic.

The conspirators had hired a few trusted assistants to help them carry out their plans, and a rumour had got abroad - in the unaccountable way of rumours - that there was danger to the King. It was of this rumour that Lord Robert brought him word, telling him bluntly that unless he escaped quickly from this place, he would leave his life there. Yet when Darnley had repeated this to the Queen, and the Queen indignantly had sent for Lord Robert and demanded to know his meaning, his lordship denied that he had uttered any such warning, protested that his words must have been misunderstood - that they referred solely to the King's condition, which demanded, he thought, different treatment and healthier air.

Knowing not what to believe, Darnley's uneasiness abode with him. Yet, trusting Mary, and feeling secure so long as she was by his side, he became more and more insistent upon her presence, more and more fretful in her absence. It was to quiet him that she consented to sleep as often as might be at Kirk o' Field. She slept there on the Wednesday of that week, and again on Friday, and she was to have done so yet again on that fateful Sunday, February 9th, but that her servant Sebastien - one who had accompanied her from France, and for whom she had a deep affection - was that day married, and Her Majesty had promised to be present at the masque that night at Holyrood, in honour of his nuptials.

Nevertheless, she did not utterly neglect her husband on that account. She rode to Kirk o' Field early in the evening, accompanied by Bothwell, Huntly, Argyll, and some others; and leaving the lords at cards below to while away the time, she repaired to Darnley, and sat beside his bed, soothing a spirit oddly perturbed, as if with some premonition of what was brewing.

"Ye'll not leave me the night, " he begged her once.

"Alas, " she said, "I must! Sebastien is being wed, and I have promised to be present. "

He sighed and shifted uneasily.

"Soon I shall be well, and then these foolish humours will cease to haunt me. But just now I cannot bear you from my sight. When you are with me I am at peace. I know that all is well. But when you go I am filled with fears, lying helpless here. "

"What should you fear? " she asked him.

"The hate that I know is alive against me. "

"You are casting shadows to affright yourself, " said she.

"What's that? " he cried, half raising himself in sudden alarm. "Listen! "

From the room below came faintly a sound of footsteps, accompanied by a noise as of something being trundled.

"It will be my servants in my room - putting it to rights. "

"To what purpose since you do not sleep there tonight? " he asked. He raised his voice and called his page.

"Why, what will you do? " she asked him, steadying her own alarm.

He answered her by bidding the youth who had entered go see what was doing in the room below. The lad departed, and had he done his errand faithfully, he would have found Bothwell's followers, Hay and Hepburn, and the Queen's man, Nicholas Hubert better known as French Paris - emptying a keg of gunpowder on the floor immediately under the King's bed. But it happened that in the passage he came suddenly face to face with the splendid figure of Bothwell, cloaked and hatted, and Bothwell asked him whither he went.

The boy told him.

"It is nothing, " Bothwell said. "They are moving Her Grace's bed in accordance with her wishes. "

And the lad, overborne by that commanding figure which so effectively blocked his path, chose the line of lesser resistance. He went back to bear the King that message as if for himself he had seen what my Lord Bothwell had but told him.

Darnley was pacified by the assurance, and the lad withdrew.

"Did I not tell you how it was? " quoth Mary. "Is not my word enough? "

"Forgive the doubt, " Darnley begged her. "Indeed, there was no doubt of you, who have shown me so much charity in my affliction. " He sighed, and looked at her with melancholy eyes.

"I would the past had been other than it has been between you and me, " he said. "I was too young for kingship, I think. In my green youth I listened to false counsellors, and was quick to jealousy and the follies it begets. Then, when you cast me out and I wandered friendless, a devil took possession of me. Yet, if you will but consent to bury all the past into oblivion, I will make amends, and you shall find me worthier hereafter. "

She rose, white to the lips, her bosom heaving under her long cloak. She turned aside and stepped to the window. She stood there, peering out into the gloom of the close, her knees trembling under her.

"Why do you not answer me? " he cried.

"What answer do you need? " she said, and her voice shook. "Are you not answered already? " And then, breathlessly, she added: "It is time to go, I think. "

They heard a heavy step upon the stairs and the clank of a sword against the rails. The door opened, and Bothwell, wrapped in his scarlet cloak, stood bending his tall shoulders under the low lintel. His gleaming eyes, so oddly mocking in their glance, for all that his face was set, fell upon Darnley, and with their look flung him into an inward state of blending fear and rage.

"Your Grace, " said Bothwell's deep voice, "it is close upon midnight. "

He came no more than in time; it needed the sight of him with its reminder of all that he meant to her to sustain a purpose that was being sapped by pity.

"Very well, " she said. "I come. "

Bothwell stood aside to give her egress and to invite it. But the King delayed her.

"A moment - a word! " he begged, and to Bothwell: "Give us leave apart, sir! "

Yet, King though he might be, there was no ready obedience from the arrogant Border lord, her lover. It was to Mary that Bothwell looked for commands, nor stirred until she signed to him to go. And even then he went no farther than the other side of the door, so that he might be close at hand to fortify her should any weakness assail her now in this supreme hour.

Darnley struggled up in bed, caught her hand, and pulled her to him.

"Do not leave me, Mary. Do not leave me! " he implored her.

"Why, what is this? " she cried, but her voice lacked steadiness. "Would you have me disappoint poor Sebastien, who loves me? "

"I see. Sebastien is more to you than I? "

"Now this is folly. Sebastien is my faithful servant. "

"And am I less? Do you not believe that my one aim henceforth will be to serve you and faithfully? Oh, forgive this weakness. I am full of evil foreboding to-night. Go, then, if go you must, but give me at least some assurance of your love, some pledge of it in earnest that you will come again to-morrow nor part from me again. "

She looked into the white, piteous young face that had once been so lovely, and her soul faltered. It needed the knowledge that Bothwell waited just beyond the door, that he could overhear what was being said, to strengthen her fearfully in her tragic purpose.

She has been censured most for what next she did. Murray himself spoke of it afterwards as the worst part of the business. But it is possible that she was concerned only at the moment to put an end to a scene that was unnerving her, and that she took the readiest means to it.

She drew a ring from her finger and slipped it on to one of his.

"Be this the pledge, then, " she said; "and so content and rest yourself. "

With that she broke from him, white and scared, and reached the door. Yet with her hand upon the latch she paused. Looking at him she saw that he was smiling, and perhaps horror of her betrayal of him overwhelmed her. It must be that she then desired to warn him, yet with Bothwell within earshot she realized that any warning must precipitate the tragedy, with direst consequences to Bothwell and herself.

To conquer her weakness, she thought of David Rizzio, whom Darnley had murdered almost at her feet, and whom this night was to avenge. She thought of the Judas part that he had played in that affair, and sought persuasion that it was fitting he should now be

37

paid in kind. Yet, very woman that she was, failing to find any such persuasion, she found instead in the very thought of Rizzio the very means to convey her warning.

Standing tense and white by the door, regarding him with dilating eyes, she spoke her last words to him.

"It would be just about this time last year that Davie was slain, " she said, and on that passed out to the waiting Bothwell.

Once on the stairs she paused and set a hand upon the shoulder of the stalwart Borderer.

"Must it be? Oh, must it be? " she whispered fearfully.

She caught the flash of his eyes in the half gloom as he leaned over her, his arm about her waist drawing her to him.

"Is it not just? Is it not full merited? " he asked her.

"And yet I would that we did not profit by it, " she complained.

"Shall we pity him on that account? " he asked, and laughed softly and shortly. "Come away, " he added abruptly. "They wait for you! " And so, by the suasion of his arm and his imperious will, she was swept onward along the road of her destiny.

Outside the horses were ready. There was a little group of gentlemen to escort her, and half a dozen servants with lighted torches, whilst Lady Reres was in waiting. A man stood forward to assist her to mount, his face and hands so blackened by gunpowder that for a moment she failed to recognize him. She laughed nervously when he named himself.

"Lord, Paris, how begrimed you are! " she cried; and, mounting, rode away towards Holyrood with her torchbearers and attendants.

In the room above, Darnley lay considering her last words. He turned them over in his thoughts, assured by the tone she had used and how she had looked that they contained some message.

"It would be just about this time last year that Davie was slain. "

In themselves, those words were not strictly accurate. It wanted yet a month to the anniversary of Rizzio's death. And why, at parting, should she have reminded him of that which she had agreed should be forgotten? Instantly came the answer that she sought to warn him that retribution was impending. He thought again of the rumours that he had heard of a bond signed at Craigmillar; he recalled Lord Robert's warning to him, afterwards denied.

He recalled her words to himself at the time of Rizzio's death: "Consider well what I now say. Consider and remember. I shall never rest until I give you as sore a heart as I have presently. " And further, he remembered her cry at once agonized and fiercely vengeful: "Jamais, jamais je n'oublierai. "

His terrors mounted swiftly, to be quieted again at last when he looked at the ring she had put upon his finger in pledge of her renewed affection. The past was dead and buried, surely. Though danger might threaten, she would guard him against it, setting her love about him like a panoply of steel. When she came to-morrow, he would question her closely, and she should be more frank and open with him, and tell him all. Meanwhile, he would take his precautions for to-night.

He sent his page to make fast all doors. The youth went and did as he was bidden, with the exception of the door that led to the garden. It had no bolts, and the key was missing; yet, seeing his master's nervous, excited state, he forbore from any mention of that circumstance when presently he returned to him.

Darnley requested a book of Psalms, that he might read himself to sleep. The page dozed in a chair, and so the hours passed; and at last the King himself fell into a light slumber. Out of this he started suddenly at a little before two o'clock, and sat upright in bed, alarmed without knowing why, listening with straining ears and throbbing pulses.

He caught a repetition of the sound that had aroused him, a sound akin to that which had drawn his attention earlier, when Mary had been with him. It came up faintly from the room immediately beneath: her room. Some one was moving there, he thought. Then, as he continued to listen, all became quiet again, save his fears, which would not be quieted. He extinguished the light, slipped from the bed, and, crossing to the window, peered out into the close that was faintly illumined by a moon in its first quarter. A shadow moved, he thought. He watched with increasing panic for confirmation, and presently saw that he had been right. Not one, but several shadows were shifting there among the trees. Shadows of men, they were, and as he peered, he saw one that went running from the house across the lawn and joined the others, now clustered together in a group. What could be their purpose here? In the silence, he seemed to hear again the echo of Mary's last words to him:

"It would be just about this time last year that Davie was slain. "

In terror, he groped his way to the chair where the page slept and shook the lad vigorously.

"Afoot, boy! " he said, in a hoarse whisper. He had meant to shout it, but his voice failed him, his windpipe clutched by panic. "Afoot - we are beset by enemies! "

At once the youth was wide awake, and together the King just in his shirt as he was - they made their way from the room in the dark, groping their way, and so reached the windows at the back. Darnley opened one of these very softly, then sent the boy back for a sheet. Making this fast, they descended by it to the garden, and started towards the wall, intending to climb it, that they might reach the open.

The boy led the way, and the King followed, his teeth chattering as much from the cold as from the terror that possessed him. And then, quite suddenly, without the least warning, the ground, it seemed to them, heaved under their feet, and they were flung violently forward on their faces. A great blaze rent the darkness of the night, accompanied by the thunders of an explosion so terrific that it seemed as if the whole world must have been shattered by it.

For some instants the King and his page lay half stunned where they had fallen, and well might it have been for them had they so continued. But Darnley, recovering, staggered to his feet, pulling the boy up with him and supporting him. Then, as he began to move, he heard a soft whistle in the gloom behind him. Over his shoulder he looked towards the house, to behold a great, smoking gap now yawning in it. Through this gap he caught a glimpse of shadowy men moving in the close beyond, and he realized that he had been seen. The white shirt he wore had betrayed his presence to them.

With a stifled scream, he began to run towards the wall, the page staggering after him. Behind them now came the clank and thud of a score of overtaking feet. Soon they were surrounded. The King turned this way and that, desperately seeking a way out of the murderous human ring that fenced them round.

"What d'ye seek? What d'ye seek? " he screeched, in a pitiful attempt to question with authority.

A tall man in a trailing cloak advanced and seized him.

"We seek thee, fool! " said the voice of Bothwell.

The kingliness that he had never known how to wear becomingly now fell from him utterly.

"Mercy - mercy! " he cried.

"Such mercy as you had on David Rizzio! " answered the Border lord.

Darnley fell on his knees and sought to embrace the murderer's legs. Bothwell stooped over him, seized the wretched man's shirt, and pulled it from his shivering body; then, flinging the sleeves about the royal neck, slipped one over the other and drew them tight, nor relaxed his hold until the young man's struggles had entirely ceased.

Four days later, Mary went to visit the body of her husband in the chapel of Holyrood House, whither it had been conveyed, and there, as a contemporary tells us, she looked upon it long, "not only without grief, but with greedy eyes. " Thereafter it was buried secretly in the night by Rizzio's side, so that murderer and victim lay at peace together in the end.

III. THE NIGHT OF BETRAYAL

Antonio Perez and Philip II of Spain

You a Spaniard of Spain? " had been her taunt, dry and contemptuous. "I do not believe it. "

And upon that she had put spur to the great black horse that bore her and had ridden off along the precipitous road by the river.

After her he had flung his answer on a note of laughter, bitter and cynical as the laughter of the damned, laughter that expressed all things but mirth.

"Oh, a Spaniard of Spain, indeed, Madame la Marquise. Very much a Spaniard of Spain, I assure you. "

The great black horse and the woman in red flashed round a bend of the rocky road and were eclipsed by a clump of larches. The man leaned heavily upon his ebony cane, sighed wearily, and grew thoughtful. Then, with a laugh and a shrug, he sat down in the shade of the firs that bordered the road. Behind him, crowning the heights, loomed the brown castle built by Gaston Phoebus, Count of Foix, two hundred years ago, and the Tower of Montauzet, its walls scarred by the shots of the rebellious Biscayans. Below him, nourished by the snows that were dissolving under the sunshine of early spring, sped the tumbling river; beyond this spread pasture and arable land to the distant hills, and beyond those stood the gigantic sharp-summited wall of the Pyrenees, its long ridge dominated by the cloven cone of the snow clad Pic du Midi. There was in the sight of that great barrier, at once natural and political, a sense of security for this fugitive from the perils and the hatreds that lurked in Spain beyond. Here in Bearn he was a king's guest, enjoying the hospitality of the great Castle of Pau, safe from the vindictive persecution of the mean tyrant who ruled in Spain. And here, at last, he was at peace, or would have been but for the thought of this woman - this Marquise de Chantenac - who had gone to such lengths in her endeavours to soften his exile that her ultimate object could never have been in doubt to a coxcomb, though it was in some doubt to Antonio Perez, who had been cured for all time of Coxcombry by suffering and misfortune, to say nothing of increasing age. It was when he bethought him of that age of his that he was chiefly intrigued by the amazing ardour of this great lady of Bearn. A dozen years ago - before misfortune overtook him - he would have accepted her flagrant wooing as a proper tribute. For then he had been the handsome, wealthy, witty, profligate Secretary of State to His Catholic Majesty King Philip II, with a power in Spain second only to the King's, and sometimes even greater. In those days he would have welcomed her as her endowments merited. She was radiantly lovely, in the very noontide of her resplendent youth, the well-born widow of a gentleman of Bearn. And it would not have lain within the strength or inclinations of Antonio Perez, as he once had been, to have resisted the temptation that she offered. Ever avid of pleasure, he had denied himself no single cup of it that favouring Fortune had proffered him. It was, indeed, because of this that he was fallen from his high estate; it was a woman who had pulled him down in ruin, tumbling with him to her doom. She, poor soul, was dead at last, which was the best that any lover could have wished her. But he lived on, embittered, vengeful, with gall in his veins instead of blood. He was the pale, faded shadow of that arrogant, reckless, joyous Antonio Perez beloved of Fortune. He was fifty, gaunt, hollow-eyed, and grey, half crippled by torture, sickly from long years of incarceration.

What, he asked himself, sitting there, his eyes upon the eternal snows of the barrier that shut out his past, was there left in him to awaken love in such a woman as Madame de Chantenac? Was it that his tribulations stirred her pity, or that the fame of him which rang through Europe shed upon his withering frame some of the transfiguring radiance of romance?

It marked, indeed, the change in him that he should pause to question, whose erstwhile habit had been blindly to accept the good things tossed by Fortune into his lap. But question he did, pondering that parting taunt of hers to which, for emphasis, she had given an odd redundancy - "You a Spaniard of Spain! " Could her meaning have been plainer? Was not a Spaniard proverbially as quick to love as to jealousy? Was not Spain, that scented land of warmth and colour, of cruelty and blood, of throbbing lutes under lattices ajar, of mitred sinners doing public penance, that land where lust and piety went hand in hand, where passion and penitence lay down together - was not Spain the land of love's most fruitful growth? And was not a Spaniard the very hierophant of love?

His thoughts swung with sudden yearning to his wife Juana and their children, held in brutal captivity by Philip, who sought to slake upon them some of the vindictiveness from which their husband and father had at last escaped. Not that Antonio Perez observed marital fidelity more closely than any other Spaniard of his time, or of any time. But Antonio Perez was growing old, older than he thought, older than his years. He knew it. Madame de Chantenac had proved it to him.

She had reproached him with never coming to see her at Chantenac, neglecting to return the too assiduous visits that she paid him here at Pau.

"You are very beautiful, madame, and the world is very foul, " he had excused himself. "Believe one who knows the world, to his bitter cost. Tongues will wag. "

"And your Spanish pride will not suffer that clods may talk of you? "

"I am thinking of you, madame. "

"Of me? " she had answered. "Why, of me they talk already - talk their fill. I must pretend blindness to the leering eyes that watch me each time I come to Pau; feign unconsciousness of the impertinent glances of the captain of the castle there as I ride in. "

"Then why do you come? " he had asked point-blank. But before her sudden change of countenance he had been quick to add: "Oh, madame, I am full conscious of the charity that brings you, and I am deeply, deeply grateful; but - "

"Charity? " she had interrupted sharply, on a laugh that was self-mocking. "Charity? "

"What else, madame? "

"Ask yourself, " she had answered, reddening and averting her face from his questioning eyes.

"Madame, " he had faltered, "I dare not. "

"Dare not? "

"Madame, how should I? I am an old man, broken by sickness, disheartened by misfortune, daunted by tribulation - a mere husk cast aside by Fortune, whilst you are lovely as one of the angels about the Throne of Heaven. "

She had looked into the haggard face, into the scars of suffering that seared it, and she had answered gently: "Tomorrow you shall come to me at Chantenac, my friend. "

"I am a Spaniard, for whom to-morrow never comes. "

"But it will this time. To-morrow I shall expect you. "

He looked up at her sitting her great black horse beside which he had been pacing.

"Better not, madame! Better not! " he had said.

And then he saw the eyes that had been tender grow charged with scorn; then came her angry taunt:

"You a Spaniard of Spain! I do not believe it! "

Oh, there was no doubt that he had angered her. Women of her temperament are quick to anger as to every emotion. But he had not wished to anger her. God knows it was never the way of Antonio Perez to anger lovely women - at least not in this fashion. And it was an ill return for her gentleness and attention to himself. Considering this as he sat there now, he resolved that he must make amends - the only amends it was possible to make.

An hour later, in one of the regal rooms of the castle, where he enjoyed the hospitality of King Henri IV of France and Navarre, he announced to that most faithful equerry, Gil de Mesa, his intention of riding to Chantenac to-morrow.

"Is it prudent? " quoth Mesa, frowning.

"Most imprudent, " answered Don Antonio. "That is why I go. "

And on the morrow he went, escorted by a single groom. Gil de Mesa had begged at first to be allowed to accompany him. But for Gil he had other work, of which the instructions he left were very full. The distance was short - three miles along the Gave de Pau - and Don Antonio covered it on a gently ambling mule, such as might have been bred to bear some aged dignitary of Holy Church.

The lords of Chantenac were as noble, as proud, and as poor as most great lords of Bearn. Their lineage was long, their rent-rolls short. And the last marquis had suffered more from this dual complaint than any of his forbears, and he had not at all improved matters by a certain habit of gaming contracted in youth. The chateau bore abundant signs of it. It was a burnt red pile standing four-square on a little eminence, about the base of which the river went winding turbulently; it was turreted at each of its four angles, imposing in its way, but in a sad state of dilapidation and disrepair.

The interior, when Don Antonio reached it, was rather better; the furnishings, though sparse, were massive and imposing; the tapestries on the walls, if old, were rich and choice. But everywhere the ill-assorted marriage of pretentiousness and neediness was apparent. The floors of hall and living-room were strewn with fresh-cut rushes, an obsolescent custom which served here alike to save the heavy cost of carpets and to lend the place an ancient baronial dignity. Whilst pretence was made of keeping state, the servitors were all old, and insufficient in number to warrant the retention of the infirm seneschal by whom Don Antonio was ceremoniously received. A single groom, aged and without livery, took charge at once of Don Antonio's mule, his servant's horse, and the servant himself.

The seneschal, hobbling before him, conducted our Spaniard across the great hall, gloomy and half denuded, through the main living-room of the chateau into a smaller, more intimate apartment, holding some trace of luxury, which he announced as madame's own room. And there he left him to await the coming of the chatelaine.

She, at least, showed none of the outward disrepair of her surroundings. She came to him sheathed in a gown of shimmering silk that was of the golden brown of autumn tints, caught to her waist by a slender girdle of hammered gold. Eyes of deepest blue pondered him questioningly, whilst red lips smiled their welcome. "So you have come in spite of all? " she greeted him. "Be very welcome to my poor house, Don Antonio. "

And regally she proffered her hand to his homage.

He took it, observing the shapely, pointed fingers, the delicately curving nails. Reluctantly, almost, he admitted to himself how complete was her beauty, how absolute her charm. He sighed - a sigh for that lost youth of his, perhaps - as he bowed from his fine, lean height to press cold lips of formal duty on that hand.

"Your will, madame, was stronger than my prudence, " said he.

"Prudence? " quoth she, and almost sneered. "Since when has Antonio Perez stooped to prudence? "

"Since paying the bitter price of imprudence. You know my story? "

"A little. I know, for instance, that you murdered Escovedo - all the world knows that. Is that the imprudence of which you speak? I have heard it said that it was for love of a woman that you did it. "

"You have heard that, too? " he said. He had paled a little. "You have heard a deal, Marquise. I wonder would it amuse you to hear more, to hear from my own lips this story of mine which all Europe garbles? Would it? "

There was a faint note of anxiety in his voice, a look faintly anxious in his eyes.

She scanned him a moment gravely, almost inscrutably. "What purpose can it serve? " she asked; and her tone was forbidding - almost a tone of fear.

"It will explain, " he insisted.

"Explain what? "

"How it comes that I am not this moment prostrate at your feet; how it happens that I am not on my knees to worship your heavenly beauty; how I have contrived to remain insensible before a loveliness that in happier times would have made me mad. "

"Vive Dieu! " she murmured, half ironical. "Perhaps that needs explaining. "

"How it became necessary, " he pursued, never heeding the interruption, "that yesterday you should proclaim your disbelief that

47

I could be, as you said, a Spaniard of Spain. How it happens that Antonio Perez has become incapable of any emotion but hate. Will you hear the story - all of it? "

He was leaning towards her, his white face held close to her own, a smouldering fire in the dark, sunken eyes that now devoured her.

She shivered, and her own cheeks turned very pale. Her lips were faintly twisted as if in an effort to smile.

"My friend - if you insist, " she consented.

"It is the purpose for which I came, " he announced.

For a long moment each looked into the other's eyes with a singular intentness that nothing here would seem to warrant.

At length she spoke.

"Come, " she said, "you shall tell me. "

And she waved him to a chair set in the embrasure of the mullioned window that looked out over a tract of meadowland sweeping gently down to the river.

Don Antonio sank into the chair, placing his hat and whip upon the floor beside him. The Marquise faced him, occupying the padded window-seat, her back to the light, her countenance in shadow.

And here, in his own words, follows the story that he told her as she herself set it down soon after. Whilst more elaborate and intimate in parts, it yet so closely agrees throughout with his own famous "Relacion, " that I do not hesitate to accept the assurance she has left us that every word he uttered was burnt as if by an acid upon her memory.

THE STORY OF ANTONIO PEREZ

As a love-story this is, I think, the saddest that ever was invented by a romancer intent upon wringing tears from sympathetic hearts. How sad it is you will realize when I tell you that daily I thank God on my knees - for I still believe in God, despite what was alleged against me by the inquisitors of Aragon - that she who inspired this love of which I am to tell you is now in the peace of death. She died in exile at Pastrana a year ago. Anne de Mendoza was what you call in France a great parti. She came of one of the most illustrious families in Spain, and she was a great heiress. So much all the world knew. What the world forgot was that she was a woman, with a woman's heart and mind, a woman's natural instincts to select her mate. There are fools who envy the noble and the wealthy. They are little to be envied, those poor pawns in the game of statecraft, moved hither and thither at the will of players who are themselves no better. The human nature of them is a negligible appendage to the names and rent-rolls that predetermine their place upon the board of worldly ambition, a board befouled by blood, by slobberings from the evil mouth of greed, and by infamy of every kind.

So, because Anne was a daughter of the House of Mendoza, because her endowments were great, they plucked her from her convent at the age of thirteen years, knowing little more of life than the merest babe, and they flung her into the arms of Ruy Gomez, Prince of Eboli, who was old enough to have been her father. But Eboli was a great man in Spain, perhaps the greatest; he was, first Minister to Philip II, and between his House and that of Mendoza an alliance was desired. To establish it that tender child was sacrificed without ruth. She discovered that life held nothing of all that her maiden dreamings had foreseen; that it was a thing of horror and greed and lovelessness and worse. For there was much worse to come.

Eboli brought his child-princess to Court. He wore her lightly as a ribbon or a glove, the insignificant appendage to the wealth and powerful alliance he had acquired with her. And at Court she came under the eye of that pious satyr Philip. The Catholic King is very devout - perfervidly devout. He prays, he fasts, he approaches the sacraments, he does penance, all in proper season as prescribed by Mother Church; he abominates sin and lack of faith - particularly in others; he has drenched Flanders in blood that he might wash it clean of the heresy of thinking differently from himself in spiritual matters, and he would have done the same by England but that God - Who cannot, after all, be quite of Philip's way of thinking - willed otherwise. All this he has done for the greater honour and glory of his Maker, but he will not tolerate his Maker's interference with his own minor pleasures of the flesh. He is, as you would say, a Spaniard of Spain.

This satyr's protruding eyes fell upon the lovely Princess of Eboli - for lovely she was, a very pearl among women. I spare you details. Eboli was most loyal and submissive where his King was concerned, most complacent and accommodating. That was but logical, and need not shock you at all. To advance his worldly ambitions had he taken Anne to wife; why should he scruple, then, to yield her again that thus he might advance those ambitions further?

If poor Anne argued at all, she must have argued thus. For the rest, she was told that to be loved by the King was an overwhelming honour, a matter for nightly prayers of thankfulness. Philip was something very exalted, hardly human in fact; almost, if not quite, divine. Who and what was Anne that she should dispute with those who knew the world, and who placed these facts before her? Never in all her little life had she belonged to herself. Always had she been the property of somebody else, to be dealt with as her owner might consider best. If about the Court she saw some men more nearly of her own age - though there were not many, for Philip's Court was ever a gloomy, sparsely peopled place - she took it for granted that such men were not for her. This until I taught her otherwise, which, however, was not yet a while. Had I been at Court in those days, I think I should have found the means, at whatever cost, of preventing that infamy; for I know that I loved her from the day I saw her. But I was of no more than her own age, and I had not yet been drawn into that whirlpool.

So she went to the arms of that rachitic prince, and she bore him a son - for, as all the world knows, the Duke of Prastana owns Philip for his father. And Eboli increased in power and prosperity and the favour of his master, and also, no doubt, in the contempt of posterity. There are times when the thought of posterity and its vengeances is of great solace.

It would be some six years later when first I came to Court, brought thither by my father, to enter the service of the Prince of Eboli as one of his secretaries. As I have told you, I loved the Princess from the moment I beheld her. From the gossip of the Court I pieced together her story, and pitied her, and, pitying her, I loved her the more. Her beauty dazzled me, her charm enmeshed me, and she had grown by now in worldly wisdom and mental attainments. Yet I set a mask upon my passion, and walked very circumspectly, for all that by nature I was as reckless and profligate as all the world could ever call me. She was the wife of the puissant Secretary of State, the mistress of the King. Who was I to dispute their property to those exalted ones?

And another consideration stayed me. She seemed to love the King. Young and lacking in wisdom, this amazed me. In age he compared favourably with her husband he was but thirteen years older than herself - but in nothing else. He was a weedy, unhealthy-looking man, weakly of frame, rachitic, undersized, with spindle-shanks, and a countenance that was almost grotesque, with its protruding jaw, gaping mouth, great, doglike eyes, and yellow tuft of beard. A great king, perhaps, this Philip, having so been born; but a ridiculous man and an unspeakable lover. And yet this incomparable woman seemed to love him.

Let me pass on. For ten years I nursed that love of mine in secret. I was helped, perhaps, by the fact that in the mean time I had married - oh, just as Eboli himself had married, an arrangement dictated by worldly considerations - and no better, truer mate did ever a man find than I in Juana Coello. We had children and we were happy, and for a season - for years, indeed - I began to think that my unspoken passion for the Princess of Eboli was dead and done with. I saw her rarely now, and my activities increased with increasing duties. At twenty-six I was one of the Ministers of the Crown, and one of the chief supporters of that party of which Eboli was the leader in Spanish politics. I sat in Philip's Council, and I came under the spell of that taciturn, suspicious man, who, utterly unlovable as he was, had yet an uncanny power of inspiring devotion. From the spell of it I never quite escaped until after long years of persecution. Yet the discovery that one by nature so entirely antipathetic to me should have obtained such sway over my mind helped me to understand Anne's attachment to him.

When Eboli died, in 1573, I had so advanced in ability and Royal favour that I took his place as Secretary of State, thus becoming all but the supreme ruler of Spain. I do not believe that there was ever in Spain a Minister so highly favoured by the reigning Prince, so powerful as I became. Not Eboli himself in his halcyon days had been so deeply esteemed of Philip, or had wielded such power as I now made my own. All Europe knows it - for it was to me all Europe addressed itself for affairs that concerned the Catholic King.

And with my power came wealth - abundant, prodigious wealth. I was housed like a Prince of the blood, and no Prince of the blood ever kept greater state than I, was ever more courted, fawned upon, or t flattered. And remember I was young, little more than thirty, with all the strength and zest to enjoy my intoxicating eminence. I was to my party what Eboli had been, though the nominal leader of it remained Quiroga, Archbishop of Toledo. On the other side was the Duke of Alva with his following.

You must know that it was King Philip's way to encourage two rival parties in the State, between which he shared his confidence and sway. Thus he stimulated emulation and enlightened his own views in the opposing opinions that were placed before him. But the power of my party was absolute in those days, and Alva himself was as the dust beneath our feet.

Such eminences, they say, are perilous. Heads that are very highly placed may at any moment be placed still higher - upon a pike. I am all but a living witness to the truth of that, and yet I wonder would it so have fallen out with me had I mistrusted that slumbering passion of mine for Anne. I should have known that where such fires have once been kindled in a man they never quite die out as long as life endures. Time and preoccupations may overlay them as with a film of ashes, but more or less deeply down they smoulder on, and the first breath will fan them into flame again.

It was at the King's request I went to see her in her fine Madrid house opposite Santa Maria Mayor some months after her husband's death. There were certain matters of heritage to be cleared up, and, having regard to her high rank, it was Philip's wish that I - who was by now Eboli's official successor - should wait on her in person.

There were documents to be conned and signed, and the matter took some days, for Eboli's possessions were not only considerable, but scattered, and his widow displayed an acquired knowledge of affairs and a natural wisdom that inspired her to probe deeply. To my undoing, she probed too deeply in one matter. It concerned some land - a little property - at Velez. She had been attached to the place, it seemed, and she missed all mention of it from the papers that I brought her. She asked the reason.

"It is disposed of, " I told her.

"Disposed of! " quoth she. "But by whom? "

"By the Prince, your husband, a little while before he died. "

She looked up at me - she was seated at the wide, carved writing-table, I standing by her side - as if expecting me to say more. As I left my utterance there, she frowned perplexedly.

"But what mystery is this? " she asked me. "To whom has it gone? "

"To one Sancho Gordo. "

"To Sancho Gordo? " The frown deepened. "The washerwoman's son? You will not tell me that he bought it? "

"I do not tell you so, madame. It was a gift from the Prince, your husband. "

"A gift! " She laughed. "To Sancho Gordo! So the washerwoman's child is Eboli's son! "

And again she laughed on a note of deep contempt.

"Madame! " I cried, appalled and full of pity, "I assure you that you assume too much. The Prince - "

"Let be, " she interrupted me. "Do you dream I care what rivals I may have had, however lowly they may have been? The Prince, my husband, is dead, and that is very well. He is much better dead, Don Antonio. The pity of it is that he ever lived, or else that I was born a woman. "

She was staring straight before her, her hands fallen to her lap, her face set as if carved and lifeless, and her voice came hard as the sound of one stone beating upon another.

"Do you dream what it can mean to have been so nurtured on indignities that there is no anger left, no pride to wound by the discovery of yet another nothing but cold, cold hate? That, Don Antonio, is my case. You do not know what my life has been. That man - "

"He is dead, madame, " I reminded her, out of pity.

"And damned, I hope, " she answered me in that same cold, emotionless voice. "He deserves no less for all the wrongs he did to me, the least of which was the great wrong of marrying me. For advancement he acquired me; for his advancement he bartered and used me and made of me a thing of shame. "

I was so overwhelmed with grief and love and pity that a groan escaped me almost before I was aware of it. She broke off short, and stared at me in haughtiness.

"You presume to pity me, I think, " she reproved me. "It is my own fault. I was wrong to talk. Women should suffer silently, that they may preserve at least a mask of dignity. Otherwise they incur pity - and pity is very near contempt. "

And then I lost my head.

"Not mine, not mine! " I cried, throwing out my arms; and though that was all I said, there was such a ring in my choking voice that she rose stiffly from her seat and stood tense and tall confronting me, almost eye to eye, reproof in every line of her.

"Princess, forgive me! " I cried. "It breaks my heart in pieces to hear you utter things that have been in my mind these many years, poisoning the devotion that I owed to the late Prince, poisoning the very loyalty I owe my King. You say I pity you. If that were so, none has the better right. "

"Who gave it you? " she asked me, breathless.

"Heaven itself, I think, " I answered recklessly. "What you have suffered, I have suffered for you. When I came to Court the infamy was a thing accomplished - all of it. But I gathered it, and gathering it, thanked Heaven I had been spared the pain and misery of witnessing it, which must have been more than ever I could have endured. Yet when I saw you, when I watched you - your wistful beauty, your incomparable grace - there was a time when the thought to murder stirred darkly in my mind that I might at least avenge you. "

She fell away before me, white to the very lips, her eyes dilating as they regarded me.

"In God's name, why? " she asked me in a strangled voice.

"Because I loved you, " I replied, "always, always, since the day I saw you. Unfortunately, that day was years too late, even had I dared to hope - "

"Antonio! " Something in her voice drew my averted eyes. Her lips had parted, her eyes kindled into life, a flush was stirring in her cheeks.

"And I never knew! I never knew! " she faltered piteously.

I stared.

"Dear Heaven, why did you withhold a knowledge that would have upheld me and enheartened me through all that I have suffered? Once, long, long agog I hoped - "

"You hoped! "

"I hoped, Antonio - long, long ago. "

We were in each other's arms, she weeping on my shoulder as if her heart would burst, I almost mad with mingling joy and pain - and as God lives there was more matter here for pain than joy.

We sat long together after that, and talked it out. There was no help for it. It was too late on every count. On her side there was the King, most jealous of all men, whose chattel she was become; on mine, there was my wife and children, and so deep and true was my love for Anne that it awakened in me thoughts of the loyalty I owed Juana, thoughts that had never troubled me hitherto in my pleasure-loving life - and this not only as concerned Anne herself, but as concerned all women. There was something so ennobling and sanctifying about our love that it changed at once the whole of my life, the whole tenor of my ways. I abandoned profligacy, and became so staid and orderly in my conduct that I was scarcely recognizable for the Antonio Perez whom the world had known hitherto.

We parted there that day with a resolve to put all this behind us; to efface from our minds all memory of what had passed between us! Poor fools were we to imagine we could resist the vortex of circumstance which had caught us. For three months we kept our engagement scrupulously; and then, at last, resistance mutually exhausted, we yielded each to the other, both to Fate.

But because we cherished our love we moved with caution. I was circumspect in my comings and goings, and such were the precautions we observed, that for four years the world had little suspicion, and certainly no knowledge, that I had inherited from the Prince of Eboli more than his office as Secretary of State. This secrecy was necessary as long as Philip lived, for we were both fully aware of what manner of vengeance we should have to reckon with did knowledge of our relations reach the jealous King. And I think that but for Don John of Austria's affairs, and the intervention in them of the Escovedo whom you say - whom the world says I murdered, all might have been well to this day.

Escovedo had been, like myself, one of Eboli's secretaries in his day, and it was this that won him after Eboli's death a place at the Royal Council board. It was but an inferior place, yet the King remarked him for a man shrewd and able, who might one day have his uses.

That day was not very long in coming, though the opportunity it afforded Escovedo was scarcely such as, in his greedy, insatiable ambition, he had hoped for. Yet the opportunity, such as it was, was afforded him by me, and had he used it properly it should have carried him far, certainly much farther than his talent and condition warranted.

It came about through Don John of Austria's dreams of sovereignty. You will have heard - as who has not? - so much of Don John, the natural son of Charles V, that I need tell you little concerning him. In body and soul he was a very different man, indeed, from his half-brother Philip of Spain. As joyous as Philip was gloomy, as open and frank as Philip was cloudy and suspicious, and as beautiful as Philip was grotesque, Don John was the Bayard of our day, the very mirror of all knightly graces. To the victory of Lepanto, which had made him illustrious as a soldier, he had added, in '73 - the year of Eboli's death the conquest of Tunis, thereby completing the triumph of Christianity over the Muslim in the Mediterranean. Success may have turned his head a little. He was young, you know, and an emperor's son. He dreamt of an empire for himself, of sovereignty, and of making Tunis the capital of the kingdom he would found.

We learnt of this. Indeed, Don John made little secret of his intentions. But they went not at all with Philip's views. It was far from his notions that Don John should go founding kingdoms of his own. His valour and talents were required to be employed for the greater honour and glory of the Crown of Spain, and nothing further.

Philip consulted me, who was by then the depositary of all his secrets, the familiar of his inmost desires. There was evidence that Don John's ambitions were being fomented by his secretary, who dreamt, no doubt, of his own aggrandizement in the aggrandizement of his master. Philip proposed the man's removal.

"That would be something, " I agreed. "But not enough. He must be replaced by a man of our own, a man loyal to Your Majesty, who will not only seek to guide Don John in the course that he should follow, but will keep close watch upon his projects, and warn you should they threaten to neglect your interests the interests of Spain for his own. "

"And such a man? Where shall we find him? "

I considered a moment, and bethought me of Escovedo. He was able; he had charm and an ingratiating manner; I believed him loyal, and imagined that I could quicken that loyalty by showing him that advancement would wait upon its observation; he could well be spared from the Council, where, as I have said, he occupied a quite inferior post; lastly, we were friends, and I was glad of the opportunity to serve him, and place him on the road to better things.

All this I said to Philip, and so the matter was concluded. But Escovedo failed me. His abilities and ingratiating manner endeared him quickly to Don John, whilst himself he succumbed entirely, not only to Don John of Austria's great personal charm, but also to Don John's ambitious projects. The road to advancement upon which I had set him seemed to him long and toilsome by contrast with the shorter cut that was offered by his new master's dreams. He fell as the earlier secretary had fallen, and more grievously, for he was the more ambitious of the two, and from merely seconding Don John's projects, it was not long before he spurred them on, not long before he was dreaming dreams of his own for Don John to realize.

From Tunis, which had by now been recovered by the Turks, and any hopes concerned with which King Philip had discouraged, the eyes of Don John were set, at Escovedo's bidding, I believe, upon the crown of England.

He had just been invited by Philip to make ready to take in hand the affairs of Flanders, sadly disorganized under the incompetent rule of Alva. It occurred to him that if he were to issue victoriously from that enterprise - and so far victory had waited upon his every venture - if he were to succeed in restoring peace and Spanish order in rebellious Flanders, he would then be able to move against England with the Spanish troops under his command, overthrow Elizabeth, deliver Mary Stuart from the captivity in which she languished, and by marriage with her set the crown of England on his brow. To this great project he sought the support of Rome, and Rome accorded it very readily being naturally hostile to the heretic daughter of Anne Boleyn.

It was Escovedo himself who went as Don John's secret ambassador to the Vatican in this affair Escovedo, who had been placed with Don John to act as a curb on that young man's ambitions. Nor did he move with the prudence he should have observed.

Knowledge of what was brewing reached us from the Papal Nuncio in Madrid, who came to see me one day in the matter.

"I have a dispatch from Rome, " he announced, "in which His Holiness instructs me to enjoin upon the King that the expedition against England be now executed, and that he consider bestowing its crown upon Don John of Austria for the greater honour and glory of Holy Church. "

I was thunderstruck. The expedition against England, I knew, was no new project. Three years before a secret envoy from the Queen of Scots, an Italian named Ridolfi, had come to propose to Philip that, in concert with the Pope, he should reestablish the Catholic faith in England and place Mary Stuart upon the throne. It was a scheme attractive to Philip, since it agreed at once with his policy and his religion. But it had been abandoned under the dissuasions of Alva, who accounted that it would be too costly even if successful. Here it was again, emanating now directly from the Holy See, but in a slightly altered form.

"Why Don John of Austria? " I asked him.

"A great soldier of the faith. And the Queen of Scots must have a husband. "

"I should have thought that she had had husbands enough by now, " said I.

"His Holiness does not appear to share that view, " he answered tartly.

"I wonder will the King, " said I.

"The Catholic King is ever an obedient child of Mother Church, " the oily Nuncio reminded me, to reprove my doubt.

But I knew better - that the King's own policy was the measure of his obedience. This the Nuncio should learn for himself; for if I knew anything of Philip's mind, I knew precisely how he would welcome this proposal.

"Will you see the King now? " I suggested maliciously, anxious to witness the humbling of his priestly arrogance.

"Not yet. It is upon that I came to see you. I am instructed first to consult with one Escoda as to the manner in which this matter shall be presented to His Majesty. Who is Escoda? "

"I never heard of him, " said I. "Perhaps he comes from Rome. "

"No, no. Strange! " he muttered, frowning, and plucked a parchment from his sleeve. "It is here. " He peered slowly at the writing, and slowly spelled out the name: "Juan de Escoda. "

In a flash it came to me.

"Escovedo you mean, " I cried,

"Yes, yes - Escovedo, to be sure, " he agreed, having consulted the writing once more. "Where is he? "

"On his way to Madrid with Don John, " I informed him. "He is Don John's secretary. "

"I will do nothing, then, until he arrives, " he said, and took his leave.

Oh, monstrous indiscretion! That dispatch from Rome so cunningly and secretly contrived in cipher had yet contained no warning that Escovedo's share in this should be concealed. There are none so imprudent as the sly. I sought the King at once, and told him all that I had learnt. He was aghast. Indeed, I never saw him more near to anger. For Philip of Spain was not the man to show wrath or any other emotion. He had a fish-like, cold, impenetrable inscrutability. True, his yellow skin grew yellower, his gaping mouth gaped wider, his goggle eyes goggled more than usual. Left to himself, I think he would have disgraced Don John and banished Escovedo there and then, as he did, indeed, suggest. And I have since had cause enough to wish to God that I had left him to himself.

"Who will replace Don John in Flanders? " I asked him quietly. He stared at me. "He is useful to you there. Use him, Sire, to your own ends. "

"But they will press this English business. "

"Acquiesce. "

"Acquiesce? Are you mad? "

"Seem to acquiesce. Temporize. Answer them, 'One thing at a time. ' Say, 'When the Flanders business is happily concluded, we will think of England. ' Give them hope that success in Flanders will dispose you to support the other project. Thus you offer Don John an incentive to succeed, yet commit yourself to nothing. "

"And this dog Escovedo? "

"Is a dog who betrays himself by his bark. We will listen for it. "

And thus it was determined; thus was Don John suckled on the windy pap of hope when presently he came to Court with Escovedo at his heels. Distended by that empty fare he went off to the Low Countries, leaving Escovedo in Madrid to represent him, with secret instructions to advance his plans.

Now Escovedo's talents were far inferior to my conception of them.

He was just a greedy schemer, without the wit to dissemble his appetite or the patience necessary to secure attainment.

Affairs in Flanders went none too well, yet that did not set a curb upon him. He pressed his master's business upon the King with an ardour amounting to disrespect, and disrespect was a thing the awful majesty of Philip could never brook. Escovedo complained of delays, of indecision, and finally - in the summer of '76 - he wrote the King a letter of fierce upbraidings, criticizing his policy in terms that were contemptuous, and which entirely exasperated Philip.

It was in vain I strove to warn the fellow of whither he was drifting; in vain I admonished and sought to curb his headlong recklessness. I have said that I had a friendship for him, and because of that I took more pains, perhaps, than I should have taken in another's case.

"Unless you put some judgment into that head of yours, my friend, you will leave it in this business, " I told him one day.

He flung into a passion at the admonition, heaped abuse upon me, swore that it was I who thwarted him, I who opposed the fulfilment of Don John's desires and fostered the dilatory policy of the King.

I left him after that to pursue his course, having no wish to quarrel with this headstrong upstart; yet, liking him as I did, I spared no endeavour to shield him from the consequences he provoked. But that letter of his to Philip made the task a difficult one. Philip showed it to me.

"If that man, " he said, "had uttered to my face what he has dared to write, I do not think I should have been able to contain myself without visible change of countenance. It is a sanguinary letter. "

I set myself to calm him as best I could.

"The man is indiscreet, which has its advantage, for we always know whither an indiscreet man is heading. His zeal for his master blinds him and makes him rash. It is better, perhaps, than if he were secretive and crafty. "

With such arguments I appeased his wrath against the secretary. But I knew that his hatred of Escovedo, his thirst for Escovedo's blood, dated from that moment in which Escovedo had forgotten the reverence due to majesty. I was glad when at last he took himself off to Flanders to rejoin Don John. But that was very far from setting a term to his pestering. The Flanders affair was going so badly that the hopes of an English throne to follow were dwindling fast. Something else must be devised against the worst, and now Don John and Escovedo began to consider the acquisition of power in Spain itself. Their ambition aimed at giving Don John the standing of an Infante. Both of them wrote to me to advance this fresh project of theirs, to work for their recall, so that they could ally themselves with my party - the Archbishop's party - and ensure its continuing supreme. Escovedo wrote me a letter that was little better than an attempt to bribe me. The King was ageing, and the Prince was too young to relieve him of the heavy duties of State. Don John should shoulder these, and in so doing Escovedo and myself should be hoisted into greater power.

I carried all those letters to the King, and at his suggestion I even pretended to lend an ear to these proposals that we might draw from Escovedo a fuller betrayal of his real ultimate aims. It was dangerous, and I enjoined the King to move carefully.

"Be discreet, " I warned him, "for if my artifice were discovered, I should not be of any further use to you at all. In my conscience I am satisfied that in acting as I do I am performing no more than my duty. I require no theology other than my own to understand that much. "

"My theology, " he answered me, "takes much the same view. You would have failed in your duty to God and me had you failed to enlighten me on the score of this deception. These things, " he added in a dull voice, "appal me. "

So I wrote to Don John, urging him as one who counselled him for his good, who had no interest but his own at heart, to remain in Flanders until the work there should be satisfactorily completed. He did so, since he was left no choice in the matter, but the intrigues continued. Later we saw how far he was from having forsaken his dreams of England, when I discovered that he had engaged the Pope to assist him with six thousand men and one hundred and fifty thousand ducats when the time for that adventure should be ripe.

And then, quite suddenly, entirely unheralded, Escovedo reappeared in Madrid, having come to press Philip in person for reinforcements that should enable Don John to finish the campaign. He brought news that there had been a fresh rupture of the patched-up peace, that Don John had taken the field once more, and had forcibly made himself master of Namur. This was contrary to all the orders we had sent, a direct overriding of Philip's wishes. The King desired peace in the Low Countries because he was in no case just then to renew the war, and Escovedo's impudently couched demands completed his exasperation.

"My will, " he said, "is as naught before the ambitions of these two. You sent my clear instructions to Escovedo, who was placed with Don John that he might render him pliant to my wishes. Instead, he stiffens him in rebellion. There must be an end to this man. "

"Sire, " I cried, "it may be they think to advance your interests. "

"Heaven help me! " he cried. "Did ever villain wear so transparent a mask as this dog Escovedo? To advance my interests - that will be his tale, no doubt. He will advance them where I do not wish them advanced; he will advance them to my ruin; he will stake all on a success in Flanders that shall be the preliminary to a descent upon England in the interests of Don John. I say there must be an end to this man before he works more mischief. "

Again I set myself to calm him, as I had so often done before, and again I was the shield between Escovedo and the royal lightnings, of whose menace to blot him out the fool had no suspicion. For months things hung there, until, in January of '78, when war had been forced in earnest upon Spain by Elizabeth's support of the Low Countries, Don John won the great victory of Gemblours. This somewhat raised the King's depression, somewhat dissipated his overgrowing mistrust of his half-brother, and gave him patience to read the letters in which Don John urged him to send money - to throw wood on the fire whilst it was alight, or else resign himself to the loss of Flanders for all time. As it meant also resigning himself to the loss of all hope of England for all time, Escovedo's activities were just then increased a hundredfold.

"Send me money and Escovedo, " was the burden of the almost daily letters from Don John to me, and at my elbow was Escovedo, perpetually pressing me to bend the King to his master's will. Another matter on which he pressed me then was that I should obtain for himself the governorship of the Castle of Mogro, which commands the port of Santander, an ambition this which intrigued me deeply, for I confess I could not fathom what it had to do with all the rest.

And then something else happened. From the Spanish Ambassador at the Louvre we learnt one day of a secret federation entered into between Don John and the Guises, known as the Defence of the Two Crowns. Its object was as obscure as its title. But it afforded the last drop to the cup of Philip's mistrust. This time it was directly against Don John that he inveighed to me. And to defend Don John, in the interests of common justice, I was forced to place the blame where it belonged.

"Nay, Sire, " I assured him, "these ambitions are not Don John's. With all his fevered dreams of greatness, Don John has ever been, will ever be, loyal to his King. "

"If you know anything of temptation, " he answered me, "you should know that there is a breaking-point to every man's resistance of it. How long will Don John remain loyal while Escovedo feeds his disloyalty, adds daily to the weight of temptation the burden of a fresh ambition? I tell you, man, I feel safe no longer. " He rose up before me, a blotch on his sallow face, his fingers tugging nervously at the tuft of straw-coloured beard. "I tell you some blow is about to fall unless we avert it. This man this fellow Escovedo - must be dispatched before he can kill us. "

I shrugged and affected carelessness to soothe him.

"A contemptible dreamer, " I said. "Pity him, Sire. He has his uses. To remove him would be to remove a channel through which we can always obtain knowledge precisely of what is doing. "

Again I prevailed, and there the matter hung a while. But the King was right, his fears were well inspired. Escovedo, always impatient, was becoming desperate under persistent frustration. I reasoned with him - was he not still my friend? - I held him off, urged prudence and patience upon him, and generally sought to temporize. I was as intent upon saving him from leaving his skin in this business as I was, on the other hand, intent upon doing my duty without pause or scruple to my King. But the fool forced my hand. A Court is a foul place always, even so attenuated a Court as that which Philip of Spain encouraged. Rumour thrives in it, scandal blossoms luxuriantly in its fetid atmosphere. And rumour and scandal had been busy with the Princess of Eboli and me, though I did not dream it.

We had been indiscreet, no doubt. We had been seen together in public too often. We had gone to the play together more than once; she had been present with me at a bull-fight on one occasion, and it was matter of common gossip, as I was to learn, that I was a too frequent visitor at her house.

Another visitor there was Escovedo when in Madrid. Have I not said that in his early days he had been one of Eboli's secretaries? On that account the house of Eboli remained open to him at all times. The Princess liked him, was kindly disposed towards him, and encouraged his visits. We met there more than once. One day we left together, and that day the fool set spark to a train that led straight to the mine on which, all unconsciously, he stood.

"A word of advice in season, Don Antonio, " he said as we stepped forth together. "Do not go so often to visit the Princess. "

I sought to pull my arm from his, but he dung to it and pinned it to his side.

"Nay, now - nay, now! " he soothed me. "Not so hot, my friend. What the devil have I said to provoke resentment? I advise you as your friend. "

"In future advise that other friend of yours, the devil, " I answered angrily, and pulled my arm away at last. "Don Juan, you have presumed, I think. I did not seek your advice. It is yourself that stands in need of advice this moment more than any man in Spain. "

"Lord of the World, " he exclaimed in amiable protest, "listen to him! I speak because I owe friendship to the Princess. Men whisper of your comings and goings, I tell you. And the King, you know well, should he hear of this I am in danger of losing my only friend at Court, and so - "

"Another word of this, " I broke in fiercely, "now or at any other time, and I'll skewer you like a rabbit! "

I had stopped. My face was thrust within a hand's-breadth of his own; I had tossed back my cloak, and my fingers clutched the hilt of my sword. He became grave. His fine eyes - he had great, sombre, liquid eyes, such as you'll scarcely ever see outside of Spain - considered me thoughtfully a moment. Then he laughed lightly and fell back a pace.

"Pish! " said he. "Saint James! I am no rabbit for your skewering. If it comes to skewers, I am a useful man of my hands, Antonio. Come, man" - and again he took my arm - "if I presume, forgive it out of the assurance that I am moved solely by interest and concern for you. We have been friends too long that I should be denied. "

I had grown cool again, and I realized that perhaps my show of anger had been imprudent. So I relented now, and we went our ways together without further show of ill-humour on my part, or further advice on his. But the matter did not end there. Indeed, it but began. Going early in the afternoon of the morrow to visit Anne, I found her in tears - tears, as I was to discover, of anger.

Escovedo had been to visit her before me, and he had dared to reproach her on the same subject.

"You are talked about, you and Perez, " he had informed her, "and the thing may have evil consequences. It is because I have eaten our bread that I tell you this for your own good. "

She had risen up in a great passion.

"You will leave my house, and never set foot in it again, " she had told him. "You should learn that grooms and lackeys have no concern in the conduct of great ladies. It is because you have eaten my bread that I tell you this for your own good. "

It drove him out incontinently, but it left her in the condition in which I was later to discover her. I set myself to soothe her. I swore that Escovedo should be punished. But she would not be soothed. She blamed herself for an unpardonable rashness. She should not have taken that tone with Escovedo. He could avenge himself by telling Philip, and if he told Philip, and Philip believed him - as Philip would, being jealous and mistrustful beyond all men - my ruin must follow. She had thought only of herself in dismissing him in that high-handed manner. Coming since to think of me it was that she had fallen into this despair. She clung to me in tears.

"Forgive me, Antonio. The fault is all mine - the fault of all. Always have I known that this danger must overhang you as a penalty for loving me. Always I knew it, and, knowing it, I should have been stronger. I should have sent you from me at the first. But I was so starved of love from childhood till I met you. I hungered so for love - for your love, Antonio - that I had not the strength. I was weak and selfish, and because I was ready and glad to pay the price myself, whatever it should be and whenever asked, I did not take thought enough for you. "

"Take no thought now, " I implored her, holding her close.

"I must. I can't help it. I have raised this peril for you. He will go to Philip. "

"Not he; he dare not. I am his only hope. I am the ladder by which he hopes to scale the heaven of his high ambition. If he destroys me, there is the kennel for himself. He knows it. "

"Do you say that to comfort me, or is it really true? "

"God's truth, sweetheart, " I swore, and drew her closer.

She was comforted long before I left her. But as I stepped out into the street again a man accosted me. Evidently he had been on the watch, awaiting me. He fell into step beside me almost before I realized his presence. It was Escovedo.

"So, " he said, very sinister, "you'll not be warned. "

"Nor will you, " I answered, no whit less sinister myself.

It was broad daylight. A pale March sunshine was beating down upon the cobbled streets, and passers-by were plentiful. There was no fingering of hilts or talk of skewering on either side. Nor must I show any of the anger that was boiling in me. My face was too well known in Madrid streets, and a Secretary of State does not parade emotions to the rabble. So I walked stiff and dignified amain, that dog in step with me the while.

"She will have told you what I have said to her, " he murmured.

"And what she said to you. It was less than your deserts. "

"Groom and lackey, eh? " said he. "And less than I deserve - a man of my estate. Oh, ho! Groom and lackey! Those are epithets to be washed out in blood and tears. "

"You rant, " I said.

"Or else to be paid for - handsomely. " His tone was sly - so sly that I answered nothing, for to answer a sly man is to assist him, and my business was to let him betray the cause of this slyness. Followed a spell of silence. Then, "Do you know, " said he, "that several of her relatives are thinking seriously of killing you? "

"Many men have thought seriously of that - so seriously that they never attempted it. Antonio Perez is not easily murdered, Don Juan, as you may discover. "

It was a boast that I may claim to have since justified.

"Shall I tell you their names? " quoth he.

"If you want to ruin them. "

"Ha! " It was a short bark of a laugh. "You talk glibly of ruining - but then you talk to a groom and lackey. " The epithets rankled in his mind; they were poison to his blood, it seemed. It takes a woman to find words that burn and blister a man. "Yet groom and lackey that I am, I hold you both in the hollow of my hand. If I close that hand, it will be very bad for you, very bad for her. If, for instance, I were to tell King Philip that I have seen her in your arms -"

"You dog! "

"I have - I swear to God I have, with these two eyes - at least with one of them, applied to the keyhole half an hour ago. Her servants passed me in; a ducat or two well bestowed - you understand? "

We had reached the door of my house. I paused and turned to him.

"You will come in? " I invited.

"As the wolf said to the lamb, eh? Well, why not? " And we went in.

"You are well housed, " he commented, his greedy, envious eyes considering all the tokens of my wealth. "It were a pity to lose so much, I think. The King is at the Escurial, I am told. "

He was. He had gone thither into retreat, that he might cleanse his pious, murky soul against the coming of Eastertide.

"You would not, I am sure, compel me to undertake so tedious a journey, " said he.

"Will you put off this slyness and be plain? " I bade him. "You have some bargain in your mind. Propound it. "

He did, and left me aghast.

"You have temporized long enough, Perez, " he began. "You have been hunting with the dogs and running with the stag. There must be an end to all that. Stand by me now, and I will make you greater than you are, greater than you could ever dream to be. Oppose me, betray me - for I am going to be very frank - and the King shall hear things from me that will mean your ruin and hers. You understand? "

Then came his demands. First of all the command of the fortress of Mogro for himself. I must obtain him that at once. Secondly, I must see to it that Philip pledged himself to support Don John's expedition against England and Elizabeth and to seat Don John upon the throne with Mary Stuart for his wife. These things must come about, and quickly, or I perished. Nor was that all. Indeed, no more than a beginning. He opened out the vista of his dreams, that having blackmailed me on the one hand, he might now bribe me on the other. Once England was theirs, he aimed at no less than a descent upon Spain itself. That was why he wanted Mogro to facilitate a landing at Santander. Thus, as the Christians had originally come

69

down from the mountains of the Asturias to drive the Moors from the Peninsula, so should the forces of Don John descend again to reconquer it for himself.

It was a madman's fancy utterly - fruit of a brain that ambition had completely addled; and I do not believe that Don John had any part in it or even knowledge of it. Escovedo saw himself, perhaps, upon the throne of one or the other of the two kingdoms as Don John's vice-regent - for himself and for me, if I stood by him, there was such power in store as no man ever dreamed of. If I refused, he would destroy me.

"And if I go straight to the Escurial and lay this project before the King? " I asked him.

He smiled.

"You will force me to tell him that it is a lie invented to deliver you from a man who can destroy you by the knowledge he possesses, knowledge which I shall at once impart to Philip. Think what that will mean to you. Think, " he added very wickedly, "what it will mean to her. "

As I am a Christian, I believe that had it been but the consideration of myself I would have flung him from my house upon the instant and bade him do his worst. But he was well advised to remind me of her. Whatever Philip's punishment of me, it would be as nothing to his punishment of that long-suffering woman who had betrayed him. Oh, I assure you it is a very evil, ill judged thing to have a king for rival, particularly a fish-souled tyrant of King Philip's kind.

I was all limp with dread. I passed a hand across my brow, and found it chill and moist.

"I am in your hands, Escovedo, " I confessed miserably.

"Say, rather, that we are partners. Forget all else. " He was eager, joyous, believing all accomplished, such was his faith in my influence with Philip. "And now, Mogro for me, and England for Don John. About it with dispatch. "

"The King is in retreat. We must wait some days. "

"Till Easter, then. " And he held out his hand. I took it limply, thus clenching the bargain of infamy between us. What else was there for me. What, otherwise, was to become of Anne?

Oh, I may have been self-seeking and made the most of my position, as was afterwards urged against me. I may have been extortionate and venal, and I may have taken regal bribes to expedite affairs. But always was I loyal and devoted to the King. Never once had I been bribed to aught that ran counter to his interests; never until now, when at a stroke I had sold my honour and pledged myself to this betrayal of my trust.

Not in all Spain was there a more miserable man than I. All night I sat in the room where I was wont to work, and to my wife's entreaties that I should take some rest I answered that the affairs of Spain compelled attention. And when morning found me haggard and distraught came a courier from Philip with a letter.

"I have letters from Don John, " he wrote, "more insistent than ever in their tone. He demands the instant dispatch of money and Escovedo. I have been thinking, and this letter confirms my every fear. I have cause to apprehend some stroke that may disturb the public peace and ruin Don John himself if he is allowed to retain Escovedo any longer in his service. I am writing to Don John that I will see to it that Escovedo is promptly dispatched as he requests. Do you see him dispatched, then, in precise accordance with his deserts, and this at once, before the villain kills us. "

My skin bristled as I read. Here was fatality itself at work. Philip was at his old fears - and, Heaven knows, he was not without justification of his intuitions, as I had learnt by now - that Escovedo meditated the most desperate measures. He was urging me again, as he had urged me before, and more than once, to dispatch this traitor whose restless existence so perpetually perturbed him. I was not deceived as to the meaning he set upon that word "dispatch. " I knew quite well the nature of the dispatch he bade me contrive.

Conceive now my temptation. Escovedo dead, I should be safe, and Anne would be safe, and this without any such betrayal as was being forced upon me. And that death the King himself commanded a secret, royal execution, such as his confessor Frey Diego de Chaves has since defended as an expedient measure within the royal prerogative. He had commanded it before quite unequivocally, but always I had stood between Escovedo and the sword. Was I to continue in that attitude? Could it humanly be expected of me in all the circumstances again to seek to deflect the royal wrath from that too daring head? I was, after all, only a man, subject to the temptations of the flesh, and there was a woman whom I loved better than my own salvation to whose peace and happiness that fellow Escovedo was become a menace.

If he lived, and for as long as he lived, she and I were to be as slaves of his will, and I was to drag my honour and my loyalty through the foul kennels of his disordered ambitions. And the King my master was bidding me clearly see to it that he died immediately.

I sat down and wrote at once, and the burden of my letter was: "Be more explicit, Sire. What manner of dispatch is it your will that Escovedo should be given? "

On the morrow, which was Thursday of Holy Week, that note of mine was returned to me, and on the margin of it, in Philip's own hand, Escovedo's death-warrant. "I mean that it would be well to hasten the death of this rascal before some act of his should render it too late; for he never rests, nor will anything turn him from his usual ways. Do it, then, and do it quickly, before he kills us. "

There was no more to be said. My instructions were clear and definite. Obedience alone remained. I went about it.

Just as all my life I have been blessed with the staunchest friends, so have I, too, been blessed with the most faithful servants. And of these none was more faithful than my steward, Diego Martinez, unless, indeed, it be my equerry, Gil de Mesa, who to this day follows my evil fortunes. But Mesa at that time was as yet untried, whilst in Diego I knew that I had a man devoted to me heart and soul, a man who would allow himself to be torn limb from limb on the rack on my behalf.

I placed the affair in Diego's hands. I told him that I was acting under orders from the King, and that the thing at issue was the private execution of a dangerous traitor, who could not be brought to trial lest there he should impeach of complicity one whose birth and blood must be shielded from all scandal. I bade him get what men he required, and see the thing done with the least possible delay. And thereupon I instantly withdrew from Madrid and went to Alcala.

Diego engaged five men to assist him in the task; these were a young officer named Enriquez, a lackey named Rubio, the two Aragonese - Mesa and Insausti - and another whose name was Bosque. He clearly meant to take no chances, but I incline to think that he overdid precaution, and employed more hands than were necessary for the job. However, the six of them lurked in waiting on three successive nights for Escovedo near his house in the little square of Santiago. At last, on the night of Easter Monday, March 31st, they caught him and dispatched him. He died almost before he realized himself beset, from a sword-thrust with which Insausti transfixed him. But there were at least half a dozen wounds in the body when it was found. Diego, I have said, was a man who made quite certain.

No sooner was it done than they dispersed, whilst the lackey Rubio, instantly quitting Madrid, brought me news of the deed to Alcala, and the assurance that no arrests had been made. But there was a great ado in Madrid upon the morrow, as you may imagine, for it is no everyday occurrence to find a royal secretary murdered in the streets.

The alcaldes set out upon a rigorous search, and they began by arresting and questioning all who attempted to leave the city. On the next day they harassed with their perquisitions all those who let lodgings. They were still at this work in the evening when I returned to Madrid, brought back - as it would seem - from my country rest by the news of this murder of my friend and colleague. I bore myself as I should have done had I no knowledge of how the thing had been contrived. That was a necessity as imperative as it was odious, and no part of it more odious than the visit of condolence I was forced to pay to the Escovedo family, which I found plunged in grief.

From the very outset suspicion pointed its finger at me, although there were no visible traces to connect me with the deed. Rumour, however, was astir, and as I had powerful friends, so, too, I had the powerful enemies which envy must always be breeding for men in high places such as mine. Escovedo's wife mistrusted me, though at first she seems equally to have suspected in this deed the hand of the Duke of Alva, who was hostile to Don John and all his creatures. Very soon, as a result of this, came the Court alcalde to visit and question me. His stated object was in the hope that I might give him information which would lead to the discovery of the assassin; but his real object, rendered apparent by the searching, insistent nature of his questions, was to lead me to incriminate myself. I presented a bold front. I pretended to see in this, perhaps, the work of the Flemish States. I deplored - that I might remind him of it - my absence from Madrid at the time.

He was followed by another high official, who came in simulated friendship to warn me that certain rumours linking me with the deed were in circulation, in reality to trap me into some admission, to watch my countenance for some betraying sign.

I endured it stoutly, but inwardly I was shaken, as I wrote to Philip, giving him full details of what had been said and what answers I had returned, what bitter draughts I had been forced to swallow.

He wrote in reply: "I find that you answered very well. Continue to be prudent. They will tell you a thousand things, not for the sake of telling them, but in the hope of drawing something out of you. The bitter draughts you mention are inevitable. But use all the dissimulation and address of which you are capable. "

We corresponded daily after that, and I told him of every step I took; how I kept my men about me, for fear that if they attempted to leave Madrid they would be arrested, and how, finally, I contrived their departure one by one, under conditions that placed them beyond all suspicion. Juan de Mesa set out for Aragon on a mission concerned with the administration of some property of the Princess of Eboli's. Rubio, Insausti, and Enriquez were each given an ensign's commission, bearing the King's own signature, and ordered to join the armies in various parts of Italy; the first was sent to Milan, the second to Sicily, and the last to Naples. Bosque went back to Aragon. Thus all were placed beyond the reach of the active justice of Castile, all save myself - and the King, who wrote to me expressing his satisfaction that there had been no arrests.

But rumour continued to give tongue, and the burden of its tale was that the murder had been my work, in complicity with the Princess of Eboli. How they came to drag her name into the affair I do not know. It may have been pure malice trading upon its knowledge of the relations between us. She may have lent colour to the charge by her own precipitancy in denying it. She announced indignantly that she was being accused, almost before this had come to pass, and as indignantly protested against the accusation, and threatened those who dared to voice it.

The end of it all was that, a month later, the Escovedo family drew up a memorial for the consideration of the King, in which they laid the murder to my charge, and Philip consented to receive Don Pedro de Escovedo - the dead man's son - and promised him that he would consider the memorial, and that he would deliver up to justice whomsoever he thought right. He was embarrassed by these demands of the Escovedos, my own danger, his duty as king, and his interests as an accomplice, or, rather, as the originator of the deed.

The Escovedos were powerfully seconded by Vasquez, the Secretary of the Council, a member of Alva's party, a secret enemy of my own, consumed by jealousy of my power, and no longer fearing to disclose himself and assail me since he believed himself possessed of the means of ruining me. He spoke darkly to the King of a woman concerned in this business, without yet daring to mention Anne by name, and urged him for the satisfaction of the State, where evil rumours were abroad, to order an inquiry that should reveal the truth of the affair.

It was Philip himself who informed me of what had passed, sneering at the wildness of rumours that missed the truth so wildly, and when I evinced distress at my position, he sought to reassure me; he even wrote to me after I had left him: "As long as I live you have nothing to fear. Others may change, but I never change, as you should know who know me. "

That was a letter that epitomized many others written me in those days to Madrid from the Escurial, whither he had returned. And those letters comforted me not only by their expressed assurances, but by the greater assurance implicit in them of the King's good faith. I had by now a great mass of his notes dealing with the Escovedo business, in almost every one of which he betrayed his own share as the chief murderer, showing that I was no more than his dutiful instrument in that execution. With those letters in my power what need I ever fear? Not Philip himself would dare to betray me.

But I went now in a new dread - the dread of being myself murdered. There were threats of it in the air. The Escovedo family and their partisans, who included all my enemies, and even some members of the Eboli family, who considered that I had sullied the honour of their name by my relations with Anne, talked openly of vengeance, so that I was driven to surround myself by armed attendants whenever now I went abroad.

I appealed again to Philip to protect me. I even begged him to permit me to retire from my Ministerial office, that thus the clamant envy that inspired my persecution might be deprived of its incentive. Finally, I begged him to order me to stand my trial, that thus, since I was confident that no evidence could be produced against me, I should force an acquittal from the courts and lay the matter to rest for all time.

"Go and see the President of Castile, " he bade me. "Tell him the causes that led to the death of Escovedo, and then let him talk to Don Pedro de Escovedo and to Vasquez, so as to induce them to desist. "

I did as I was bidden, and when the president, who was the Bishop of Pati, had heard me, he sent for my two chief enemies.

"I have, Don Pedro, " he said, "your memorial to the King in which you accuse Don Antonio Perez of the murder of your father. And I am to assure you in the King's name that justice will be done upon the murderer, whoever he may be, without regard to rank. But I am first to engage you to consider well what evidence you have to justify your charge against a person of such consideration. For should your proofs be insufficient I warn you that matters are likely to take a bad turn for yourself. Finally, before you answer me, let me add, upon my word as a priest, that Antonio Perez is as innocent as I am. "

It was the truth - the absolute truth, so far as it was known to Philip and to the Bishop - for, indeed, I was no more than the instrument of my master's will.

Don Pedro looked foolish, almost awed. He was as a man who suddenly becomes aware that he has missed stepping over the edge of a chasm in which destruction awaited him. He may have bethought him at last that all his rantings had no better authority than suspicions which no evidence could support.

"Sir, " he faltered, "since you tell me this, I pledge you my word on behalf of myself and my family to make no more mention of this death against Don Antonio. "

The Bishop swung then upon Vasquez, and his brow became furrowed with contemptuous anger.

"As for you, sir, you have heard - which was more than your due, for it is not your business by virtue of your office, nor have you any obligations towards the deceased, such as excuse Don Pedro's rashness, to pursue the murderers of Escovedo. Your solicitude in this matter brings you under a suspicion the more odious since you are a priest. I warn you, sir, to abstain, for this affair is different far from anything that you imagine. "

But envy is a fierce goad, a consuming, irresistible passion, corroding wisdom and deaf to all prudent counsels. Vasquez could not abstain. Ridden by his devil of spite and jealousy, he would not pause until he had destroyed either himself or me.

Since Escovedo's immediate family now washed their hands of the affair, Vasquez sought out more distant relatives of the murdered man, and stirred them up until they went in their turn to pester the courts, not only with accusations against myself, but with accusations that now openly linked with mine the name of the Princess of Eboli.

We were driven to the brink of despair, and in this Anne wrote to Philip. It was a madness. She made too great haste to excuse herself. She demanded protection from Vasquez and the evil rumours he was putting abroad, implored the King to make an example of men who could push so far their daring and irreverence, and to punish that Moorish dog Vasquez - I dare say there was Moorish blood in the fellow's veins - as he deserved.

I think our ruin dated from that letter. Philip sent for me to the Escurial. He wished to know more precisely what the accusations were. I told him, denying them. Then he desired of the Princess proof of what she alleged against Vasquez, and she had no difficulty in satisfying him. He seemed to believe our assurance that all was lies. Yet he did not move to punish Vasquez. But then I knew that sluggishness was his great characteristic. "Time and I are one, " he would say when I pressed on matters.

After that it was open war in the Council between me and Vasquez. The climax came when I was at the Escurial. I had sent a servant to Vasquez for certain State papers to be submitted to the King. He brought them, and folded in them a fiercely denunciatory letter full of insults and injuries, not the least of which was the imputation that my blood was not clean, my caste not good.

In a passion I sought Philip, beside myself almost, trembling under the insult.

"See, Sire, what this Moorish thief has dared to write me. It transcends all bearing. Either you take satisfaction for me of these insults or you permit me to take it for myself. "

He appeared to share my indignation, promised to give me leave to proceed against the man, but bade me first wait a while until certain business in the competent hands of Vasquez should be transacted. But weeks grew into months, and nothing was done. We were in April of '79, a year after the murder, and I was grown so uneasy, so sensitive to dangers about me, that I dared no longer visit Anne. And then Philip's confessor, Frey Diego de Chaves, came to me one day with a request on the King's part that I should make my peace with Vasquez.

"If he will retract, " was my condition. And Chaves went to see my enemy. What passed between them, what Vasquez may have told him, what he may have added to those rumours of my relations with Anne, I do not know. But I know that from that date there was a change in the King's attitude towards me, a change in the tone of the letters that he sent me, and, this continuing, I wrote to him at last releasing him from his promise to afford me satisfaction against Vasquez, assuring him that since, himself, he could forgive the injuries against us both, I could easily forgive those I had received myself, and finally begging his permission to resign my office and retire.

Anne had contributed to this. She had sent for me, and in tears had besought me to make my peace with Vasquez since the King desired it, and this was no time in which to attempt resistance to his wishes. I remained with her some hours, comforting her, for she was in the very depths of despair, persuaded that we were both ruined, and inconsolable in the thought that the blame of this was all her own.

It may be that I was watched, perhaps more closely than I imagined. It may be that spies were close about us, set by the jealous Philip, who desired confirmation or refutation of the things he had been told, the rumours that were gnawing at his vitals.

I left her, little dreaming that I was never to see her again in this life. That night I was arrested at my house by the Court alcalde upon an order from the King. The paltry reason advanced was my refusal to make my peace with Vasquez, and this when already the King was in possession of my letter acknowledging my readiness to do so; for the King was in Madrid, unknown to me. He came, it seems, that he might be present at another arrest effected that same night. From the porch of the Church of Santa Maria Mayor, he watched his alguazils enter the house of the Princess of Eboli, bring her forth, bestow her in a waiting carriage that was to bear her away to the fortress of Pinto, to an imprisonment which was later exchanged for exile to Pastrana lasting as long as life itself.

To sin against a Prince is worse, it seems, than to sin against God Himself. For God forgives, but princes, wounded in their vanity and pride, know nothing of forgiveness.

I was kept for four months a prisoner by the alcalde, no charge being preferred against me. Then, because my health was suffering grievously from confinement and the anxiety of suspense, I was moved to my own house, and detained there for another eight months under close guard. My friends besought the King in vain either to restore me to liberty or to bring me to trial. He told them the affair was of a nature very different from anything they deemed, and so evaded all demands.

In the summer of 1580, Philip went to Lisbon to take formal possession of the crown of Portugal, which he had inherited. I sent my wife to him to intercede for me. But he refused to see her, and so I was left to continue the victim of his vindictive lethargy. After a year of this, upon my giving a formal promise to renounce all hostility towards Vasquez, and never seek to do him harm in any way, I was accorded some degree of liberty. I was allowed to go out and to receive visitors, but not to visit any one myself.

Followed a further pause. Vasquez was now a man of power, for my party had fallen with me, and his own had supplanted it in the royal councils. It was by his work that at last, in '84, I was brought to trial upon a charge of corruption and misappropriation. I knew that my enemies had, meanwhile, become possessed of Enriquez, and that he was ready to give evidence, that he was making no secret of his share in the death of Escovedo, and that the King was being pressed by the Escovedos to bring me to trial upon the charge of murder. Instead, the other charge alone was preferred.

It was urged against me that I had kept a greater state than any grandee of Spain, that when I went abroad I did so with a retinue befitting a prince, that I had sold my favour and accepted bribes from foreign princes to guard their interests with the King of Spain.

They sentenced me to two years' imprisonment in a fortress, to be followed by ten years of exile, and I was to make, within nine days, restitution of some twenty million maravedis* - the alleged extent of my misappropriations - besides some jewels and furniture which I had received from the Princess of Eboli, and which I was now ordered to deliver up to the heirs of the late Prince.

*Ten thousand pounds, but with at least five times the present purchasing power of that sum.

Perquisitions had been made in my house, and my papers ransacked. Well I knew what they had sought. For the thought of the letters that had passed between Philip and myself at the time of Escovedo's death must now be troubling his peace of mind. I had taken due precautions when first I had seen the gathering clouds foreshadowing this change of weather. I had bestowed those papers safely in two iron-bound chests which had been concealed away against the time when I might need them to save my neck. And because now he failed to find what he sought - the evidence of his own share in the deed and his present base duplicity - Philip dared not slip the leash from those dogs who would be at my throat for the murder of Escovedo. That was why he bade them proceed against me only on the lesser charge of corruption.

I was taken to the fortress of Turruegano, and there they came to demand of me the surrender of my papers which the alcalde had failed to discover at my house. I imagined the uneasiness of Philip in dispatching those emissaries. I almost laughed as I refused. Those papers were my buckler against worse befalling me than had befallen already. Even now, if too hard pressed, I might find the opportunity of breaking my bonds by means of them. I sometimes

80

wonder why I did not apply myself to that. Yet there is small cause for wonder, really. From boyhood, almost, King Philip had been my master. Loyalty to him was a habit that went to the very roots of my being. I had served him without conscience and without scruple, and the notion of betraying him, save as a very last and very desperate resource, was inconceivable. I do not think he ever knew the depth and breadth of that loyalty of mine.

My refusal led those sons of dogs to attempt to frighten my wife with threats of unmentionable horrors unless she delivered up the papers I had secreted. She and our children were threatened with perpetual imprisonment on bread and water if she persisted in refusing to surrender them. But she held out against all threats, and remained firm even under the oily persecution to the same end of Philip's confessor, Frey Diego. Finally, I was notified that, in view of her stubbornness and my own, she and our children were cast into prison, and that there they would remain until I saw fit to become submissive to the royal will.

It is a subtle form of mental torture that will bid a man contemplate the suffering for his sake to which those who are dear to him are being subjected.

I raged and stormed before the officer who brought me this infamous piece of news. I gave vent to my impotent anger in blasphemous expressions that were afterwards to be used against me. The officer was subtly sympathetic.

"I understand your grief, Don Antonio, " he said. "Believe me, I feel for you - so much that I urge you to set an end to the captivity of those dear ones who are innocent, who are suffering for your sake. "

"And so make an end of myself? " I asked him fiercely.

"Reflection may show that even that is your duty in the circumstances. "

I looked into his smug face, and I was within an ace of striking him. Then I controlled myself, and my will was snapped.

"Very well, " I said. "The papers shall be surrendered. Let my steward, Diego Martinez, come to me here, and he shall receive my instructions to deliver the chests containing them to my wife, that she in turn may deliver them to the King. "

He withdrew, well pleased. No doubt he would take great credit to himself for this. Within three days, such haste did they make, my faithful steward stood before me in my prison at Turruegano.

You conceive the despair that had overwhelmed me after giving my consent, the consciousness that it was my life I was surrendering with those papers, - that without them I should be utterly defenceless. But in the three days that were sped I had been thinking, and not quite in vain.

Martinez left me with precise instructions, as a result of which those two iron-bound chests, locked and sealed, were delivered, together with the keys, to the royal confessor. Martinez was asked what they contained.

"I do not know, " he answered. "My orders are merely to deliver them. "

I can conceive the King's relief and joy in his conviction that thus had he drawn my teeth, that betide now what might, I could never defend or justify myself. The immediate sequel took me by surprise. We were at the end of '85, and my health was suffering from my confinement and its privations. And now my captivity was mitigated. My wife Juana even succeeded in obtaining permission that I should be taken home to Madrid, and there for fourteen months I enjoyed a half liberty, and received the visits of my old friends, among whom were numbered most of the members of the Court.

I imagined at first that since my teeth were drawn the King despised me, and intended nothing further. But I was soon to be disillusioned on that score. It began with the arrest of Martinez on a charge of complicity in the murder of Escovedo. And then one day I was again arrested, without warning, and carried off for a while to the fortress of Pinto. Thence I was brought back in close captivity to Madrid, and there I learnt at last what had been stirring.

In the previous summer King Philip had gone into Aragon to preside over the Cortes, and Vasquez, who had gone with him, had seized the opportunity to examine the ensign Enriquez, who had, meanwhile, denounced himself of complicity in the murder of Escovedo. Enriquez made a full confession - turned accuser under a promise of full pardon for himself and charged Mesa, Rubio, and my steward Martinez with complicity, denouncing Martinez as the ringleader of the business. The other two, Insausti and Bosque, were already dead.

Immediately Vasquez attempted to seize the survivors. But Mesa had gone to earth in Aragon, and Rubio was with him. Martinez alone remained, and him they seized and questioned. He remained as cool and master of himself as he was true and loyal to me. Their threats made no impression on him. He maintained that the tale was all a lie, begotten of spite, that I had been Escovedo's best friend, that I had been greatly afflicted by his death, and that no man could have done more than I to discover his real murderers. They confronted him with Enriquez, and the confrontation no whit disturbed him. He handled the traitor contemptuously as a perjured, suborned witness, a false servant, a man who, as he proceeded to show, was a scoundrel steeped in crime, whose word was utterly worthless, and who, no doubt, had been bought to bring these charges against his sometime master.

The situation, thanks to Martinez's stoutness, had reached a deadlock. Between the assertions of one man, who was revealed to the judges for a worthless scoundrel, and the denials of the other, against whom nothing was known, it was impossible for the court of inquiry to reach any conclusion. At least another witness must be obtained. And Vasquez laboured with all his might and arts and wiles to draw Rubio out of Aragon into the clutches of the justice of Castile. But he laboured in vain, for I had secretly found the means to instruct my trusty Mesa to retain the fellow where he was.

In this inconclusive state of things the months dragged on and my captivity continued. I wrote to Philip, imploring his mercy, complaining of these unjust delays on the part of Vasquez, which threatened to go on forever, and begging His Majesty to command the conclusion of the affair. That was in August of '8g. You see how time had sped. All that came of my appeal was at first an increased rigour of imprisonment, and then a visit from Vasquez to examine and question me upon the testimony of Enriquez. As you can imagine, the attempt to lure me into self-betrayal was completely fruitless. My enemy withdrew, baffled, to go question my wife, but without any better success.

Nevertheless, Vasquez proclaimed the charge established against myself and Martinez, and allowed us ten days in which to prepare our answer. Immediately upon that Don Pedro de Escovedo lodged a formal indictment against us, and I was put into irons.

To rebut the evidence of one single, tainted witness I produced six witnesses of high repute, including the Secretary of the Council of Aragon. They testified for me that I was at Alcala at the time of Escovedo's death, that I had always been Escovedo's friend, that I was a good Christian incapable of such a deed, and that Enriquez as an evil man whose word was worthless, a false witness inspired by vengeance.

Thus, in spite of the ill-will of my judges and the hatred of my enemies, it was impossible legally to condemn me upon the evidence. There were documents enough in existence to have proved my part in the affair; but not one of them dared the King produce, since they would also show me to have been no more than his instrument. And so, desiring my death as it was now clear he did, he must sit impotently brooding there with what patience he could command, like a gigantic, evil spider into whose web I obstinately refused to fling myself.

My hopes began to revive. When at last the court announced that it postponed judgment whilst fresh evidence was sought, there was an outcry of indignation on all sides. This was a tyrannical abuse of power, men said; and I joined my voice to theirs to demand that judgment be pronounced and my liberty restored to me, pointing out that I had already languished years in captivity without any charge against me - beyond that of corruption, which had been purged by now - having been established.

Then at last the King stirred in his diabolical underground manner. He sent his confessor to me in prison. The friar was mild and benign.

"My poor friend, " he said, "why do you allow yourself to suffer in this fashion, when a word from you can set a term to it? Confess the deed without fear, since at the same time you can advance a peremptory reason of State to justify it. "

It was too obvious a trap. Did I make confession, indeed, upon such grounds, they would demand of me proof of what I asserted; and meanwhile the documents to prove it had been extorted from me and had passed into the King's possession. In the result I should be ruined completely as one who, to the crime of murder, added a wicked, insidious falsehood touching the honour of his King.

But I said naught of this. I met guile with guile. "Alas! I have been tempted, " I answered him. "But I thank Heaven I have known even in my extremity how to resist the temptation of such disloyalty. I cannot forget, Brother Diego, that amongst the letters from the King was one that said, 'Be not troubled by anything your enemies may do against you. I shall not abandon you, and be sure their animosity cannot prevail. But you must understand that it must not be discovered that this death took place by my order. '"

"But if the King were to release you from that command? " he asked.

"When His Majesty in his goodness and generosity sends me a note in his own hand to say, 'You may confess that it was by my express order that you contrived the death of Escovedo, ' then I shall thankfully account myself absolved from the silence his service imposes on me. "

He looked at me narrowly. He may have suspected that I saw through the transparent device to ruin me, and that in a sense I mocked him with my answer.

He withdrew, and for some days nothing further happened. Then the rigours of my captivity were still further increased. I was allowed to communicate with no one, and even the alguazil who guarded me was forbidden, under pain of death, to speak to me.

And in January I was visited by Vasquez, who brought me a letter from the King, not, indeed, addressed to me and in the terms I had suggested, but to Vasquez himself, and it ran:

You may tell Antonio Perez from me, and, if necessary, show him this letter, that he is aware of my knowledge of having ordered him to put Escovedo to death and of the motives which he told me existed for this measure; and that as it imports for the satisfaction of my conscience that it be ascertained whether or not those motives were sufficient, I order him to state them in the fullest detail, and to advance proof of what he then alleged to me, which is not unknown to yourself, since I have clearly imparted it to you. When I shall have seen his answers, and the reasons he advances, I shall give order that such measures be taken as may befit. I, THE KING

You see what a twist he had given to the facts. It was I who had urged the death of Escovedo; it was I who had advanced reasons which he had considered sufficient, trusting to my word; and it was because of this he had consented to give the order. Let me confess so much, let me prove it, and prove, too, that the motives I had advanced were sound ones, or I must be destroyed. That was all clear. And that false king held fast the two trunks of papers that would have given the lie to this atrocious note of his, that would have proved that again and again I had shielded Escovedo from the death his king designed for him.

I looked into the face of my enemy, and there was a twisted smile on my lips.

"What fresh trap is this? " I asked him. "King Philip never wrote that note. "

"You should know his hand. Look closer, " he bade me harshly.

"I know his hand - none better. But I claim, too, to know something of his heart. And I know that it is not the heart of a perjured liar such as penned those lines. "

That was as near as a man dared to go in expressing his true opinion of a prince.

"For the rest, " I said, "I do not understand it. I know nothing of the death of Escovedo. I have nothing to add to what already I have said in open court unless it be to protest against you, who are a passionate, hostile judge. "

Six times in the month that followed did Vasquez come to me, accompanied now by a notary, to press me to confess. At last, seeing that no persuasions could bend my obstinacy, they resorted to other measures.

"You will drive us to use the torture upon you so that we may loosen your tongue! " snarled Vasquez fiercely, enraged by my obduracy.

I laughed at the threat. I was a noble of Spain, by birth immune from torture. They dared not violate the law. But they did dare. There was no law, human or divine, the King was not prepared to violate so that he might slake his vengeance upon the man who had dared to love where he had loved.

They delivered me naked into the hands of the executioner, and I underwent the question at the rope. They warned me that if I lost my life or the use of any of my limbs, it would be solely by my own fault. I advanced my nobility and the state of my health as all-sufficient reasons why the torture should not be applied to me, reminding them that for eleven years already I had suffered persecution and detention, so that my vigour was all gone.

For the last time they summoned me to answer as the King desired. And then, since I still refused, the executioner was recalled, he crossed my arms upon my breast, bound them securely, thrust a long rod beneath the cord, and, seizing one end of this in either hand, gave the first turn.

I screamed. I could not help it, enfeebled as I was. But my spirit being stouter than my flesh, I still refused to answer. Not indeed, until they had given the rope eight turns, not until it had sliced through my muscles and crushed the bone of one of my arms, so that to this day it remains of little use to me, did they conquer me. I had reached the limit of endurance.

"In Christ's name, release me! " I gasped. "I will say anything you wish. "

Released at last, half swooning, smothered in blood, agonized by pain, I confessed that it was myself had procured the death of Escovedo for reasons of State and acting upon the orders of the King. The notary made haste to write down my words, and, when I had done, it was demanded of me that I should advance proof of the State reasons which I had alleged.

Oh, I had never been under any delusion on that score, as I have shown you. The demand did not take me by surprise at all. I was waiting for it, knowing that my answer to it would pronounce my doom. But I delivered it none the less.

"My papers have been taken from me, and without them I can prove nothing. With them I could prove my words abundantly. "

They left me then. On the morrow, as I afterwards learnt, they read my confession to my devoted Martinez, and the poor fellow, who hitherto had remained staunch and silent under every test, seeing that there was no further purpose to be served by silence, gave them the confirmation they desired of Enriquez's accusation.

Meanwhile, I was very ill, in a raging fever as you may well conceive, and in answer to my prayer my own doctor was permitted to visit me in prison. He announced that he found my case extremely grave, and that I must perish unless I were relieved. As a consequence, and considering my weakness and the uselessness just then of both my arms, one of which was broken, first a page of my own, then other servants, and lastly my wife were allowed to come and tend me.

That was at the end of February. By the middle of April my wounds had healed, I had recovered the use of my limbs, though one remains half maimed for life, and my condition had undergone a very considerable improvement. But of this I allowed no sign to show, no suspicion even. I continued to lie there day after day in a state of complete collapse, so that whilst I was quickly gathering strength it was believed by my gaolers that I was steadily sinking, and that I should soon be dead.

My only hope, you see, lay now in evasion, and it was for this that I was thus craftily preparing. Once out of Castile I could deal with Philip, and he should not find me as impotent, as toothless as he believed. But I go too fast.

One night at last, on April 20th, by when all measures had been concerted, and Gil de Mesa awaited me outside with horses - the whole having been contrived by my dear wife - I made the attempt. My apparent condition had naturally led to carelessness in guarding me. Who would guard a helpless, dying man? Soon after dark I rose, donned over my own clothes a petticoat and a hooded cloak belonging to my wife, and thus mufed walked out of my cell, past the guards, and so out of the prison unchallenged. I joined Gil de Mesa, discarded my feminine disguise, mounted and set out with him upon that ninety-mile journey into Aragon.

We reached Saragossa in safety, and there my first act was to surrender myself to the Grand Justiciary of Aragon to stand my trial for the murder of Escovedo with which I was charged.

It must have sent a shudder through the wicked Philip when he received news of that. A very stricken man he must have been, for he must have suspected something of the truth, that if I dared, after all the evidence amassed now against me, including my own confession under torture, openly to seek a judgment, it was because I must possess some unsuspected means of establishing all the truth - the truth that must make his own name stink in the nostrils of the world. And so it was. Have you supposed that Antonio Perez, who had spent his life in studying the underground methods of burrowing statecraft, had allowed himself to be taken quite so easily in their snare? Have you imagined that when I sent for Diego Martinez to come to me at Turruegano and instructed him touching the surrender of those two chests of documents, that I did not also instruct him carefully touching the abstraction in the first instance of a few serviceable papers and the renewal of the seals that should conceal the fact that he had tampered with the chests? If you have thought that, you have done me less than justice. There had been so much correspondence between Philip and myself, so many notes had passed touching the death of Escovedo, and there was that habit of Philip's of writing his replies in marginal notes to my own letters and so returning them, that it was unthinkable he should have kept them all in his memory, and the abstraction of three or four could not conceivably be detected by him.

Ever since then those few letters, of a most deeply incriminating character, selected with great acumen by my steward, had secretly remained in the possession of my wife. Yet I had not dared produce them in Castile, knowing that I should instantly have been deprived of them, and with them of my last hope. They remained concealed against precisely such a time as this, when, beyond the immediate reach of Philip's justice, I should startle the world and clear my own character by their production.

You know the ancient privileges enjoyed by Aragon, privileges of which the Aragonese are so jealous that a King of Castile may not assume the title of King of Aragon until, bareheaded, he shall have received from the Grand Justiciary of Aragon the following admonition: "We, who are of equal worth and greater power than you, constitute you our king on the condition that you respect our privileges, and not otherwise. " And to that the king must solemnly bind himself by oath, whose violation would raise in revolt against him the very cobbles of the streets. No king of Spain had ever yet been found to dare violate the constitution and the fueros of Aragon, the independence of their cortes, or parliament, composed of the four orders of the State. The Grand Justiciary's Court was superior to any royally constituted tribunal in the kingdom; to that court it was the privilege of any man to appeal for justice in any cause; and there justice was measured out with a stern impartiality that had not its like in any other State of Europe.

That was the tribunal to which I made surrender of my, person and my cause. There was an attempt on the part of Philip to seize me and drag me back to Castile and his vengeance. His officers broke into the prison for that purpose, and already I was in their power, when the men of the Justiciary, followed by an excited mob, which threatened open rebellion at this violation of their ancient rights, delivered me from their hands.

Baffled in this - and I can imagine his fury, which has since been vented on the Aragonese - Philip sent his representatives and his jurists to accuse me before the Court of the Grand Justiciary and to conduct my prosecution.

The trial began, exciting the most profound interest, not only in Aragon, but also in Castile, which, as I afterwards learnt, had openly rejoiced at my escape. It proceeded with the delays and longueurs that are inseparable from the sluggish majesty of the law. one of these pauses I wrote to Philip, inviting him to desist, and to grant me the liberty to live out my days in peace with my family in some remote corner of his kingdom. I warned him that I was not helpless before his persecution, as he imagined; that whilst I had made surrender of two chests of papers, I yet retained enough authentic documents - letters in his own hand - to make my innocence and his guilt apparent in a startling degree, with very evil consequences to himself.

His answer was to seize my wife and children and cast them into prison, and then order the courts of Madrid to pronounce sentence of death against me for the murder of Escovedo. Such were the sops with which he sought to quench his vindictive rage.

Thereupon the trial proceeded. I prepared my long memorial of the affair, supporting it with proofs in the shape of those letters I had retained. And then at last Philip of Spain took fright. He was warned by one of his representatives that there was little doubt I should be acquitted on all counts, and, too late, he sought to save his face by ordering the cessation of the prosecution he had instructed.

He stated that since I had chosen a line of defence, to answer which - as it could be answered - it would be necessary to touch upon matters of a secrecy that was inviolable, and to introduce personages whose reputation and honour was of more consequence to the State than the condemnation of Antonio Perez, he preferred to renounce the prosecution before the tribunal of Aragon. But he added a certificate upon his royal word to the effect that my crimes were greater than had ever been the crimes of any man, and that, whilst he renounced the prosecution before the courts of Aragon, he retained the right to demand of me an account of my actions before any other tribunal at any future time.

My acquittal followed immediately. And immediately again that was succeeded by fresh charges against me on behalf of the King. First it was sought to prove that I had procured the death of two of my servants - a charge which I easily dispersed by proving them to have died natural deaths. Then it was sought to prosecute me on the charge of corruption, for which I had once already been prosecuted, condemned, and punished. Confidently I demanded my release, and Philip must have ground his teeth in rage to see his prey escaping him, to see himself the butt of scorn and contempt for the wrongs that it became clear he had done me.

One weapon remained to him, and a terrible weapon this - the Holy Office of the Inquisition, a court before which all temporal courts must bow and quail. He launched its power against me, and behold me, in the moment when I accounted myself the victor in the unequal contest, accused of the dread sin of heresy. Words lightly weighed - uttered by me in prison under stress - had been zealously gathered up y spies.

On one occasion I had exclaimed: "I think God sleeps where my affairs are concerned, and I am in danger of losing my faith. " The Holy Office held this to be a scandalous proposition, offensive to pious ears.

Again, when I heard of the arrest of my wife and children I had cried out in rage: "God sleeps! God sleeps! There cannot be a God! "

This they argued at length to be rank heresy, since it is man's duty positively to believe, and who does not believe is an infidel.

Yet again it seems I had exclaimed: "Should things so come to pass, I shall refuse to believe in God! " This was accounted blasphemous, scandalous, and not without suspicion of heresy.

Upon these grounds the Supreme Council of the Inquisition at Madrid drew up its impeachment, and delivered it to the inquisitors of Aragon at Saragossa. These at once sent their familiars to demand the surrender of me from the Grand Justiciary, in whose hands I still remained. The Grand Justiciary incontinently refused to yield me up.

Thereupon the three Inquisitors drew up a peremptory demand, addressed to the lieutenants of the Justiciary, summoning them by virtue of holy obedience, under pain of greater excommunication, of a fine in the case of each of them of one thousand ducats, and other penalties to which they might later be condemned, to deliver me up within three hours to the pursuivants of the Holy Office.

This was the end of the Justiciary's resistance. He dared not refuse a demand so framed, and surrender of me was duly made. But the news of what was doing had run abroad. I had no lack of friends, whom I instantly warned of what was afoot, and they had seen to it that the knowledge spread in an inflammatory manner. Saragossa began to stir at once. Here was a thinly masked violation of their ancient privileges. If they suffered this precedent of circumventing their rights, what was to become of their liberties in future, who would be secure against an unjust persecution? For their sympathies were all with me throughout that trial.

I was scarcely in the prison of the Holy Office before the dread cry of Contrafueros! was ringing through the streets of Saragossa, summoning the citizens to arm and come forth in defence of their inviolable rights. They stormed the palace of the Grand Justiciary, demanded that he should defend the fueros, to whose guardianship he had been elected. Receiving no satisfaction, they attacked the palace of the Inquisition, clamouring insistently that I should immediately be returned to the Justiciary's prison, whence I had so unwarrantably been taken.

The Inquisitors remained firm a while, but the danger was increasing hourly. In the end they submitted, for the sake of their skins, and considering, no doubt, a later vengeance for this outrage upon their holy authority. But it was not done until faggots had been stacked against the Holy House, and the exasperated mob had threatened to burn them out of it.

"Castilian hypocrites! " had been the insurgent roar. "Surrender your prisoner, or you shall be roasted in the fire in which you roast so many! "

Blood was shed in the streets. The King's representative died of wounds that he received in the affray, whilst the Viceroy himself was assailed and compelled to intervene and procure my deliverence.

For the moment I was out of danger. But for the moment only. There was no question now of my enlargement. The Grand Justiciary, intimidated by what had taken place, by the precise expression of the King's will, dared not set me at liberty. And then the Holy Office, under the direction of the King, went to work in that subterranean way which it has made its own; legal quibbles were raised to soothe the sensibilities of the Aragonese with respect to my removal from the Justiciary's prison to that of the Holy Office. Strong forces of troops were brought to Saragossa to overawe the plebeian insolence, and so, by the following September, all the preliminaries being concluded, the Inquisition came in force and in form to take possession of me.

The mob looked on and murmured; but it was intimidated by the show of ordered force; it had perhaps tired a little of the whole affair, and did not see that it should shed its blood and lay up trouble for itself for the sake of one who, after all, was of no account in the affairs of Aragon. I stood upon the threshold of my ruin. All my activities were to go unrewarded. Doom awaited me. And then the unexpected happened. The alguazil of the Holy Office was in the very act of setting the gyves upon my legs when the first shot was fired, followed almost at once by a fusillade.

It was Gil de Mesa, faithfullest servant that ever any man possessed. He had raised an armed band, consisting of some Aragonese gentlemen and their servants, and with this he fell like a thunderbolt upon the Castilian men-at-arms and the familiars of the Inquisition.

The alguazil fled, leaving me one leg free, the other burdened by the gyve, and as he fled so fled all others, being thus taken unawares. The Inquisitors scuttled to the nearest shelter; the Viceroy threw himself into his house and barricaded the door. There was no one to guide, no one to direct. The soldiery in these circumstances, and accounting themselves overpowered, offered no resistance. They, too, fled before the fusillade and the hail of shot that descended on them.

Before I realized what had happened, the iron had been struck from my leg, I was mounted on a horse, and, with Gil at my side, I was galloping out of Saragossa by the gate of Santa Engracia, and breasting the slopes with little cause to fear pursuit just yet, such was the disorder we had left behind.

And there, very briefly, you have the story of my sufferings and my escapes. Not entirely to be baulked, numerous arrests were made by the Inquisitors in Saragossa when order was at last restored. There followed an auto-da-fe, the most horrible and vindictive of all those horrors, in which many suffered for having displayed the weakness of charity towards a persecuted man. And, since my body was no longer in their clutches, they none the less sentenced me to death as contumaciously absent, and my effigy was burnt in the holy fires they lighted, amongst the human candles which they offered up for the greater honour and glory of a merciful God. Let me say no more, lest I blaspheme in earnest.

After months of wandering and hiding, Gil and I made our way here into Navarre, where we remain the guests of Protestant King Henri IV, who does not love King Philip any better since he has heard my story.

Still King Philip's vengeance does not sleep. Twice has he sent after me his assassins - since assassination is the only weapon now remaining to him. But his poor tools have each time been taken, exposed to Philip's greater infamy and shame - and hanged as they deserve who can so vilely serve so vile a master. It has even been sought to bribe my faithful Gil de Mesa into turning his hand against me, and that attempt, too, has been given the fullest publication. Meanwhile, my death to-day could no longer avail Philip very much. My memorial is published throughout Europe for all to read. It has been avidly read until Philip of Spain has earned the contempt of every upright man. In his own dominions the voice of execration has been raised against him. One of his own nobles has contemptuously announced that Spain under Philip has become unsafe for any gentleman, and that a betrayal of a subject by his king is without parallel in history.

That is some measure of vengeance. But if I am spared I shall not leave it there. Henry of Navarre is on the point of turning Catholic that his interests may be better served. Elizabeth of England remains. In her dominions, where thrives the righteous hatred of Philip and all the evil that he stands for, I shall find a welcome and a channel for the activities that are to show him that Antonio Perez lives. I have sent him word that when he is weary of the conflict he can signify his surrender by delivering from their prison my wife and children, upon whom he seeks still to visit some of the vengeance I have succeeded in eluding. When he does that, then will I hold my hand. But not before.

"That, madame, is my story, " said Don Antonio, after a pause, and from narrowing eyes looked at the beauty who had heard him through.

Daylight had faded whilst the tale was telling. Night was come, and lights had long since been fetched, the curtains drawn over the long windows that looked out across the parkland to the river.

Twice only had he paused in all that narrative. Once when he had described the avowal of his love for Anne, Princess of Eboli, when a burst of sobs from her had come to interrupt him; again when a curious bird-note had rung out upon the gathering dusk. Then he stopped to listen.

"Curious that, " he had said - "an eagle's cry. I have not heard it these many months, not since I left the hills of Aragon. "

Thereafter he had continued to the end.

Considering her now, his glance inscrutable, he said:

"You weep, madame. Tell me, what is it that has moved you - the contemplation of my sufferings, or of your own duplicity? "

She started up, very white, her eyes scared.

"I do not understand you. What do you mean, sir? "

"I mean, madame, that God did not give you so much beauty that you should use it in the decoying of an unfortunate, that you should hire it at an assassin's fee to serve the crapulous King of Spain. "

He rose and towered before her, a figure at once of anger, dignity, and some compassion.

"So much ardour from youth and beauty to age and infirmity was in itself suspicious. The Catholic King has the guile of Satan, I remembered. I wondered, and hoped my suspicions might be unfounded. Yet prudence made me test them, that the danger, if it existed, should manifest itself and be destroyed. So I came to tell you all my story, so that if you did the thing I feared, you might come to the knowledge of precisely what it was you did. I have learnt whilst here that what I suspected is - alas! quite true. You were a lure, a decoy sent to work my ruin, to draw me into a trap where daggers waited for me. Why did you do this? What was the bribe that could corrupt you, lovely lady? "

Sobs shook her. Her will gave way before his melancholy sternness.

"I do not know by what wizardry you have discovered it! " she cried. "It was true; but it is true no longer. I knew not what I did. By that window, across the meadows, you can reach the river in safety. "

She rose, controlling her emotion that she might instruct him. "They wait for you in the enclosed garden. "

He smiled wistfully.

"They waited, madame. They wait no longer, unless it be for death. That eagle's cry, thrice repeated, was the signal from my faithful Gil, not only that the trap was discovered, but that those who baited it were taken. Suspecting what I did, I took my measures ere I came. Antonio Perez, as I have told you, is not an easy man to murder. Unlike Philip, I do not make war on women, and I have no reckoning to present to you. But I am curious, madame, to know what led you to this baseness. "

"I - I thought you evil, and - and they bribed me. I was offered ten thousand ducats for your head. We are very poor, we Chantenacs, and so I fell. But, sir - sir" - she was on her knees to him now, and she had caught his hand in hers- "poor as I am, all that I have is yours to do with as you will, to help to avenge yourself upon that Spanish monster. Take what you will. Take all I have. "

His smile grew gentler. Gently he raised her.

"Madame, " he said, "I am myself a sinner, as I have shown you, a man unequal to resisting temptation when it took me in its trammels. Of all that you offer, I will take only the right to this kiss. "

And bending, be bore her hand to his lips.

Then he went out to join Gil and his men, who waited in the courtyard, guarding three prisoners they had taken.

Perez considered them by the light of the lantern that Gil held aloft for him.

"One of you, " he announced, "shall return to Castile and give tidings to Philip, his master, that Antonio Perez leaves for England and the Court of Elizabeth, to aid her, by his knowledge of the affairs of Spain, in her measures against the Catholic King, and to continue his holy work, which is to make the name of Philip II stink in the nostrils of all honest men. One of you I will spare for that purpose. You shall draw lots for it in the morning. The other two must hang. "

IV. THE NIGHT OF CHARITY

The Case of the Lady Alice Lisle

Of all the cases tried in the course of that terrible circuit, justly known as the Bloody Assizes, the only one that survives at all in the popular memory is the case of the Lady Alice Lisle. Her advanced age, the fact that she was the first woman known in English history to have suffered death for no worse an offence than that of having exercised the feminine prerogative of mercy, and the further fact that, even so, this offence - technical as it was - was never fully proved against her, are all circumstances which have left their indelible stamp of horror upon the public mind. There is also the further circumstance that hers was the first case tried in the West by that terrible Chief Justice, Baron Jeffreys of Wem.

But the feature that renders her case peculiarly interesting to the historical psychologist - and it is a feature that is in danger of being overlooked - is that she cannot really be said to have suffered for the technical offence for which she took her trial. That was the pretext rather than the cause. In reality she was the innocent victim of a relentless, undiscerning Nemesis.

The battle of Sedgemoor had been fought and lost by the Protestant champion, James, Duke of Monmouth. In the West, which had answered the Duke's summons to revolt, there was established now a horrible reign of terror reflecting the bigoted, pitiless, vindictive nature of the King. Faversham had left Colonel Percy Kirke in command at Bridgwater, a ruthless ruffian, who at one time had commanded the "Tangier garrison, and whose men were full worthy of their commander. Kirke's Lambs they were called, in an irony provoked by the emblem of the Paschal Lamb on the flag of this, the First Tangier Regiment, originally levied to wage war upon the infidel.

From Bridgwater Colonel Kirke made a horrible punitive progress to Taunton, where he put up at the White Hart Inn. Now, there was a very solid signpost standing upon a triangular patch of green before the door of the White Hart, and Colonel Kirke conceived the quite facetious notion of converting this advertisement of hospitality into a gallows - a signpost of temporal welfare into a signpost of eternity. So forth he fetched the prisoners he had brought in chains from

Bridgwater, and proceeded, without any form of trial whatsoever, to string them up before the inn. The story runs that as they were hoisted to that improvised gibbet, Kirke and his officers, standing at the windows, raised their glasses to pledge their happy deliverance; then, when the victims began to kick convulsively, Kirke would order the drums to strike up, so that the gentlemen might have music for their better dancing.

The colonel, you see, was a humorist, as humour was then understood upon the northern shores of Africa, where he had been schooled.

When, eventually, Colonel Kirke was recalled and reprimanded, it was not because of his barbarities many of which transcend the possibilities of decent print - but because of a lenity which this venal gentleman began to display when he discovered that many of his victims were willing to pay handsomely for mercy.

Meanwhile, under his reign of terror, men who had cause to fear the terrible hand of the King's vengeance went into hiding wherever they could. Among those who escaped into Hampshire, thinking themselves safer in a county that had not participated in the war, were a dissenting parson named George Hicks, who had been in Monmouth's army, and a lawyer named Richard Nelthorp, outlawed for participation in the Rye House Plot. In his desperate quest for shelter, Hicks bethought him of the charitable Nonconformist lady of Moyle's Court, the widow of that John Lisle who had been one of Cromwell's Lords Commissioners of the Great Seal, and most active in bringing King Charles I to justice.

John Lisle had fled to Switzerland at the Restoration; but Stuart vengeance had followed him, set a price upon his head, and procured his murder at Lausanne. That was twenty years ago. Since then his lady, because she was known to have befriended and sheltered many Royalists, and because she had some stout Tory friends to plead for her, was allowed to remain in tranquil possession of her estates. And there the Lady Alice Lisle - so called by courtesy, since Cromwell's titles did not at law survive the Restoration - might have ended her days in peace, but that it was written that those who hated her - innocent and aged though she was - for the name she bore, who included her in the rancour which had procured her husband's assassination, were to be fully satisfied. And the instrument of fate was this parson Hicks. He prevailed upon

Dunne, a baker of Warminster, and a Nonconformist, to convey to the Lady Lisle his prayer for shelter. With that message Dunne set out on July 25th for Ellingham, a journey of some twenty miles. He went by way of Fovant and Chalk to Salisbury Plain. But as he did not know the way thence, he sought out a co-religionist named Barter, who undertook, for a consideration, to go with him and direct him.

Together the pair came in the late afternoon of that Saturday to the handsome house of Moyle's Court, and to my lady's steward, who received them. Dunne, who appears to have been silly and imprudent, states that he is sent to know if my lady will entertain a minister named Hicks.

Carpenter, the steward, a staid, elderly fellow, took fright at once. Although he may not have associated an absconding Presbyterian parson with the late rebellion, he must have supposed at least that he was one of those against whom there were warrants for preaching in forbidden private meetings. So to her ladyship above stairs Carpenter conveyed a warning with the message.

But that slight, frail, homely lady of seventy, with kindly eyes of a faded blue, smiled upon his fears. She had sheltered fugitives before - in the old days of the Commonwealth - and nothing but good had ever come of it. She would see this messenger.

With misgivings, Carpenter haled Dunne into her presence, and left them alone together. The impression conveyed by Dunne was that Hicks was in hiding from the warrants that were out against all Nonconformist preachers. But when he mentioned that Hicks had a companion, she desired to know his name.

"I do not know, my lady. But I do not think he has been in the army, either. "

She considered a while. But in the end pity conquered doubt in her sweetly charitable soul.

"Very well, " she said, "I will give them entertainment for a week. Bring them on Tuesday after dark, and come by the back way through the orchard, that they may not be seen. "

And upon this she rose, and took up an ebony cane, herself to reconduct him and to see to his entertainment before he left. Not until they came to the kitchen did she realize that he had a companion. At sight of Barter, who rose respectfully when she entered, she checked, turned to Dunne, and whispered something, to which his answer provoked from her a laugh.

Now Barter, intrigued by this whispering and laughing, of which he deemed himself the object, questioned Dunne upon it as they rode forth again together.

"She asked me if you knew aught of the business, " replied Dunne; "and I answered 'No. '"

"Business, say'st thou? " quoth Barter. "What business? "

"Sure, the business on which we came, " Dunne evaded; and he laughed.

It was an answer that left Barter uneasy. Nor was his mind set at rest by the parting words with which Dunne accompanied the half-crown for his services.

"This is but an earnest of what's to come if you will meet me here on Tuesday to show me the way to Moyle's Court again. I shall be bringing two gentlemen with me - wealthy men, of a half-score thousand pounds a year apiece. I tell you there will be a fine booty for my part, so fine that I shall never want for money again all the days of my life. And, so that you meet us here, you too may count upon a handsome reward. "

Consenting, Barter went his ways home. But as he pondered Dunne's silly speech, and marvelled that honest men should pay so disproportionately for an honest service, he came to the reasonable conclusion that he had to do with rebels. This made him so uneasy that he resolved at last to lodge information with the nearest justice.

Now, it happened, by the irony of Fate, that the justice sought by Barter was one Colonel Penruddock - the vindictive son of that Penruddock whom the late John Lisle - whilst Lord President of the High Court - had sentenced to death some thirty years ago for participation in an unsuccessful Wiltshire rising against the Commonwealth.

The colonel, a lean, stark man of forty-five, heard with interest Barter's story.

"Art an honest fellow! " he commended him. "What are the names of these rogues? "

"The fellow named no names, sir. "

"Well, well, we shall discover that for ourselves when we come to take them at this trysting-place. Whither do you say you are to conduct them? "

"To Moyle's Court, sir, where my Lady Lisle is to give them entertainment. "

The colonel stared a moment; then a heavy smile came to light the saturnine face under the heavy periwig. Beyond that he gave no sign of what was passing in his mind.

"You may go, " he said slowly, at last. "Be sure we shall be at the tryst to take these rascals. "

But the colonel did not keep his promise. To Barter's surprise, there were no soldiers at the tryst on Salisbury Plain on the following Tuesday; and he was suffered to lead Dunne and the two men with him the short, corpulent Mr. Hicks and the long, lean Nelthorp - to Moyle's Court without interference.

The rich reward that Dunne had promised him amounted in actual fact to five shillings, that he had from Nelthorpe at parting. Puzzled by Colonel Penruddock's failure to do his part, Barter went off at once to the colonel's house to inform him that the pair were now at Lady Lisle's.

"Why, that is very well, " said the colonel, his smile more sinister than ever. "Trouble not yourself about that. "

And Barter, the unreasoning instrument of Fate, was not to know that the apprehending of a couple of traitorous Jack Presbyters was of small account to Colonel Penruddock by comparison with the satisfaction of the blood-feud between himself and the House of Lisle.

Meanwhile the fugitives were being entertained at Moyle's Court, and whilst they sat at supper in a room above-stairs, Dunne being still of the party, my lady came in person to see that they had all that they required, and stayed a little while in talk with them. There was some mention of Monmouth and the battle of Sedgemoor, which was natural, that being the topic of the hour.

My lady asked no questions at the time regarding Hicks's long, lean companion. But it occurred to her later that perhaps she should know more about him. Early next morning, therefore, she sent for Hicks as he was in the act of sitting down to breakfast, and by her direct questions elicited from him that this companion was that Richard Nelthorp outlawed for his share in the Rye House Plot. Not only was the information alarming, but it gave her a sense that she had not been dealt with fairly, as indeed she told him.

"You will see, sir, " she concluded, "that you cannot bide here. So long as I thought it was on the score of Nonconformity alone that you were suffering persecution, I was willing to take some risk in hiding you. But since your friend is what he is, the risk is greater than I should be asked to face, for my own sake and for that of my daughters. Nor can I say that I have ever held plottings and civil war in anything but abhorrence - as much in the old days as now. I am a loyal woman, and as a loyal woman I must bid you take your friend hence as soon as your fast is broken. "

The corpulent and swarthy Hicks stood dejectedly before her. He might have pleaded, but at that moment there came a loud knocking at the gates below, and instantly Carpenter flung into the room with a white, scared face and whirling gestures.

"Soldiers, my lady! " he panted in affright. "We have been betrayed. The presence of Mr. Hicks here is known. What shall we do? What shall we do? "

She stood quite still, her countenance entirely unchanged, unless it were to smile a little upon Carpenter's terror. The mercy of her nature rose dominant now.

"Why, we must hide these poor fellows as best we can, " said she; and Hicks flung down upon one knee to kiss her hand with protestations that he would sooner be hanged than bring trouble upon her house.

But she insisted, calm and self-contained; and Carpenter carried Hicks away to bestow him, together with Dunne, in a hole in the malt-house under a heap of sacking. Nelthorp had already vanished completely on his own initiative.

Meanwhile, the insistent knocking at the gate continued. Came shouted demands to open in the name of the King, until from a window my lady's daughters looked out to challenge those who knocked.

Colonel Penruddock, who had come in person with the soldiers to raid the house of his hereditary foe, stood forth to answer, very stiff and brave in his scarlet coat and black plumed hat.

"You have rebels in the house, " he announced, "and I require you in the King's name to deliver them up to me. "

And then, before they could answer him, came Carpenter to, unbar the door, and admit them to the court. Penruddock, standing squarely before the steward, admonished him very sternly.

"Friend, " said he, "you had best be ingenuous with me and discover who are in your lady's house, for it is within my knowledge that some strangers came hither last night. "

The stricken Carpenter stood white-faced and trembling.

"Sir - sir -" he faltered.

But the colonel was impatient.

"Come, come, my friend. Since I know they are here, there's an end on't. Show me where they are hid if you would save your own neck from the halter. "

It was enough for Carpenter. The pair in the malthouse might have eluded all search but for the steward's pusillanimity. Incontinently, he betrayed the hiding-place.

"But, sir, of your charity do not tell my mistress that I have told you. Pray, sir - "

Penruddock brushed him aside as if he had been a pestering fly, and with his men went in, and straight to the spot where Hicks and Dunne were lurking. When he had taken them, he swung round on Carpenter, who had followed.

"These be but two, " he said, "and to my knowledge three rogues came hither last night. No shufing with me, rascal. Where have you bestowed the other? "

"I swear, as Heaven's my witness, I do not know where he is, " protested the afflicted steward, truly enough.

Penruddock turned to his men.

"Make search, " he bade them; and search was made in the ruthless manner of such searches.

The brutal soldiers passed from room to room beating the wainscoting with pike and musket-butts, splintering and smashing heedlessly. Presses were burst open and their contents scattered; chests were broken into and emptied, the searchers appropriating such objects as took their fancy, with true military cynicism. A mirror was shattered, and some boards of the floor were torn up because a sergeant conceived that the blows of his halbert rang hollow.

When the tumult was at its height, came her ladyship at last into the room, where Colonel Penruddock stood watching the operations of his men. She stood in the doorway leaning upon her ebony cane, her faded eyes considering the gaunt soldier with reproachful question.

"Sir, " she asked him with gentle irony, masking her agitation, "has my house been given over to pillage? "

He bowed, doffing his plumed hat with an almost excessive courtesy.

"To search, madame, " he corrected her. And added: "In the King's name. "

"The King, " she answered, "may give you authority to search my house, but not to plunder it. Your men are robbing and destroying. "

105

He shrugged. It was the way of soldiers. Fine manners, he suggested, were not to be expected of their kind. And he harangued her upon the wrong she had done in harbouring rebels and giving entertainment to the King's enemies.

"That is not true, " said she. "I know of no King's enemies. "

He smiled darkly upon her from his great height. She was so frail a body and so old that surely it was not worth a man's while to sacrifice her on the altar of revenge. But not so thought Colonel Penruddock. Therefore he smiled.

"Two of them, a snivelling Jack Presbyter named Hicks and a rascal named Dunne, are taken already. Pray, madame, be so free and ingenuous with me aye, and so kind to yourself - as if there be any other person concealed in your house - and I am sure there is somebody else - to deliver him up, and you shall come to no further trouble. "

She looked up at him, and returned him smile for smile.

"I know nothing, " she said, "of what you tell me, or of what you ask. "

His countenance hardened.

"Then, mistress, the search must go on. "

But a shout from the adjoining room announced that it was at an end. Nelthorp had been discovered and dragged from the chimney into which he had crept.

Almost exactly a month later - on August 27th the Lady Alice Lisle was brought to the bar of the court-house at Winchester upon a charge of high treason.

The indictment ran that secretly, wickedly, and traitorously she did entertain, conceal, comfort, uphold, and maintain John Hicks, knowing him to be a false traitor, against the duty of her allegiance and against the peace of "our sovereign lord the King that now is. "

Demurely dressed in grey, the little white-haired lady calmly faced the Lord Chief Justice Jeffreys and the four judges of oyer and

106

terminer who sat with him, and confidently made her plea of "Not Guilty. "

It was inconceivable that Christian men should deal harshly with her for a technical offence amounting to an act of Christian charity. And the judge, sitting there in his robe of scarlet reversed with ermine, looked a gentle, kindly man; his handsome, oval, youthful face - Jeffreys was in his thirty-sixth year - set in the heavy black periwig, was so pale that the mouth made a vivid line of scarlet; and the eyes that now surveyed her were large and liquid and compassionate, as it seemed to her.

She was not to know that the pallor which gave him so interesting an air, and the dark stains which lent his eyes that gentle wistfulness, were the advertisements at once of the debauch that had kept him from his bed until after two o'clock that morning and of the inexorable disease that slowly gnawed away his life and enraged him out of all humanity.

And the confidence his gentle countenance inspired was confirmed by the first words he had occasion to address to her. She had interrupted counsel to the Crown when, in his opening address to the jury - composed of some of the most considerable gentlemen of Hampshire - he seemed to imply that she had been in sympathy with Monmouth's cause. She was, of course, without counsel, and must look herself to her defence.

"My lord, " she cried, "I abhorred that rebellion as much as any woman in the world! "

Jeffreys leaned forward with a restraining gesture.

"Look you, Mrs. Lisle, " he admonished her sweetly, "because we must observe the common and usual methods of trial in your case I must interrupt you now. " And upon that he promised that she should be fully heard in her own defence at the proper time, and that himself he would instruct her in the forms of law to her advantage. He reassured her by reverent allusions to the great Judge of Heaven and Earth, in whose sight they stood, that she should have justice. "And as to what you say concerning yourself, " he concluded, "I pray God with all my heart you may be innocent. "

He was benign and reassuring. But she had the first taste of his true quality in the examination of Dunne — a most unwilling witness.

Reluctantly, under the pressure put upon him, did Dunne yield up the tale of how he had conducted the two absconders to my lady's house with her consent, and it was sought to prove that she was aware of their connection with the rebellion. The stubbornly evasive Dunne was asked at last:

"Do you believe that she knew Mr. Hicks before? "

He returned the answer that already he had returned to many questions of the sort.

"I cannot tell truly. "

Jeffreys stirred in his scarlet robes, and his wistful eyes grew terrible as they bent from under beetling brows upon the witness.

"Why, " he asked, "dost thou think that she would entertain any one she had no knowledge of merely upon thy message? Mr. Dunne, Mr. Dunne! Have a care. It may be more is known to me of this matter than you think for. "

"My lord, I speak nothing but the truth! " bleated the terrified Dunne.

"I only bid you have a care, " Jeffreys smiled; and his smile was more terrible than his frown. "Truth never wants a subterfuge; it always loves to appear naked; it needs no enamel nor any covering. But lying and snivelling and canting and Hicksing always appear in masquerade. Come, go on with your evidence. "

But Dunne was reluctant to go on, and out of his reluctance he lied foolishly, and pretended that both Hicks and Nelthorp were unknown to him. When pressed to say why he should have served two men whom he had never seen before, he answered:

"All the reason that induced me to it was that they said they were men in debt, and desired to be concealed for a while. "

Then the thunder was heard in Jeffreys' voice.

"Dost thou believe that any one here believes thee? Prithee, what trade art thou? "

"My lord, " stammered the unfortunate, "I - I am a baker by trade. "

"And wilt thou bake thy bread at such easy rates? Upon my word, then, thou art very kind. Prithee, tell me. I believe thou dost use to bake on Sundays, dost thou not? "

"No, my lord, I do not! " cried Dunne indignantly.

"Alackaday! Art precise in that, " sneered the judge. "But thou canst travel on Sundays to lead rogues into lurking-holes. "

Later, when to implicate the prisoner, it was sought to draw from Dunne a full account of the reception she had given his companions, his terror under the bullying to which he was subjected made him contradict himself more flagrantly than ever. Jeffreys addressed the jury.·

"You see, gentlemen, what a precious fellow this is; a very pretty tool to be employed upon such an errand; a knave that nobody would trust for half a crown. A Turk has more title to an eternity of bliss than these pretenders to Christianity. "

And as there was no more to be got from Dunne just then, he was presently dismissed, and Barter's damning evidence was taken. Thereafter the wretched Dunne was recalled, to be bullied by Jeffreys in blasphemous terms that may not be printed here.

Barter had told the Court how my lady had come into the kitchen with Dunne, and how, when he had afterwards questioned Dunne as to why they had whispered and laughed together, Dunne told him she had asked "If he knew aught of the business. " Jeffreys sought now to wring from Dunne what was this business to which he had so mysteriously alluded - this with the object of establishing Lady Lisle's knowledge of Hicks's treason.

Dunne resisted more stubbornly than ever. Jeffreys, exasperated - since without the admission it would be difficult to convict her ladyship —invited the jury to take notice of the strange, horrible carriage of the fellow, and heaped abuse upon the snivelling, canting sect of which he was a member. Finally, he reminded Dunne of his oath to tell the truth, and addressed him with a sort of loving ferocity.

"What shall it profit a man to gain the whole world and lose his own soul? " bellowed that terrible judge, his eyes aflame. "Is not this the voice of Scripture itself? And wilt thou hazard so dear and precious a thing as thy soul for a lie? Thou wretch! All the mountains and hills of the world heaped upon one another will not cover thee from the vengeance of the Great God for this transgression of false-witness bearing. "

"I cannot tell what to say, my lord, " gasped Dunne.

In his rage to see all efforts vain, the judge's language became that of the cockpit. Recovering at last, he tried gentleness again, and very elaborately invited Dunne, in my lady's own interest, to tell him what was the business to which he had referred to Barter.

"She asked me whether I did not know that Hicks was a Nonconformist. "

"That cannot be all. There must be something more in it. "

"Yes, my lord, " Dunne protested, "it is all. I know nothing more. "

"Was there ever such an impudent rascal? " roared the judge. "Dolt think that, after all the pains I have been at to get an answer, thou canst banter me with such sham stuff as this? Hold the candle to his brazen face, that we may see it clearly. "

Dunne stood terrified and trembling under the glance of those terrible eyes.

"My lord, " he cried, "I am so baulked, I am cluttered out of my senses. "

Again he was put down whilst Colonel Penruddock gave his evidence of the apprehension of the rebels. When he had told how he found Hicks and Dunne concealed under some stuff in the malt-house, Dunne was brought back yet again, that Jeffreys might resume his cross-examination.

"Dunne, how came you to hide yourself in the malthouse? "

"My lord, " said Dunne foolishly, "I was frighted by the noise. "

"Prithee, what needest thou be afraid of, for thou didst not know Hicks nor Nelthorp; and my lady only asked thee whether Hicks were a Nonconformist parson. Surely, so very innocent a soul needed no occasion to be afraid. I doubt there was something in the case of that business we were talking of before. If we could but get out of thee what it was. "

But Dunne continued to evade.

"My lord, I heard a great noise in the house, and did not know what it meant. So I went and hid myself. "

"It is very strange thou shouldst hide thyself for a little noise, when thou knewest nothing of the business. "

Again the witness, with a candle still held close to his nose, complained that he was quite cluttered out of his senses, and did not know what he was saying.

"But to tell the truth would not rob thee of any of thy senses, if ever thou hadst any, " Jeffreys told him angrily. "But it would seem that neither thou nor thy mistress, the prisoner, had any; for she knew nothing of it either, though she had sent for them thither. "

"My lord, " cried her ladyship at that, "I hope I shall not be condemned without being heard. "

"No, God forbid, Mrs. Lisle, " he answered; and then viciously flashed forth a hint of the true forces of Nemesis at work against her. "That was a sort of practice in your late husband's time - you know very well what I mean - but God be thanked it is not so now. "

Came next the reluctant evidence of Carpenter and his wife, and after that there was yet a fourth equally futile attempt to drag from Dunne an admission that her ladyship was acquainted with Hicks's share in the rebellion. But if stupid, Dunne at least was staunch, and so, with a wealth of valedictory invective, Jeffreys dismissed him, and addressed at last the prisoner, inviting her to speak in her own defence.

She rose to do so, fearlessly yet gently.

111

"My lord, what I have to say is this. I knew of nobody's coming to my house but Mr. Hicks, and for him I was informed that he did abscond by reason of warrants that were out against him for preaching in private meetings; for that reason I sent to him to come by night. But I had never heard that Nelthorp was to come with him, nor what name Nelthorp had till after he had come to my house. I could die upon it. As for Mr. Hicks, I did not in the least suspect that he had been in the army, being a Presbyterian minister that used to preach and not to fight. "

"But I will tell you, " Jeffreys interrupted her, "that there is not one of those lying, snivelling, canting Presbyterian rascals but one way or the other had a hand in the late horrid conspiracy and rebellion. "

"My lord, I abhorred both the principles and the practices of the late rebellion, " she protested; adding that if she had been tried in London, my Lady Abergavenny and many other persons of quality could have testified with what detestation she had spoken of the rebellion, and that she had been in London until Monmouth had been beheaded.

"If I had known the time of my trial in the country, " she pursued, "I could have had the testimony of those persons of honour for me. But, my lord, I have been told, and so I thought it would have been, that I should not have been tried for harbouring Mr. Hicks until he should himself be convict as a traitor. I did abhor those that were in the plot and conspiracy against the King. I know my duty to my King better, and have always exercised it. I defy anybody in the world that ever knew contrary to come and give testimony. "

His voice broke harshly upon the pause. "Have you any more to say? "

"As to what they say to my denying Nelthorp to be in the house, " she resumed. "I was in very great consternation and fear of the soldiers, who were very rude and violent. I beseech your lordship to make that construction of it, and not harbour an ill opinion of me because of those false reports that go about of me, relating to my carriage towards the old King, that I was anyways consenting to the death of King Charles I; for, my lord, that is as false as God is true. I was not out of my chamber all the day in which that king was beheaded, and I believe I shed more tears for him than any other woman then living.

"And I do repeat it, my lord, as I hope to attain salvation, I never did know Nelthorp, nor did I know of anybody's coming but Mr. Hicks. Him I knew to be a Nonconformist minister, and there being, as is well known, warrants out to apprehend all Nonconformist ministers, I was willing to give him shelter from these warrants, which I knew was no treason. "

"Have you any more to say for yourself? " he asked her.

"My lord, " she was beginning, "I came but five days before this into the country. "

"Nay, " he broke in, "I cannot tell when you came into the country, nor I don't care. It seems you came in time to harbour rebels. "

She protested that if she would have ventured her life for anything, it would have been to serve the King.

"But, though I could not fight for him myself, my son did; he was actually in arms on the King's side in this business. It was I that bred him in loyalty and to fight for the King. "

"Well, have you done? " he asked her brutally.

"Yes, my lord, " she answered; and resumed her seat, trembling a little from the exertion and emotion of her address.

His charge to the jury began. It was very long, and the first half of it was taken up with windy rhetoric in which the Almighty was invoked at every turn. It degenerated at one time into a sermon upon the text of "render unto Caesar, " inveighing against the Presbyterian religion. And the dull length of his lordship's periods, combined with the monotone in which he spoke, lulled the wearied lady at the bar into slumber. She awakened with a start when suddenly his fist crashed down and his voice rose in fierce denunciation of the late rebellion. But she was dozing again - so calm and so little moved was she - before he had come to apply his denunciations to her own case, and this in spite of all her protests that she had held the rebellion in abhorrence.

It was all calculated to prejudice the minds of the jurymen before he came to the facts and the law of the case. And that charge of his throughout, far from being a judicial summing-up, was a virulent address for the prosecution, just as his bearing hitherto in examining and cross-examining witnesses had been that of counsel for the Crown. The statement that she had made in her own defence he utterly ignored, save in one particular, where he saw his opportunity further to prejudice her case.

"I am sorry, " he said, his face lengthening, "to remember something that dropped even from the gentlewoman herself. She pretends to religion and loyalty very much - how greatly she wept at the death of King Charles the Martyr - and owns her great obligations to the late king and his royal brother. And yet no sooner is one in the grave than she forgets all gratitude and entertains those that were rebels against his royal successor.

"I will not say, " he continued with deliberate emphasis, "what hand her husband had in the death of that blessed martyr; she has enough to answer for her own guilt; and I must confess that it ought not, one way or other, to make any ingredient into this case what she was in former times. "

But he had dragged it in, protesting that it should not influence the case, yet coldly, calculatingly intending it to do so. She was the widow of a regicide, reason and to spare in the views of himself and his royal master why she should be hounded to her death upon any pretext.

Thereafter he reviewed the evidence against her, dwelt upon the shuffling of Dunne, deduced that the reason for so much lying was to conceal the damning truth - namely, that she knew Hicks for a rebel when she gave him shelter, and thus became the partner of his horrible guilt. Upon that he charged them to find their verdict "without any consideration of persons, but considering only the truth. "

Nevertheless, although his commands were clear, some of the jury would seem to have feared the God whom Jeffreys invoked so constantly. One of them rose to ask him pertinently, in point of law, whether it was treason to have harboured Hicks before the man had been convicted of treason.

Curtly he answered them that beyond doubt it was, and upon that assurance the jury withdrew, the Court settled down into an expectant silence, and her ladyship dozed again in her chair.

The minutes passed. It was growing late, and Jeffreys was eager to be done with this prejudged affair, that he might dine in peace. His voice broke the stillness of the court, protesting his angry wonder at the need to deliberate in so plain a case. He was threatening to adjourn and let the jury lie by all night if they did not bring in their verdict quickly. When, at the end of a half-hour, they returned, his fierce, impatient glance found them ominously grave.

"My lord, " said Mr. Whistler, the foreman, "we have to beg of your lordship some directions before we can bring our verdict. We have some doubt upon us whether there be sufficient proof that she knew Hicks to have been in the army. "

Well might they doubt it, for there was no proof at all. Yet he never hesitated to answer them.

"There is as full proof as proof can be. But you are judges of the proof. For my part, I thought there was no difficulty in it. "

"My lord, " the foreman insisted, "we are in some doubt about it. "

"I cannot help your doubts, " he said irritably. "Was there not proved a discourse of the battle and of the battle and of the army at supper-time? "

"But, my lord, we are not satisfied that she had notice that Hicks was in the army. "

He glowered upon them in silence for a moment. They deserved to be themselves indicted for their slowness to perceive where lay their duty to their king.

"I cannot tell what would satisfy you, " he said; and sneered. "Did she not inquire of Dunne whether Hicks had been in the army? And when he told her he did not know, she did not say she would refuse if he had been, but ordered him to come by night, by which it is evident she suspected it. "

He ignored, you see, her own complete explanation of that circumstance.

"And when Hicks and Nelthorp came, did she not discourse with them about the battle and the army? " (As if that were not at the time a common topic of discussion.) "Come, come, gentlemen, " he said, with amazing impudence, "it is plain proof. "

But Mr. Whistler was not yet satisfied.

"We do not remember, my lord, that it was proved that she asked any such question. "

That put him in a passion.

"Sure, " he bellowed, "you do not remember anything that has passed. Did not Dunne tell you there was such a discourse, and she was by? But if there were no such proof, the circumstances and management of the thing are as full proof as can be. I wonder what it is you doubt of! "

Mrs. Lisle had risen. There was a faint flush of excitement on her grey old face.

"My lord, I hope - " she began, in trembling tones, to get no further.

"You must not speak now! " thundered her terrible judge; and thus struck her silent.

The brief resistance to his formidable will was soon at an end. Within a quarter of an hour the jury announced their verdict. They found her guilty.

"Gentlemen, " said his lordship, "I did not think I should have occasion to speak after your verdict, but, finding some hesitancy and doubt among you, I cannot but say I wonder it should come about; for I think, in my conscience, the evidence was as full and plain as it could be, and if I had been among you, and she had been my own mother, I should have found her guilty. "

She was brought up for sentence on the morrow, together with several others subsequently convicted. Amid fresh invectives against the religion she practised, he condemned her to be burned alive - which was the proper punishment for high treason - ordering the sheriff to prepare for her execution that same afternoon.

"But look you, Mrs. Lisle, " he added, "we that are the judges shall stay in town an hour or two. You shall have pen, ink, and paper, and if, in the mean time, you employ that pen, ink, and paper and that hour or two well - you understand what I mean it may be that you shall hear further from us in a deferring of this execution. "

What was this meaning that he assumed she understood? Jeffreys had knowledge of Kirke's profitable traffic in the West, and it is known that he spared no means of acquiring an estate suitable to his rank which he did not possess by way of patrimony. Thus cynically he invited a bribe.

It is the only inference that explains the subsequent rancour he displayed against her, aroused by her neglect to profit by his suggestions. The intercession of the divines of Winchester procured her a week's reprieve, and in that week her puissant friends in London, headed by the Earl of Abergavenny, petitioned the King on her behalf. Even Feversham, the victor of Sedgemoor, begged her life of the King - bribed to it, as men say, by an offer of a thousand pounds. But the King withheld his mercy upon the plea that he had promised Lord Jeffreys he would not reprieve her, and the utmost clemency influential petitions could wring from James II was that she should be beheaded instead of burned.

She suffered in the market-place of Winchester on September 2d. Christian charity was all her sin, and for this her head was demanded in atonement. She yielded it with a gentle fortitude and resolution. In lieu of speech, she left with the sheriff a pathetic document wherein she protests her innocence of all offence against the King, and forgives her enemies specifically - the judge, who prejudiced her case, and forgot that "the Court should be counsel for the prisoner, " and Colonel Penruddock, "though he told me he could have taken those men before they came to my house. "

Between those lines you may read the true reason why the Lady Alice Lisle died. She died to slake the cruelly vindictive thirst of King James II on the one hand, and Colonel Penruddock on the other, against her husband who had been dead for twenty years.

V. THE NIGHT OF MASSACRE

The Story of the Saint Bartholomew

There are elements of mystery about the massacre of Saint Bartholomew over which, presumably, historians will continue to dispute as long as histories are written. Indeed, it is largely of their disputes that the mystery is begotten. Broadly speaking, these historians may be divided into two schools - Catholic and anti-Catholic. The former have made it their business to show that the massacre was purely a political affair, having no concern with religion; the latter have been equally at pains to prove it purely an act of religious persecution having no concern with politics. Those who adopt the latter point of view insist that the affair was long premeditated, that it had its source in something concerted some seven years earlier between Catherine of Medicis and the sinister Duke of Alva. And they would seem to suggest that Henry of Navarre, the nominal head of the Protestant party, was brought to Paris to wed Marguerite de Valois merely so that by this means the Protestant nobles of the kingdom, coming to the capital for the wedding, should be lured to their destruction.

It does not lie within the purview of the present narrative to enter into a consideration of the arguments of the two schools, nor will it be attempted.

But it may briefly be stated that the truth lies probably in a middle course of reasoning - that the massacre was political in conception and religious in execution; or, in other words, that statecraft deliberately made use of fanaticism as of a tool; that the massacre was brought about by a sudden determination begotten of opportunity which is but another word for Chance.

Against the theory of premeditation the following cardinal facts may be urged:

(a) The impossibility of guarding for seven years a secret that several must have shared;

(b) The fact that neither Charles IX nor his mother Catherine were in any sense bigoted Catholics, or even of a normal religious sincerity.

(c) The lack of concerted action - so far as the kingdom generally was concerned - in the execution of the massacre.

A subsidiary disproof lies in the attempted assassination of Coligny two days before the massacre, an act which might, by putting the Huguenots on their guard, have caused the miscarriage of the entire plan - had it existed.

It must be borne in mind that for years France had been divided by religious differences into two camps, and that civil war between Catholic and Huguenot had ravaged and distracted the country. At the head of the Protestant party stood that fine soldier Gaspard de Chatillon, Admiral de Coligny, virtually the Protestant King of France, a man who raised armies, maintaining them by taxes levied upon Protestant subjects, and treated with Charles IX as prince with prince. At the head of the Catholic party - the other imperium in imperio - stood the Duke of Guise. The third and weakest party in the State, serving, as it seemed, little purpose beyond that of holding the scales between the other turbulent two, was the party of the King.

The motives and events that precipitated the massacre are set forth in the narration of the King's brother, the Duke of Anjou (afterwards Henri III). It was made by him to Miron, his physician and confidential servant in Cracow, when he ruled there later as King of Poland, under circumstances which place it beyond suspicion of being intended to serve ulterior aims. For partial corroboration, and for other details of the massacre itself, we have the narratives, among others, of Sully, who was then a young man in the train of the King of Navarre, and of Lusignan, a gentleman of the Admiral's household. We shall closely follow these in our reconstruction of the event and its immediate causes.

The gay chatter of the gallants and ladies thronging the long gallery of the Louvre sank and murmured into silence, and a movement was made to yield a free passage to the King, who had suddenly made his appearance leaning affectionately upon the shoulder of the Admiral de Coligny.

The Duke of Anjou, a slender, graceful young man in a gold-embroidered suit of violet, forgot the interest he was taking in his beautiful hands to bend lower over the handsome Madame de

Nemours what time the unfriendly eyes of both were turned upon the Admiral.

The King and the great Huguenot leader came slowly down the gallery, an oddly contrasting pair. Coligny would have been the taller by a half-head but for his stoop, yet in spite of it there was energy and military vigour in his carriage, just as there was a severe dignity amounting to haughtiness in his scarred and wrinkled countenance. A bullet that had pierced his cheek and broken three of his teeth at the battle of Moncontour had left a livid scar that lost itself in his long white beard. His forehead was high and bald, and his eyes were of a steely keenness under their tufted brows. He was dressed with Calvinistic simplicity entirely in black, and just as this contrasted with the King's suit of sulphur-coloured satin, so did the gravity of his countenance contrast with the stupidity of his sovereign's.

Charles IX, a slimly built young man in his twenty-fourth year, was of a pallid, muddy complexion, with great, shifty, greenish eyes, and a thick, pendulous nose. The protruding upper lip of his long, thin mouth gave him an oafish expression, which was increased by his habit of carrying his head craned forward.

His nature was precisely what you would have expected from his appearance - dull and gross. He was chiefly distinguished among men of birth for general obscenity of speech and morphological inventiveness in blasphemy.

At the end of the gallery Coligny stooped to kiss the royal hand in leave-taking. With his other hand Charles patted the Admiral's shoulder.

"Count me your friend, " he said, "body and soul, heart and bowels, even as I count you mine. Fare you well, my father. "

Coligny departed, and the King retraced his steps, walking quickly, his head hunched between his shoulders, his baleful eyes looking neither to left nor right. As he passed out, the Duke of Anjou quitted the side of Madame de Nemours, and went after him. Then at last the suspended chatter of the courtiers broke loose again.

The King was pacing his cabinet - a simple room furnished with a medley of objects appertaining to study, to devotion, and to hunting.

A large picture of the Virgin hung from a wall flanked on either side by an arquebus, and carrying a hunting-horn on one of its upper corners. A little alabaster holy-water font near the door, crowned by a sprig of palm, seemed to serve as a receptacle for hawk-bells and straps. There was a writing-table of beautifully carved walnut near the leaded window, littered with books and papers - a treatise on hunting lay cheek by jowl with a Book of Hours; a string of rosary beads and a dog-whip lay across an open copy of Ronsard's verses. The King was quite the vilest poetaster of his day.

Charles looked over his shoulder as his brother entered. The scowl on his face deepened when he saw who came, and with a grunt he viciously kicked the liver-coloured hound that lay stretched at his feet. The hound fled yelping to a corner, the Duke checked, startled, in his advance.

"Well? " growled the King. "Well? Am I never to have peace? Am I never to be alone? What now? Bowels of God! What do you want? "

His green eyes smouldered, his right hand opened and closed on the gold hilt of the dagger at his girdle:

Scared by the maniac ferocity of this reception, the young Duke precipitately withdrew.

"It is nothing. Another time, since I disturb you now. " He bowed and vanished, followed by an evil, cackling laugh.

Anjou knew how little his brother loved him, and he confesses how much he feared him in that moment. But under his fear it is obvious that there was lively resentment. He went straight in quest of his mother, whose darling he was, to bear her the tale of the King's mood, and what he accounted, no doubt rightly, the cause of it.

"It is the work of that pestilential Huguenot admiral, " he announced, at the end of a long tirade, "It is always thus with him after he has seen Coligny. "

Catherine of Medicis considered. She was a fat, comfortable woman, with a thick nose, pinched lips, and sleepy eyes.

"Charles, " she said at length, in her monotonous, emotionless voice, "is a weathercock that turns with every wind that blows upon him.

You should know him by now. " And she yawned, so that one who did not know her and her habit of perpetually yawning might have supposed that she was but indifferently interested.

They were alone together in the intimate little tapestried room she called her oratory. She half sat, half reclined upon a couch of rose brocade. Anjou stood over by the window, his back to it, so that his pale face was in shadow. He considered his beautiful hands, which he was reluctant to lower, lest the blood should flow into them and mar their white perfection.

"The Admiral's influence over him is increasing, " he complained, "and he uses it to lessen our own. "

"Do I not know it? " came her dull voice.

"It is time to end it, " said Anjou passionately, "before he ends us. Your influence grows weaker every day and the Admiral's stronger. Charles begins to take sides with him against us. We shall have him a tool of the Huguenot party before all is done. Ah, mon Dieu! You should have seen him leaning upon the shoulder of that old parpaillot, calling him 'my father, ' and protesting himself his devoted friend 'body and soul, heart and bowels, ' in his own words. And when I seek him afterwards, he scowls and snarls at me, and fingers his dagger as if he would have it in my throat. It is plain to see upon what subject the old scoundrel entertained him. " And again he repeated, more fiercely than before: "It is time to end it! "

"I know, " she said, ever emotionless before so much emotion. "And it shall be ended. The old assassin should have been hanged years ago for guiding the hand that shot Francois de Guise. Daily he becomes a greater danger, to Charles, to ourselves, and to France. He is embroiling us with Spain through this Huguenot army he is raising to go and fight the battles of Calvinism in Flanders. A fine thing that. Ah, per Dio! " For a moment her voice was a little warmed and quickened. "Catholic France at war with Catholic Spain for the sake of Huguenot Flanders! " She laughed shortly. Then her voice reverted to its habitual sleepy level. "You are right. It is time to end it. Coligny is the head of this rebellious beast. If we cut off the head, perhaps the beast will perish. We will consult the Duke of Guise. " She yawned again. "Yes, the Duke of Guise will be ready to lend us his counsel and his aid. Decidedly we must get rid of the Admiral. "

That was on Monday, August 18th of that year 1572, and such was the firm purpose and energy of that fat and seemingly sluggish woman, that within two days all necessary measures were taken, and Maurevert, the assassin, was at his post in the house of Vilaine, in the Cloisters of Saint-Germain l'Auxerrois, procured for the purpose by Madame de Nemours, who bore the Admiral a mortal hatred.

It was not, however, until the following Friday that Maurevert was given the opportunity of carrying out the task to which he had been hired. On that morning, as the Admiral was passing, accompanied by a few gentlemen of his household, returning from the Louvre to his house in the Rue Betisy, the assassin did his work. There was a sudden arquebusade from a first-floor window, and a bullet smashed two fingers of the Admiral's right hand, and lodged itself in the muscles of his left arm.

With his maimed and bleeding hand he pointed to the window whence the shot had been fired, bidding his gentlemen to force a way into the house and take the assassin. But whilst they were breaking in at the front, Maurevert was making his escape by the back, where a horse waited for him, and, though pursued, he was never overtaken.

News of the event was instantly borne to the King. It found him at tennis with the Duke of Guise and the Admiral's son-in-law, Teligny.

"In this assassin's work, Sire, " said the blunt gentleman whom Coligny had sent, "the Admiral desires you to see the proof of the worth of the agreement between himself and Monsieur de Guise that followed upon the treaty of peace of Saint-Germain. "

The Duke of Guise drew himself stiffly up, but said no word. The King, livid with rage, looked at him balefully a moment, then to vent some of his fury he smashed his racket against the wall.

"God's Blood! " he cried, mouthing horribly. "Am I then never to have rest? " He flung away the broken remnants of his racket, and went out cursing. Questioning the messenger further, he learnt that the shot had been fired from the house of Vilaine, a sometime tutor to the Duke of Guise, and that the horse upon which the assassin had fled had been held for him by a groom in the Guise livery.

Meanwhile the Duke and Monsieur de Teligny had gone their ways with no word spoken between them - Guise to shut himself up in his hotel and assemble his friends, Teligny to repair at once to his father-in-law.

At two o'clock in the afternoon, in response to an urgent request from the Admiral, the King went to visit him, accompanied by the Queen-Mother, by his brothers Anjou and Alencon, and a number of officers and courtiers. The royal party saw nothing of the excitement which had been prevailing in the city ever since the morning's event, an excitement which subsided at their approach. The King was gloomy, resentful, and silent, having so far refused to discuss the matter with any one, denying audience even to his mother. Catherine and Anjou were vexed by the miscarriage of the affair, anxious and no less silent than the King.

They found the Admiral awaiting them, calm and composed. The famous Ambroise Pare had amputated the two broken fingers, and had dealt with the wound in the arm. But although Coligny might be considered to have escaped lightly, and not to be in any danger, a rumour was abroad that the bullet was poisoned; and neither the Admiral nor his people seem to have rejected the possibility. One suspects, indeed, that capital was made out of it. It was felt, perhaps, that thus should the Admiral maintain a greater influence with the King. For in any uncertainty as to whether Coligny would live or die, the King's feelings must be more deeply stirred than if he knew that the wound carried no peril to life.

Followed closely by his mother and his brothers, Charles swept through the spacious ante-chamber, thronged now with grim-faced, resentful Huguenot gentlemen, and so entered the room where Coligny reclined upon a day bed near the window. The Admiral made shift to rise, but this the King hurried forward to prevent.

"Rest yourself, my dear father! " he cried, in accents of deep concern. "Heart of God! What is this they have done to you? Assure me, at least, that your life is safe, or, by the Mass, I'll - "

"I hold my life from God, " the Admiral replied gravely, "and when He requires it of me I will yield it up. That is nothing. "

124

"Nothing? God's Blood! Nothing? The hurt is yours, my father, but the outrage mine; and I swear to you, by the Blood and the Death, that I will take such a vengeance as shall never be forgotten! "

Thereupon he fell into such a storm of imprecation and blasphemy that the Admiral, a sincerely devout, God-fearing heretic, shuddered to hear him.

"Calm, Sire! " he begged at last, laying his sound hand upon the King's velvet sleeve. " Be calm and listen, for it is not to speak of myself, of these wounds, or of the wrong done me, that I have presumed to beg you to visit me. This attempt to murder me is but a sign of the evil that is stirring in France to sap your authority and power. But - " He checked and looked at the three who stood immediately behind the King. "What I have to say is, if you will deign to listen, for your private ear. "

The King jerked round in a fashion peculiar to him; his every action was abrupt and spasmodic. He eyed his mother and brothers shiftily. It was beyond his power to look any one directly in the face.

"Outside! " he commanded, waving an impatient hand almost in their faces. "Do you hear? Leave me to talk with my father the Admiral. "

The young dukes fell back at once, ever in dread of provoking the horrible displays of passion that invariably followed upon any resistance of his feeble will. But the sluggish Catherine was not so easily moved.

"Is Monsieur de Coligny strong enough, do you think, to treat of affairs at present? Consider his condition, I beg, " she enjoined in her level voice.

"I thank you for your consideration, madame, " said the Admiral, the ghost of an ironic smile about his lips. "But I am strong enough, thank God! And even though my strength were less than it is, it would be more heavily taxed by the thought that I had neglected my duty to His Majesty than it ever could be by the performance of that duty. "

"Ha! You hear? " snapped the King. "Go, then; go! "

They went, returning to the ante-chamber to wait until the audience should conclude. The three stood there in the embrasure of a window that looked out upon the hot, sunlit courtyard. There, as Anjou himself tells us, they found themselves hemmed about by some two hundred sullen, grim-faced gentlemen and officers of the Admiral's party, who eyed them without dissembling their hostility, who preserved a silence that was disturbed only by the murmurs of their constant whisperings, and who moved to and fro before the royal group utterly careless of the proper degree of deference and respect.

Isolated thus in that hostile throng, Catherine and her sons became more and more uneasy, so that, as the Queen-Mother afterwards confessed, she was never in any place where her tarrying was attended by so much fear, or her departure thence by so much pleasure.

It was this fear that spurred her at last to put an end to that secret conference in the room beyond. She did it in characteristic manner. In the most complete outward composure, stifling a yawn as she went, she moved deliberately across to the door, her sons following, rapped shortly on the panel, and entered without waiting to be bidden.

The King, who was standing by the Admiral's side, wheeled sharply at the sound of the opening door. His eyes blazed with sudden anger when he beheld his mother, but she was the first to speak.

"My son, " she said, "I am concerned for the poor Admiral. He will have the fever if you continue to permit him to weary himself with affairs at present. It is not to treat him as a friend to prolong this interview. Let business wait until he is recovered, which will be the sooner if he is given rest at present. "

Coligny stroked his white beard in silence, while the King flared out, striding towards her:

"Par la Mort Dieu! What is this sudden concern for the Admiral? "

"Not sudden, my son, " she answered in her dull voice, her eyes intent upon him, with something magnetic in their sleepy glance that seemed to rob him of half his will. "None knows more accurately than I the Admiral's precise, value to France. "

Anjou behind her may have smiled at that equivocal phrase.

"God's Bowels! Am I King, or what am I? "

"It ill becomes a king to abuse the strength of a poor wounded subject, " she returned, her eyes ever regarding him steadily. "Come, Charles. Another day, when the Admiral shall have recovered more fully, you may continue this discourse. Come now. "

His anger was subdued to mere sullenness, almost infantile in its outward petulant expression. He attempted to meet her glance, and he was completely lost.

"Perhaps . .. Ah, Ventre Dieu, my mother is right! Let the matter rest, then, my father. We will talk of it again as soon as you are well. "

He stepped up to the couch, and held out his hand.

Coligny took it, and his eyes looked up wistfully into the weak young face of his King.

"I thank you, Sire, for coming and for hearing me. Another day, if I am spared, I may tell you more. Meanwhile, bear well in mind what I have said already. I have no interests in this world but your own, Sire. " And he kissed the royal hand in farewell.

Not until they were back in the Louvre did the Queen attempt to break upon the King's gloomy abstraction, to learn - as learn she must - the subject of the Admiral's confidential communication.

Accompanied by Anjou, she sought him in his cabinet, nor would she be denied. He sat at his writing-table, his head sunken between his shoulders, his receding chin in his cupped palms. He glared at the pair as they entered, swore savagely, and demanded their business with him.

Catherine sat down with massive calm. Anjou remained standing beside and slightly behind her, leaning upon the back of her tall chair.

"My son, " she said bluntly, "I have come to learn what passed between you and Coligny. "

"What passed? What concern is that of yours? "

"All your concerns are mine, " she answered tranquilly. "I am your mother. "

"And I am your king! " he answered, banging the table. "And I mean to be king! "

"By the grace of God and the favour of Monsieur de Coligny, " she sneered, with unruffled calm.

"What's that? " His mouth fell open, and his eyes stared. A crimson flush overspread his muddy complexion. "What's that? "

Her dull glance met and held his own whilst calmly she repeated her sneering words.

"And that is why I have come to you, " she added. "If you are unable to rule without guidance, I must at least do what I can so that the guidance shall not be that of a rebel, of one who guides you to the end that he may master you. "

"Master me! " he screamed. He rose in his indignation and faced her. But his glance, unable to support her steady eyes, faltered and fell away. Foul oaths poured from his royal lips. "Master me! " he repeated.

"Aye - master you, " she answered him. "Master you until the little remnant of your authority shall have been sapped; until you are no more than a puppet in the hands of the Huguenot party, a roi faineant, a king of straw. "

"By God, madame, were you not my mother - "

"It is because I am your mother that I seek to save you. "

He looked at her again, but again his glance faltered. He paced the length of the room and back, mouthing and muttering. Then he came to stand, leaning on the prie-dieu, facing her.

"By God's Death, madame, since you demand to know what the Admiral said, you shall. You prove to me that what he told me was no more than true. He told me that a king is only recognized in

France as long as he is a power for good or ill over his subjects; that this power, together with the management of all State affairs, is slipping, by the crafty contrivances of yourself and Anjou there, out of my hands into your own; that this power and authority which you are both stealing from me may one day be used against me and my kingdom. And he bade me be on my guard against you both and take my measures. He gave me this counsel, madame, because he deemed it his duty as one of my most loyal and faithful servants at the point of death, and - "

"The shameless hypocrite! " her dull, contemptuous voice interrupted him. "At the point of death! Two broken fingers and a flesh-wound in the arm and he represents himself as in articulo mortis that he may play upon you, and make you believe his lies. "

Her stolidity of manner and her logic, ponderous and irresistible, had their effect. His big, green eyes seemed to dilate, his mouth fell open.

"If - " he began, and checked, rapped out an oath, and checked again. "Are they lies, madame? " he asked slowly.

She caught the straining note of hope in that question of his - a hope founded upon vanity, the vanity to be king in fact, as well as king in name. She rose.

"To ask me that - me, your mother - is to insult me. Come, Anjou. "

And on that she departed, craftily, leaving her suggestion to prey upon his mind.

But once alone in her oratory with Anjou, her habitual torpor was sloughed away. For once she quivered and crimsoned and raised her voice, whilst for once her sleepy eyes kindled and flashed as she inveighed against Coligny and the Huguenots.

For the moment, however, there was no more to be done. The stroke had failed; Coligny had survived the attempt upon his life, and there was danger that on the recoil the blow might smite those who had launched it. But on the morrow, which was Saturday, things suddenly assumed a very different complexion.

That great Catholic leader, the powerful, handsome Duke of Guise, who, more than suspected of having inspired the attempted assassination, had kept his hotel since yesterday, now sought the Queen-Mother with news of what was happening in the city. Armed bands of Huguenot nobles were riding through the streets, clamouring:

"Death to the assassins of the Admiral! Down with the Guisards! "

And, although a regiment of Gardes Francaises had been hastily brought to Paris to keep order, the Duke feared grave trouble in a city which the royal wedding had filled with Huguenot gentlemen and their following. Then, too, there were rumours that the Huguenots were arming everywhere - rumours which, whether true or not, were, under the circumstances, sufficiently natural and probable to be taken seriously.

Leaving Guise in her oratory, and summoning her darling Anjou, Catherine at once sought the King. She may have believed the rumours, and she may even have stated them as facts beyond dispute so as to strengthen and establish her case against Gaspard de Coligny.

"King Gaspard I, " she told him, "is already taking his measures. The Huguenots are arming; officers have been dispatched into the provinces to levy troops. The Admiral has ordered the raising of ten thousand horse in Germany, and another ten thousand Swiss mercenaries in the Cantons. "

He stared at her vacuously. Some such rumour had already reached him, and he conceived that here was definite confirmation of it.

"You may determine now who are your friends, who your loyal servants, " she told him. "How is so much force to be resisted in the state in which you find yourself? The Catholics exhausted, and weary as they are by a civil war in which their king was of little account to them, are going to arm so as to offer what resistance they can without depending upon you. Thus, within your State you will have two great parties under arms, neither of which can be called your own. Unless you stir yourself, and quickly, unless you choose now between friends and foes, you will find yourself alone, isolated, in grave peril, without authority or power. "

He sank overwhelmed to a chair, and took his head in his hands, cogitating. When next he looked at her there was positive fear in his great eyes, a fear evoked by contemplation of the picture which her words had painted for him.

He looked from her to Anjou.

"What then? " he asked. "What then? How is the danger to be averted? "

"By a simple stroke of the sword, " she answered calmly. "Slice off at a blow the head of this beast of rebellion, this hydra of heresy. "

He huddled back, horror in his eyes. His hands slid slowly along the carved arms of his chair, and clenched the ends so tightly that his knuckles looked like knobs of marble.

"Kill the Admiral? " he said slowly.

"The Admiral and the chief Huguenot leaders, " she said, much in the tone she might have used, were it a matter of wringing the necks of a dozen capons.

"Ah, ca! Par la Mort Dieu! " He heaved himself up, raging. "Thus would your hatred of him be served. Thus would you - "

Coolly she sliced into his foaming speech.

"Not I - not I! " she said. "Do nothing upon my advice. Summon your Council. Send for Tavannes, Biragues, Retz, and the others. Consult with them. They are your friends; you trust and believe in them. When they know the facts, see if their counsel will differ from your mother's. Send for them; they are in the Louvre now. "

He looked at her a moment.

"Very well, " he said; and reeled to the door, bawling hoarsely his orders.

They came, one by one - the Marshal de Tavannes, the Duke of Retz, the Duke of Nevers, the Chancellor de Biragues, and lastly the Duke of Guise, upon whom the King scowled a jealous hatred that was now fully alive.

The window, which overlooked the quay and the river, stood open to admit what air might be stirring on that hot day of August.

Charles sat at his writing-table, sullen and moody, twining a string of beads about his fingers. Catherine occupied the chair over beyond the table, Anjou sitting near her on a stool. The others stood respectfully awaiting that the King should make known his wishes. The shifty royal glance swept over them from under lowering brows; then it rested almost in challenge upon his mother.

"Tell them, " he bade her curtly.

She told them what already she had told her son, relating all now with greater detail and circumstance. For some moments nothing was heard in that room but the steady drone of her unemotional voice. When she had finished, she yawned and settled herself to hear what might be answered.

"Well, " snapped the King, "you have heard. What do you advise? Speak out! "

Nevers was the first to answer.

"There is no other way, " he said stiffly, "but that which Her Majesty advises. The danger is grave. If it is to be averted, action must be prompt and effective. "

Tavannes clasped his hands behind him and said much the same, as did presently the Chancellor.

Twisting and untwisting his chaplet of beads about his long fingers, his eyes averted, the King heard each in turn. Then he looked up. His glance, deliberately ignoring Guise, settled upon the Duke of Retz, who held aloof.

"And you, Monsieur le Marechal, what is your counsel? "

Retz drew himself up, as if bracing himself to meet opposing forces. He was a little pale, but quite composed.

"If there is a man whom I should hate, " he said, "it is this Gaspard de Coligny, who has defamed me and all my family by the foul accusations he has put abroad. But I will not, " he added firmly, "take vengeance upon my enemies at the expense of my king and master. I cannot counsel a course so disastrous to Your Majesty and the whole kingdom. Did we act as we have been advised, Sire, can you doubt that we should be taxed - and rightly taxed in view of the treaty that has been signed - with perfidy and disloyalty? "

Dead silence followed that bombshell of opposition, coming from a quarter whence it was least expected. For Catherine and Anjou had confidently counted upon the Duke's hatred of Coligny to ensure his support of their designs.

A little colour crept into the pale cheeks of the King. His glance kindled out of its sullenness. He was as one who sees sudden hope amid despair.

"That is the truth, " he said. "Messieurs, and you, madame my mother, you have heard the truth. How do you like it? "

"Monsieur de Retz is deceived by an excess of loyalty, " said Anjou quickly. "Because he bears a personal enmity to the Admiral, he conceives that it would hurt his honour to speak otherwise. It must savour to him, as he has said, of using his king and master to avenge his own personal wrongs. We can respect Monsieur de Retz's view, although we hold it mistaken. "

"Will Monsieur de Retz tell us what other course lies open? " quoth the bluff Tavannes.

"Some other course must be found, " cried the King, rousing himself. "It must be found, do you hear? I will not have you touch the life of my friend the Admiral. I will not have it - by the Blood! "

A hubbub followed, all speaking at once, until the King banged the table, and reminded them that his cabinet was not a fish-market.

"I say that there is no other way, " Catherine insisted. "There cannot be two kings in France, nor can there be two parties. For your own safety's sake, and for the safety of your kingdom, I beseech you so to contrive that in France there be but one party with one head - yourself. "

"Two kings in France? " he said. "What two kings? "

"Yourself and Gaspard I - King Coligny, the King of the Huguenots. "

"He is my subject - my faithful, loyal subject, " the King protested, but with less assurance.

"A subject who raises forces of his own, levies taxes of his own, garrisons Huguenot cities, " said Biragues. "That is a very dangerous type of subject, Sire. "

"A subject who forces you into war with Protestant Flanders against Catholic Spain, " added the blunt Tavannes.

"Forces me? " roared the King, half rising, his eyes aflash. "That is a very daring word. "

"It would be if the proof were absent. Remember, Sire, his very speech to you before you permitted him to embark upon preparations for this war. 'Give us leave, ' he said, 'to make war in Flanders, or we shall be compelled to make war upon yourself. '"

The King winced and turned livid. Sweat stood in beads upon his brow. He was touched in his most sensitive spot. That speech of Coligny's was of all things the one he most desired to forget. He twisted the chaplet so that the beads bit deeply into his fingers.

"Sire, " Tavannes continued, "were I a king, and did a subject so address me, I should have his head within the hour. Yet worse has happened since, worse is happening now. The Huguenots are arming. They ride arrogantly through the streets of your capital, stirring up rebellion. They are here in force, and the danger grows acute and imminent. "

Charles writhed before them. He mopped his brow with a shaking hand.

"The danger - yes. I see that. I admit the danger. But Coligny - "

"Is it to be King Gaspard or King Charles? " rasped the voice of Catherine.

The chaplet snapped suddenly in the King's fingers. He sprang to his feet, deathly pale.

"So be it! " he cried. "Since it is necessary to kill the Admiral, kill him, then. Kill him! " he screamed, in a fury that seemed aimed at those who forced this course upon him. "Kill him - but see to it also that at the same time you kill every Huguenot in France, so that not one shall be left to reproach me. Not one, do you hear? Take your measures and let the thing be done at once. " And on that, his face livid and twitching, his limbs shaking, he flung out of the room and left them.

It was all the warrant they required, and they set to work at once there in the King's own cabinet, where he had left them. Guise, who had hitherto been no more than a silent spectator, assumed now the most active part. Upon his own shoulders he took the charge of seeing the Admiral done to death.

The remainder of the day and a portion of the evening were spent in concerting ways and means. They assured themselves of the Provost of the merchants of Paris, of the officers of the Gardes Francaises and the three thousand Swiss, of the Captains of the quarters and other notoriously factious persons who could be trusted as leaders. By ten o'clock at night all preparations were made and it was agreed that the ringing of the bell of Saint-Germain l'Auxerrois for matins was to be the signal for the massacre.

A gentleman of the Admiral's household taking his way homeward that night passed several men bearing sheaves of pikes upon their shoulders, and never suspected whom these weapons were to arm. He met several small companies of soldiers marching quietly, their weapons shouldered, their matches glowing, and still he suspected nothing, whilst in one quarter he stopped to watch a man whose behaviour seemed curious, and discovered that he was chalking a white cross upon the doors of certain houses.

Meeting soon afterwards another man with a bundle of weapons on his shoulder, the intrigued Huguenot gentleman asked him bluntly what he carried and whither he went.

"It is for the divertissement at the Louvre tonight, " he was answered.

But in the Louvre the Queen-Mother and the Catholic leaders, the labours of preparation ended, were snatching a brief rest. Between two and three o'clock in the morning Catherine and Anjou repaired again to the King's cabinet. They found him waiting there, his face haggard and his eyes fevered.

He had spent a part of the evening at billiards, and among the players had been La Rochefoucauld, of whom he was fond, and who had left him with a jest at eleven o'clock, little dreaming that it was for the last time.

The three of them crossed to the window overlooking the river. They opened it, and peered out fearfully. Even Catherine trembled now that the hour approached. The air was fresh and cool, swept clean by the stirring breeze of the dawn, whose first ghostly gleams were already in the sky. Suddenly, somewhere near at hand, a pistol cracked. The noise affected them oddly. The King fell into an ague and his teeth chattered audibly. Panic seized him.

"By the Blood, it shall not be! It shall not be! " he cried suddenly.

He looked at his mother and his brother and they looked at him; ghastly were the faces of all three, their eyes wide and staring with horror.

Charles swore in his terror that he would cancel all commands. And since Catherine and Anjou made no attempt to hinder him, he summoned an officer and bade him seek out the Duke of Guise at once and command him to stay his hand.

The messenger eventually found the Duke in the courtyard of the Admiral's house, standing over the Admiral's dead body, which his assassins had flung down from the bedroom window. Guise laughed, and stirred the head of the corpse with his foot, answering that the message came too late. Even as he spoke the great bell of Saint-Germain l'Auxerrois began to ring for matins.

The royal party huddled at that window of the Louvre heard it at the same moment, and heard, as if in immediate answer, shots of arquebus and pistol, cries and screams near at hand, and then, gradually swelling from a murmur, the baying of the fierce multitude. Other bells gave tongue, until from every steeple in Paris the alarm rang out. The red glow from thousands of torches flushed the heavens with a rosy tint as of dawn, the air grew heavy with the smell of pitch and resin.

The King, clutching the sill of the window, poured out a stream of blasphemy from between his chattering teeth. Then the hubbub rose suddenly near at hand. The neighbourhood of the Louvre was populous with Huguenots, and into it now poured the excited Catholic citizens and soldiers. Soon the quay beneath the palace windows presented the fiercest spectacle of any quarter, of Paris.

Half-clad men, women, and children fled screaming before the assassins, until they were checked by the chains that everywhere had been placed across the streets. Some sought the river, hoping to find a way of escape. But with Satanic foresight, the boats usually moored there had been conveyed to the other side. Thus some hundreds of Huguenots were brought to bay, and done to death under the very eyes of the King who had unleashed this horror. Doors were crashed open, flames rose to heaven, men and women were shot down under the palace wall, bodies were flung from windows, and on every side - in the words of D'Aubigne - the blood now flowed, seeking the river.

The King watched a while, screams and curses pouring from his lips to be lost in the horrible uproar. He turned, perhaps to upbraid his mother and his brother, but found that they were no longer at his side. Behind him in the room a page was crouching, watching him with a white, horrified face.

Suddenly the King laughed - it was the fierce, hysterical laugh of a madman. His eyes fell on the arquebuses flanking the picture of the Mother of Mercy. He took one of them down, then caught the boy by the collar of his doublet and dragged him forward to the window.

"Hither, and load for me! " he bade him, between peals of his terrible laughter. Then he levelled the weapon across the sill of the window. "Parpaillots! Parpaillots! " he screamed. "Kill! Kill! " and he discharged the arquebus into a fleeing group of Huguenots.

Five days later, the King - who by now had thrown the blame of the whole affair, with its slaughter of some two thousand Huguenots, upon the Guises and their hatred of Coligny - rode out to Montfaucon to behold the decapitated body of the Admiral, which hung from the gallows in chains. A courtier of a poor but obtrusive wit leaned towards him.

"The Admiral becomes noisome, I think, " he said.

The King's green eyes considered him, his lips curling grimly.

"The body of a dead enemy always smells sweet, " he said.

VI. THE NIGHT OF WITCHCRAFT

Louis XIV and Madame de Montespan

If you scrape the rubbish-heap of servile, coeval flattery that usually smothers the personality of a monarch, you will discover a few kings who have been truly great; many who have achieved greatness because they were wisely content to serve as masks for the great intellects of their time; and, for the rest, some bad kings, some foolish kings, and some ridiculous kings. But in all that royal gallery of history you will hardly find a more truly absurd figure than that of the resplendent Roi Soleil, the Grand Monarque, the Fourteenth Louis of France.

I am not aware that he has ever been laughed at; certainly never to the extent which he deserves. The flatterers of his day, inevitable products of his reign, did their work so thoroughly that even in secret they do not appear to have dared to utter - possibly they did not even dare to think - the truth about him. Their work survives, and when you have assessed the monstrous flattery at its true worth, swept it aside and come down to the real facts of his life, you make the discovery that the proudest title their sycophancy could bestow and his own fatuity accept - Le Roi Soleil, the Sun-King - makes him what indeed he is: a king of opera bouffe. There is about him at times something almost reminiscent of the Court buffoons of a century before, who puffed themselves out with mock pride, and aped a sort of sovereignty to excite laughter; with this difference, however, that in his own case it was not intended to be amusing.

A heartless voluptuary of mediocre intelligence, he contrived to wrap himself in what Saint-Simon has called a "terrible majesty. " Hewas obsessed by the idea of the dignity, almost the divinity - of kingship. I cannot believe that he conceived himself human. He appears to have held that being king was very like being God, and he duped the world by ceremonials of etiquette that were very nearly sacramental. We find him burdening the·most simple and personal acts of everyday life with a succession of rites of an amazing complexity. Thus, when he rose in the morning, princes of the blood and the first gentlemen of France were in attendance: one to present to him his stockings, another to proffer on bended knee the royal garters, a third to perform the ceremony of handing him his wig, and so on until the toilette of his plump, not unhandsome person was complete. You miss the incense, you feel that some noble thurifer should have fumigated him at each stage. Perhaps he never thought of it.

The evil fruits of his reign - evil, that is to say, from the point of view of his order, which was swept away as so much anachronistic rubbish - did not come until a hundred years later. In his own day France was great, and this not because but in spite of him. After all, he was not the absolute ruler he conceived himself. There were such capable men as Colbert and Louvois at the King's side'; there was the great genius of France which manifests itself when and as it will, whatever the regime - and there was Madame de Montespan to whose influence not a little of Louis's glory may be ascribed, since the most splendid years of his reign were those between 1668 and 1678 when she was maitresse en titre and more than Queen of France. The women played a great part at the Court of Louis XIV, and those upon whom he turned his dark eyes were in the main as wax under the solar rays of the Sun-King. But Madame de Montespan had discovered the secret of reversing matters, so that in her hands it was the King who became as wax for her modelling. It is with this secret - a page of the secret history of France that we are here concerned.

Francoises Athenais de Tonnay-Charente had come to Court in 1660 as a maid of honour to the Queen. Of a wit and grace to match her superb beauty, she was also of a perfervid piety, a daily communicant, a model of virtue to all maids of honour. This until the Devil tempted her. When that happened, she did not merely eat an apple; she devoured an entire orchard. Pride and ambition brought about her downfall. She shared the universal jealousy of which Louise de la Valliere was a victim, and coveted the honours and the splendour by which that unfortunate favourite was surrounded.

Not even her marriage with the Marquis de Montespan some three years after her coming to Court sufficed to overcome the longings born of her covetousness and ambition. And then, when the Sun-King looked with favour upon her opulent charms, when at last she saw the object of her ambition within reach, that husband of hers went very near to wrecking everything by his unreasonable behaviour. This preposterous marquis had the effrontery to dispute his wife with Jupiter, was so purblind as not to appreciate the honour the Sun-King proposed to do him.

In putting it thus, I but make myself the mouthpiece of the Court.

When Montespan began to make trouble by railing furiously against the friendship of the King for his wife, his behaviour so amazed the King's cousin, Mademoiselle de Montpensier, that she called him "an extravagant and extraordinary man. " To his face she told him that he must be mad to behave in this fashion; and so incredibly distorted were his views, that he did not at all agree with her. He provoked scenes with the King, in which he quoted Scripture, made opposite allusions to King David which were in the very worst taste, and even ventured to suggest that the Sun-King might have to reckon with the judgment of God. If he escaped a lettre de cachet and a dungeon in the Bastille, it can only have been because the King feared the further spread of a scandal injurious to the sacrosanctity of his royal dignity.

The Marchioness fumed in private and sneered in public. When Mademoiselle de Montpensier suggested that for his safety's sake she should control her husband's antics, she expressed her bitterness.

"He and my parrot, " she said, "amuse the Court to my shame. "

In the end, finding that neither by upbraiding the King nor by beating his wife could he prevail, Monsieur de Montespan resigned himself after his own fashion. He went into widower's mourning, dressed his servants in black, and came ostentatiously to Court in a mourning coach to take ceremonious leave of his friends. It was an affair that profoundly irritated the Sun-King, and very nearly made him ridiculous.

Thereafter Montespan abandoned his wife to the King. He withdrew first to his country seat, and, later, from France, having received more than a hint that Louis was intending to settle his score with him. By that time Madame de Montespan was firmly established as maitresse en titre, and in January of 1669 she gave birth to the Duke of Maine, the first of the seven children she was to bear the King. Parliament was to legitimize them all, declaring them royal children of France, and the country was to provide titles, dignities, and royal rent-rolls for them and their heirs forever. Do you wonder that there was a revolution a century later, and that the people, grown weary of the parasitic anachronism of royalty, should have risen to throw off the intolerable burden it imposed upon them?

The splendour of Madame de Montespan in those days was something the like of which had never been seen at the Court of France. On her estate of Clagny, near Versailles, stood now a magnificent chateau. Louis had begun by building a country villa, which satisfied her not at all.

"That, " she told him, "might do very well for an opera-girl"; whereupon the infatuated monarch had no alternative but to command its demolition, and call in the famous architect, Mansard, to erect in its place an ultraroyal residence.

At Versailles itself, whilst the long-suffering Queen had to be content with ten rooms on the second floor, Madame de Montespan was installed in twice that number on the first; and whilst a simple page sufficed to carry the Queen's train at Court, nothing less than the wife of a marshal of France must perform the same office for the favourite. She kept royal state as few queens have ever kept it. She was assigned a troop of royal bodyguards for escort, and when she travelled there was a never-ending train to follow her six-horse coach, and officers of State came to receive her with royal honours wherever she passed.

In her immeasurable pride she became a tyrant, even over the King himself.

"Thunderous and triumphant, " Madame de Sevigne describes her in those days when the Sun-King was her utter and almost timid slave.

But constancy is not a Jovian virtue. Jupiter grew restless, and then, shaking off all restraint, plunged into inconstancy of the most scandalous and flagrant kind. It is doubtful if the history of royal amours, with all its fecundity, can furnish a parallel. Within a few months, Madame de Soubise, Mademoiselle de Rochefort-Theobon, Madame de Louvigny, Madame de Ludres, and some lesser ones passed in rapid succession through the furnace of the Sun-King's affection - which is to say, through the royal bed - and at last the Court was amazed to see the Widow Scarron, who had been appointed governess to Madame de Montespan's royal children, empanoplied in a dignity and ceremony that left no doubt on the score of her true position at Court.

And so, after seven years of absolute sway in which homage had been paid her almost in awe by noble and simple alike, Madame de Montespan, neglected now by Louis, moved amid reflections of that neglect, with arrogantly smiling lips and desperate rage in her heart. She sneered openly at the royal lack of taste, allowed her barbed wit to make offensive sport with the ladies who supplanted her; yet, ravaged by jealousy, she feared for herself the fate which through her had overtaken La Valliere.

That fear was with her now as she sat in the window embrasure, hell in her heart and a reflection of it in her eyes, as, fallen almost to the rank of a spectator in that comedy wherein she was accustomed to the leading part, she watched the shifting, chattering, glittering crowd. And as she watched, her line of vision was crossed to her undoing by the slender, wellknit figure of de Vanens, who, dressed from head to foot in black, detached sharply from that dazzling throng. His face was pale and saturnine, his eyes dark, very level, and singularly piercing. Thus his appearance served to underline the peculiar fascination which he exerted, the rather sinister appeal which he made to the imagination.

This young Provencal nobleman was known to dabble in magic, and there were one or two dark passages in his past life of which more than a whisper had gone abroad. Of being a student of alchemy, a "philosopher" - that is to say, a seeker after the philosopher's stone, which was to effect the transmutation of metals - he made no secret. But if you taxed him with demoniacal practices he would deny it, yet in a way that carried no conviction.

To this dangerous fellow Madame de Montespan now made appeal in her desperate need.

Their eyes met as he was sauntering past, and with a lazy smile and a languid wave of her fan she beckoned him to her side.

"They tell me, Vanens, " said she, "that your philosophy succeeds so well that you are transmuting copper into silver. "

His piercing eyes surveyed her, narrowing; a smile flickered over his thin lips.

"They tell you the truth, " he said. "I have cast a bar which has been purchased as good silver by the Mint. "

143

Her interest quickened. "By the Mint! " she echoed, amazed. "But, then, my friend - " She was breathless with excitement. "It is a miracle. "

"No less, " he admitted. "But there is the greater miracle to come - the transmutation of base metal into gold. "

"And you will perform it? "

"Let me but conquer the secret of solidifying mercury, and the rest is naught. I shall conquer it, and soon. "

He spoke with easy confidence, a man stating something that he knew beyond the possibility of doubt. The Marquise became thoughtful. She sighed.

"You are the master of deep secrets, Vanens. Have you none that will soften flinty hearts, make them responsive? "

He considered this woman whom Saint-Simon has called "beautiful as the day, " and his smile broadened.

"Look in your mirror for the alchemy needed there, " he bade her.

Anger rippled across the perfect face. She lowered

"I have looked - in vain. Can you not help me, Vanens, you who know so much? "

"A love-philtre? " said he, and hummed. "Are you in earnest? "

"Do you mock me with that question? Is not my need proclaimed for all to see? "

Vanens became grave.

"It is not an alchemy in which myself I dabble, " he said slowly. "But I am acquainted with those who do. "

She clutched his wrist in her eagerness.

"I will pay well, " she said.

"You will need to. Such things are costly. " He glanced round to see that none was listening, then bending nearer: "There is a sorceress named La Voisin in the Rue de la Tannerie, well known as a fortuneteller to many ladies of the Court, who at a word from me will do your need. "

La Montespan turned white. The piety in which she had been reared - the habits of which clung to her despite the irregularity of her life- made her recoil before the thing that she desired. Sorcery was of the Devil. She told him so. But Vanens laughed.

"So that it be effective . .. " said he with a shrug.

And then across the room floated a woman's trilling laugh. She looked in the direction of the sound and beheld the gorgeous figure of the King bending - yet haughty and condescending even in adoration - over handsome Madame de Ludres. Pride and ambition rose up in sudden fury to trample on religious feeling. Let Vanens take her to this witch of his, for be the aid what it might, she must have it.

And so, one dark night late in the year, Louis de Vanens handed a masked and muffled lady from a coach at the corner of the Rue de la Tannerie, and conducted her to the house of La Voisin.

The door was opened for them by a young woman of some twenty years of age - Marguerite Monvoisin, the daughter of the witch - who led them upstairs to a room that was handsomely furnished and hung with fantastic tapestry of red designs upon a black ground - designs that took monstrous shapes in the flickering light of a cluster of candles. Black curtains parted, and from between them stepped a short, plump woman, of a certain comeliness, with two round black beads of eyes. She was fantastically robed in a cloak of crimson velvet, lined with costly furs and closely studded with double- headed eagles in fine gold, which must have been worth a prince's ransom; and she wore red shoes on each of which there was the same eagle design in gold.

"Ah, Vanens! " she said familiarly.

He bowed.

"I bring you, " he announced, "a lady who has need of your skill. "

And he waved a hand towards the tall cloaked figure at his side.

La Voisin looked at the masked face.

"Velvet faces tell me little, Madame la Marquise, " she said calmly. "Nor, believe me, will the King look at a countenance that you conceal from me. "

Therewas an exclamation of surprise and anger from Madame de Montespan. She plucked off her mask.

"You knew me? "

"Can you wonder? " asked La Voisin, "since I have told you what you carry concealed in your heart? "

Madame de Montespan was as credulous as only the very devout can be.

"Since that is so, since you know already what I seek, tell me can you procure it me? " she asked in a fever of excitement. "I will pay well. "

La Voisin smiled darkly.

"Obdurate, indeed, is the case that will not yield to such medicine as mine, " she said. "Let me consider first what must be done. In a few days I shall bring you word. But have you courage for a great ordeal? "

"For any ordeal that will give me what I want. "

"In a few days, then, you shall hear from me, " said the witch, and so dismissed the great lady.

Leaving a heavy purse behind her, as Vanens had instructed her, the Marchioness departed with her escort. And there, with that initiation, as far as we can ascertain, ended Louis de Vanens's connection with the affair.

At Clagny Madame de Montespan waited for three days in a fever of impatience for the coming of the witch. But when at last La Voisin presented herself, the proposal that she had to make was one before which the Marchioness recoiled in horror and some indignation.

146

The magic that La Voisin suggested involved a coadjutor, the Abbe Guibourg, and the black mass to be celebrated by him. Madame de Montespan had heard something of these dread sacrificial rites to Satan; sufficient to fill her with loathing and disgust of the whitefaced, beady-eyed woman who dared to insult her by the proposal. She fumed and raged a while, and even went near to striking La Voisin, who looked on with inscrutable face and stony, almost contemptuous, indifference. Before that impenetrable, almost uncanny, calm, Madame de Montespan's fury at last abated. Then the urgency of her need becoming paramount, she desired more clearly to be told what would be expected of her. What the witch told her was more appalling than anything she could have imagined. But La Voisin argued:

"Can anything be accomplished without cost? Can anything be gained in this life without payment of some kind? "

"But the price of this is monstrous! " Madame de Montespan protested.

"Measure it by the worldly advantages to be gained. They are not small, madame. To enjoy boundless wealth, boundless power, and boundless honour, to be more than queen - is not all this worth some sacrifice? "

To Madame de Montespan it must have been worth any sacrifice in this world or the next, since in the end she conquered her disgust, and agreed to lend herself to this horror.

Three masses, she was told, would be necessary to ensure success, and it was determined that they should be celebrated in the chapel of the Chateau de Villebousin, where Guibourg had been almoner, to which he had access, and which was at the time untenanted.

The chateau was a gloomy mediaeval fortress, blackened by age, and standing, surrounded by a moat, in a lonely spot some two miles to the south of Paris. Thither on a dark, gusty night of March came Madame de Montespan, accompanied by her confidential waiting-woman, Mademoiselle Desceillets. They left the coach to await them on the Orleans road, and thence, escorted by a single male attendant, they made their way by a rutted, sodden path towards the grim castle looming faintly through the enveloping gloom.

The wind howled dismally about the crenellated turrets; and a row of poplars, standing like black, phantasmal guardians of the evil place, bent groaning before its fury. From the running waters of the moat, swollen by recent rains, came a gurgling sound that was indescribably wicked.

Desocillets was frightened by the dark, the desolate loneliness and eeriness of the place; but she dared utter no complaint as she stumbled forward over the uneven ground, through the gloom and the buffeting wind, compelled by the suasion of her mistress's imperious will. Thus, by a drawbridge spanning dark, oily waters, they came into a vast courtyard and an atmosphere as of mildew. A studded door stood ajar, and through the gap, from a guiding beacon of infamy, fell a rhomb of yellow light, suddenly obscured by a squat female figure when the steps of the Marchioness and her companions fell upon the stones of the yard.

It was La Voisin who stood on the threshold to receive her client. In the stone-flagged hall behind her the light of a lantern revealed her daughter, Marguerite Monvoisin, and a short, crafty-faced, misshapen fellow in black homespun and a red wig - a magician named Lesage, one of La Voisin's coadjutors, a rogue of some talent who exploited the witches of Paris to his own profit.

Leaving Leroy - the Marchioness's male attendant below in this fellow's company, La Voisin took up a candle and lighted Madame de Montespan up the broad stone staircase, draughty and cold, to the ante-room of the chapel on the floor above. Mademoiselle Desceillets followed closely and fearfully, and Marguerite Monvoisin came last.

They entered the ante-room, a spacious chamber, bare of furniture save for an oaken table in the middle, some faded and mildewed tapestries, and a cane-backed settle of twisted walnut over against the wall. An alabaster lamp on the table made an island of light in that place of gloom, and within the circle of its feeble rays stood a gross old man of some seventy years of age in sacerdotal garments of unusual design: the white alb worn over a greasy cassock was studded with black fir-cones; the stole and maniple were of black satin, with fir-cones wrought in yellow thread.

His inflamed countenance was of a revolting hideousness: his cheeks were covered by a network of blue veins, his eyes squinted horribly, his lips vanished inwards over toothless gums, and a fringe of white hair hung in matted wisps from his high, bald crown. This was the infamous Abbe Guibourg, sacristan of Saint Denis, an ordained priest who had consecrated himself to the service of the Devil.

He received the great lady with a low bow which, despite herself, she acknowledged by a shudder. She was very pale, and her eyes were dilating and preternaturally bright. Fear began to possess her, yet she suffered herself to be ushered into the chapel, which was dimly illumined by a couple of candles standing beside a basin on a table. The altar light had been extinguished. Her maid would have hung back, but that she feared to be parted from her mistress. She passed in with her in the wake of Guibourg, and followed by La Voisin, who closed the door, leaving her daughter in the ante-room.

Although she had never been a participant in any of the sorceries practised by her mother, yet Marguerite was fully aware of their extent, and more than guessed what horrors were taking place beyond the closed doors of the chapel. The very thought of them filled her with loathing and disgust as she sat waiting, huddled in a corner of the settle. And yet when presently through the closed doors came the drone of the voice of that unclean celebrant, to blend with the whine of the wind in the chimney, Marguerite, urged by a morbid curiosity she could not conquer, crept shuddering to the door, which directly faced the altar, and going down on her knees applied her eye to the keyhole.

What she saw may very well have appalled her considering the exalted station of Madame de Montespan. She beheld the white, sculptural form of the royal favourite lying at full length supine upon the altar, her arms outstretched, holding a lighted candle in each hand. Immediately before her stood the Abbe Guibourg, his body screening the chalice and its position from the eye of the watching girl.

She heard the whine of his voice pattering the Latin of the mass, which he was reciting backwards from the last gospel; and occasionally she heard responses muttered by her mother, who with Mademoiselle Desceillets was beyond Marguerite's narrow range of vision.

Apart from the interest lent to the proceedings by the presence of the royal favourite the affair must have seemed now very stupid and pointless to Marguerite, although she would certainly not have found it so had she known enough Latin to understand the horrible perversion of the Credo. But when the Offertory was reached, matters suddenly quickened. In stealing away from the door, she was no more than in time to avoid being caught spying by her mother, who now issued from the chapel.

La Voisin crossed the ante-room briskly and went out.

Within a very few minutes she was back again, her approach now heralded by the feeble, quavering squeals of a very young child.

Marguerite Monvoisin was sufficiently acquainted with the ghastly rites to guess what was impending. She was young, and herself a mother. She had her share of the maternal instinct alive in every female animal - with the occasional exception of the human pervert - and the hoarse, plaintive cries of that young child chilled her to the soul with horror. She felt the skin roughening and tightening upon her body, and a sense of physical sickness overcame her. That and the fear of her mother kept her stiff and frozen in an angle of the settle until La Voisin had passed through and reentered the chapel bearing that piteous bundle in her arms.

Then, when the door had closed again, the girl, horrified and fascinated, sped back to watch. She saw that unclean priest turn and receive the child from La Voisin. As it changed hands its cries were stilled.

Guibourg faced the altar once more, that little wisp of humanity that was but a few days old held now aloft, naked, in his criminal hands. His muttering, slobbering voice pronouncing the words of that demoniac consecration reached the ears of the petrified girl at the keyhole.

Ashtaroth, Asmodeus, Princes of Affection, I conjure you to acknowledge the sacrifice I offer to you of this child for the things I ask of you, which are that the King's love for me shall be continued, and that honoured by princes and princesses nothing shall be denied me of all that I may ask. "

A sudden gust of wind smote and rattled the windows of the chapel and the ante-room, as if the legions of hell had flung themselves against the walls of the chateau. There was a rush and clatter in the chimney of the ante-room's vast, empty fireplace, and through the din Marguerite, as her failing limbs sank under her and she slithered down in a heap against the chapel door, seemed to hear a burst of exultantly cruel satanic laughter. With chattering teeth and burning eyes she sat huddled, listening in terror. The child began to cry again, more violently, more piteously; then, quite suddenly, there was a little choking cough, a gurgle, the chink of metal against earthenware, and silence.

When some moments later the squat figure of La Voisin emerged from the chapel, Marguerite was back in the shadows, hunched on the settle to which she had crawled. She saw that her mother now carried a basin under her arm, and she did not need the evidence of her eyes to inform her of the dreadful contents that the witch was bearing away in it.

Meanwhile in the chapel the ineffably blasphemous rites proceeded. To the warm human blood which had been caught in the consecrated chalice, Guibourg had added, among other foulnesses, powdered cantharides, the dust of desiccated moles, and the blood of bats. By the addition of flour he had wrought the ingredients into an ineffable paste, and over this, through the door, which La Voisin had left ajar, Marguerite heard his voice pronouncing the dread words of Transubstantiation.

Marguerite's horror mounted until it threatened to suffocate her. It was as if some hellish miasma, released by Guibourg's monstrous incantations, crept through to permeate and poison the air she breathed.

It would be a half-hour later when Madame de Montespan at last came out. She was of a ghastly pallor, her limbs shook and trembled under her as she stepped forth, and there was a wild horror in her staring eyes. Yet she contrived to carry herself almost defiantly erect, and she spoke sharply to the half-swooning Desceillets, who staggered after her.

She took her departure from that unholy place bearing with her the host compounded of devilish ingredients which when dried and reduced to powder was to be administered to the King to ensure the renewal of his failing affection for her.

The Marchioness contrived that a creature of her own, an officer of the buttery in her pay, should introduce it into the royal soup. The immediate and not unnatural result was that the King was taken violently ill, and Madame de Montespan's anxiety and suspense were increased thereby. On his recovery, however, it would seem that the demoniac sacrament - thrice repeated by then - had not been in vain.

The sequel, indeed, appeared to justify Madame de Montespan's faith in sorcery, and to compensate her for all the horror to which in her despair she had submitted. Madame de Ludres found herself coldly regarded by the convalescent King. Very soon she was discarded, the Widow Scarron neglected, and the fickle monarch was once more at the feet of the lovely marchioness, her utter and devoted slave.

Thus was Madame de Montespan "thunderously triumphant" once more, and established as firmly as 'ever in the Sun-King's favour. Madame de Sevigne, in speaking of this phase of their relations, dilates upon the completeness of the reconciliation, and tells us that the ardour of the first years seemed now to have returned. And for two whole years it continued thus. Never before had Madame de Montespan's sway been more absolute, no shadow came to trouble, the serenity of her rule.

But it proved, after all, to be no more than the last flare of an expiring fire that was definitely quenched at last, in 1679, by Mademoiselle de Fontanges. A maid of honour to madame, she was a child of not more than eighteen years, fair and flaxen, with pink cheeks and large, childish eyes; and it was for this doll that the regal Montespan now found herself discarded.

Honours rained upon the new favourite. Louis made her a duchess with an income of twenty thousand livres, and deeply though this may have disgusted his subjects, it disgusted Madame de Montespan still more. Blinded by rage she openly abused the new duchess, and provoked a fairly public scene with Louis, in which she gave him her true opinion of him with a disturbing frankness.

"You dishonour yourself, " she informed him among other things. "And you betray your taste when you make love to a pink-and-white doll, a little fool that has no more wit nor manners than if she were painted on canvas! " Then, with an increase of scorn, she delivered herself of an unpardonable apostrophe: "You, a king, to accept the inheritance of that chit's rustic lovers! "

He flushed and scowled upon her.

"That is an infamous falsehood! " he exclaimed. "Madame, you are unbearable! " He was very angry, and it infuriated him the more that she should stand so coldly mocking before an anger that could bow the proudest heads in France. "You have the pride of Satan, your greed is insatiable, your domineering spirit utterly insufferable, and you have the most false and poisonous tongue in the world! "

Her brutal answer bludgeoned that high divinity to earth.

"With all my imperfections, " she sneered, "at least I do not smell as badly as you do! "

It was an answer that extinguished her last chance. It was fatal to the dignity, to the "terrible majesty" of Louis. It stripped him of all divinity, and revealed him authoritatively as intensely and even unpleasantly human. It was beyond hope of pardon.

His face turned the colour of wax. A glacial silence hung over the agonized witnesses of that royal humiliation. Then, without a word, in a vain attempt to rescue the dignity she had so cruelly mauled, he turned, his red heels clicked rapidly and unsteadily across the polished floor, and he was gone.

When Madame de Montespan realized exactly what she had done, nothing but rage remained to her - rage and its offspring, vindictiveness. The Duchess of Fontanges must not enjoy her victory, nor must Louis escape punishment for his faithlessness. La Voisin should afford her the means to accomplish this. And so she goes once more to the Rue de la Tannerie.

Now, the matter of Madame de Montespan's present needs was one in which the witches were particularly expert. Were you troubled with a rival, did your husband persist in surviving your affection for him, did those from whom you had expectations cling obstinately and inconsiderately to life, the witches by incantations and the use of powders - in which arsenic was the dominant charm - could usually put the matter right for you. Indeed, so wide and general was the practice of poisoning become, that the authorities, lately aroused to the fact by the sensational revelations of the Marchioness de Brinvilliers, had set up in this year 1670 the tribunal known as the Chambre Ardente to inquire into the matter, and to conduct prosecutions.

La Voisin promised help to the Marchioness. She called in another witch of horrible repute, named La Filastre, her coadjutor Lesage, and two expert poisoners, Romani and Bertrand, who devised an ingenious plot for the murder of the Duchess of Fontanges. They were to visit her, Romani as a cloth merchant, and Bertrand as his servant, to offer her their wares, including some Grenoble gloves, which were the most beautiful gloves in the world and unfailingly irresistible to ladies. These gloves they prepared in accordance with certain magical recipes in such a way that the Duchess, after wearing them, must die a lingering death in which there could be no suspicion of poisoning.

The King was to be dealt with by means of a petition steeped in similar powders, and should receive his death by taking it into his hands. La Voisin herself was to go to Saint-Germain to present this petition on Monday, March 13th, one of those days on which, according to ancient custom, all comers were admitted to the royal presence.

Thus they disposed. But Fate was already silently stalking La Voisin.

It is to the fact that an obscure and vulgar woman had drunk one glass of wine too many three months earlier that the King owed his escape.

If you are interested in the almost grotesque disparity that can lie between cause and effect, here is a subject for you. Three months earlier a tailor named Vigoureux, whose wife secretly practised magic, had entertained a few friends to dinner, amongst whom was an intimate of his wife's, named Marie Bosse. This Marie Bosse it was who drank that excessive glass of wine which, drowning prudence, led her to boast of the famous trade she drove as a fortune-teller to the nobility, and even to hint of something further.

"Another three poisonings, " she chuckled, "and I shall retire with my fortune made! "

An attorney who was present pricked up his ears, bethought him of the tales that were afloat, and gave information to the police. The police set a trap for Marie Bosse, and she betrayed herself. Later, under torture, she betrayed La Vigoureux. La Vigoureux betrayed others, and these others again.

The arrest of Marie Bosse was like knocking down the first of a row of ninepins, but none could have suspected that the last of these stood in the royal apartments.

On the day before she was to repair to Saint-Germain, La Voisin, betrayed in her turn, received a surprise visit from the police - who, of course, had no knowledge of the regicide their action was thwarting - and she was carried off to the Chatelet. Put to the question, she revealed a great deal; but her terror of the horrible punishment reserved for regicides prevented her to the day of her death at the stake - in February of 1680 from saying a word of her association with Madame de Montespan.

But there were others whom she betrayed under torture, and whose arrest followed quickly upon her own, who had not her strength of character. Among these were La Filastre and the magician Lesage. When it was found that these two corroborated each other in the incredible things which they related, the Chambre Ardente took fright. La Reynie, who presided over it, laid the matter before the King, and the King, horror-stricken by the discovery of the revolting practices in which the mother of his children had been engaged, suspended the sittings of the Chambre Ardente, and commanded that no further proceedings should be taken against Lesage and La Filastre, and none initiated against Romani, Bertrand, the Abbe Guibourg, and the scores of other poisoners and magicians who had been arrested, and who were acquainted with Madame de Montespan's unholy traffic.

But it was not out of any desire to spare Madame de Montespan that the King proceeded in this manner; he was concerned only to spare himself and his royal dignity. He feared above all things the scandal and ridicule which must touch him as a result of publicity, and because he feared it so much, he could impose no punishment upon Madame de Montespan.

This he made known to her at the interview between them procured by his minister Louvois, at about the time that the sittings of the Chambre Ardente were suspended.

To this interview that proud, domineering woman came in dread, and in tears and humility for once. The King's bearing was cold and hard. Cold and hard were the words in which he declared the extent of his knowledge of her infamy, words which revealed the loathing and disgust this knowledge brought him. If at first she was terror-stricken, crushed under the indictment, yet she was never of a temper to bear reproaches long. Under his scorn her anger kindled and her humility was sloughed.

"What then? " she cried at last, eyes aflash through lingering tears. "Is the blame all mine? If all this is true, it is no less true that I was driven to it by my love for you and the despair to which your heartlessness and infidelity reduced me. To you, " she continued, gathering force at every word, "I sacrificed everything - my honour, a noble husband who loved me, all that a woman prizes. And what did you give me in exchange? Your cruel fickleness exposed me to the low mockery of the lick-spittles of your Court. Do you wonder that I went mad, and that in my madness I sacrificed what shreds of self-respect you had left me? And now it seems I have lost all but life. Take that, too, if it be your pleasure. Heaven knows it has little value left for me! But remember that in striking me you strike the mother of your children - the legitimate children of France. Remember that! "

He remembered it. Indeed, he was never in danger of forgetting it; for she might have added that he would be striking also at himself and at that royal dignity which was his religion. And so that all scandalous comment might be avoided she was actually allowed to remain at Court, although no longer in her first-floor apartments; and it was not until ten years later that she departed to withdraw to the community of Saint Joseph.

But even in her disgrace this woman, secretly convicted among other abominations of attempting to procure the poisoning of the King and of her rival, enjoyed an annual pension of 1,200.000 livres; whilst none dared proceed against those who shared her guilt - not even the infamous Guibourg, the poisoners Romani and Bertrand, and La Filastre - nor yet against some scores of associates of these, who were known to live by sorcery and poisonings, and who might be privy to the part played by Madame de Montespan in that horrible night of magic at the Chateau de Villebousin.

The hot blast of revolution was needed to sweep France clean.

VII. THE NIGHT OF GEMS

The "Affairs" of the Queen's Necklace

Under the stars of a tepid, scented night of August of 1784, Prince Louis de Rohan, Cardinal of Strasbourg, Grand Almoner of France, made his way with quickened pulses through the Park of Versailles to a momentous assignation in the Grove of Venus.

This illustrious member of an illustrious House, that derived from both the royal lines of Valois and Bourbon, was a man in the prime of life, of a fine height, still retaining something of the willowy slenderness that had been his in youth, and of a gentle, almost womanly beauty of countenance.

In a grey cloak and a round, grey hat with gold cords, followed closely by two shadowy attendant figures, he stepped briskly amain, eager to open those gates across the path of his ambition, locked against him hitherto by the very hands from which he now went to receive the key.

He deserves your sympathy, this elegant Cardinal-Prince, who had been the victim of the malice and schemings of the relentless Austrian Empress since the days when he represented the King of France at the Court of Vienna.

The state he had kept there had been more than royal and royal in the dazzling French manner, which was perturbing to a woman of Marie Therese's solid German notions. His hunting-parties, his supper-parties, the fetes he gave upon every occasion, the worldly inventiveness, the sumptuousness and reckless extravagance that made each of these affairs seem like a supplement to "The Arabian Nights' Entertainments, " the sybaritic luxury of his surroundings, the incredible prodigality of his expenditure, all served profoundly to scandalize and embitter the Empress.

That a priest in gay, secular clothes should hunt the stag on horseback filled her with horror at his levity; that he should flirt discreetly with the noble ladies of Vienna made her despair of his morals; whilst his personal elegance and irresistible charm were proofs to her of a profligacy that perverted the Court over which she ruled.

She laboured for the extinction of his pernicious brilliance, and intrigued for his recall. She made no attempt to conceal her hostility, nor did she love him any the better because he met her frigid haughtiness with an ironical urbanity that seemed ever to put her in the wrong. And then one day he permitted his wit to be bitingly imprudent.

"Marie Therese, " he wrote to D'Aiguillon, "holds in one hand a handkerchief to receive her tears for the misfortunes of oppressed Poland, and in the other a sword to continue its partition. "

To say that in this witticism lay one of the causes of the French Revolution may seem at first glance an outrageous overstatement. Yet it is certain that, but for that imprudent phrase, the need would never have arisen that sent Rohan across the Park of Versailles on that August night to an assignation that in the sequel was to place a terrible weapon in the hands of the Revolutionary party.

D'Aiguillon had published the gibe. It had reached the ears of Marie Antoinette, and from her it had travelled back to her mother in Vienna. It aroused in the Empress a resentment and a bitterness that did not rest until the splendid Cardinal-Prince was recalled from his embassy. It did not rest even then. By the ridicule to which the gibe exposed her - and if you know Marie Therese at all, you can imagine what that meant - it provoked a hostility that was indefatigably to labour against him.

The Cardinal was ambitious, he had confidence in his talents and in the driving force of his mighty family, and he looked to become another Richelieu or Mazarin, the first Minister of the Crown, the empurpled ruler of France, the guiding power behind the throne. All this he looked confidently to achieve; all this he might have achieved but for the obstacle that Marie Therese's resentment flung across his path. The Empress saw to it that, through the person of her daughter, her hatred should pursue him even into France.

Obedient ever to the iron will of her mother, sharing her mother's resentment, Marie Antoinette exerted all her influence to thwart this Cardinal whom her mother had taught her to regard as a dangerous, unprincipled man.

On his return from Vienna bearing letters from Marie Therese to Louis XVI and Marie Antoinette, the Cardinal found himself coldly

159

received by the dull King, and discouraged from remaining at Court, whilst the Queen refused to grant him so much as the audience necessary for the delivery of these letters, desiring him to forward them instead.

The chagrined Cardinal had no illusions. He beheld here the hand of Marie Therese controlling Marie Antoinette, and, through Marie Antoinette, the King himself. Worse followed. He who had dreamt himself another Richelieu could only with difficulty obtain the promised position of Grand Almoner of France, and this solely as a result of the powerful and insistent influence exerted by his family.

He perceived that if he was to succeed at all he must begin by softening the rigorous attitude which the Queen maintained towards him. To that end he addressed himself. But three successive letters he wrote to the Queen remained unanswered. Through other channels persistently he begged for an audience that he might come in person to express his regrets for the offending indiscretion. But the Queen remained unmoved, ruled ever by the Austrian Empress, who through her daughter sought to guide the affairs of France.

Rohan was reduced to despair, and then in an evil hour his path was crossed by Jeanne de la Motte de Valois, who enjoyed the reputation of secretly possessing the friendship of the Queen, exerting a sort of back-stair influence, and who lived on that reputation.

As a drowning man clutches at a straw, so the Cardinal-Prince Louis de Rohan, Grand Almoner of France, Landgrave of Alsace, Commander of the Order of the Holy Ghost, clutched at this faiseuse d'affaires to help him in his desperate need.

Jeanne de la Motte de Valois - perhaps the most astounding adventuress that ever lived by her wits and her beauty - had begun life by begging her bread in the streets. She laid claim to left-handed descent from the royal line of Valois, and, her claim supported by the Marchioness Boulainvilliers, who had befriended her, she had obtained from the Crown a small pension, and had married the unscrupulous Marc Antoine de la Motte, a young soldier in the Burgundy regiment of the Gendarmerie.

Later, in the autumn of 1786, her protectress presented her to Cardinal de Rohan. His Eminence, interested in the lady's extraordinary history, in her remarkable beauty, vivacity, and wit, received the De la Mottes at his sumptuous chateau at Saverne, near Strasbourg, heard her story in greater detail, promised his protection, and as an earnest of his kindly intentions obtained for her husband a captain's commission in the Dragoons.

Thereafter you see the De la Mottes in Paris and at Versailles, hustled from lodging to lodging for failure to pay what they owe; and finally installed in a house in the Rue Neuve Saint-Gilles. There they kept a sort of state, spending lavishly, now the money borrowed from the Cardinal, or upon the Cardinal's security; now the proceeds of pawned goods that had been bought on credit, and of other swindles practised upon those who were impressed by the lady's name and lineage and the patronage of the great Cardinal which she enjoyed.

To live on your wits is no easy matter. It demands infinite address, coolness, daring, and resource qualities which Madame de la Motte possessed in the highest degree, so that, harassed and pressed by creditors, she yet contrived to evade their attacks and to present a calm and, therefore, confidence-inspiring front to the world.

The truth of Madame de la Motte de Valois's reputation for influence at Court was never doubted. There was nothing in the character of Marie Antoinette to occasion such doubts. Indiscreet in many things, Her Majesty was most notoriously so in her attachments, as witness her intimacy with Madame de Polignac and the Princesse de Lambelle. And the public voice had magnified - as it will - those indiscretions until it had torn her character into shreds.

The fame of the Countess Jeanne de Valois - as Madame de la Motte now styled herself - increasing, she was employed as an intermediary by place-seekers and people with suits to prefer, who gratefully purchased her promises to interest herself on their behalf at Court.

And then into her web of intrigue blundered the Cardinal de Rohan, who, as he confessed, "was completely blinded by his immense desire to regain the good graces of the Queen. " She aroused fresh hope in his despairing heart by protesting that, as some return for all the favours she had received from him, she would not rest until she had disposed the Queen more favourably towards him.

Later came assurances that the Queen's hostility was melting under her persuasions, and at last she announced that she was authorized by Her Majesty to invite him to submit the justification which so long and so vainly he had sought permission to present.

Rohan, in a vertigo of satisfaction, indited his justification, forwarded it to the Queen by the hand of the Countess, and some days later received a note in the Queen's hand upon blue-edged paper adorned by the lilies of France.

"I rejoice, " wrote Marie Antoinette, "to find at last that you were not in fault. I cannot yet grant you the audience you desire, but as soon as the circumstances allow of it I shall let you know. Be discreet. "

Upon the advice of the Countess of Valois, His Eminence sent a reply expressive of his deep gratitude and joy.

Thus began a correspondence between Queen and Cardinal which continued regularly for a space of three months, growing gradually more confidential and intimate. As time passed his solicitations of an audience became more pressing, until at last the Queen wrote announcing that, actuated by esteem and affection for him who had so long been kept in banishment, she herself desired the meeting. But it must be secret. An open audience would still be premature; he had numerous enemies at Court, who, thus forewarned, might so exert themselves against him as yet to ruin all.

To receive such a letter from a beautiful woman, and that woman a queen whose glories her inaccessibility had magnified a thousandfold in his imagination, must have all but turned the Cardinal's head. The secrecy of the correspondence, culminating in a clandestine meeting, seemed to establish between them an intimacy impossible under other circumstances.

Into the warp of his ambition was now woven another, tenderly romantic, though infinitely respectful, feeling.

You realize, I hope, the frame of mind in which the Cardinal-Prince took his way through that luminous, fragrant summer night towards the Grove of Venus. He went to lay the cornerstone of the proud edifice of his ambitions. To him it was a night of nights - a night of gems, he pronounced it, looking up into the jewelled vault of heaven. And in that phrase he was singularly prophetic.

By an avenue of boxwood and yoke-elm he entered into an open glade, in the middle of which there was a circle where the intended statue of Venus was never placed. But if the cold marble effigy of a goddess were absent, the warm, living figure of a queen stood, all in shimmering white amid the gloom, awaiting him.

Rohan checked a moment, his breath arrested, his pulses quickened. Then he sped forward, and, flinging off his wide-brimmed hat, he prostrated himself to kiss the hem of her white cambric gown. Something - a rose that she let fall - brushed lightly past his cheek. Reverently he recovered it, accounting it a tangible symbol of her favour, and he looked up into the proud, lovely face - which, although but dimly discernible, was yet unmistakable to him protesting his gratitude and devotion. He perceived that she was trembling, and caught the quiver in the voice that answered him.

"You may hope that the past will be forgiven. "

And then, before he could drink more deeply of this cup of delight, came rapid steps to interrupt them. A slender man, in whom the Cardinal seemed to recognize the Queen's valet Desclaux, thrust through the curtains of foliage into the grove.

"Quick, madame! " he exclaimed in agitation. "Madame la Comtesse and Mademoiselle d'Artois are approaching! "

The Queen was whirled away, and the Cardinal discreetly effaced himself, his happiness tempered by chagrin at the interruption.

When, on the morrow, the Countess of Valois brought him a blue-bordered note with Her Majesty's wishes that he should patiently await a propitious season for his public restoration to royal favour, he resigned himself with the most complete and satisfied submission. Had he not the memory of her voice and the rose she had given him? Soon afterwards came a blue-bordered note in which Marie Antoinette advised him to withdraw to his Bishopric of Strasbourg until she should judge that the desired season of: his reinstatement had arrived.

Obediently Rohan withdrew.

It was in the following December that the Countess of Valois's good offices at Court were solicited by a new client, and that she first beheld the famous diamond necklace.

It had been made by the Court jewellers of the Rue Vendome - Bohmer and Bassenge - and intended for the Countess du Barry. On the assembling of its component gems Bohmer had laboured for five years and travelled all over Europe, with the result that he had achieved not so much a necklace as a blaziing scarf of diamonds of a splendour outrivalling any jewel that the world had ever seen.

Unfortunately, Bohmer was too long over the task. Louis XV died inopportunely, and the firm found itself with a necklace worth two million livres on its hands.

Hopes were founded upon Marie Antoinette's reputed extravagance. But the price appalled her, while Louis XVI met the importunities of the jeweller with the reply that the country needed a ship of war more urgently than a necklace.

Thereafter Bohmer offered it in various Courts of Europe, but always without success. Things were becoming awkward. The firm had borrowed heavily to pay for the stones, and anxiety seems to have driven Bohmer to the verge of desperation. Again he offered the necklace to the King, announcing himself ready to make terms, and to accept payment in instalments; but again it was refused.

Bohmer now became that pest to society, the man with a grievance that he must be venting everywhere. On one occasion he so far forgot himself as to intrude upon the Queen as she was walking in the gardens of the Trianon. Flinging himself upon his knees before her, he protested with sobs that he was in despair, and that unless she purchased the necklace he would go and drown himself. His tears left her unmoved to anything but scorn.

"Get up, Bohmer! " she bade him. "I don't like such scenes. I have refused the necklace, and I don't want to hear of it again. Instead of drowning yourself, break it up and sell the diamonds separately. "

He did neither one nor the other, but continued to air his grievance; and among those who heard him was one Laporte, an impecunious visitor at the house of the Countess of Valois.

Bohmer had said that he would pay a thousand louis to any one who found him a purchaser for the necklace. That was enough to stir the needy Laporte. He mentioned the matter to the Countess, and enlisted her interest. Then he told Bohmer of her great influence with the Queen, and brought the jeweller to visit her with the necklace.

Dazzled by the fire of those gems, the Countess nevertheless protested - but in an arch manner calculated to convince Bohmer of the contrary - that she had no power to influence Her Majesty. Yet yielding with apparent reluctance to his importunities, she, nevertheless, ended by promising to see what could be done.

On January 3d the Cardinal came back from Strasbourg. Correspondence with the Queen, through Madame de Valois, had continued during his absence, and now, within a few days of his return, an opportunity was to be afforded him of proving his readiness to serve Her Majesty, and of placing her under a profound obligation to him.

The Countess brought him a letter from Marie Antoinette, in which the Queen expressed her desire to acquire the necklace, but added that, being without the requisite funds at the moment, it would be necessary to settle the terms and arrange the instalments, which should be paid at intervals of three months. For this she required an intermediary who in himself would be a sufficient guarantee to the Bohmers, and she ended by inviting His Eminence to act on her behalf.

That invitation the Cardinal, who had been waiting ever since the meeting in the Grove of Venus for an opportunity of proving himself, accepted with alacrity.

And so, on January 24th, the Countess drives up to the Grand Balcon, the jewellers' shop in the Rue Vendome. Her dark eyes sparkle, the lovely, piquant face is wreathed in smiles.

"Messieurs, " she greets the anxious partners, "I think I can promise you that the necklace will very shortly be sold. "

The jewellers gasp in the immensity of the hope her words arouse.

"The purchase, " she goes on to inform them, "will be effected by a very great nobleman. "

Bassenge bursts into voluble gratitude. She cuts it short.

"That nobleman is the Cardinal-Prince Louis de Rohan. It is with him that you will arrange the affair, and I advise you, " she adds in a confidential tone, "to take every precaution, especially in the matter of the terms of payment that may be proposed to you. That is all, I think, messieurs. You will, of course, bear in mind that it is no concern of mine, and that I do not so much as want my name mentioned in connection with it. "

"Perfectly, madame, " splutters Bohmer, who is perspiring, although the air is cold - "perfectly! We understand, and we are profoundly grateful. If - " His hands fumble nervously at a case. "If you would deign, madame, to accept this trifle as an earnest of our indebtedness, we - "

There is a tinge of haughtiness in her manner as she interrupts him.

"You do not appear to understand, Bohmer, that the matter does not at all concern me. I have done nothing, " she insists; then, melting into smiles, "My only desire, " she adds, "was to be of service to you. "

And upon that she departs, leaving them profoundly impressed by her graciousness and still more by her refusal to accept a valuable jewel.

On the morrow the great nobleman she had heralded, the Cardinal himself, alighted at the Grand Balcon, coming, on the Queen's behalf, to see the necklace and settle the terms. By the end of the week the bargain was concluded. The price was fixed at 1,600,000 livres, which the Queen was to pay in four instalments extending over two years, the first falling due on the following August 1st.

These terms the Cardinal embodied in a note which he forwarded to Madame de la Motte, that they might be ratified by the Queen.

The Countess returned the note to him next day.

"Her Majesty is pleased and grateful, " she announced, "and she approves of all that you have done. But she does not wish to sign anything. "

On that point, however, the Cardinal was insistent. The magnitude of the transaction demanded it, and he positively refused to move further without Her Majesty's signature.

The Countess departed to return again on the last day of the month with the document completed as the Cardinal required, bearing now the signature "Marie Antoinette de France, " and the terms marked "approved" in the Queen's hand.

"The Queen, " Madame de la Motte informed him, "is making this purchase secretly, without the King's knowledge, and she particularly begs that this note shall not leave Your Eminence's hands. Do not, therefore, allow any one to see it. "

Rohan gave the required promise, but, not conceiving that the Bohmers were included in it, he showed them the note and the Queen's signature when they came to wait upon him with the necklace on the morrow.

In the dusk of evening a closed carriage drew up at the door of Madame de la Motte Valois's lodging on the Place Dauphine at Versailles. Rohan alighted, and went upstairs with a casket under his arm.

Madame awaited him in a white-panelled, indifferently lighted room, to which there was an alcove with glass doors.

"You have brought the necklace? "

"It is here, " he replied, tapping the box with his gloved hand.

"Her Majesty is expecting it to-night. Her messenger should arrive at any moment. She will be pleased with Your Eminence. "

"That is all that I can desire, " he answered gravely; and sat down in answer to her invitation, the precious casket on his knees.

Waiting thus, they talked desultorily for some moments. At last came steps upon the stairs.

"Quick! The alcove! " she exclaimed. "You must not be seen by Her Majesty's messenger. "

Rohan, with ready understanding, a miracle of discretion, effaced himself into the alcove, through the glass doors of which he could see what passed.

The door was opened by madame's maid with the announcement:

"From the Queen. "

A tall, slender young man in black, the Queen's attendant of that other night of gems - the night of the Grove of Venus - stepped quickly into the room, bowed like a courtier to Madame de la Motte, and presented a note.

Madame broke the seal, then begged the messenger to withdraw for a moment. When he had gone, she turned to the Cardinal, who stood in the doorway of the alcove.

"That is Desclaux, Her Majesty's valet, " she said; and held out to him the note, which requested the delivery of the necklace to the bearer.

A moment later the messenger was reintroduced to receive the casket from the hands of Madame de la Motte. Within five minutes the Cardinal was in his carriage again, driving happily back to Paris with his dreams of a queen's gratitude and confidence.

Two days later, meeting Bohmer at Versailles, the Cardinal suggested to him that he should offer his thanks to the Queen for having purchased the necklace.

Bohmer sought an opportunity for this in vain. None offered. It was also in vain that he waited to hear that the Queen had worn the necklace. But he does not appear to have been anxious on that score. Moreover, the Queen's abstention was credibly explained by Madame de la Motte to Laporte with the statement that Her Majesty did not wish to wear the necklace until it was paid for.

With the same explanation she answered the Cardinal's inquiries in the following July, when he returned from a three months' sojourn in Strasbourg.

And she took the opportunity to represent to him that one of the reasons why the Queen could not yet consider the necklace quite her own was that she found the price too high.

"Indeed, she may be constrained to return it, after all, unless the Bohmers are prepared to be reasonable. "

If His Eminence was a little dismayed by this, at least any nascent uneasiness was quieted. He consented to see the jewellers in the matter, and on July 10th - three weeks before the first instalment was due - he presented himself at the Grand Balcon to convey the Queen's wishes to the Bohmers.

Bohmer scarcely troubled to prevent disgust from showing on his keen, swarthy countenance. Had not his client been a queen and her intermediary a cardinal, he would, no doubt, have afforded it full expression.

"The price agreed upon was already greatly below the value of the necklace, " he grumbled. "I should never have accepted it but for the difficulties under which we have been placed by the purchase of the stones - the money we owe and the interest we are forced to pay. A further reduction is impossible. "

The handsome Cardinal was suave, courtly, regretful, but firm. Since that was the case, there would be no alternative but to return the necklace.

Bohmer took fright. The annulment of the sale would bring him face to face with ruin. Reluctantly, feeling that he was being imposed upon, he reduced the price by two hundred thousand livres, and even consented to write the Queen the following letter, whose epistolary grace suggests the Cardinal's dictation:

MADAME, - We are happy to hazard the thought that our submission with zeal and respect to the last arrangement proposed constitutes a proof of our devotion and obedience to the orders of Your Majesty. And we have genuine satisfaction in thinking that the most beautiful set of diamonds in existence will serve to adorn the greatest and best of queens.

Now it happened that Bohmer was about to deliver personally to the Queen some jewels with which the King was presenting her on the occasion of the baptism of his nephew. He availed himself of that opportunity, two days later, personally to hand his letter to Her Majesty. But chance brought the Comptroller-General into the room before she had opened it, and as a result the jeweller departed while the letter was, still unread.

Afterwards, in the presence of Madame de Campan, who relates the matter in her memoirs, the Queen opened the note, pored over it a while, and then, perhaps with vivid memories of Bohmer's threat of suicide:

"Listen to what that madman Bohmer writes to me, " she said, and read the lines aloud. "You guessed the riddles in the 'Mercure' this morning. I wonder could you guess me this one. "

And, with a half-contemptuous shrug, she held the sheet in the flame of one of the tapers that stood alight on the table for the purpose of sealing letters.

"That man exists for my torment, " she continued. "He has always some mad notion in his head, and must always be visiting it upon me. When next you see him, pray convince him how little I care for diamonds. "

And there the matter was dismissed.

Days passed, and then a week before the instalment of 350,000 livres was due, the Cardinal received a visit from Madame de la Motte on the Queen's behalf.

"Her Majesty, " madame announced, "seems embarrassed about the instalment. She does not wish to trouble you by writing about it. But I have thought of a way by which you could render yourself agreeable to her and, at the same time, set her mind at rest. Could you not raise a loan for the amount? "

Had not the Cardinal himself dictated to Bohmer a letter which Bohmer himself had delivered to the Queen, he must inevitably have suspected by now that all was not as it should be. But, satisfied as he was by that circumstance, he addressed himself to the matter which Madame de la Motte proposed. But, although Rohan was extraordinarily wealthy, he had ever been correspondingly lavish.

Moreover, to complicate matters, there had been the bankruptcy of his nephew, the Prince de Guimenee, whose debts had amounted to some three million livres. Characteristically, and for the sake of the family honour, Rohan had taken the whole of this burden upon his own shoulders. Hence his resources were in a crippled condition, and it was beyond his power to advance so considerable a sum at such short notice. Nor did he succeed in obtaining a loan within the little time at his disposal.

His anxieties on this score were increased by a letter from the Queen which Madame de la Motte brought him on July 30th, in which Her Majesty wrote that the first instalment could not be paid until October 1st; but that on that date a payment of seven hundred thousand livres - half of the revised price -would unfailingly be made. Together with this letter, Madame de la Motte handed him thirty thousand livres, interest on the instalment due, with which to pacify the jewellers.

But the jewellers were not so easily to be pacified. Bohmer, at the end of his patience, definitely refused to grant the postponement or to receive the thirty thousand livres other than as on account of the instalment due.

The Cardinal departed in vexation. Something must be done at once, or his secret relations with the Queen would be disclosed, thus precipitating a catastrophe and a scandal. He summoned Madame de la Motte, flung her into a panic with his news and sent her away to see what she could do. What she actually did would have surprised him. Realizing that a crisis had been reached calling for bold measures, she sent for Bassenge, the milder of the two partners. He came to the Rue Neuve Saint-Gilles, protesting that he was being abused.

"Abused? " quoth she, taking him up on the word. "Abused, do you say? " She laughed sharply. "Say duped, my friend; for that is what has happened to you. You are the victim of a swindle. "

Bassenge turned white; his prominent eyes bulged in his rather pasty face.

"What are you saying, madame? " His voice was husky.

"The Queen's signature on the note in the Cardinal's possession is a forgery."

"A forgery! The Queen's signature? Oh, mon Dieu!" He stared at her, and his knees began to tremble. "How do you know, madame?"

"I have seen it," she answered.

"But - but - "

His nerveless limbs succumbing under him, he sank without ceremony to a chair that was opportunely near him. With the same lack of ceremony, mechanically, in a dazed manner, he mopped the sweat that stood in beads on his brow, then raised his wig and mopped his head.

"There is no need to waste emotion," said she composedly. "The Cardinal de Rohan is very rich. You must look to him. He will pay you."

"Will he?"

Hope and doubt were blended in the question.

"What else?" she asked. "Can you conceive that he will permit such a scandal to burst about his name and the name of the Queen?"

Bassenge saw light. The rights and wrongs of the case, and who might be the guilty parties, were matters of very secondary importance. What mattered was that the firm should recover the 14,000,000 livres for which the necklace had been sold; and Bassenge was quick to attach full value to the words of Madame de la Motte.

Unfortunately for everybody concerned, including the jewellers themselves, Bohmer's mind was less supple. Panic-stricken by Bassenge's report, he was all for the direct method. There was no persuading him to proceed cautiously, and to begin by visiting the Cardinal. He tore away to Versailles at once, intent upon seeing the Queen. But the Queen, as we know, had had enough of Bohmer. He had to content himself with pouring his mixture of intercessions and demands into the ears of Madame de Campan.

"You have been swindled, Bohmer, " said the Queen's lady promptly. "Her Majesty never received the necklace. "

Bohmer would not be convinced. Disbelieving, and goaded to fury, he returned to Bassenge.

Bassenge, however, though perturbed, retained his calm. The Cardinal, he insisted, was their security, and it was impossible to doubt that the Cardinal would fulfil his obligations at all costs, rather than be overwhelmed by a scandal.

And this, no doubt, is what would have happened but for that hasty visit of Bohmer's to Versailles. It ruined everything. As a result of it, Bohmer was summoned to wait instantly upon the Queen in the mater of some paste buckles.

The Queen received the jeweller in private, and her greeting proved that the paste buckles were a mere pretext. She demanded to know the meaning of his words to Madame de Campan.

Bohmer could not rid himself of the notion that he was being trifled with. Had he not written and himself delivered to the Queen a letter in which he thanked her for purchasing the necklace, and had not that letter remained unanswered - a silent admission that the necklace was in her hands? In his exasperation he became insolent.

"The meaning, madame? The meaning is that I require payment for my necklace, that the patience of my creditors is exhausted, and that unless you order the money to be paid, I am a ruined man! "

Marie Antoinette considered him in cold, imperious anger.

"Are you daring to suggest that your necklace is in my possession? "

Bohmer was white to the lips, his hands worked nervously.

"Does Your Majesty deny it? "

"You are insolent! " she exclaimed. "You will be good enough to answer questions, not to ask them. Answer me, then. Do you suggest that I have your necklace? "

But a desperate man is not easily intimidated.

"No, madame; I affirm it! It was the Countess of Valois who - "

"Who is the Countess of Valois? "

That sudden question, sharply uttered, was a sword of doubt through the heart of Bohmer's confidence. He stared wide-eyed a moment at the indignant lady before him, then collected himself, and made as plain a tale as he could of the circumstances under which he had parted with the necklace Madame de la Motte's intervention, the mediation of the Cardinal de Rohan with Her Majesty's signed approval of the terms, and the delivery of the necklace to His Eminence for transmission to the Queen.

Marie Antoinette listened in increasing horror and anger. A flush crept into her pale cheeks.

"You will prepare and send me a written statement of what you have just told me, " she said. "You have leave to go. "

That interview took place on August 9th. The 15th was the Feast of the Assumption, and also the name-day of the Queen, therefore a gala day at Court, bringing a concourse of nobility to Versailles. Mass was to be celebrated in the royal chapel at ten o'clock, and the celebrant, as by custom established for the occasion, was the Grand Almoner of France, the Cardinal de Rohan.

But at ten o'clock a meeting was being held in the King's cabinet, composed of the King and Queen, the Baron de Breteuil, and the Keeper of the Seals, Miromesnil. They were met, as they believed, to decide upon a course of action in the matter of a diamond necklace. In reality, these puppets in the hands of destiny were helping to decide the fate of the French monarchy.

The King, fat, heavy, and phlegmatic, sat in a gilded chair by an ormolu-encrusted writing-table. His bovine eyes were troubled. Two wrinkles of vexation puckered the flesh above his great nose. Beside, and slightly behind him, stood the Queen, white and imperious, whilst facing them stood Monsieur de Breteuil, reading aloud the statement which Bohmer had drawn up.

When he had done, there was a moment's utter silence. Then the King spoke, his voice almost plaintive.

"What is to be done, then? But what is to be done? "

It was the Queen who answered him, harshly and angrily.

"When the Roman purple and a princely title are but masks to cover a swindler, there is only one thing to be done. This swindler must be exposed and punished. "

"But, " the King faltered, "we have not heard the Cardinal. "

"Can you think that Bohmer, that any man, would dare to lie upon such a matter? "

"But consider, madame, the Cardinal's rank and family, " calmly interposed the prudent Miromesnil; "consider the stir, the scandal that must ensue if this matter is made public. "

But the obedient daughter of Marie Therese, hating Rohan at her mother's bidding and for her mother's sake, was impatient of any such wise considerations.

"What shall the scandal signify to us? " she demanded. The King looked at Breteuil.

"And you, Baron? What is your view? "

Breteuil, Rohan's mortal enemy, raised his shoulders and flipped the document.

"In the face of this, Sire, it seems to me that the only course is to arrest the Cardinal. "

"You believe, then - " began the King, and checked, leaving the sentence unfinished.

But Breteuil had understood.

"I know that the Cardinal must be pressed for money, " he said. "Ever prodigal in his expenditure, he is further saddled with the debts of the Prince de Guimenee. "

"And you can believe, " the King cried, "that a Prince of the House of Rohan, however pressed for money, could - Oh, it is unimaginable! "

"Yet has he not stolen my name? " the Queen cut in. "Is he not proven a common, stupid forger? "

"We have not heard him, " the King reminded her gently.

"And His Eminence might be able to explain, " ventured Miromesnil. "It were certainly prudent to give him the opportunity. "

Slowly the King nodded his great, powdered head. "Go and find him. Bring him at once! " he bade Breteuil; and Breteuil bowed and departed.

Very soon he returned, and he held the door whilst the handsome Cardinal, little dreaming what lay before him, serene and calm, a commanding figure in his cassock of scarlet watered silk, rustled forward into the royal presence, and so came face to face with the Queen for the first time since that romantic night a year ago in the Grove of Venus.

Abruptly the King launched his thunderbolt.

"Cousin, " he asked, "what purchase is this of a diamond necklace that you are said to have made in the Queen's name? "

King and Cardinal looked into each other's eyes, the King's narrowing, the Cardinal's dilating, the King leaning forward in his chair, elbows on the table, the Cardinal standing tense and suddenly rigid.

Slowly the colour ebbed from Rohan's face, leaving it deathly pale. His eyes sought the Queen, and found her contemptuous glance, her curling lip. Then at last his handsome head sank a little forward.

"Sire, " he said unsteadily, "I see that I have been duped. But I have duped nobody. "

"You have no reason to be troubled, then. You need but to explain. "

Explain! That was precisely what he could not do. Besides, what was the nature of the explanation demanded of him? Whilst he stood stricken there, it was the Queen who solved this question.

"If, indeed, you have been duped, " she said scornfully, her colour high, her eyes like points of steel, "you have been self-duped. But even then it is beyond belief that self-deception could have urged you to the lengths of passing yourself off as my intermediary - you, who should know yourself to be the last man in France I should employ, you to whom I have not spoken once in eight years. " Tears of anger glistened in her eyes; her voice shrilled up. "And yet, since you have not denied it, since you put forward this pitiful plea that you have been duped, we must believe the unbelievable. "

Thus at a blow she shattered the fond hopes he had been cherishing ever since the night of gems - of gems, forsooth! - in the Grove of Venus; thus she laid his ambition in ruins about him, and left the man himself half stunned.

Observing his disorder, the ponderous but kindly monarch rose.

"Come, my cousin, " he said more gently, "collect yourself. Sit down here and write what you may have to say in answer. "

And with that he passed into the library beyond, accompanied by the Queen and the two Ministers.

Alone, Rohan staggered forward and sank nervelessly into the chair. He took up a pen, pondered a moment, and began to write. But he did not yet see clear. He could not yet grasp the extent to which he had been deceived, could not yet believe that those treasured notes from Marie Antoinette were forgeries, that it was not the Queen who had met him in the Grove of Venus and given him the rose whose faded petals kept those letters company in a portfolio of red morocco. But at least it was clear to him that, for the sake of honour - the Queen's honour - he must assume it so; and in that assumption he now penned his statement.

When it was completed, himself he bore it to the King in the library.

Louis read it with frowning brows; then passed it to the Queen.

"Have you the necklace now? " he asked Rohan.

"Sir, I left it in the hands of this woman Valois. "

"Where is this woman? "

"I do not know, Sire. "

"And the letter of authority bearing the Queen's signature, which the jewellers say you presented to them - where is that? "

"I have it, Sire. I will place it before you. It is only now that I realize that it is a forgery. "

"Only now! " exclaimed the Queen in scorn.

"Her Majesty's name has been compromised, " said the King sternly. "It must be cleared. As King and as husband my duty is clear. Your Eminence must submit to arrest. "

Rohan fell back a step in stupefaction. For disgrace and dismissal he was prepared, but not for this.

"Arrest? " he whispered. "Ah, wait, Sire. The publicity! The scandal! Think of that! As for the necklace, I will pay for it myself, and so pay for my credulous folly. I beseech you, Sire, to let the matter end here. I implore it for my own sake, for the sake of the Prince de Soubise and the name of Rohan, which would be smirched unjustly and to no good purpose. "

He spoke with warmth and force; and, without adding more, yet conveyed an impression that much more could be said for the course he urged.

The King hesitated, considering. Noting this, the prudent, far-seeing Miromesnil ventured to develop the arguments at which Rohan had hinted, laying stress upon the desirability of avoiding scandal.

Louis was nodding, convinced, when Marie Antoinette, unable longer to contain her rancour, broke into opposition of those prudent measures.

"This hideous affair must be disclosed, " she insisted. "It is due to me that it should publicly be set right. The Cardinal shall tell the world how he came to suppose that, not having spoken to him for eight years, I could have wished to make use of his services in the purchase of this necklace. "

She was in tears, and her weak, easily swayed husband accounted her justified in her demand. And so, to the great consternation of all the world, Prince Louis de Rohan was arrested like a common thief.

A foolish, indiscreet, short-sighted woman had allowed her rancour to override all other considerations - careless of consequences, careless of injustice so that her resentment, glutted by her hatred of the Cardinal, should be gratified. The ungenerous act was terribly to recoil upon her. In tears and blood was she to expiate her lack of charity; very soon she was to reap its bitter fruits.

Saint-Just, a very prominent counsellor of the Parliament, one of the most advanced apostles of the new ideas that were to find full fruition in the Revolution, expressed the popular feeling in the matter.

"Great and joyful affair! A cardinal and a queen implicated in a forgery and a swindle! Filth on the crosier and the sceptre! What a triumph for the ideas of liberty! "

At the trial that followed before Parliament, Madame de la Motte, a man named Reteaux de Villette - who had forged the Queen's hand and impersonated Desclaux and a Mademoiselle d'Oliva - who had used her striking resemblance to Marie Antoinette to impersonate the Queen in the Grove of Venus were found guilty and sentenced. But the necklace was not recovered. It had been broken up, and some of the diamonds were already sold; others were being sold in London by Captain de la Motte, who had gone thither for the purpose, and who prudently remained there.

The Cardinal was acquitted, amid intense public joy and acclamation, which must have been gall and wormwood to the Queen. His powerful family, the clergy of France, and the very people, with whom he had ever been popular, had all laboured strenuously to vindicate him. And thus it befell that the one man the Queen had aimed at crushing was the only person connected with the affair who came out of it unhurt. The Queen's animus against the Cardinal aroused against her the animus of his friends of all classes. Appalling libels of her were circulated throughout Europe. It was thought and argued that she was more deeply implicated in the swindle than had transpired, that Madame de la Motte was a scapegoat, that the Queen should have stood her trial with the others, and that she was saved only by the royalty that hedged her.

Conceive what a weapon this placed in the hands of the men of the new ideas of liberty - men who were bent on proving the corruption of a system they sought to destroy!

Marie Antoinette should have foreseen something of this. She might have done so had not her hatred blinded her, had she been less intent upon seizing the opportunity at all costs to make Rohan pay for his barbed witticism upon her mother. She might have been spared much had she but spared Rohan when the chance was hers. As it was, the malevolent echoes of the affair and of Saint-Just's exultation were never out of her ears. They followed her to her trial eight years later before the revolutionary tribunal. They followed her to the very scaffold, of which they had undoubtedly supplied a plank.

VIII. THE NIGHT OF TERROR

The Drownings at Nantes under Carrier

The Revolutionary Committee of the city of Nantes, reinforced by some of the administrators of the district and a few members of the People's Society, sat in the noble hall of the Cour des Comptes, which still retained much of its pre-republican sumptuousness. They sat expectantly - Goullin, the attorney, president of the committee, a frail, elegant valetudinarian, fierily eloquent; Grandmaison, the fencing-master, who once had been a gentleman, fierce of eye and inflamed of countenance; Minee, the sometime bishop, now departmental president; Pierre Chaux, the bankrupt merchant; the sans-culotte Forget, of the People's Society, an unclean, ill-kempt ruffian; and some thirty others called like these from every walk of life.

Lamps were lighted, and under their yellow glare the huddled company - for the month was December, and the air of the vast room was chill and dank - looked anxious and ill at ease.

Suddenly the doors were thrown open by an usher; and his voice rang loud in announcement -

"The Citizen Representative Carrier. "

The great man came in, stepping quickly. Of middle height, very frail and delicate, his clay-colored face was long and thin, with arched eyebrows, a high nose, and a loose, coarse mouth. His deeply sunken dark eyes glared fiercely, and wisps of dead-black hair, which had escaped the confining ribbon of his queue, hung about his livid brow. He was wrapped in a riding-coat of bottle-green, heavily lined with fur, the skirts reaching down to the tops of his Hessian boots, and the enormous turned-up collar almost touching the brim of his round hat. Under the coat his waist was girt with the tricolour of office, and there were gold rings in his ears.

Such at the age of five-and-thirty was Jean Baptiste Carrier, Representative of the Convention with the Army of the West, the attorney who once had been intended by devout parents for the priesthood. He had been a month in Nantes, sent thither to purge the body politic.

He reached a chair placed in the focus of the gathering, which sat in a semicircle. Standing by it, one of his lean hands resting upon the back, he surveyed them, disgust in his glance, a sneer curling his lip, so terrible and brutal of aspect despite his frailness that more than one of those stout fellows quailed now before him.

Suddenly he broke into torrential speech, his voice shrill and harsh:

"I do not know by what fatality it happens, but happen it does, that during the month that I have been in Nantes you have never ceased to give me reason to complain of you. I have summoned you to meet me here that you may justify yourselves, if you can, for your ineptitude! " And he flung himself into the chair, drawing his fur-lined coat about him. "Let me hear from you! " he snapped.

Minee, the unfrocked bishop, preserving still a certain episcopal portliness of figure, a certain episcopal oiliness of speech, respectfully implored the representative to be more precise.

The invitation flung him into a passion. His irascibility, indeed, deserved to become a byword.

"Name of a name! " he shrilled, his sunken eyes ablaze, his face convulsed. "Is there a thing I can mention in this filthy city of yours that is not wrong? Everything is wrong! You have failed in your duty to provide adequately for the army of Vendee. Angers has fallen, and now the brigands are threatening Nantes itself. There is abject want in the city, disease is rampant; people are dying of hunger in the streets and of typhus in the prisons. And sacre nom! - you ask me to be precise! I'll be precise in telling you where lies the fault. It lies in your lousy administration. Do you call yourselves administrators? You - " He became unprintable. "I have come here to shake you out of your torpor, and by — I'll shake you out of it or I'll have the blasted heads off the lot of you. "

They shivered with chill fear under the wild glare of his sunken eyes.

"Well? " he barked after a long pause. "Are you all dumb as well as idiots? "

It was the ruffian Forget who had the courage to answer him:

"I have told the People's Society that if the machine works badly it is because the Citizen Carrier refuses to consult with the administration. "

"You told them that, did you, you — liar? " screeched Carrier. "Am I not here now to consult with you? And should I not have come before had you suggested it? Instead, you have waited until, of my own accord, I should come to tell you that your administration is ruining Nantes. "

Goullin, the eloquent and elegant Goullin, rose to soothe him:

"Citizen Representative, we admit the truth of all that you have said. There has been a misunderstanding. We could not take it upon ourselves to summon the august representative of the Sacred People. I We have awaited your own good pleasure, and now that you have made this manifest, there is no reason why the machine should not work effectively. The evils of which you speak exist, alas! But they are not so deeply rooted that, working under your guidance and advice, we cannot uproot them, rendering the soil fertile once more of good under the beneficent fertilizing showers of liberty. "

Mollified, Carrier grunted approval.

"That is well said, Citizen Goullin. The fertilizer needed by the soil is blood - the bad blood of aristocrats and federalists, and I can promise you, in the name of the august people, that it shall be abundantly provided. "

The assembly broke into applause, and his vanity melted to it. He stood up, expressed his gratification at being so completely understood, opened his arms, and invited the departmental president, Minee, to come down and receive the kiss of brotherhood.

Thereafter they passed to the consideration of measures of improvement, of measures to combat famine and disease. In Carrier's view there was only one way of accomplishing this - the number of mouths to be fed must be reduced, the diseased must be eliminated. It was the direct, the radical, the heroic method.

That very day six prisoners in Le Bouffay had been sentenced to death for attempting to escape.

"How do we know, " he asked, "that those six include all the guilty? How do we know that all in Le Bouffay do not share the guilt? The prisoners are riddled with disease, which spreads to the good patriots of Nantes; they eat bread, which is scarce, whilst good patriots starve. We must have the heads off all those blasted swine! " He took fire at his own suggestion. "Aye, that would be a useful measure. We'll deal with it at once. Let some one fetch the President of the Revolutionary Tribunal. "

He was fetched - a man of good family and a lawyer, named Francois Phelippes.

"Citizen President, " Carrier greeted him, "the administration of Nantes has been considering an important measure. To-day you sentenced to death six prisoners in Le Bouffay for attempting to escape. You are to postpone execution so as to include all the Bouffay prisoners in the sentence. "

Although an ardent revolutionary, Phelippes was a logically minded man with a lawyer's reverence for the sacredness of legal form. This command, issued with such cynical coldness, and repudiated by none of those present, seemed to him as grotesque and ridiculous as it was horrible.

"But that is impossible, Citizen Representative, " said he.

"Impossible! " snarled Carrier. "A fool's word. The administration desires you to understand that it is not impossible. The sacred will of the august people - "

Phelippes interrupted him without ceremony.

"There is no power in France that can countermand the execution of a sentence of the law. "

"No - no power! "

Carrier's loose mouth fell open. He was too amazed to be angry.

"Moreover, " Phelippes pursued calmly, "there is the fact that all the other prisoners in Le Bouffay are innocent of the offence for which the six are to die. "

184

"What has that to do with it? " roared Carrier. "Last year I rode a she-ass that could argue better than you! In the name of —, what has that to do with it? "

But there were members of the assembly who thought with Phelippes, and who, whilst lacking the courage to express themselves, yet found courage to support another who so boldly expressed them.

Carrier sprang up quivering with rage before that opposition. "It seems to me, " he snarled, "that there are more than the scoundrels in Le Bouffay who need to be shortened by a head for the good of the nation. I tell you that you are slaying the commonweal by your slowness and circumspection. Let all the scoundrels perish! "

A handsome, vicious youngster named Robin made chorus.

"Patriots are without bread! It is fitting that the scoundrels should die, and not eat the bread of starving patriots. "

Carrier shook his fist at the assembly.

"You hear, you —! I cannot pardon whom the law condemns. "

It was an unfortunate word, and Phelippes fastened on it.

"That is the truth, Citizen Representative, " said Phelippes. "And as for the prisoners in Le Bouffay, you will wait until the law condemns them. "

And without staying to hear more, he departed as firmly as he had come, indifferent to the sudden uproar.

When he had gone, the Representative flung himself into his chair again, biting his lip.

"There goes a fellow who will find his way to the guillotine in time, " he growled.

But he was glad to be rid of him, and would not have him brought back. He saw how the opposition of Phelippes had stiffened the weaker opposition of some of those in the assembly. If he was to have his way he would contrive better without the legal-minded

185

President of the Revolutionary Tribunal. And his way he had in the end, though not until he had stormed and cursed and reviled the few who dared to offer remonstrances to his plan of wholesale slaughter.

When at last he took his departure, it was agreed that the assembly should proceed to elect a jury which was to undertake the duty of drawing up immediately a list of those confined in the prisons of Nantes. This list they were to deliver when ready to the committee, which would know how to proceed, for Carrier had made his meaning perfectly clear. The first salutary measure necessary to combat the evils besetting the city was to wipe out at once the inmates of all the prisons in Nantes.

In the chill December dawn of the next day the committee - which had sat all night under the presidency of Goullin forwarded a list of some five hundred prisoners to General Boivin, the commandant of the city of Nantes, together with an order to collect them without a moment's delay, take them to L'Eperonniere, and there have them shot.

But Boivin was a soldier, and a soldier is not a sans-culotte. He took the order to Phelippes, with the announcement that he had no intention of obeying it. Phelippes, to Boivin's amazement, agreed with him. He sent the order back to the committee, denouncing it as flagrantly illegal, and reminding them that it was illegal to remove any prisoner, no matter by whose order, without such an order as might follow upon a decision of the Tribunal.

The committee, intimidated by this firmness on the part of the President of the Revolutionary Tribunal, dared not insist, and there the matter remained.

When Carrier learnt of it the things he said were less than ever fit for publication. He raved like a madman at the very thought that a quibbling lawyer should stand in the very path of him, the august representative of the Sacred People.

It had happened that fifty-three priests, who had been brought to Nantes a few days before, were waiting in the sheds of the entrepot for prison accommodation, so that their names did not yet appear upon any of the prison registers. As a solatium to his wounded feelings, he ordered his friends of the Marat Company to get rid of them.

Lamberty, the leader of the Marats, asked him how it should be done.

"How? " he croaked. "Not so much mystery, my friend. Fling the swine into the water, and so let's be rid of them. There will be plenty of their kind left in France. "

But he seems to have explained himself further, and what precisely were his orders, and how they were obeyed, transpires from a letter which he wrote to the Convention, stating that those fifty-three wretched priests, "being confined in a boat on the Loire, were last night swallowed up by the river. " And he added the apostrophe, "What a revolutionary torrent is the Loire! "

The Convention had no illusions as to his real meaning; and when Carrier heard that his letter had been applauded by the National Assembly, he felt himself encouraged to break down all barriers of mere legality that might obstruct his path. And, after all, what the Revolutionary Committee as a body - intimidated by Phelippes - dared not do could be done by his faithful and less punctilious friends of the Marat Company.

This Marat Company, the police of the Revolutionary Committee, enrolled from the scourings of Nantes' sans-culottism, and captained by a ruffian named Fleury, had been called into being by Carrier himself with the assistance of Goullin.

On the night of the 24th Frimaire of the year III (December 14, 1793, old style), which was a Saturday, Fleury mustered some thirty of his men, and took them to the Cour des Comptes, where they were awaited by Goullin, Bachelier, Grandmaison, and some other members of the committee entirely devoted to Carrier. From these the Marats received their formal instructions.

"Plague, " Goullin informed them, "is raging in the gaols, and its ravages must be arrested. You will therefore proceed this evening to the prison of Le Bouffay in order to take over the prisoners whom you will march up to the Quay La Fosse, whence they will be shipped to Belle Isle. "

In a cell of that sordid old building known as Le Bouffay lay a cocassier, an egg and poultry dealer, arrested some three years before upon a charge of having stolen a horse, and since forgotten.

His own version was that a person of whom he knew very little had entrusted him with the sale of the stolen animal in possession of which he was discovered.

The story sounds familiar; it is the sort of story that must have done duty many times; and it is probable that the cocassier was no better than he should have been. Nevertheless Fate selected him to be one of her unconscious instruments. His name was Leroy, and we have his own word for it that he was a staunch patriot. The horse business was certainly in the best vein of sans-culottism.

Leroy was awakened about ten o'clock that night by sounds that were very unusual in that sombre, sepulchral prison. They were sounds of unbridled revelry - snatches of ribald song, bursts of coarse, reverberating laughter and they proceeded, as it seemed to him, from the courtyard and the porter's lodge.

He crawled from the dank straw which served him for a bed, and approached the door to listen. Clearly the porter Laqueze was entertaining friends and making unusually merry. It was also to be gathered that Laqueze's friends were getting very drunk. What the devil did it mean?

His curiosity was soon to be very fully gratified. Came heavy steps up the stone staircase, the clatter of sabots, the clank of weapons, and through the grille of his door an increasing light began to beat.

Some one was singing the "Carmagnole" in drunken, discordant tones. Keys rattled, bolts were drawn; doors were being flung open. The noise increased. Above the general din he heard the detestable voice of the turnkey.

"Come and see my birds in their cages. Come and see my pretty birds. "

Leroy began to have an uneasy premonition that the merrymaking portended sinister things.

"Get up, all of you! " bawled the turnkey. "Up and pack your traps. You're to go on a voyage. No laggards, now. Up with you! "

The door of Leroy's cell was thrown open in its turn, and he found himself confronting a group of drunken ruffians. One of these - a red-capped giant with long, black mustaches and a bundle of ropes over one arm suddenly pounced upon him. The cocassier was an active, vigorous young man. But, actuated by fear and discretion, he permitted himself tamely to be led away.

Along the stone-flagged corridor he went, and on every hand beheld his fellow-prisoners in the same plight, being similarly dragged from their cells and similarly hurried below. At the head of the stairs one fellow, perfectly drunk, was holding a list, hiccupping over names which he garbled ludicrously as he called them out. He was lighted in his task by a candle held by another who was no less drunk. The swaying pair seemed to inter-support one another grotesquely.

Leroy suffered himself to be led down the stairs, and so came to the porter's lodge, where he beheld a half-dozen Marats assembled round a table, with bumpers of wine before them, bawling, singing, cursing, and cracking lewd jests at the expense of each prisoner as he entered. The place was in a litter. A lamp had been smashed, and there was a puddle of wine on the floor from a bottle that had been knocked over. On a bench against the wall were ranged a number of prisoners, others lay huddled on the floor, and all of them were pinioned.

Two or three of the Marats lurched up to Leroy, and ran their hands over him, turning out his pockets, and cursing him foully for their emptiness. He saw the same office performed upon others, and saw them stripped of money, pocket-books, watches, rings, buckles, and whatever else of value they happened to possess. One man, a priest, was even deprived of his shoes by a ruffian who was in want of foot-gear.

As they were pinioning his wrists, Leroy looked up. He confesses that he was scared.

"What is this for? " he asked. "Does it mean death? "

With an oath he was bidden to ask no questions.

"If I die, " he assured them, "you will be killing a good republican. "

A tall man with an inflamed countenance and fierce, black eyes, that were somewhat vitreous, now leered down upon him.

"You babbling fool! It's not your life, it's your property we want. "

This was Grandmaison, the fencing-master, who once had been a gentleman. He had been supping with Carrier, and he had only just arrived at Le Bouffay, accompanied by Goullin. He found the work behind time, and told them so.

"Leave that fellow now, Jolly. He's fast enough. Up and fetch the rest. It's time to be going . .. time to be going. "

Flung aside now that he was pinioned, Leroy sat down on the floor and looked about him. Near him an elderly man was begging for a cup of water. They greeted the prayer with jeering laughter.

"Water! By Sainte Guillotine, he asks for water! " The drunken sans-culottes were intensely amused. "Patience, my friend - patience, and you shall drink your fill. You shall drink from the great cup. "

Soon the porter's lodge was crowded with prisoners, and they were overflowing into the passage.

Came Grandmaison cursing and swearing at the sluggishness of the Marats, reminding them - as he had been reminding them for the last hour - that it was time to be off, that the tide was on the ebb.

Stimulated by him, Jolly - the red-capped giant with the black mustaches - and some others of the Marat Company, set themselves to tie the prisoners into chains of twenty, further to ensure against possible evasion. They were driven into the chilly courtyard, and there Grandmaison, followed by a fellow with a lantern, passed along the ranks counting them.

The result infuriated him.

"A hundred and five! " he roared, and swore horribly. "You have been here nearly five hours, and in all that time you have managed to truss up only a hundred and five. Are we never to get through with it? I tell you the tide is ebbing. It is time to be off. "

Laqueze, the porter of Le Bouffay, with whose food and wine those myrmidons of the committee had made so disgracefully free, came to assure him that he had all who were in the prison.

"All? " cried Grandmaison, aghast. "But according to the list there should have been nearer two hundred. " And he raised his voice to call: "Goullin! Hola, Goullin! Where the devil is Goullin? "

"The list, " Laqueze told him, "was drawn up from the register. But you have not noted that many have died since they came - we have had the fever here - and that a few are now in hospital. "

"In hospital! Bah! Go up, some of you, and fetch them. We are taking them somewhere where they will be cured. " And then he hailed the elegant Goullin, who came up wrapped in a cloak. "Here's a fine bathing-party! " he grumbled. "A rare hundred of these swine! "

Goullin turned to Laqueze.

"What have you done with the fifteen brigands I sent you this evening? "

"But they only reached Nantes to-day, " said Laqueze, who understood nothing of these extraordinary proceedings. "They have not yet been registered, not even examined. "

"I asked you what you have done with them? " snapped Goullin.

"They are upstairs. "

"Then fetch them. They are as good as any others. "

With these, and a dozen or so dragged from sick-beds, the total was made up to about a hundred and thirty.

The Marats, further reinforced now by half a company of National Guards, set out from the prison towards five o'clock in the morning; urging their victims along with blows and curses.

Our cocassier found himself bound wrist to wrist with a young Capuchin brother, who stumbled along in patient resignation, his head bowed, his lips moving as if he were in prayer.

"Can you guess what they are going to do with us? " murmured Leroy.

He caught the faint gleam of the Capuchin's eyes in the gloom.

"I do not know, brother. Commend yourself to God, and so be prepared for whatever may befall. "

The answer was not very comforting to a man of Leroy's temperament. He stumbled on, and they came now upon the Place du Bouffay, where the red guillotine loomed in ghostly outline, and headed towards the Quai Tourville. Thence they were marched by the river the whole length of the Quai La Fosse. Fear spreading amongst them, some clamours were raised, to be instantly silenced by blows and assurances that they were to be shipped to Belle Isle, where they were to be set to work to build a fort.

The cocassier thought this likely enough, and found it more comforting than saying his prayers - a trick which he had long since lost.

As they defiled along the quays, an occasional window was thrown up, and an inquisitive head protruded, to be almost instantly withdrawn again.

On the Cale Robin at last they were herded into a shed which opened on to the water. Here they found a large lighter alongside, and they beheld in the lantern-light the silhouettes of a half-dozen shipwrights busily at work upon it, whilst the place rang with the blows of hammers and the scream of saws.

Some of those nearest the barge saw what was being done. Two great ports were being opened in the vessel's side, and over one of these thus opened the shipwrights were nailing planks. They observed that these ports, which remained above the water-line now that the barge was empty, would be well below it once she were laden, and conceiving that they perceived at last the inhuman fate awaiting them, their terror rose again. They remembered snatches of conversation and grim jests uttered by the Marats in Le Bouffay, which suddenly became clear, and the alarm spreading amongst them, they writhed and clamoured, screamed for mercy, cursed and raved.

Blows were showered upon them. In vain was it sought to quiet them again with that fable of a fort to be constructed on Belle Isle. One of them in a frenzy of despair tore himself free of his bonds, profited by a moment of confusion, and vanished so thoroughly that Grandmaison and his men lost a quarter of an hour seeking him in vain, and would have so spent the remainder of the night but for a sharp word from a man in a greatcoat and a round hat who stood looking on in conversation with Goullin.

"Get on, man! Never mind that one! We'll have him later. It will be daylight soon. You've wasted time enough already. "

It was Carrier.

He had come in person to see the execution of his orders, and at his command Grandmaison now proceeded to the loading. A ladder was set against the side of the lighter by which the prisoners were to descend. The cords binding them in chains were now severed, and they were left pinioned only by the wrists. They were ordered to embark. But as they were slow to obey, and as some, indeed, hung back wailing and interceding, he and Jolly took them by their collars, thrust them to the edge, and bundled them neck and crop down into the hold, recking nothing of broken limbs. Finding this method of embarkation more expeditious, the use of the ladder was neglected thenceforth.

Among the last to be thus flung aboard was our cocassier Leroy. He fell soft upon a heaving, writhing mass of humanity, which only gradually shook down and sorted itself out on the bottom of the lighter when the hatches overhead were being nailed down. Yet by an odd chance the young Capuchin and Leroy, who had been companions in the chain, were not separated even now. Amid the human welter in that agitated place of darkness, the cries and wails that rang around him, Leroy recognized the voice of the young friar exhorting them to prayer.

They were in the stern of the vessel, against one of the sides, and Leroy, who still kept a grip on the wits by which he had lived, bade the Capuchin hold up his wrists. Then he went nosing like a dog, until at last he found them, and his strong teeth fastened upon the cord that bound them, and began with infinite patience to gnaw it through.

Meanwhile that floating coffin had left its moorings and was gliding with the stream. On the hatches sat Grandmaison, with Jolly and two other Marats, howling the "Carmagnole" to drown the cries of the wretches underneath, and beating time with their feet upon the deck.

Leroy's teeth worked on like a rat's until at last the cord was severed. Then, lest they should be parted in the general heaving and shifting of that human mass, those teeth of his fastened upon the Capuchin's sleeve.

"Take hold of me! " he commanded as distinctly as he could; and the Capuchin gratefully obeyed. "Now untie my wrists! "

The Capuchin's hands slid along Leroy's arms until they found his hands, and there his fingers grew busy, groping at the knots. It was no easy matter to untie them in the dark, guided by sense of touch alone. But the friar was persistent and patient, and in the end the last knot ran loose, and our cocassier was unpinioned.

It comforted him out of all proportion to the advantage. At least his hands were free for any emergency that might offer. That he depended in such a situation, and with no illusions as to what was to happen, upon emergency, shows how tenacious he was of hope.

He had been released not a moment too soon. Overhead, Grandmaison and his men were no longer singing. They were moving about. Something bumped against the side of the vessel, near the bow, obviously a boat, and voices came up from below the level of the deck. Then the lighter shuddered under a great blow upon the planks of the forecastle port. The cries in the hold redoubled. Panting, cursing, wailing men hurtled against Leroy, and almost crushed him for a moment under their weight as the vessel heaved to starboard. Came a succession of blows, not only on the port in the bow, but also on that astern. There was a cracking and rending of timbers, and the water rushed in.

Then the happenings in that black darkness became indescribably horrible. In their frenzy not a few had torn themselves free of their bonds. These hurled themselves towards the open ports through which the water was pouring. They tore at the planks with desperate, lacerated hands. Some got their arms through, seeking convulsively to widen the openings and so to gain an egress. But outside in the shipwrights' boat stood Grandmaison, the fencing-master, brandishing a butcher's sword.

With derision and foul objurgations he slashed at protruding arms and hands, thrust his sword again and again through the port into

194

that close-packed, weltering mass, until at last the shipwrights backed away the boat to escape the suction of the sinking lighter.

The vessel, with its doomed freight of a hundred and thirty human lives, settled down slowly by the head, and the wailing and cursing was suddenly silenced as the icy waters of the Loire eddied over it and raced on.

Caught in the swirl of water, Leroy had been carried up against the deck of the lighter. Instinctively he had clutched at a crossbeam. The water raced over his head, and then, to his surprise, receded, beat up once or twice as the lighter grounded, and finally settled on a level with his shoulders.

He was quick to realize what had happened. The lighter had gone down by the head on a shallow. Her stern remained slightly protruding, so that in that part of her between the level of the water and the deck there was a clear space of perhaps a foot or a foot and a half. Yet of the hundred and thirty doomed wretches on board he was the only one who had profited by this extraordinary chance.

Leroy hung on there; and thereafter for two hours, to use his own expression, he floated upon corpses. A man of less vigorous mettle, moral and physical, could never have withstood the ordeal of a two hours' immersion in the ice-cold water of that December morning. Leroy clung on, and hoped. I have said that he was tenacious of hope. And soon after daybreak he was justified of his confidence in his luck. As the first livid gleams of light began to suffuse the water in which he floated, a creaking of rowlocks and a sound of voices reached his ears. A boat was passing down the river.

Leroy shouted, and his voice rang hollow and sepulchral on the morning stillness. The creak of oars ceased abruptly. He shouted again, and was answered. The oars worked now at twice their former speed. The boat was alongside. Blows of a grapnel tore at the planking of the deck until there was a hole big enough to admit the passage of his body.

He looked through the faint mist which he had feared never to see again, heaved himself up with what remained him of strength until his breast was on a level with the deck, and beheld two men in a boat.

But, exhausted by the effort, his numbed limbs refused to support him. He sank back, and went overhead, fearing now, indeed, that help had arrived too late. But as he struggled to the surface the bight of a rope smacked the water within the hold. Convulsively he clutched it, wound it about one arm, and bade them haul.

Thus they dragged him out and aboard their own craft, and put him ashore at the nearest point willing out of humanity to do so much, but daring to do no more when he had told them how he came where they had found him.

Half naked, numbed through and through, with chattering teeth and failing limbs, Leroy staggered into the guard-house at Chantenay. Soldiers of the Blues stripped him of his sodden rags, wrapped him in a blanket, thawed him outwardly before a fire and inwardly with gruel, and then invited him to give an account of himself.

The story of the horse will have led you to suppose him a ready liar. He drew now upon that gift of his, represented himself as a mariner from Montoir, and told a harrowing tale of shipwreck. Unfortunately, he overdid it. There was present a fellow who knew something of the sea, and something of Montoir, to whom Leroy's tale did not ring quite true. To rid themselves of responsibility, the soldiers carried him before the Revolutionary Committee of Nantes.

Even here all might have gone well with him, since there was no member of that body with seacraft to penetrate his imposture. But as ill-chance would have it, one of the members sitting that day was the black-mustached sans-culotte Jolly, the very man who had dragged Leroy out of his cell last night and tied him up.

At sight of him Jolly's eyes bulged in his head.

"Where the devil have you come from? " he greeted him thunderously.

Leroy quailed. Jolly's associates stared. But Jolly explained to them:

"He was of last night's bathing party. And he has the impudence to come before us like this. Take him away and shove him back into the water. "

But Bachelier, a man who, next to the President Goullin, exerted the greatest influence in the committee, was gifted with a sense of humour worthy of the Revolution. He went off into peals of laughter as he surveyed the crestfallen cocassier, and, perhaps because Leroy's situation amused him, he was disposed to be humane.

"No, no! " he said. "Take him back to Le Bouffay for the present. Let the Tribunal deal with him. "

So back to Le Bouffay went Leroy, back to his dungeon, his fetid straw and his bread and water, there to be forgotten again, as he had been forgotten before, until Fate should need him.

It is to him that we owe most of the materials from which we are able to reconstruct in detail that first of Carrier's drownings on a grand scale, conceived as an expeditious means of ridding the city of useless mouths, of easing the straitened circumstances resulting from misgovernment.

Very soon it was followed by others, and, custom increasing Carrier's audacity, these drownings - there were in all some twenty-three noyades - ceased to be conducted in the secrecy of the night, or to be confined to men. They were made presently to include women - of whom at one drowning alone, in Novose, three hundred perished under the most revolting circumstances - and even little children. Carrier himself admitted that during the three months of his rule some three thousand victims visited the national bathing-place, whilst other, and no doubt more veracious, accounts treble that number of those who received the National Baptism.

Soon these wholesale drownings had become an institution, a sort of national spectacle that Carrier and his committee felt themselves in duty bound to provide.

But at length a point was reached beyond which it seemed difficult to continue them. So expeditious was the measure, that soon the obvious material was exhausted. The prisons were empty. Yet habits, once contracted, are not easily relinquished. Carrier would be looking elsewhere for material, and there was no saying where he might look, or who would be safe. Soon the committee heard a rumour that the Representative intended to depose it and to appoint a new one, whereupon many of its members, who were conscious of lukewarmness, began to grow uneasy.

Uneasy, too, became the members of the People's Society. They had sent a deputation to Carrier with suggestions for the better conduct of the protracted campaign of La Vendee. This was a sore point with the Representative. He received the patriots with the foulest abuse, and had them flung downstairs by his secretaries.

Into this atmosphere of general mistrust and apprehension came the most ridiculous Deus ex machina that ever was in the person of the very young and very rash Marc Antoine Jullien. His father, the Deputy Jullien, was an intimate of Robespierre's, by whose influence Marc Antoine was appointed to the office of Agent of the Committee of Public Safety, and sent on a tour of inspection to report upon public feeling and the conduct of the Convention's Representatives.

Arriving in Nantes at the end of January of '94, one of Marc Antoine's first visits happened to be to the People's Society, which was still quivering with rage at the indignities offered by Carrier to its deputation.

Marc Antoine was shocked by what he heard, so shocked that instead of going to visit the Representative on the morrow, he spent the morning inditing a letter to Robespierre, in which he set forth in detail the abuses of which Carrier was guilty, and the deplorable state of misery in which he found the city of Nantes.

That night, as Marc Antoine was sinking into the peaceful slumber of the man with duty done, he was rudely aroused by an officer and a couple of men of the National Guard, who announced to him that he was under arrest, and bade him rise and dress.

Marc Antoine flounced out of bed in a temper, and flaunted his credentials. The officer remained unmoved. He was acting upon orders from the Citizen Representative.

Still in a temper, Marc Antoine hurriedly dressed himself. He would soon show this Representative that it is not safe to trifle with Agents of the Public Safety. The Citizen Representative should hear from him. The officer, still unimpressed, bundled him into a waiting carriage, and bore him away to the Maison Villetreux, on the island where Carrier had his residence.

Carrier had gone to bed. But he was awake, and he sat up promptly when the young muscadin from Paris was roughly thrust into his room by the soldiers. The mere sight of the Representative sufficed to evaporate Marc Antoine's anger, and with it his courage.

Carrier's pallor was of a grey-green from the rage that possessed him. His black eyes smouldered like those of an animal seen in the gloom, and his tumbled black hair, fluttering about his moist brow, increased the terrific aspect of his countenance. Marc Antoine shrank and was dumb.

"So, " said Carrier, regarding him steadily, terribly, "you are the thing that dares to denounce me to the Safety, that ventures to find fault with my work! " From under his pillow he drew Marc Antoine's letter to Robespierre. "Is this yours? "

At the sight of this violation of his correspondence with the Incorruptible, Marc Antoine's indignation awoke, and revived his courage.

"It is mine, " he answered. "By what right have you intercepted it? "

"By what right? " Carrier put a leg out of bed. "So you question my right, do you? You have so imposed yourself upon folk that you are given powers, and you come here to air them, by "

"You shall answer to the Citizen Robespierre for your conduct, " Marc Antoine threatened him.

"Aha! " Carrier revealed his teeth in a smile of ineffable wickedness. He slipped from the bed, and crouching slightly as if about to spring, he pointed a lean finger at his captive.

"You are of those with whom it is dangerous to deal publicly, and you presume upon that. But you can be dealt with privily, and you shall. I have you, and, by —, you shall not escape me, you —! "

Marc Antoine looked into the Representative's face, and saw there the wickedness of his intent. He stiffened. Nature had endowed him with wits, and he used them now.

"Citizen Carrier, " he said, "I understand. I am to be murdered to-night in the gloom and the silence. But you shall perish after me in daylight, and amid the execrations of the people. You may have intercepted my letters to my father and to Robespierre. But if I do not

199

leave Nantes, my father will come to ask an account of you, and you will end your life on the scaffold like the miserable assassin that you are. "

Of all that tirade, but one sentence had remained as if corroded into the mind of Carrier. "My letters to my father and to Robespierre, " the astute Marc Antoine had said. And Marc Antoine saw the Representative's mouth loosen, saw a glint of fear replace the ferocity in his dark eyes.

What Marc Antoine intended to suggest had instantly leapt to Carrier's mind - that there had been a second letter which his agents had missed. They should pay for that. But, meanwhile, if it were true, he dare not for his neck's sake go further in this matter. He may have suspected that it was not true. But he had no means of testing that suspicion. Marc Antoine, you see, was subtle.

"Your father? "growled the Representative. "Who is your father? "

"The Deputy Jullien. "

"What? " Carrier straightened himself, affecting an immense astonishment. "You are the son of the Deputy Julien? " He burst into a laugh. He came forward, holding out both his hands. He could be subtle, too, you see. "My friend, why did you not say so sooner? See in what a ghastly mistake you have let me flounder. I imagined you - of course, it was foolish of me - to be a proscribed rascal from Angers, of the same name. "

He had fallen upon Marc Antoine's neck, and was embracing him.

"Forgive me, my friend! " he besought him. "Come and dine with me to-morrow, and we will laugh over it together. "

But Marc Antoine had no mind to dine with Carrier, although he promised to do so readily enough. Back at his inn, scarce believing that he had got away alive, still sweating with terror at the very thought of his near escape, he packed his valise, and, by virtue of his commission, obtained post-horses at once.

On the morrow from Angers, safe beyond the reach of Carrier, he wrote again to Robespierre, and this time also to his father.

"In Nantes, " he wrote, "I found the old regime in its worst form. " He knew the jargon of Liberty, the tune that set the patriots a-dancing. "Carrier's insolent secretaries emulate the intolerable haughtiness of a ci-devant minister's lackeys. Carrier himself lives surrounded by luxury, pampered by women 'and parasites, keeping a harem and a court. He tramples justice in the mud. He has had all those who filled the prisons flung untried into the Loire. The city of Nantes, " he concluded, "needs saving. The Vendean revolt must be suppressed, and Carrier the slayer of Liberty recalled. "

The letter had its effect, and Carrier was recalled to Paris, but not in disgrace. Failing health was urged as the solicitous reason for his retirement from the arduous duties of governing Nantes.

In the Convention his return made little stir, and even when early in the following July he learnt that Bourbotte, his successor at Nantes, had ordered the arrest of Goullin, Bachelier, Grandmaison, and his other friends of the committee, on the score of the drownings and the appropriation of national property confiscated from emigres, he remained calm, satisfied that his own position was unassailable.

But the members of the Committee of Nantes were sent to Paris for trial, and their arrival there took place on that most memorable date in the annals of the Revolution, the 10th Thermidor (July 29, 1794, O. S.), the day on which Robespierre fell and the floodgates of vengeance upon the terrorists were flung open.

You have seen in the case of Marc Antoine Jullien how quick Carrier could be to take a cue. In a coach he followed the tumbril that bore Robespierre to execution, radiant of countenance and shouting with the loudest, "Death to the traitor! " On the morrow from the rostrum of the Convention, he passionately represented himself as a victim of the fallen tyrant, cleverly turning to his own credit the Marc Antoine affair, reminding the Convention how he had himself been denounced to Robespierre. He was greeted with applause in that atmosphere of Thermidorean reaction.

But Nemesis was stalking him relentlessly if silently.

Among a batch of prisoners whom a chain of curious chances had brought from Nantes to Paris was our old friend Leroy the cocassier, required now as a witness against the members of the committee.

Having acquainted the court with the grounds of his arrest, and the fact that for three years he had lain forgotten and without trial in the pestilential prison of Le Bouffay, Leroy passed on to a recital of his sufferings on that night of terror when he had gone down the Loire in the doomed lighter. He told his tale with an artlessness that rendered it the more moving and convincing. The audience crowding the chamber of justice shuddered with horror, and sobbed over the details of his torments, wept for joy over his miraculous preservation. At the close he was applauded on all sides, which bewildered him a little, for he had never known anything but abuse in all his chequered life.

And then, at the promptings of that spirit of reaction that was abroad in those days when France was awakening from the nightmare of terror, some one made there and then a collection on his behalf, and came to thrust into his hands a great bundle of assignats and bank bills, which to the humble cocassier represented almost a fortune. It was his turn to weep.

Then the crowd in the court which had heard his story shouted for the head of Carrier. The demand was taken up by the whole of Paris, and finally his associates of the Convention handed him over to the Revolutionary Tribunal.

He came before it on November 25th, and he could not find counsel to defend him. Six advocates named in succession by the President refused to plead the cause of so inhuman a monster. In a rage, at last Carrier announced that he would defend himself. He did.

He took the line that his business in Nantes had been chiefly concerned with provisioning the Army of the West; that he had had little to do with the policing of Nantes, which he left entirely to the Revolutionary Committee; and that he had no knowledge of the things said to have taken place. But Goullin, Bachelier, and the others were there to fling back the accusation in their endeavours to save their own necks at the expense of his.

He was sentenced on the very anniversary of that terrible night on which the men of the Marat Company broke into the prison of Le Bouffay, and he was accompanied in the tumbril by Grandmaison the pitiless, who was now filled with self-pity to such an extent that he wept bitterly.

The crowd, which had hooted and insulted him from the Conciergerie to the Place de Greve, fell suddenly silent as he mounted the scaffold, his step firm, but his shoulders bowed, and his eyes upon the ground.

Suddenly upon the silence, grotesquely, horribly merry, broke the sound of a clarinet playing the "Ca ira! "

Jerking himself erect, Carrier turned and flung the last of his terrible glances at the musician.

A moment later the knife fell with a thud, and a bleeding head rolled into the basket, the eyes still staring, but powerless now to inspire terror.

Upon the general silence broke an echo of the stroke.

"Vlan! " cried a voice. "And there's a fine end to a great drowner! "

It was Leroy the cocassier. The crowd took up the cry.

IX. THE NIGHT OF NUPTIALS

Charles the Bold and Sapphira Danvelt

When Philip the Good succumbed at Bruges of an apoplexy in the early part of the year 1467, the occasion was represented to the stout folk of Flanders as a favourable one to break the Burgundian yoke under which they laboured. It was so represented by the agents of that astute king, Louis XI, who ever preferred guile to the direct and costly exertion of force.

Charles, surnamed the Bold (le Temeraire), the new Duke of Burgundy, was of all the French King's enemies by far the most formidable and menacing just then; and the wily King, who knew better than to measure himself with a foe that was formidable, conceived a way to embarrass the Duke and cripple his resources at the very outset of his reign. To this end did he send his agents into the Duke's Flemish dominions, there to intrigue with the powerful and to stir up the spirit of sedition that never did more than slumber in the hearts of those turbulent burghers.

It was from the Belfry Tower of the populous, wealthy city of Ghent - then one of the most populous and wealthy cities of Europe - that the call to arms first rang out, summoning the city's forty thousand weavers to quit their looms and take up weapons - the sword, the pike, and that arm so peculiarly Flemish, known as the goedendag. >From Ghent the fierce flame of revolt spread rapidly to the valley of the Meuse, and the scarcely less important city of Liege, where the powerful guilds of armourers and leather workers proved as ready for battle as the weavers of Ghent.

They made a brave enough show until Charles the Bold came face to face with them at Saint-Trond, and smashed the mutinous burgher army into shards, leaving them in their slaughtered thousands upon the stricken field.

The Duke was very angry. He felt that the Flemings had sought to take a base advantage of him at a moment when it was supposed he would not be equal to protecting his interests, and he intended to brand it for all time upon their minds that it was not safe to take such liberties with their liege lord. Thus, when a dozen of the most important burghers of Liege came out to him very humbly in their shirts, with halters round their necks, to kneel in the dust at his feet and offer him the keys of the city, he spurned the offer with angry disdain.

"You shall be taught, " he told them, "how little I require your keys, and I hope that you will remember the lesson for your own good. "

On the morrow his pioneers began to smash a breach, twenty fathoms wide, in one of the walls of the city, rolling the rubble into the ditch to fill it up at the spot. When the operation was complete, Charles rode through the gap, as a conqueror, with vizor lowered and lance on thigh at the head of his Burgundians, into his city of Liege, whose fortifications he commanded should be permanently demolished.

That was the end of the Flemish rising of 1467 against Duke Charles the Bold of Burgundy. The weavers returned to their looms, the armourers to their forges, and the glove-makers and leather workers to their shears. Peace was restored; and to see that it was kept, Charles appointed military governors of his confidence where he deemed them necessary.

One of these was Claudius von Rhynsault, who had followed the Duke's fortunes for some years now, a born leader of men, a fellow of infinite address at arms and resource in battle, and of a bold, reckless courage that nothing could ever daunt. It was perhaps this last quality that rendered him so esteemed of Charles, himself named the Bold, whose view of courage was that it was a virtue so lofty that in the nature of its possessor there could, perforce, be nothing mean.

So now, to mark his esteem of this stalwart German, the Duke made him Governor of the province of Zeeland, and dispatched him thither to stamp out there any lingering sparks of revolt, and to rule it in his name as ducal lieutenant.

Thus, upon a fair May morning, came Claud of Ryhnsault and his hardy riders to the town of Middelburg, the capital of Zeeland, to take up his residence at the Gravenhof in the main square, and thence to dispense justice throughout that land of dykes in his master's princely name. This justice the German captain dispensed with merciless rigour, conceiving that to be the proper way to uproot rebellious tendencies. It was inevitable that he should follow such a course, impelled to it by a remorseless cruelty in his nature, of which the Duke his master had seen no hint, else he might have thought twice before making him Governor of Zeeland, for Charles - despite his rigour when treachery was to be punished - was a just and humane prince.

Now, amongst those arrested and flung into Middelburg gaol as a result of Rhynsault's ruthless perquisitions and inquisitions was a wealthy young burgher named Philip Danvelt. His arrest was occasioned by a letter signed "Philip Danvelt" found in the house of a marked rebel who had been first tortured and then hanged. The letter, of a date immediately preceding the late rising, promised assistance in the shape of arms and money.

Brought before Rhynsault for examination, in a cheerless hall of the Gravenhof, Danvelt's defence was a denial upon oath that he had ever taken or offered to take any part in the rebellion. Told of the letter found, and of the date it bore, he laughed. That letter made everything very simple and clear. At the date it bore he had been away at Flushing marrying a wife, whom he had since brought thence to Middelburg. It was ludicrous, he urged, to suppose that in such a season - of all seasons in a man's life - he should have been concerned with rebellion or correspondence with rebels, and, urging this, he laughed again.

Now, the German captain did not like burghers who laughed in his presence. It argued a lack of proper awe for the dignity of his office and the importance of his person. From his high seat at the Judgment-board, flanked by clerks and hedged about by men-at-arms, he scowled upon the flaxen-haired, fresh-complexioned young burgher who bore himself so very easily. He was a big, handsome man, this Rhynsault, of perhaps some thirty years of age. His thick hair was of a reddish brown, and his beardless face was cast in bold lines and tanned by exposure to the colour of mahogany, save where the pale line of a scar crossed his left cheek.

"Yet, I tell you, the letter bears your signature, " he grumbled sourly.

"My name, perhaps, " smiled the amiable Danvelt, "but assuredly not my signature. "

"Herrgott! " swore the German captain. "Is this a riddle? What is the difference? "

Feeling himself secure, that very foolish burgher ventured to be mildly insolent.

"It is a riddle that the meanest of your clerks there can read for you, " said he.

The Governor's blue eyes gleamed like steel as they, fastened upon Danvelt, his heavy jaw seemed to thrust itself forward, and a dull flush crept into his cheeks. Then he swore.

"Beim blute Gottes! " quoth he, "do you whet your trader's wit upon me, scum? "

And to the waiting men-at-arms:

"Take him back to his dungeon, " he commanded, "that in its quiet he may study a proper carriage before he is next brought before us. "

Danvelt was haled away to gaol again, to repent him of his pertness and to reflect that, under the governorship of Claudius von Rhynsault, it was not only the guilty who had need to go warily.

The Governor sat back in his chair with a grunt. His secretary, on his immediate right, leaned towards him.

"It were easy to test the truth of the man's assertion, " said he. "Let his servants and his wife attend and be questioned as to when he was in Flushing and when married. "

"Aye, " growled von Rhynsault. "Let it be done. I don't doubt we shall discover that the dog was lying. "

But no such discovery was made when, on the morrow, Danvelt's household and his wife stood before the Governor to answer his questions. Their replies most fully bore out the tale Danvelt had told, and appeared in other ways to place it beyond all doubt that he had taken no part, in deed or even in thought, in the rebellion against the Duke of Burgundy. His wife protested it solemnly and piteously.

"To this I can swear, my lord, " she concluded. "I am sure no evidence can be brought against him, who was ever loyal and ever concerned with his affairs and with me at the time in question. My lord" - she held out her hands towards the grim German, and her

207

lovely eyes gleamed with unshed tears of supplication - "I implore you to believe me, and in default of witnesses against him to restore my husband to me. "

Rhynsault's blue eyes kindled now as they considered her, and his full red lips slowly parted in the faintest and most inscrutable of smiles. She was very fair to look upon - of middle height and most exquisite shape. Her gown, of palest saffron, edged with fur, high-waisted according to the mode, and fitted closely to the gently swelling bust, was cut low to display the white perfection of her neck. Her softly rounded face looked absurdly childlike under the tall-crowned hennin, from which a wispy veil floated behind her as she moved.

In silence, then, for a spell, the German mercenary pondered her with those slowly kindling eyes, that slowly spreading, indefinite smile. Then he stirred, and to his secretary he muttered shortly:

"The woman lies. In private I may snare the truth from her. "

He rose - a tall, massively imposing figure in a low-girdled tunic of deep purple velvet, open at the breast, and gold-laced across a white silken undervest.

"There is some evidence, " he informed her gruffly. "Come with me, and you shall see it for yourself. "

He led the way from that cheerless hall by a dark corridor to a small snug room, richly hung and carpeted, where a servant waited. He dismissed the fellow, and in the same breath bade her enter, watching her the while from under lowered brows. One of her women had followed; but admittance was denied her. Danvelt's wife must enter his room alone.

Whilst she waited there, with scared eyes and fluttering bosom, he went to take from an oaken coffer the letter signed "Philip Danvelt. " He folded the sheet so that the name only was to be read, and came to thrust it under her eyes.

"What name is that? " he asked her gruffly.

Her answer was very prompt.

is my husband's, but not the writing - it is another hand; some her Philip Danvelt; there will be others in Zeeland. "

He laughed softly, looking at her ever with that odd intentness, and under his gaze she shrank and cowered in terror; it spoke to her of some nameless evil; the tepid air of the luxurious room was stifling her.

"If I believed you, your husband would be delivered from his prison - from all danger; and he stands, I swear to you, in mortal peril. "

"Ah, but you must believe me. There are others who can bear witness. "

"I care naught for others, " he broke in, with harsh and arrogant contempt. Then he softened his voice to a lover's key. "But I might accept your word that this is not your husband's hand, even though I did not believe you. "

She did not understand, and so she could only stare at him with those round, brown eyes of hers dilating, her lovely cheeks blanching with horrid fear.

"Why, see, " he said at length, with an easy, gruff good-humour, "I place the life of Philip Danvelt in those fair hands to do with as you please. Surely, sweeting, you will not be so unkind as to destroy it. "

And as he spoke his face bent nearer to her own, his flaming eyes devoured her, and his arm slipped softly, snake-like round her to draw her to him. But before it had closed its grip she had started away, springing back in horror, an outcry already on her pale lips.

"One word, " he admonished her sharply, "and it speaks your husband's doom! "

"Oh, let me go, let me go! " she cried in anguish.

"And leave your husband in the hangman's hands? " he asked.

"Let me go! Let me go! " was all that she could answer him, expressing the only thought of which in that dread moment her mind was capable.

That and the loathing on her face wounded his vanity for this beast was vain. His manner changed, and the abysmal brute in him was revealed in the anger he displayed. With foul imprecations he drove her out.

Next day a messenger from the Governor waited upon her at her house with a brief note to inform her that her husband would be hanged upon the morrow. Incredulity was succeeded by a numb, stony, dry-eyed grief, in which she sat alone for hours - a woman entranced. At last, towards dusk, she summoned a couple of her grooms to attend and light her, and made her way, ever in that odd somnambulistic state, to the gaol of Middelburg. She announced herself to the head gaoler as the wife of Philip Danvelt, lying under sentence of death, and that she was come to take her last leave of him. It was not a thing to be denied, nor had the gaoler any orders to deny it.

So she was ushered into the dank cell where Philip waited for his doom, and by the yellow wheel of light of the lantern that hung from the shallow vaulted ceiling she beheld the ghastly change that the news of impending death had wrought in him. No longer was he the self-assured young burgher who, conscious of his innocence and worldly importance, had used a certain careless insolence with the Governor of Zeeland. Here she beheld a man of livid and distorted face, wild-eyed, his hair and garments in disarray, suggesting the physical convulsions to which he had yielded in his despair and rage.

"Sapphira! " he cried at sight of her. A sigh of anguish and he flung himself, shuddering and sobbing, upon her breast. She put her arms about him, soothed him gently, and drew him back to the wooden chair from which he had leapt to greet her.

He took his head in his hands and poured out the fierce anguish of his soul. To die innocent as he was, to be the victim of an arbitrary, unjust power! And to perish at his age!

Hearing him rave, she shivered out of an agony of compassion and also of some terror for herself. She would that he found it less hard to die. And thinking this she thought further, and uttered some of her thought aloud.

"I could have saved you, my poor Philip. "

He started up, and showed her again that livid, di

"What do you mean? " he asked hoarsely. "You
me, do you say? Then - then why - "

"Ah, but the price, my dear, " she sobbed.

"Price? " quoth he in sudden, fierce contempt. "W
great to pay for life? Does this Rhynsault want all
yield it to him yield it so that I may live - "

"Should I have hesitated had it been but that? " she in

And then she told him, whilst he sat there hunched and snu

"The dog! The foul German dog! " he muttered through clenched
teeth.

"So that you see, my dear, " she pursued brokenly, "it was too great
a price. Yourself, you could not have condoned it, or done aught else
but loathe me afterwards. "

But he was not as stout-mettled as she deemed him, or else the all-
consuming thirst of life, youth's stark horror of death, made him a
temporizing craven in that hour.

"Who knows? " he answered. "Certes, I do not. But a thing so done,
a thing in which the will and mind have no part, resolves itself
perhaps into a sacrifice - "

He broke off there, perhaps from very shame. After all he was a man,
and there are limits to what manhood will permit of one.

But those words of his sank deeply into her soul. They rang again
and again in her ears as she took her anguished way home after the
agony of their farewells, and in the end they drove her out again that
very night to seek the Governor of Zeeland.

Rhynsault was at supper when she came, and without quitting the
table bade them usher her into his presence. He found her very
white, but singularly calm and purposeful in her bearing.

"Well, mistress? "

"May I speak to you alone?"

Her voice was as steady as her glance.

He waved away the attendants, drank a deep draught from the cup at his elbow, wiped his mouth with the back of his hand, and sat back in his tall chair to hear her.

"Yesterday, " she said, "you made me a certain proposal. "

He looked up at first in surprise, then with a faint smile on his wide, red mouth. His glance had read her meaning clearly.

"Look you, mistress, here I am lord of life and death. Yet in the case of your husband I yield up that power to you. Say but the word and I sign the order for his gaol delivery at dawn. "

"I have come to say that word, " she informed him.

A moment he looked up at her, his smile broadening, a flush mounting to his cheek-bones. Then he rose and sent his chair crashing behind him to the ground.

"Herrgott! " he grunted; and he gathered her slim, trembling body to his massive gold-laced breast.

Soon after sunrise on the morrow she was beating at the gates of Middelburg gaol, a paper clutched convulsively in her left hand.

She was admitted, and to the head gaoler she showed the paper that she carried.

"An order from the Governor of Zeeland for the gaol delivery of Philip Danvelt! " she announced almost hysterically.

The gaoler scanned the paper, then her face. His lips tightened.

"Come this way, " he said; and led her down a gloomy corridor to the cell where yesterday she had seen her husband.

He threw wide the door, and Sapphira sprang in.

"Philip! " she cried, and checked as suddenly.

He lay supine and still upon the miserable pallet, his hands folded upon his breast, his face waxen, his eyes staring glassily through half-closed lids.

She sped to his side in a sudden chill of terror. She fell on her knees and touched him.

"Dead! " she screamed, and, kneeling, span round questioning to face the gaoler in the doorway. "Dead! "

"He was hanged at daybreak, mistress, " said the gaoler gently.

She rocked a moment, moaning, then fell suddenly forward across her husband's body in a swoon.

That evening she was again at the Gravenhof to see Rhynsault, and again she was admitted - a haggard faced woman now, in whom there was no trace of beauty left. She came to stand before the Governor, considered him in silence a moment with a loathing unutterable in her glance, then launched into fierce recriminations of his broken faith.

He heard her out, then shrugged and smiled indulgently.

"I performed no less than I promised, " said he. "I pledged my word to Danvelt's gaol delivery, and was not my gaol delivery effective? You could hardly suppose that I should allow it to be of such a fashion as to interfere with our future happy meetings. "

Before his leering glance she fled in terror, followed by the sound of his bestial laugh.

For a week thereafter she kept her house and brooded. Then one day she sallied forth all dressed in deepest mourning and attended by a train of servants, and, embarking upon a flat-bottomed barge, was borne up the river Scheldt towards Antwerp. Bruges was her ultimate destination, of which she left no word behind her, and took the longest way round to reach it. From Antwerp her barge voyaged on to Ghent, and thence by canal, drawn by four stout Flemish horses, at last to the magnificent city where the Dukes of Burgundy kept their Court.

Under the June sunshine the opulent city of Bruges hummed with activity like the great human hive it was. For Bruges at this date was the market of the world, the very centre of the world's commerce, the cosmopolis of the age. Within its walls were established the agencies of a score of foreign great trading companies, and the ambassadors of no less a number of foreign Powers. Here on a day you might hear every language of civilization spoken in the broad thoroughfares under the shadow of such imposing buildings as you would not have found together in another city of Europe. To the harbour came the richly laden argosies from Venice and Genoa, from Germany and the Baltic, from Constantinople and from England, and in her thronged markets Lombard and Venetian, Levantine, Teuton, and Saxon stood jostling one another to buy and sell.

It was past noon, and the great belfry above the Gothic Cloth Hall in the Grande Place was casting a lengthening shadow athwart the crowded square. Above the Babel of voices sounded on a sudden the note of a horn, and there was a cry of "The Duke! The Duke! " followed by a general scuttle of the multitude to leave a clear way down the middle of the great square.

A gorgeous cavalcade some twoscore strong came into sight, advancing at an amble, a ducal hunting party returning to the palace. A hush fell upon the burgher crowd as it pressed back respectfully to gaze; and to the din of human voices succeeded now the clatter of hoofs upon the kidney-stones of the square, the jangle of hawkbells, the baying of hounds, and the occasional note of the horn that had first brought warning of the Duke's approach.

It was a splendid iridescent company, flaunting in its apparel every colour of the prism. There were great lords in silks and velvets of every hue, their legs encased in the finest skins of Spain; there were great ladies, in tall, pointed hennins or bicorne headdresses and floating veils, with embroidered gowns that swept down below the bellies of their richly harnessed palfreys. And along the flanks of this cavalcade ran grooms and huntsmen in green and leather, their jagged liripipes flung about their necks, leading the leashed hounds.

The burghers craned their necks, and Levantine merchant argued with Lombard trader upon an estimate of the wealth paraded thus before them. And then at last came the young Duke himself, in black, as if to detach himself from the surrounding splendour. He was of middle stature, of a strong and supple build, with a lean, swarthy face and lively eyes. Beside him, on a white horse, rode a dazzling youth dressed from head to foot in flame-coloured silk, a peaked bonnet of black velvet set upon his lovely golden head, a hooded falcon perched upon his left wrist, a tiny lute slung behind him by a black ribbon. He laughed as he rode, looking the very incarnation of youth and gaiety.

The cavalcade passed slowly towards the Prinssenhof, the ducal residence. It had all but crossed the square when suddenly a voice - a woman's voice, high and tense - rang out.

"Justice, my Lord Duke of Burgundy! Justice, Lord Duke, for a woman's wrongs! "

It startled the courtly riders, and for a moment chilled their gaiety. The scarlet youth at the Duke's side swung round in his saddle to obtain a view of her who called so piteously, and he beheld Sapphira Danvelt.

She was all in black, and black was the veil that hung from her steeple head-dress, throwing into greater relief her pallid loveliness which the youth's glance was quick to appraise. He saw, too, from her air and from the grooms attending her, that she was a woman of some quality, and the tragic appeal of her smote home in his gay, poetic soul. He put forth a hand and clutched the Duke's arm, and, as if yielding to this, the Duke reined up.

"What is it that you seek? " Charles asked her not unkindly, his lively dark eyes playing over her.

"Justice! " was all she answered him very piteously, and yet with a certain fierceness of insistence.

"None asks it of me in vain, I hope, " he answered gravely. "But I do not dispense it from the saddle in the public street. Follow us. "

And he rode on.

She followed to the Prinssenhof with her grooms and her woman Catherine. There she was made to wait in a great hall, thronged with grooms and men-at-arms and huntsmen, who were draining the measure sent them by the Duke. She stood apart, wrapped in her tragic sorrow, and none molested her. At last a chamberlain came to summon her to the Duke's presence.

In a spacious, sparsely furnished room she found the Duke awaiting her, wearing now a gown of black and gold that was trimmed with rich fur. He sat in a tall chair of oak and leather, and leaning on the back of it lounged gracefully the lovely scarlet youth who had ridden at his side.

Standing before him, with drooping eyes and folded hands, she told her shameful story. Darker and darker grew his brow as she proceeded with it. But it was the gloom of doubt rather than of anger.

"Rhynsault? " he cried when she had done. "Rhynsault did this? "

There was incredulity in his voice and nothing else.

The youth behind him laughed softly, and shifted his attitude.

"You are surprised. Yet what else was to be looked for in that Teuton swine? Me he never could deceive, for all his - "

"Be silent, Arnault, " said the Duke sharply. And to the woman: "It is a grave, grave charge, " he said, "against a man I trusted and have esteemed, else I should not have placed him where he is. What proof have you? "

She proffered him a strip of parchment - the signed order for the gaol delivery of Philip Danvelt.

"The gaoler of Middelburg will tell Your Grace that he was hanged already when I presented this. My woman Catherine, whom I have with me, can testify to part. And there are some other servants who can bear witness to my husband's innocence. Captain von Rhynsault had ceased to doubt it. "

He studied the parchment, and fell very grave and thoughtful.

"Where are you lodged? " he asked.

She told him.

"Wait there until I send for you again, " he bade her. "Leave this order with me, and depend upon it, justice shall be done. "

That evening, a messenger rode out to Middelburg to summon von Rhynsault to Bruges, and the arrogant German came promptly and confidently, knowing nothing of the reason, but conceiving naturally that fresh honours were to be conferred upon him by a master who loved stout-hearted servants. And that Rhynsault was stout-hearted he showed most of all when the Duke taxed him without warning with the villainy he had wrought.

If he was surprised, he was not startled. What was the life of a Flemish burgher more or less? What the honour of a Flemish wife? These were not considerations to daunt a soldier, a valiant man of war. And because such was his dull mood - for he was dull, this Rhynsault, as dull as he was brutish - he considered his sin too venial to be denied. And the Duke, who could be crafty, perceiving that mood of his, and simulating almost an approval of it, drew the German captain into self-betrayal.

"And so this Philip Danvelt may have been innocent? "

"He must have been, for we have since taken the guilty man of the same name, " said the German easily. "It was unfortunate, but - "

"Unfortunate! " The Duke's manner changed from silk to steel. He heaved himself out of his chair, and his dark eyes flamed. "Unfortunate! Is that all, you dog? "

"I conceived him guilty when I ordered him to be hanged, " spluttered the captain, greatly taken aback.

"Then, why this? Answer me - why this? "

And under his nose the Duke thrust the order of gaol delivery Rhynsault had signed.

The captain blenched, and fear entered his glance. The thing was becoming serious, it seemed.

"Is this the sort of justice you were sent to Middelburg to administer in my name? Is this how you dishonour me? If you conceived him guilty, why did you sign this and upon what terms? Bah, I know the terms. And having made such foul terms, why did you not keep your part of the bargain, evil as it was? "

Rhynsault had nothing to say. He was afraid, and he was angry too. Here was a most unreasonable bother all about nothing, it seemed to him.

"I - I sought to compromise between justice and - and - "

"And your own vile ends, " the Duke concluded for him. "By Heaven, you German dog, I think I'll have you shortened by a head! "

"My lord! " It was a cry of protest.

"There is the woman you have so foully wronged, and so foully swindled, " said the Duke, watching him. "What reparation will you make to her? What reparation can you make? I can toss your filthy head into her lap. But will that repair the wrong? "

The captain suddenly saw light, and quite a pleasant light it was, for he had found Sapphira most delectable.

"Why, " he said slowly, and with all a fool's audacity, "having made her a widow, I can make her a wife again. I never thought to wive, myself. But if Your Grace thinks such reparation adequate, I will afford it her. "

The Duke checked in the very act of replying. Again the expression of his countenance changed. He strode away, his head bowed in thought; then slowly he returned.

"Be it so, " he said. "It is not much, but it is all that you can do, and after a fashion it will mend the honour you have torn. See that you wed her within the week. Should she not consent, it will be the worse for you. "

She would not have consented - she would have preferred death, indeed - but for the insistence that the Duke used in private with her. And so, half convinced that it would in some sort repair her honour, the poor woman suffered herself to be led, more dead than living, to the altar in the Duke's private chapel, and there, scarcely knowing what she did, she became the wife of Captain Claudius von

Rhynsault, the man she had most cause to loathe and hate in all the world.

Rhynsault had ordered a great banquet to celebrate his nuptials, for on the whole he was well satisfied with the issue of this affair. But as he left the altar, his half-swooning bride upon his arm, the Duke in person tapped his shoulder.

"All is not yet done, " he said. "You are to come with me. "

The bridal pair were conducted to the great hall of the Prinssenhof, where there was a great gathering of the Court - to do honour to his nuptials, thought the German captain. At the broad table sat two clerkly fellows with quills and parchments, and by this table the Duke took his stand, Arnault beside him - in peacock-blue to-day - and called for silence.

"Captain von Rhynsault, " he said gravely and quietly, "what you have done is well done; but it does not suffice. In the circumstances of this marriage, and after the revelation we have had of your ways of thought and of honour, it is necessary to make provision against the future. It shall not be yours, save at grave cost, to repudiate the wife you have now taken. "

"There is no such intent - " began Rhynsault, who misliked this homily.

The Duke waved him into silence.

"You are interrupting me, " he said sharply. "You are a wealthy man, Rhynsault, thanks to the favours I have heaped upon you ever since the day when I picked you from your German kennel to set you where you stand. Here you will find a deed prepared. It is in the form of a will, whereby you bequeath everything of which you are to-day possessed - and it is all set down - to your wife on your death, or on the day on which you put her from you. Your signature is required to that. "

The captain hesitated a moment. This deed would fetter all his future. The Duke was unreasonable. But under the steady, compelling eyes of Charles he moved forward to the table, and accepted the quill the clerk was proffering. There was no alternative, he realized. He was trapped. Well, well! He must make the best of it.

He stooped from his great height, and signed in his great sprawling, clumsy, soldier's hand.

The clerk dusted the document with pounce, and handed it to the Duke. Charles cast an eye upon the signature, then taking the quill himself, signed under it, then bore the document to the half-swooning bride.

"Keep this secure, " he bade her. "It is your marriage-gift from me. "

Rhynsault's eyes gleamed. If his wife were to keep the deed, the thing was none so desperate after all. But the next moment he had other things to think of.

"Give me your sword, " the Duke requested.

Wondering, the German unsheathed the weapon, and proffered the hilt to his master. Charles took it, and a stern smile played about his beardless mouth. He grasped it, hilt in one hand and point in the other. Suddenly he bent his right knee, and, bearing sharply downward with the flat of the weapon upon his thigh, snapped in into two.

"So much for that dishonourable blade, " he said, and cast the pieces from him. Then he flung out an arm to point to Rhynsault. "Take him out, " he commanded; "let him have a priest, and half an hour in which to make his soul, then set his head on a spear above the Cloth Hall, that men may know the justice of Charles of Burgundy. "

With the roar of a 'goaded bull the German attempted to fling forward. But men-at-arms, in steel and leather, who had come up quietly behind him, seized him now. Impotent in their coiling arms, he was borne away to his doom, that thereby he might complete the reparation of his hideous offence, and deliver Sapphira from the bondage of a wedlock which Charles of Burgundy had never intended her to endure.

X. THE NIGHT OF STRANGLERS

Govanna of Naples and Andreas of Hungary

Charles, Duke of Durazzo, was one of your super chess-players, handling kings and queens, knights and prelates of flesh and blood in the game that he played with Destiny upon the dark board of Neapolitan politics. And he had no illusions on the score of the forfeit that would be claimed by his grim opponent in the event of his own defeat. He knew that his head was the stake he set upon the board, and he knew, too, that defeat must inevitably follow upon a single false move. Yet he played boldly and craftily, as you shall judge.

He made his first move in March of 1343, some three months after the death of Robert of Anjou, King of Jerusalem and Sicily, as ran the title of the ruler of Naples. He found his opportunity amid the appalling anarchy into which the kingdom was then plunged as a result of a wrong and an ill judged attempt to right it.

Good King Robert the Wise had wrested the crown of Naples from his elder brother, the King of Hungary, and had ruled as a usurper. Perhaps to quiet his conscience, perhaps to ensure against future strife between his own and his brother's descendants, he had attempted to right the wrong by a marriage between his brother's grandson Andreas and his own granddaughter Giovanna, a marriage which had taken place ten years before, when Andreas was but seven years of age and Giovanna five.

The aim had been thus to weld into one the two branches of the House of Anjou. Instead, the rivalry was to be rendered more acute than ever, and King Robert's fear of some such result contributed to it not a little. On his deathbed he summoned the Princes of the Blood - the members of the Houses of Durazzo and Taranto - and the chief nobles of the kingdom, demanding of them an oath of allegiance to Giovanna, and himself appointing a Council of Regency to govern the kingdom during her minority.

The consequence was that, against all that had been intended when the marriage was contracted, Giovanna was now proclaimed queen in her own right, and the government taken over in her name by the appointed Council. Instantly the Court of Naples was divided into two camps, the party of the Queen, including the Neapolitan nobility, and the party of Andreas of Hungary, consisting of the Hungarian nobles forming his train and a few malcontent Neapolitan barons, and guided by the sinister figure of Andreas's preceptor, Friar Robert.

This arrogant friar, of whom Petrarch has left us a vivid portrait, a red-faced, red-bearded man, with a fringe of red hair about his tonsure, short and squat of figure, dirty in his dress and habits, yet imbued with the pride of Lucifer despite his rags, thrust himself violently into the Council of Regency, demanding a voice in the name of his pupil Andreas. And the Council feared him, not only on the score of his over-bearing personality, but also because he was supported by the populace, which had accepted his general filthiness as the outward sign of holiness. His irruption occasioned so much trouble and confusion that in the end the Pope intervened, in his quality as Lord Paramount - Naples being a fief of Holy Church - and appointed a legate to rule the kingdom during Giovanna's minority.

The Hungarians, with Andreas's brother, King Ludwig of Hungary, at their head, now appealed to the Papal Court of Avignon for a Bull commanding the joint coronation of Andreas and Giovanna, which would be tantamount to placing the government in the hands of Andreas. The Neapolitans, headed by the Princes of the Blood - who, standing next in succession, had also their own interests to consider clamoured that Giovanna alone should be crowned.

In this pass were the affairs of the kingdom when Charles of Durazzo, who had stood watchful and aloof, carefully weighing the chances, resolved at last to play that dangerous game of his. He began by the secret abduction of Maria of Anjou, his own cousin and Giovanna's sister, a child of fourteen. He kept her concealed for a month in his palace, what time he obtained from the Pope, through the good offices of his uncle the Cardinal of Perigord, a dispensation to overcome the barrier of consanguinity. That dispensation obtained, Charles married the girl publicly under the eyes of all Naples, and by the marriage - to which the bride seemed nowise unwilling - became, by virtue of his wife, next heir to the crown of Naples.

That was his opening move. His next was to write to his obliging uncle the Cardinal of Perigord, whose influence at Avignon was very considerable, urging him to prevail upon Pope Clement VI not to sign the Bull in favour of Andreas and the joint coronation.

Now, the high-handed action of Charles in marrying Maria of Anjou had very naturally disposed Giovanna against him; further, it had disposed against him those Princes of the Blood who were next in the succession, and upon whom he had stolen a march by this strengthening of his own claims. It is inevitable to assume that he had counted precisely upon this to afford him the pretext that he sought - he, a Neapolitan prince - to ally himself with the Hungarian intruder.

Under any other circumstances his advances must have been viewed with suspicion by Andreas, and still more by the crafty Friar Robert. But, under the circumstances which his guile had created, he was received with open arms by the Hungarian party, and his defection from the Court of Giovanna was counted a victory by the supporters of Andreas. He protested his good-will towards Andreas, and proclaimed his hatred of Giovanna's partisans, who poisoned her mind against her husband. He hunted and drank with Andreas - whose life seems to have been largely made up of hunting and drinking - and pandered generally to the rather gross tastes of this foreigner, whom in his heart he despised for a barbarian.

From being a boon companion, Charles very soon became a counsellor to the young Prince, and the poisonous advice that he gave seemed shrewd and good, even to Friar Robert.

"Meet hostility with hostility, ride ruthlessly upon your own way, showing yourself confident of the decision in your favour that the Pope must ultimately give. For bear ever in your mind that you are King of Naples, not by virtue of your marriage with Giovanna, but in your own right, Giovanna being but the offspring of the usurping branch. "

The pale bovine eyes of Andreas would kindle into something like intelligence, and a flush would warm his stolid countenance. He was a fair-haired young giant, white-skinned and well-featured, but dull, looking, with cold, hard eyes suggesting the barbarian that he was considered by the cultured Neapolitans, and that he certainly looked by contrast with them. Friar Robert supporting the Duke of Durazzo's advice, Andreas did not hesitate to act upon it; of his own authority he delivered prisoners from gaol, showered honours upon his Hungarian followers and upon such Neapolitan barons as Count Altamura, who was ill-viewed at Court, and generally set the Queen at defiance. The inevitable result, upon which again the subtle Charles had counted, was to exasperate a group of her most prominent nobles into plotting the ruin of Andreas.

It was a good beginning, and unfortunately Giovanna's own behaviour afforded Charles the means of further speeding up his game.

The young Queen was under the governance of Filippa the Catanese, an evil woman, greedy of power. This Filippa, once a washerwoman, had in her youth been chosen for her splendid health to be the foster-mother of Giovanna's father. Beloved of her foster-child, she had become perpetually installed at Court, married to a wealthy Moor named Cabane, who was raised to the dignity of Grand Seneschal of the kingdom, whereby the sometime washerwoman found herself elevated to the rank of one of the first ladies of Naples. She must have known how to adapt herself to her new circumstances, otherwise she would hardly have been appointed, as she was upon the death of her foster-son, governess to his infant daughters. Later, to ensure her hold upon the young Queen, and being utterly unscrupulous in her greed of power, she had herself contrived that her son, Robert of Cabane, became Giovanna's lover.

One of Giovanna's first acts upon her grandfather's death had been to create this Robert Count of Evoli, and this notwithstanding that in the mean time he had been succeeded in her favour by the handsome young Bertrand d'Artois. This was the group - the Catanese, her son, and Bertrand - that, with the Princes of the Blood, governed the Queen's party.

With what eyes Andreas may have looked upon all this we have no means of determining. Possibly, engrossed as he was with his hawks and his hounds, he may have been stupidly blind to his own dishonour, at least as far as Bertrand was concerned. Another than Charles might have chosen the crude course of opening his eyes to it. But Charles was too far-seeing. Precipitancy was not one of his faults. His next move must be dictated by the decision of Avignon regarding the coronation.

This decision came in July of 1345, and it fell like a thunderbolt upon the Court. The Pope had pronounced in favour of Andreas by granting the Bull for the joint coronation of Andreas and Giovanna.

This was check to Charles. His uncle the Cardinal of Perigord had done his utmost to oppose the measure, but he had been overborne in the end by Ludwig of Hungary, who had settled the matter by the powerful argument that he was himself the rightful heir to the crown of Naples, and that he relinquished his claim in favour of his younger brother. He had backed the argument by the payment to the Pope of the enormous sum, for those days, of one hundred thousand gold crowns, and the issue, obscure hitherto, had immediately become clear to the Papal Court.

It was check to Charles, as I have said. But Charles braced himself, and considered the counter-move that should give him the advantage. He went to congratulate Andreas, and found him swollen with pride and arrogance in his triumph.

"Be welcome, Charles, " he hailed Durazzo. "I am not the man to forget those who have stood my friends whilst my power was undecided. "

"For your own sake, " said the smooth Charles, as he stepped back from that brotherly embrace, "I trust you'll not forget those who have been your enemies, and who, being desperate now, may take desperate means to avert your coronation. "

The pale eyes of the Hungarian glittered.

"Of whom do you speak? "

Charles smoothed his black beard thoughtfully, his dark eyes narrowed and pensive. There must be a victim, to strike fear into Giovanna's friends and stir them to Charles's purposes.

"Why, first and foremost, I should place Giovanna's counsellor Isernia, that man of law whose evil counsels have hurt your rights as king. Next come - "

But here Charles craftily paused and looked away, a man at fault.

"Next? " cried Andreas. "Who next? Speak out! " The Duke shrugged.

"By the Passion, there is no lack of others. You have enemies to spare among the Queen's friends. "

Andreas paled under his faint tan. He flung back his crimson robe as if he felt the heat, and stood forth, lithe as a wrestler, in his close-fitting cote-hardie and hose of violet silk.

"No need, indeed, to name them, " he said fiercely.

"None, " Charles agreed. "But the most dangerous is Isernia. Whilst he lives you walk amid swords. His death may spread a panic that will paralyze the others. "

He would say no more, knowing that he had said enough to send Andreas, scowling and sinister, to sow terror in hearts that guilt must render uneasy now, amongst which hearts be sure that he counted Giovanna's own.

Andreas took counsel with Friar Robert. Touching Isernia, there was evidence and to spare that he was dangerous, and so Isernia fell on the morrow to an assassin's sword as he was in the very act of leaving the Castel Nuovo, and it was Charles himself who bore word of it to the Court, and so plunged it into consternation.

They walked in the cool of evening in the pleasant garden of the Castel Nuovo, when Charles came upon them and touched the stalwart shoulder of Bertrand d'Artois. Bertrand the favourite eyed him askance, mistrusting and disliking him for his association with Andreas.

"The Hungarian boar, " said Charles, "is sharpening his tusks now that his authority is assured by the Holy Father. "

"Who cares? " sneered Bertrand.

"Should you care if I added that already he has blooded them? "

Bertrand changed countenance. The Duke explained himself.

226

"He has made a beginning upon Giacomo d' Isernia. Ten minutes ago he was stabbed to death within a stone's throw of the castle. " So Charles unburdened himself of his news. "A beginning, no more. "

"My God! " said Bertrand. "D' Isernia! Heaven rest him. " And devoutly he crossed himself.

"Heaven will rest some more of you if you suffer Andreas of Hungary to be its instrument, " said Charles, his lips grimly twisted.

"Do you threaten? "

"Nay, man; be not so hot and foolish. I warn. I know his mood. I know what he intends. "

"You ever had his confidence, " said Bertrand, sneering.

"Until this hour I had. But there's an end to that. I am a Prince of Naples, and I'll not bend the knee to a barbarian. He was well enough to hunt with and drink with, so long as he was Duke of Calabria with no prospect of being more. But that he should become my King, and that our lady Giovanna should be no more than a queen consort - " He made a gesture of ineffable disgust.

Bertrand's eyes kindled. He gripped the other's arm, and drew him along under a trellis of vines that formed a green cloister about the walls.

"Why, here is great news for our Queen, " he cried. "It will rejoice her, my lord, to know you are loyal to her. "

"That is no matter, " he replied. "What matters is that you should be warned - you, yourself in particular, and Evoli. No doubt there will be others, too. But the Hungarian's confidences went no further. "

Bertrand had come to a standstill. He stared at Charles, and slowly the colour left his face.

"Me? " he said, a finger on his heart.

"Aye, you. You will be the next. But not until the crown is firmly on his brow. Then he will settle his score with the nobles of Naples who have withstood him. Listen, " and Charles's voice sank as if under the awful burden of his news; "a black banner of vengeance is to precede him to his coronation. And your name stands at the head of the list of the proscribed. Does it surprise you? After all, he is a husband, and he has some knowledge of what lies between the Queen and you - "

"Stop! "

"Pish! " Charles shrugged. "What need for silence upon what all Naples knows? When have you and the Queen ever used discretion? In your place I should not need a warning. I should know what to expect from a husband become king. "

"The Queen must be told. "

"Indeed, I think so, too. It will come best from you. Go tell her, so that measures may be taken. But go secretly and warily. You are safe until he wears the crown. And above all - whatever you may decide - do nothing here in Naples. "

And on that he turned to depart, whilst Bertrand sped to Giovanna. On the threshold of the garden Charles paused and looked back. His eyes sought and found the Queen, a tall, lissome girl of seventeen, in a close-fitting, revealing gown of purple silk, the high, white gorget outlining an oval face of a surpassing loveliness, crowned by a wealth of copper-coloured hair. She was standing in a stricken attitude, looking up into the face of her lover, who was delivering himself of his news.

Charles departed satisfied.

Three days later a man of the Queen's household, one Melazzo, who was in Duke Charles's pay, brought him word that the seed he had cast had fallen upon fertile soil. A conspiracy to destroy the King had been laid by Bertrand d'Artois, Robert of Cabane, Count of Evoli, and the latter's brothers-in-law, Terlizzi and Morcone. Melazzo himself, for his notorious affection for the Queen, had been included in this band, and also a man named Pace, who was body servant to Andreas, and who, like Melazzo, was in Charles's pay.

Charles of Durazzo smiled gently to himself. The game went excellently well.

"The Court, " he sad, "goes to Aversa for a month before the coronation. That would be a favourable season to their plan. Advise it so. "

The date appointed for the coronation was September 20th. A month before - on August 20th - the Court removed itself from the heat and reek of Naples to the cooler air of Aversa, there to spend the time of waiting. They were housed in the monastery of Saint Peter, which had been converted as far as possible into a royal residence for the occasion.

On the night of their arrival there the refectory of the monastery was transfigured to accommodate the numerous noble and very jovial company assembled there to sup. The long, stone-flagged room, lofty and with windows set very high, normally so bare and austere, was hung now with tapestries, and the floor strewn with rushes that were mingled with lemon verbena and other aromatic herbs. Along the lateral walls and across the end of the room that faced the double doors were set the stone tables of the Spartan monks, on a shallow dais that raised them above the level of the floor. These tables were gay now with the gleam of crystal and the glitter of gold and silver plate. Along one side of them, their backs to the walls, sat the ladies and nobles of the Court. The vaulted ceiling was rudely frescoed to represent the open heavens - the work of a brother whose brush was more devout than cunning - and there was the inevitable cenacolo above the Abbot's table at the upper end of the room.

At this table sat the royal party, the broad-shouldered Andreas of Hungary, slightly asprawl, his golden mane somewhat tumbled now, for he was drinking deeply in accordance with his barbarian habit; ever and anon he would fling down a bone or a piece of meat to the liver-coloured hounds that crouched expectant on the rushes of the floor.

They had hunted that day in the neighbourhood of Capua, and Andreas had acquitted himself well, and was in high good-humour, giving now little thought to the sinister things that Charles of Durazzo had lately whispered, laughing and jesting with the traitor Morcone at his side. Behind him in close attendance stood his servant Pace, once a creature of Durazzo's. The Queen sat on his right, making but poor pretence to eat; her lovely young face was of a ghostly pallor, her dark eyes were wide and staring. Among the guests were the black-browed Evoli and his brother-in-law, Terlizzi;

Bertrand of Artois and his father; Melazzo, that other creature of Charles's, and Filippa the Catanese, handsome and arrogant, but oddly silent to-night.

But Charles of Durazzo was not of the company. It is not for the player, himself, to become a piece upon the board.

He had caught a whisper that the thing he had so slyly prompted to Bertrand d'Artois was to be done here at Aversa, and so Charles had remained at Naples. He had discovered very opportunely that his wife was ailing, and he developed such concern for her that he could not bring himself to leave her side. He had excused himself to Andreas with a thousand regrets, since what he most desired was to enjoy with him the cool, clean air of Aversa and the pleasures of the chase; and he had presented the young King at parting with the best of all his falcons in earnest of affection and disappointment.

The night wore on, and at last, at a sign from the Queen, the ladies rose and departed to their beds. The men settled down again. The cellarers redoubled their activities, the flagons circulated more briskly, and the noise they made must have disturbed the monks entrenched in their cells against these earthly vanities. The laughter of Andreas grew louder and more vacuous, and when at last he heaved himself up at midnight and departed to bed, that he might take some rest against the morrow's hunt, he staggered a little in his walk.

But there were other hunters there whose impatience could not keep until the morrow, whose game was to be run to death that very night. They waited - Bertrand d'Artois, Robert of Cabane, the Counts of Terlizzi and Morcone, Melazzo and Andreas's body servant Pace - until all those who lay at Aversa were deep in slumber. Then at two o'clock in the morning they made their stealthy way to the loggia on the third floor, a long colonnaded gallery above the Abbot's garden. They paused a moment before the Queen's door which opened upon this gallery, then crept on to that of the King's room at the other end. It was Pace who rapped sharply on the panels thrice before he was answered by a sleepy growl from the other side.

"It is I - Pace - my lord, " he announced. "A courier has arrived from Naples, from Friar Robert, with instant messages. "

From within there was a noisy yawn, a rustle, the sound of an overturning stool, and, lastly, the rasp of a bolt being withdrawn. The door opened, and in the faint light of the dawning day Andreas appeared, drawing a furlined robe about his body, which was naked of all but a shirt.

He saw no one but Pace. The others had drawn aside into the shadows. Unsuspecting, he stepped forth.

"Where is this messenger? "

The door through which he had come slammed suddenly behind him, and he turned to see Melazzo in the act of bolting it with a dagger to prevent any one from following that way - for the room had another door opening upon the inner corridor.

Instead, Melazzo might have employed his dagger to stab Andreas behind, and so have made an instant end. But it happened to be known that Andreas wore an amulet - a ring that his mother had given him - which rendered him invulnerable to steel or poison. And such was the credulity of his age, such the blind faith of those men in the miraculous power of that charm, that none of them so much as attempted to test it with a dagger. It was for the same reason that no recourse was had to the still easier method of disposing of him by poison. Accepting the amulet at its legendary value, the conspirators had resolved that he must be strangled.

As he turned now they leapt upon him, and, taking him unawares, bore him to the ground before he could realize what was happening. Here they grappled with him, and he with them. He was endowed with the strength of a young bull, and he made full use of it. He rose, beating them off, to be borne down again, bellowing the while for help. He smote out blindly, and stretched Morcone half senseless with a blow of his great fist.

Seeing how difficult he proved to strangle, they must have cursed that amulet of his. He struggled to his knees again, then to his feet, and, at last, with bleeding face, leaving tufts of his fair hair in their murderous hands, he broke through and went bounding down the loggia, screaming as he ran, until he came to his wife's door. Against that he hurled himself, calling her.

"Giovanna! Giovanna! For the love of God crucified! Open! Open! I am being murdered!"

From within came no answer - utter silence.

"Giovanna! Giovanna!" He beat frenziedly upon the door.

Still no answer, which yet was answer enough.

The stranglers, momentarily discomfited, scared, too, lest his cries should rouse the convent, had stood hesitating after he broke from them. But now Bertrand d'Artois, realizing that too much had been done already to admit of the business being left unfinished, sprang upon him suddenly again. Locked in each other's arms, those wrestlers swayed and panted in the loggia for a moment, then with a crash went down, Bertrand on top, Andreas striking his head against the stone floor as he fell. The Queen's lover pinned him there, kneeling upon his breast.

"The rope!" he panted to the others who came up.

One of them threw him a coil of purple silk interwrought with gold thread, in which a running noose had been tied. Bertrand slipped it over Andreas's head, drew it taut, and held it so, despite the man's desperate, convulsive struggles. The others came to his assistance. Amongst them they lifted the writhing victim to the parapet of the loggia, and flung him over; whilst Bertrand, Cabane, and Pace bore upon the rope, arresting his fall, and keeping him suspended there until he should be dead. Melazzo and Morcone came to assist them, and it was then that Cabane observed that Terlizzi held aloof, as if filled with horror.

Peremptorily he called to him:

"Hither, and lend a hand! The rope is long enough to afford you a grip. We want accomplices, not witnesses, Lord Count."

Terlizzi obeyed, and then the ensuing silence was broken suddenly by screams from the floor below the screams of a woman who slept in the room immediately underneath, who had awakened to behold in the grey light of the breaking day the figure of a man kicking and writhing at a rope's end before her window.

Yet a moment the startled stranglers kept their grip of the rope until the struggles at the end of it had ceased; then they loosed their hold and let the body go plunging down into the Abbot's garden. Thereafter they scattered and fled, for people were stirring now in the convent, aroused by the screams of the woman.

Thrice, so the story runs, came the monks to the Queen's door to knock and demand her orders for the disposal of the body of her husband without receiving any answer to their question. It remained still unanswered when later in the day she departed from Aversa in a closed litter, and returned to Naples escorted by a company of lances, and for lack of instructions the monks left the body in the Abbot's garden, where it had fallen, until Charles of Durazzo came to remove it two days later.

Ostentatiously he bore to Naples the murdered Prince - whose death he had so subtly inspired - and in the cathedral before the Hungarians, whom he had assembled, and in the presence of a vast concourse of the people, he solemnly swore over the body vengeance upon the murderers.

Having made a cat's-paw of Giovanna - through the person of her lover, Bertrand d'Artois, and his confederate assassins - and thus cleared away one of those who stood between himself and the throne, he now sought to make a cat's-paw of justice to clear away the other. Meanwhile, days grew into weeks and weeks into months, and no attempt was made by the Queen to hunt out the murderers of her husband, no inquiry instituted. Bertrand d'Artois, it is true, had fled with his father to their stronghold of Saint Agatha for safety. But the others - Cabane, Terlizzi, and Morcone - continued unabashed about Giovanna's person at the Castel Nuovo.

Charles wrote to Ludwig of Hungary, and to the Pope, demanding that justice should be done, and pointing out the neglect of all attempt to perform it in the kingdom itself, and inviting them to construe for themselves that neglect. As a consequence, Clement VI issued, on June 2d of the following year, a Bull, whereby Bertrand des Baux, the Grand Justiciary of Naples, was commanded to hunt down and punish the assassins, against whom - at the same time - the Pope launched a second Bull, of excommunication. But the Holy Father accompanied his commands to Des Baux by a private note, wherein he straitly enjoined the Grand Justiciary for reasons of State to permit nothing to transpire that might reflect upon the Queen.

Des Baux set about his task at once, and inspired, no doubt, by Charles, proceeded to the arrest of Melazzo and the servant Pace. It was not for Charles to accuse the Queen or even any of her nobles, whereby he might have aroused against himself the opposition of those who were her loyal partisans. Sufficient for him to point out the two meanest of the conspirators, and depend upon the torture to wring from them confessions that must gradually pull down the rest, and in the end Giovanna herself.

Terlizzi, alive to his danger when he heard of the arrest of those two, made a bold and desperate attempt to avert it. Riding forth with a band of followers, he attacked the escort that was bearing Pace to prison. The prisoner was seized, but not to be rescued. All that Terlizzi wanted was his silence. By his orders the wretched man's tongue was torn out, whereupon he was abandoned once more to his guards and his fate.

Had Terlizzi been able to carry out his intentions of performing the like operation upon Melazzo, Charles might have been placed in a difficult position. So much, however, did not happen, and the horrible deed upon Pace was in vain. Put to the question, Melazzo denounced Terlizzi, and together with him Cabane, Morcone, and the others. Further, his confession incriminated Filippa, the Catanese, and her two daughters, the wives of Terlizzi and Morcone. Of the Queen, however, he said nothing, because, one of the lesser conspirators, little more than a servant like Pace, he can have had no knowledge of the Queen's complicity.

The arrest of the others followed instantly, and, sentenced to death, they were publicly burned in the Square of Sant' Eligio, after suffering all the brutal, unspeakable horrors of fourteenth-century torture, which continued to the very scaffold, with the alleged intention of inducing them to denounce any further accomplices. But though they writhed and fainted under the pincers of the executioners, they confessed nothing. Indeed, they preserved a silence which left the people amazed, for the people lacked the explanation. The Grand Justiciary, Hugh des Baux, had seen to it that the Pope's injunctions should be obeyed. Lest the condemned should say too much, he had taken the precaution of having their tongues fastened down with fish-hooks.

Thus Charles was momentarily baulked, and he was further baulked by the fact that Giovanna had taken a second husband, in her cousin,

Louis of Taranto. Unless matters were to remain there and the game end in a stalemate, bold measures were required, and those measures Charles adopted. He wrote to the King of Hungary now openly accusing Giovanna of the murder, and pointing out the circumstances that in themselves afforded corroboration of his charge.

Those circumstances Ludwig embodied in a fulminating letter which he wrote to Giovanna in answer to her defence against the charge of inaction in the matter of her late husband's murderers: "Giovanna, thy antecedent disorderly life, thy retention of the exclusive power in the kingdom, thy neglect of vengeance upon the murderers of thy husband, thy having taken another husband, and thy very excuses abundantly prove thy complicity in thy husband's death. "

So far this was all as Charles of Durazzo could have desired it. But there was more. Ludwig was advancing now in arms to take possession of the kingdom, of which, under all the circumstances, he might consider himself the lawful heir, and the Princes of Italy were affording him unhindered passage through their States. This was not at all to Charles's liking. Indeed, unless he bestirred himself, it might prove to be checkmate from an altogether unexpected quarter, rendering vain all the masterly play with which he had conducted the game so far.

It flustered him a little, and in his haste to counter it he blundered.

Giovanna, alarmed at the rapid advance of Ludwig, summoned her barons to her aid, and in that summons she included Charles, realizing that at all costs he must be brought over to her side. He went, listened, and finally sold himself for a good price the title of Duke of Calabria, which made him heir to the kingdom. He raised a powerful troop of lances, and marched upon Aquila, which had already hoisted the Hungarian banner.

There it was that he discovered, and soon, his move to have been a bad one. News was brought to him that the Queen, taken with panic, had fled to Provence, seeking sanctuary at Avignon.

Charles set about correcting his error without delay, and marched out of Aquila to go and meet Ludwig that he might protest his loyalty, and range himself under the invader's banner.

At Foligno, the King of Hungary was met by a papal legate, who in the name of Pope Clement forbade him under pain of excommunication to invade a fief of Holy Church.

"When I am master of Naples, " answered Ludwig firmly, "I shall count myself a feudatory of the Holy See. Until then I render account to none but God and my conscience. " And he pushed on, preceded by a black banner of death, scattering in true Hungarian fashion murder, rape, pillage, and arson through the smiling countryside, exacting upon the whole land a terrible vengeance for the murder of his brother.

Thus he came to Aversa, and there quartered himself and his Hungarians upon that convent of Saint Peter where Andreas had been strangled a year ago. And it was here that he was joined by Charles, who came protesting loyalty, and whom the King received with open arms and a glad welcome, as was to be expected from a man who had been Andreas's one true friend in that land of enemies. Of Charles's indiscreet escapade in the matter of Aquila nothing was said. As Charles had fully expected, it was condoned upon the score both of the past and the present.

That night there was high feasting in that same refectory where Andreas had feasted on the night when the stranglers watched him, waiting, and Charles was the guest of honour. In the morning Ludwig was to pursue his march upon the city of Naples, and all were astir betimes.

On the point of setting out, Ludwig turned to Charles.

"Before I go, " he said, "I have a mind to visit the spot where my brother died.

To Charles, no doubt, this seemed a morbid notion to be discouraged. But Ludwig was insistent.

"Take me there, " he bade the Duke,

"Indeed, I scarce know - I was not here, remember, " Charles answered him, rendered faintly uneasy, perhaps by a certain grimness in the gaunt King's face, perhaps by the mutterings of his own conscience.

"I know that you were not; but surely you must know the place. It will be known to all the world in these parts. Besides, was it not yourself recovered the body? Conduct me thither, then.

Perforce, then, Charles must do his will. Arm-in-arm they mounted the stairs to that sinister loggia, a half-dozen of Ludwig's escorting officers following.

They stepped along the tessellated floor above the Abbot's garden, flooded now with sunshine which drew the perfume from the roses blooming there.

"Here the King slept, " said Charles, "and yonder the Queen. Somewhere here between the thing was done, and thence they hanged him. "

Ludwig, tall and grim, stood considering, chin in hand. Suddenly he wheeled upon the Duke who stood at his elbow. His face had undergone a change, and his lip curled so that he displayed his strong teeth as a dog displays them when he snarls.

"Traitor! " he rasped. "It is you - you who come smiling and fawning upon me, and spurring me on to vengeance - who are to blame for what happened here. "

"I? " Charles fell back, changing colour, his legs trembling under him.

"You! " the King answered him furiously. "His death would never have come about but for your intrigues to keep him out of the royal power, to hinder his coronation. "

"It is false! " cried Charles. "False! I swear it before God! "

"Perjured dog! Do you deny that you sought the aid of your precious uncle the Cardinal of Perigord to restrain the Pope from granting the Bull required? "

"I do deny it. The facts deny it. The Bull was forthcoming. "

"Then your denial but proves your guilt, " the King answered him, and from the leather pouch hanging from his belt, he pulled out a parchment, and held it under the Duke's staring eyes. It was the letter he had written to the Cardinal of Perigord, enjoining him to prevent the Pope from signing the Bull sanctioning Andreas's coronation.

The King smiled terribly into that white, twitching face.

"Deny it now, " he mocked him. "Deny, too, that, bribed by the title of Duke of Calabria, you turned to the service of the Queen, to abandon it again for ours when you perceived your danger. You think to use us, traitor, as a stepping-stone to help you to mount the throne - as you sought to use my brother even to the extent of encompassing his murder. "

"No, no! I had no hand in that. I was his friend - "

"Liar! " Ludwig struck him across the mouth.

On the instant the officers of Ludwig laid hands upon the Duke, fearing that the indignity might spur him to retaliation.

"You are very opportune, " said Ludwig; and added coldly, "Dispatch him. "

Charles screamed a moment, even as Andreas had screamed on that same spot, when he found himself staring into the fearful face of death. Then the scream became a cough as a Hungarian sword went through him from side to side.

They picked up his body from the tessellated floor of the loggia, carried it to the parapet as Andreas's had been carried, and flung it down into the Abbot's garden as Andreas's had been flung. It lay in a rosebush, dyeing the Abbot's roses a deeper red.

Never was justice more poetic.

XI. THE NIGHT OF HATE

The Murder of the Duke of Gandia

The Cardinal Vice-Chancellor took the packet proffered him by the fair-haired, scarlet-liveried page, and turned it over, considering it, the gentle, finely featured, almost ascetic face very thoughtful.

"It was brought, my lord, by a man in a mask, who will give no name. He waits below, " said the scarlet stripling.

"A man in a mask, eh? What mystery! "

The thoughtful brown eyes smiled, the fine hands broke the fragment of wax. A gold ring fell out and rolled some little way along the black and purple Eastern rug. The boy dived after it, and presented it to his lordship.

The ring bore an escutcheon, and the Cardinal found graven upon this escutcheon his own arms the Sforza lion and the flower of the quince. Instantly those dark, thoughtful eyes of his grew keen as they flashed upon the page.

"Did you see the device? " he asked, a hint of steel under the silkiness of his voice.

"I saw nothing, my lord - a ring, no more. I did not even look. "

The Cardinal continued to ponder him for a long moment very searchingly.

"Go - bring this man, " he said at last; and the boy departed, soon to reappear; holding aside the tapestry that masked the door to give passage to a man of middle height wrapped in a black cloak, his face under a shower of golden hair, covered from chin to brow by a black visor.

At a sign from the Cardinal the page departed. Then the man, coming forward, let fall his cloak, revealing a rich dress of close-fitting violet silk, sword and dagger hanging from his jewelled girdle; he plucked away the mask, and disclosed the handsome, weak face of Giovanni Sforza, Lord of Pesaro and Cotignola, the

239

discarded husband of Madonna Lucrezia, Pope Alexander's daughter.

The Cardinal considered his nephew gravely, without surprise. He had expected at first no more than a messenger from the owner of that ring. But at sight of his figure and long, fair hair he had recognized Giovanni before the latter had removed his mask.

"I have always accounted you something mad, " said the Cardinal softly. "But never mad enough for this. What brings you to Rome? "

"Necessity, my lord, " replied the young tyrant. "The need to defend my honour, which is about to be destroyed. "

"And your life? " wondered his uncle. "Has that ceased to be of value? "

"Without honour it is nothing. "

"A noble sentiment taught in every school. But for practical purposes - " The Cardinal shrugged.

Giovanni, however, paid no heed.

"Did you think, my lord, that I should tamely submit to be a derided, outcast husband, that I should take no vengeance upon, that villainous Pope for having made me a thing of scorn, a byword throughout Italy? " Livid hate writhed in his fair young face. "Did you think I should, indeed, remain in Pesaro, whither I fled before their threats to my life, and present no reckoning? "

"What is the reckoning you have in mind? " inquired his uncle, faintly ironical. "You'll not be intending to kill the Holy Father? "

"Kill him? " Giovanni laughed shortly, scornfully. "Do the dead suffer? "

"In hell, sometimes, " said the Cardinal.

"Perhaps. But I want to be sure. I want sufferings that I can witness, sufferings that I can employ as balsam for my own wounded honour. I shall strike, even as he has stricken me - at his soul, not at his body. I shall wound him where he is most sensitive. "

Ascanio Sforza, towering tall and slender in his scarlet robes, shook his head slowly.

"All this is madness - madness! You were best away, best in Pesaro. Indeed, you cannot safely show your face in Rome. "

"That is why I go masked. That is why I come to you, my lord, for shelter here until - "

"Here? " The Cardinal was instantly alert. "Then you think I am as mad as yourself. Why, man, if so much as a whisper of your presence in Rome got abroad, this is the first place where they would look nor you. If you will have your way, if you are so set on the avenging of past wrongs and the preventing of future ones, it is not for me, your kinsman, to withstand you. But here in my palace you cannot stay, for your own safety's sake. That page who brought you, now; I would not swear he did not see the arms upon your ring. I pray that he did not. But if he did, your presence is known here already. "

Giovanni was perturbed.

"But if not here, where, then, in Rome should I be safe? "

"Nowhere, I think, " answered the ironical Ascanio. "Though perhaps you might count yourself safe with Pico. Your common hate of the Holy Father should be a stout bond between you. "

Fate prompted the suggestion. Fate drove the Lord of Pesaro to act upon it, and to seek out Antonio Maria Pico, Count of Mirandola, in his palace by the river, where Pico, as Ascanio had foreseen, gave him a cordial welcome.

There he abode almost in hiding until the end of May, seldom issuing forth, and never without his mask - a matter this which excited no comment, for masked faces were common in the streets of Rome in the evening of the fifteenth century. In talk with Pico he set forth his intent, elaborating what already he had told the Cardinal Vice-Chancellor.

"He is a father - this Father of Fathers, " he said once. "A tender, loving father whose life is in his children, who lives through them and for them. Deprive him of them, and his life would become empty, worthless, a living death. There is Giovanni, who is as the apple of his eye, whom he has created Duke of Gandia, Duke of Benevento, Prince of Sessa, Lord of Teano, and more besides. There is the Cardinal of Valencia, there is Giuffredo, Prince of Squillace, and there is my wife, Lucrezia, of whom he has robbed me. There is, you see, an ample heel to our Achilles. The question is, where shall we begin? "

"And also, how, " Pico reminded him.

Fate was to answer both those questions, and that soon.

They went on June 1st - the Lord of Pesaro, with his host and his host's daughter, Antonia - to spend the day at Pico's vineyard in Trastevere. At the moment of setting out to return to Rome in the evening the Count was detained by his steward, newly returned from a journey with matters to communicate to him.

He bade his guest, with his daughter and their attendants, to ride on, saying that he himself would follow and overtake them. But the steward detained him longer than he had expected, so that, although the company proceeded leisurely towards the city, Pico had not come up with them when they reached the river. In the narrow street beyond the bridge the little escort found itself suddenly confronted and thrust aside by a magnificent cavalcade of ladies and gallants, hawk on wrist and followed by a pack of hounds.

Giovanni had eyes for one only in that gay company - a tall, splendidly handsome man in green, a Plumed bonnet on his auburn head, and a roguish, jovial eye, which, in its turn, saw nobody in that moment but Madonna Antonia, reclining in her litter, the leather curtains of which she had drawn back that she might converse with Giovanni as they rode.

The Lord of Pesaro beheld the sudden kindling of his brother-in-law's glance, for that handsome gallant was the Duke of Gandia, the Pope's eldest son, the very apple of the Holy Father's eye. He saw the Duke's almost unconscious check upon his reins; saw him turn in the saddle to stare boldly at Madonna Antonia until, grown conscious of his regard, she crimsoned under it. And when at last the litter had moved on, he saw over his shoulder a mounted servant detach from the Duke's side to follow them. This fellow dogged their heels all the way to the Parione Quarter, obviously with intent to discover for his master where the beautiful lady of the litter might be housed.

Giovanni said naught of this to Pico when he returned a little later. He was quick to perceive the opportunity that offered, but far from sure that Pico would suffer his daughter to be used as a decoy; far, indeed, from sure that he dared himself so employ her. But on the morrow, chancing to look from a window out of idle curiosity to see what horse it was that was pacing in the street below, he beheld a man in a rich cloak, in whom at once he recognized the Duke, and he accounted that the dice of destiny had fallen.

Himself unseen by that horseman, Giovanni drew back quickly. On the spur of the moment, he acted with a subtlety worthy of long premeditation. Antonia and he were by an odd fatality alone together in that chamber of the mezzanine. He turned to her.

"An odd fellow rides below here, tarrying as if expectant. I wonder should you know who he is. "

Obeying his suggestion, she rose - a tall, slim child of some eighteen years, of a delicate, pale beauty, with dark, thoughtful eyes and long, black tresses, interwoven with jewelled strands of gold thread. She rustled to the window and looked down upon that cavalier; and, as she looked, scanning him intently, the Duke raised his head. Their eyes met, and she drew back with a little cry.

"What is it? " exclaimed Giovanni.

"It is that insolent fellow who stared at me last evening in the street. I would you had not bidden me look. "

Now, whilst she had been gazing from the window, Giovanni, moving softly behind her, had espied a bowl of roses on the ebony table in the room's middle. Swiftly and silently he had plucked a blossom, which he now held behind his back. As she turned from him again, he sent it flying through the window; and whilst in his heart he laughed with bitter hate and scorn as he thought of Gandia snatching up that rose and treasuring it in his bosom, aloud he laughed at her fears, derided them as idle.

That night, in his room, Giovanni practised penmanship assiduously, armed with a model with which Antonia had innocently equipped him. He went to bed well pleased, reflecting that as a man lives so does he die. Giovanni Borgia, Duke of Gandia, had been ever an amiable profligate, a heedless voluptuary obeying no spur but that of his own pleasure, which should drive him now to his destruction. Giovanni Borgia, he considered further, was, as he had expressed it, the very apple of his father's eye; and since, of his own accord, the Duke had come to thrust his foolish head into the noose, the Lord of Pesaro would make a sweet beginning to the avenging of his wrongs by drawing it taut.

Next morning saw him at the Vatican, greatly daring, to deliver in person his forgery to the Duke. Suspicious of his mask, they asked him who he was and whence he came.

"Say one who desires to remain unknown with a letter for the Duke of Gandia which his magnificence will welcome. "

Reluctantly, a chamberlain departed with his message. Anon he was conducted above to the magnificent apartments which Gandia occupied during his sojourn there.

He found the Duke newly risen, and with him his brother, the auburn-headed young Cardinal of Valencia, dressed in a close-fitting suit of black, that displayed his lithe and gracefully athletic proportions, and a cloak of scarlet silk to give a suggestion of his ecclesiastical rank.

Giovanni bowed low, and, thickening his voice that it might not be recognized, announced himself and his mission in one.

"From the lady of the rose, " said he, proffering the letter.

Valencia stared a moment; then went off into a burst of laughter. Gandia's face flamed and his eyes sparkled. He snatched the letter, broke its seal, and consumed its contents. Then he flung away to a table, took up a pen, and sat down to write; the tall Valencia watching him with amused scorn a while, then crossing to his side and setting a hand upon his shoulder.

"You will never learn, " said the more subtle Cesare. "You must forever be leaving traces where traces are not to be desired. "

Gandia looked up into that keen, handsome young face.

244

"You are right, " he said; and crumpled the letter in his hand.

Then he looked at the messenger and hesitated.

"I am in Madonna's confidence, " said the man in the mask.

Gandia rose. "Then say - say that her letter has carried me to Heaven; that I but await her commands to come in person to declare myself. But bid her hasten, for within two weeks from now I go to Naples, and thence I may return straight to Spain. "

"The opportunity shall be found, Magnificent. Myself I shall bring you word of it. "

The Duke loaded him with thanks, and in his excessive gratitude pressed upon him at parting a purse of fifty ducats, which Giovanni flung into the Tiber some ten minutes later as he was crossing the Bridge of Sant' Angelo on his homeward way.

The Lord of Pesaro proceeded without haste. Delay and silence he knew would make Gandia the more sharp-set, and your sharp-set, impatient fellow is seldom cautious. Meanwhile, Antonia had mentioned to her father that princely stranger who had stared so offendingly one evening, and who for an hour on the following morning had haunted the street beneath her window. Pico mentioned it to Giovanni, whereupon Giovanni told him frankly who it was.

"It was that libertine brother-in-law of mine, the Duke of Gandia, " he said. "Had he persisted, I should have bidden you look to your daughter. As it is, no doubt he has other things to think of. He is preparing for his journey to Naples, to accompany his brother Cesare, who goes as papal legate to crown Federigo of Aragon. "

There he left the matter, and no more was heard of it until the night of June 14th, the very eve of the departure of the Borgia princes upon that mission.

Cloaked and masked, Giovanni took his way to the Vatican at dusk that evening, and desired to have himself announced to the Duke. But he was met with the answer that the Duke was absent; that he had gone to take leave of his mother and to sup at her villa in Trastevere. His return was not expected until late.

At first Giovanni feared that, in leaving the consummation of his plot until the eleventh hour, he had left it too late. In his anxiety he at once set out on foot, as he was, for the villa of Madonna Giovanna de Catanei. He reached it towards ten o'clock that night, to be informed that Gandia was there, at supper. The servant went to bear word to the Duke that a man in a mask was asking to see him, a message which instantly flung Gandia into agitation. Excitedly he commanded that the man be brought to him at once.

The Lord of Pesaro was conducted through the house and out into the garden to an arbour of vine, where a rich table was spread in the evening cool, lighted by alabaster lamps. About this table Giovanni found a noble company of his own relations by marriage. There was Gandia, who rose hurriedly at his approach, and came to meet him; there was Cesare, Cardinal of Valencia, who was to go to Naples to-morrow as papal legate, yet dressed tonight in cloth of gold, with no trace of his churchly dignity about him; there was their younger brother Giuffredo, Prince of Squillace, a handsome stripling, flanked by his wife, the free-and-easy Donna Sancia of Aragon, swarthy, coarse-featured, and fleshy, despite her youth; there was Giovanni's sometime wife; the lovely, golden-headed Lucrezia, the innocent cause of all this hate that festered in the Lord of Pesaro's soul; there was their mother, the nobly handsome Giovanozza de Catanei, from whom the Borgias derived their auburn heads; and there was their cousin, Giovanni Borgia, Cardinal of Monreale, portly and scarlet, at Madonna's side.

All turned to glance at this masked intruder who had the power so oddly to excite their beloved Gandia.

"From the lady of the rose, " Giovanni announced himself softly to the Duke.

"Yes, yes, " came the answer, feverishly impatient. "Well, what is your message? "

"To-night her father is from home. She will expect your magnificence at midnight. "

Gandia drew a deep breath.

"By the Host! You are no more than in time. I had almost despaired, my friend, my best of friends. To-night! " He pronounced the word ecstatically. "Wait you here. Yourself you shall conduct me. Meanwhile, go sup. "

And beating his hands, he summoned attendants.

Came the steward and a couple of Moorish slaves in green turbans, to whose care the Duke commanded his masked visitor. But Giovanni neither required nor desired their ministrations; he would not eat nor drink, but contented himself with the patience of hatred to sit for two long hours awaiting the pleasure of his foolish victim.

They left at last, a little before midnight the Duke, his brother Cesare, his cousin Monreale, and a numerous attendance, his own retinue and those of the two cardinals. Thus they rode back to Rome, the Borgias very gay, the man in the mask plodding along beside them.

They came to the Rione de Ponte, where their ways were to separate, and there, opposite the palace of the Cardinal Vice-Chancellor, Gandia drew rein. He announced to the others that he went no farther with them, summoned a single groom to attend him, and bade the remainder return to the Vatican and await him there.

There was a last jest and a laugh from Cesare as the cavalcade went on towards the papal palace. Then Gandia turned to the man in the mask, bade him get up on the crupper of his horse, and so rode slowly off in the direction of the Giudecca, the single attendant he had retained trotting beside his stirrup.

Giovanni directed his brother-in-law, not to the main entrance of the house, but to the garden gate, which opened upon a narrow alley. Here they dismounted, flinging the reins to the groom, who was bidden to wait. Giovanni produced a key, unlocked the door, and ushered the Duke into the gloom of the garden. A stone staircase ran up to the loggia on the mezzanine, and by this way was Gandia now conducted, treading softly. His guide went ahead. He had provided himself with yet another key, and so unlocked the door from the loggia which opened upon the ante-room of Madonna Antonia. He held the door for the Duke, who hesitated, seeing all in darkness.

"In, " Giovanni bade him. "Tread softly. Madonna waits for you. "

Recklessly, then, that unsuspecting fellow stepped into the trap.

Giovanni followed, closed the door, and locked it. The Duke, standing with quickened pulses in that impenetrable blackness, found himself suddenly embraced, not at all after the fond fashion he was expecting. A wrestler's arms enlaced his body, a sinewy leg coiled itself snake-wise about one of his own, pulling it from under him. As he crashed down under the weight of his unseen opponent, a great voice boomed out:

"Lord of Mirandola! To me! Help! Thieves! "

Suddenly a door opened. Light flooded the gloom, and the writhing Duke beheld a white vision of the girl whose beauty had been the lure that had drawn him into this peril which, as yet, he scarcely understood. But looking up into the face of the man who grappled with him, the man who held him there supine under his weight, he began at last to understand, or, at least, to suspect, for the face he saw, unmasked now, leering at him with hate unspeakable through the cloud of golden hair that half met across it, was the face of Giovanni Sforza, Lord of Pesaro, whom his family had so cruelly wronged. Giovanni Sforza's was the voice that now fiercely announced his doom.

"You and yours have made me a thing of scorn and laughter. Yourself have laughed at me. Go laugh in hell! "

A blade flashed up in Giovanni's hand. Gandia threw up an arm to fend his breast, and the blade buried itself in the muscles. He screamed with pain and terror. The other laughed with hate and triumph, and stabbed again, this time in the shoulder.

Antonia, from the threshold, watching in bewilderment and panic, sent a piercing scream to ring through the house, and then the voice of Giovanni, fierce yet exultant, called aloud:

"Pico! Pico! Lord of Mirandola! Look to your daughter! "

Came steps and voice, more light, flooding now the chamber, and through the mists gathering before his eyes the first-born of the house of Borgia beheld hurrying men, half dressed, with weapons in their hands. But whether they came to kill or to save, they came too late: Ten times Giovanni's blade had stabbed the Duke, yet, hindered by the Duke's struggles and by the effort of holding him there, he had been unable to find his heart, wherefore, as those others entered now, he slashed his victim across the throat, and so made an end.

He rose, covered with blood, so ghastly and terrific that Pico, thinking him wounded, ran to him. But Giovanni reassured him with a laugh, and pointed with his dripping dagger.

"The blood is his - foul Borgia blood! "

At the name Pico started, and there was a movement as of fear from the three grooms who followed him. The Count looked down at that splendid, blood-spattered figure lying there so still, its sightless eyes staring up at the frescoed ceiling, so brave and so pitiful in his gold-broidered suit of white satin, with the richly jewelled girdle carrying gloves and purse and a jewelled dagger that had been so useless in that extremity.

"Gandia" he cried; and looked at Giovanni with round eyes of fear and amazement. "How came he here? "

"How? "

With bloody hand Giovanni pointed to the open door of Antonia's chamber.

"That was the lure, my lord. Taking the air outside, I saw him slinking hither, and took him for a thief, as, indeed, he was - a thief of honour, like all his kind. I followed, and - there he lies. "

"My God! " cried Pico. And then hoarsely asked, "And Antonia? "

Giovanni dismissed the question abruptly.

"She saw, yet she knows nothing. "

And then on another note:

"Up now, Pico! " he cried. "Arouse the city, and let all men know how Gandia died the death of a thief. Let all men know this Borgia brood for what it is. "

"Are you mad? " cried Pico. "Will I put my neck under the knife? "

"You took him here in the night, and yours was the right to kill. You exercised it. "

Pico looked long and searchingly into the other's face. True, all the appearances bore out the tale, as did, too, what had gone before and had been the cause of Antonia's complaint to him. Yet, knowing what lay between Sforza and Borgia, it may have seemed to Pico too extraordinary a coincidence that Giovanni should have been so ready at hand to defend the honour of the House of Mirandola. But he asked no questions. He was content in his philosophy to accept the event and be thankful for it on every count. But as for Giovanni's suggestion that he should proclaim through Rome how he had exercised his right to slay this Tarquin, the Lord of Mirandola had no mind to adopt it.

"What is done is done, " he said shortly, in a tone that conveyed much. "Let it suffice us all. It but remains now to be rid of this. "

"You will keep silent? " cried Giovanni, plainly vexed.

"I am not a fool, " said Pico gently.

Giovanni understood. "And these your men? "

"Ate very faithful friends who will aid you now to efface all traces. "

And upon that he moved away, calling his daughter, whose absence was intriguing him. Receiving no answer, he entered her room, to find her in a swoon across her bed. She had fainted from sheer horror at what she had seen.

Followed by the three servants bearing the body, Giovanni went down across the garden very gently. Approaching the gate, he bade them wait, saying that he went to see that the coast was clear. Then, going forward alone, he opened the gate and called softly to the waiting groom:

"Hither to me! "

Promptly the man surged before him in the gloom, and as promptly Giovanni sank his dagger in the fellow's breast. He deplored the necessity for the deed, but it was unavoidable, and your cinquecentist never shrank from anything that necessity imposed upon him. To let the lackey live would be to have the bargelli in the house by morning.

The man sank with a half-uttered cry, and lay still.

Giovanni dragged him aside under the shelter of the wall, where the others would not see him, then called softly to them to follow.

When the grooms emerged from Pico's garden, the Lord of Pesaro was astride of the fine white horse on which Gandia had ridden to his death.

"Put him across the crupper, " he bade them.

And they so placed the body, the head dangling on one side, the legs on the other. And Giovanni reflected grimly how he had reversed the order in which Gandia and he had ridden that same horse an hour ago.

At a walk they proceeded down the lane towards the river, a groom on each side to see that the burden on the crupper did not jolt off, another going ahead to scout. At the alley's mouth Giovanni drew rein, and let the man emerge upon the river-bank and look to right and left to make sure that there was no one about.

He saw no one. Yet one there was who saw them Giorgio, the timber merchant, who lay aboard his boat moored to the Schiavoni, and who, three days later, testified to what he saw. You know his testimony. It has been repeated often - how he saw the man emerge from the alley and look up and down, then retire, to emerge again, accompanied now by the horseman with his burden, and the other two; how he saw them take the body from the crupper of the horse, and, with a "one, two, and three, " fling it into the river; how he heard the horseman ask them had they thrown it well into the middle, and their answer of, "Yes my lord"; and finally, when asked why he had not come earlier to report the matter, how he had answered that he had thought nothing of it, having in his time seen more than a hundred bodies flung into the Tiber at night.

Returned to the garden gate, Giovanni bade the men go in without him. There was something yet that he must do. When they had gone, he dismounted, and went to the body of the groom which he had left under the wall. He must remove that too. He cut one of the stirrup-leathers from the saddle, and attaching one end of it to the dead man's arm, mounted again, and dragged him thus - ready to leave the body and ride off at the first alarm - some little way, until he came to the Piazza della Giudecca. Here, in the very heart of the Jewish quarters, he left the body, and his movements hereafter are a little obscure. Perhaps he set out to return to Pico della Mirandola's house, but becoming, as was natural, uneasy on the way, fearing lest all traces should, after all, not have been effaced, lest the Duke should be traced to that house, and himself, if found there, dealt with summarily upon suspicion, he turned about, and went off to seek sanctuary with his uncle, the Vice-Chancellor.

The Duke's horse, which he had ridden, he turned loose in the streets, where it was found some hours later, and first gave occasion to rumours of foul play. The rumours growing, with the discovery of the body of Gandia's groom, and search-parties of armed bargelli scouring Rome, and the Giudecca in particular, in the course of the next two days, forth at last came Giorgio, that boatman of the Schiavoni, with the tale of what he had seen. When the stricken Pope heard it, he ordered the bed of the river to be dragged foot by foot, with the result that the ill-starred Duke of Gandia was brought up in one of the nets, whereupon the heartless Sanazzaro coined his terrible epigram concerning that successor of Saint Peter, that Fisherman of Men.

The people, looking about for him who had the greatest motive for that deed, were quick to fasten the guilt upon Giovanni Sforza, who by that time was far from Rome, riding hard for the shelter of his tyranny of Pesaro; and the Cardinal Ascanio Sforza, who was also mentioned, and who feared to be implicated, apprehensive ever lest his page should have seen the betraying arms upon the ring of his masked visitor - fled also, nor could be induced to return save under a safe-conduct from the Holy Father, expressing conviction of his innocence.

Later public rumour accused others; indeed, they accused in turn every man who could have been a possible perpetrator, attributing to some of them the most fantastic and incredible motives. Once, prompted no doubt by their knowledge of the libertine, pleasure-loving nature of the dead Duke, rumour hit upon the actual circumstances of the murder so closely, indeed, that the Count of Mirandola's house was visited by the bargelli and subjected to an examination, at which Pico violently rebelled, appealing boldly to the Pope against insinuations that reflected upon the honour of his daughter.

The mystery remained impenetrable, and the culprit was never brought to justice. We know that in slaying Gandia, Giovanni Sforza vented a hatred whose object was not Gandia, but Gandia's father. His aim was to deal Pope Alexander the cruellest and most lingering of wounds, and if he lacked the avenger's satisfaction of disclosing himself, at least he did not lack assurance that his blow had stricken home. He heard - as all Italy heard - from that wayfarer on the bridge of Sant' Angelo, how the Pope, in a paroxysm of grief at sight of his son's body fished from the Tiber, had bellowed in his agony like a tortured bull, so that his cries within the castle were heard upon the bridge. He learnt how the handsome, vigorous Pope staggered into the consistory of the 19th of that same month with the mien and gait of a palsied old man, and, in a voice broken with sobs, proclaimed his bitter lament:

"Had we seven Papacies we would give them all to restore the Duke to life. "

He might have been content. But he was not. That deep hate of his against those who had made him a thing of scorn was not so easily to be slaked. He waited, spying his opportunity for further hurt. It came a year later, when Gandia's brother, the ambitious Cesare Borgia, divested himself of his cardinalitial robes and rank, exchanging them for temporal dignities and the title of Duke of Valentinois. Then it was that he took up the deadly weapon of calumny, putting it secretly about that Cesare was the murderer of his brother, spurred to it by worldly ambition and by other motives which involved the principal members of the family.

Men do not mount to Borgia heights without making enemies. The evil tale was taken up in all its foul trappings, and, upon no better authority than the public voice, it was enshrined in chronicles by every scribbler of the day. And for four hundred years that lie has held its place in history, the very cornerstone of all the execration that has been heaped upon the name of Borgia. Never was vengeance more terrible, far-reaching, and abiding. It is only in this twentieth century of ours that dispassionate historians have nailed upon the counter of truth the base coin of that accusation.

XII. THE NIGHT OF ESCAPE

Casanova's Escape from the Piombi

Patrician influence from without had procured Casanova's removal in August of that year, 1756, from the loathsome cell he had occupied for thirteen months in the Piombi - so called from the leaded roof immediately above those prisons which are simply the garrets of the Doge's palace.

That cell had been no better than a kennel seldom reached by the light of day, and so shallow that it was impossible for a man of his fine height to stand upright in it. But his present prison was comparatively spacious and it was airy and well-lighted by a barred window, whence he could see the Lido.

Yet he was desperately chagrined at the change, for he had almost completed his arrangements to break out of his former cell. The only ray of hope in his present despair came from the fact that the implement to which he trusted was still in his possession, safely concealed in the upholstery of the armchair that had been moved with him into his present quarters. That implement he had fashioned for himself with infinite pains out of a door-bolt some twenty inches long, which he had found discarded in a rubbish-heap in a corner of the attic where he had been allowed to take his brief daily exercise. Using as a whetstone a small slab of black marble, similarly acquired, he had shaped that bolt into a sharp octagonal-pointed chisel or spontoon.

It remained in his possession, but he saw no chance of using it now, for the suspicions of Lorenzo, the gaoler, were aroused, and daily a couple of archers came to sound the floors and walls. True they did not sound the ceiling, which was low and within reach. But it was obviously impossible to cut through the ceiling in such a manner as to leave the progress of the work unseen.

Hence his despair of breaking out of a prison where he had spent over a year without trial or prospect of a trial, and where he seemed likely to spend the remainder of his days. He did not even know precisely why he had been arrested. All that Giacomo Casanova knew was that he was accounted a disturber of the public peace. He was notoriously a libertine, a gamester, and heavily in debt: also -

and this was more serious - he was accused of practising magic, as indeed he had done, as a means of exploiting to his own profit the credulity of simpletons of all degrees. He would have explained to the Inquisitors of State of the Most Serene Republic that the books of magic found by their apparitors in his possession - "The Clavicula of Solomon, " the "Zecor-ben, " and other kindred works - had been collected by him as curious instances of human aberration. But the Inquisitors of State would not have believed him, for the Inquisitors were among those who took magic seriously. And, anyhow, they had never asked him to explain, but had left him as if forgotten in that abominable verminous cell under the leads, until his patrician friend had obtained him the mercy of this transfer to better quarters.

This Casanova was a man of iron nerve and iron constitution. Tall and well-made, he was boldly handsome, with fine dark eyes and dark brown hair. In age he was barely one and twenty; but he looked older, as well he might, for in his adventurer's way he had already gathered more experience of life than most men gain in half a century.

The same influence that had obtained him his change of cell had also gained him latterly the privilege - and he esteemed it beyond all else - of procuring himself books. Desiring the works of Maffai, he bade his gaoler purchase them out of the allowance made him by the Inquisitors in accordance with the Venetian custom. This allowance was graduated to the social status of each prisoner. But the books being costly and any monthly surplus from his monthly expenditure being usually the gaoler's perquisite, Lorenzo was reluctant to indulge him. He mentioned that there was a prisoner above who was well equipped with books, and who, no doubt, would be glad to lend in exchange.

Yielding to the suggestion, Casanova handed Lorenzo a copy of Peteau's "Rationarium, " and received next morning, in exchange, the first volume of Wolf. Within he found a sheet bearing in six verses a paraphrase of Seneca's epigram, "Calamitosus est animus futuri anxius. " Immediately he perceived he had stumbled upon a means of corresponding with one who might be disposed to assist him to break prison.

In reply, being a scholarly rascal (he had been educated for the priesthood), he wrote six verses himself. Having no pen, he cut the long nail of his little finger to a point, and, splitting it, supplied the want. For ink he used the juice of mulberries. In addition to the verses, he wrote a list of the books in his possession, which he placed at the disposal of his fellow-captive. He concealed the written sheet in the spine of that vellum-bound volume; and on the title-page, in warning of this, he wrote the single Latin word "Latet. " Next morning he handed the book to Lorenzo, telling him that he had read it, and requesting the second volume.

That second volume came on the next day, and in the spine of it a long letter, some sheets of paper, pens, and a pencil. The writer announced himself as one Marino Balbi, a patrician and a monk, who had been four years in that prison, where he had since been given a companion in misfortune, Count Andrea Asquino.

Thus began a regular and very full correspondence between the prisoners, and soon Casanova - who had not lived on his wits for nothing - was able to form a shrewd estimate of Balbi's character. The monk's letters revealed it as compounded of sensuality, stupidity, ingratitude, and indiscretion.

"In the world, " says Casanova, "I should have had no commerce with a fellow of his nature. But in the Piombi I was obliged to make capital out of everything that came under my hands. "

The capital he desired to make in this instance was to ascertain whether Balbi would be disposed to do for him what he could not do for himself. He wrote inquiring, and proposing flight.

Balbi replied that he and his companion would do anything possible to make their escape from that abominable prison, but his lack of resource made him add that he was convinced that nothing was possible.

"All that you have to do, " wrote Casanova in answer, "is to break through the ceiling of my cell and get me out of this, then trust to me to get you out of the Piombi. If you are disposed to make the attempt, I will supply you with the means, and show you the way. "

It was a characteristically bold reply, revealing to us the utter gamester that he was in all things.

He knew that Balbi's cell was situated immediately under the leads, and he hoped that once in it he should be able readily to find a way through the roof. That cell of Balbi's communicated with a narrow corridor, no more than a shaft for light and air, which was immediately above Casanova's prison. And no sooner had Balbi written, consenting, than Casanova explained what was to do. Balbi must break through the wall of his cell into the little corridor, and there cut a round hole in the floor precisely as Casanova had done in his former cell - until nothing but a shell of ceiling remained - a shell that could be broken down by half a dozen blows when the moment to escape should have arrived.

To begin with, he ordered Balbi to purchase himself two or three dozen pictures of saints, with which to paper his walls, using as many as might be necessary for a screen to hide the hole he would be cutting.

When Balbi wrote that his walls were hung with pictures of saints, it became a question of conveying the spontoon to him. This was difficult, and the monk's fatuous suggestions merely served further to reveal his stupidity. Finally Casanova's wits found the way. He bade Lorenzo buy him an in-folio edition of the Bible which had just been published, and it was into the spine of this enormous tome that he packed the precious spontoon, and thus conveyed it to Balbi, who immediately got to work.

This was at the commencement of October. On the 8th of that month Balbi wrote to Casanova that a whole night devoted to labour had resulted merely in the displacing of a single brick, which so discouraged the faint-hearted monk that he was for abandoning an attempt whose only result must be to increase in the future the rigour of their confinement.

Without hesitation, Casanova replied that he was assured of success - although he was far from having any grounds for any such assurance. He enjoined the monk to believe him, and to persevere, confident that as he advanced he would find progress easier. This proved, indeed, to be the case, for soon Balbi found the brickwork yielding so rapidly to his efforts that one morning, a week later, Casanova heard three light taps above his head - the preconcerted signal by which they were to assure themselves that their notions of the topography of the prison were correct.

All that day he heard Balbi at work immediately above him, and again on the morrow, when Balbi wrote that as the floor was of the thickness of only two boards, he counted upon completing the job on the next day, without piercing the ceiling.

But it would seem as if Fortune were intent upon making a mock of Casanova, luring him to heights of hope, merely to cast him down again into the depths of despair. Just as upon the eve of breaking out of his former cell mischance had thwarted him, so now, when again he deemed himself upon the very threshold of liberty, came mischance again to thwart him.

Early in the afternoon the sound of bolts being drawn outside froze his very blood and checked his breathing. Yet he had the presence of mind to give the double knock that was the agreed alarm signal, whereupon Balbi instantly desisted from his labours overhead.

Came Lorenzo with two archers, leading an ugly, lean little man of between forty and fifty years of age, shabbily dressed and wearing a round black wig, whom the tribunal had ordered should share Casanova's prison for the present. With apologies for leaving such a scoundrel in Casanova's company, Lorenzo departed, and the newcomer went down upon his knees, drew forth a chaplet, and began to tell his beads.

Casanova surveyed this intruder at once with disgust and despair. Presently his disgust was increased when the fellow, whose name was Soradici, frankly avowed himself a spy in the service of the Council of Ten, a calling which he warmly defended from the contempt universally - but unjustly, according to himself - meted out to it. He had been imprisoned for having failed in his duty on one occasion through succumbing to a bribe.

Conceive Casanova's frame of mind - his uncertainty as to how long this monster, as he calls him, might be left in his company, his curbed impatience to regain his liberty, and his consciousness of the horrible risk of discovery which delay entailed! He wrote to Balbi that night while the spy slept, and for the present their operations were suspended. But not for very long. Soon Casanova's wits resolved how to turn to account the weakness which he discovered in Soradici.

The spy was devout to the point of bigoted, credulous superstition. He spent long hours in prayer, and he talked freely of his special devotion to the Blessed Virgin, and his ardent faith in miracles.

Casanova - the arch-humbug who had worked magic to delude the credulous - determined there and then to work a miracle for Soradici. Assuming an inspired air, he solemnly informed the spy one morning that it had been revealed to him in a dream that Soradici's devotion to the Rosary was about to be rewarded; that an angel was to be sent from heaven to deliver him from prison, and that Casanova himself would accompany him in his flight.

If Soradici doubted, conviction was soon to follow. For Casanova foretold the very hour at which the angel would come to break into the prison, and at that hour precisely - Casanova having warned Balbi - the noise made by the angel overhead flung Soradici into an ecstasy of terror.

But when, at the end of four hours, the angel desisted from his labours, Soradici was beset by doubts. Casanova explained to him that since angels invariably put on the garb of human flesh when descending upon earth, they labour under human difficulties. He added the prophecy that the angel would return on the last day of the month, the eve of All Saints'- two days later - and that he would then conduct them out of captivity.

By this means Casanova ensured that no betrayal should be feared from the thoroughly duped Soradici, who now spent the time in praying, weeping, and talking of his sins and of the inexhaustibility of divine grace. To make doubly sure, Casanova added the most terrible oath that if, by a word to the gaoler, Soradici should presume to frustrate the divine intentions, he would immediately strangle him with his own hands.

On October 31st Lorenzo paid his usual daily visit early in the morning. After his departure they waited some hours, Soradici in expectant terror, Casanova in sheer impatience to be at work. Promptly at noon fell heavy blows overhead, and then, in a cloud of plaster and broken laths, the heavenly messenger descended clumsily into Casanova's arms.

Soradici found this tall, gaunt, bearded figure, clad in a dirty shirt and a pair of leather breeches, of a singularly unangelic appearance; indeed, he looked far more like a devil.

When he produced a pair of scissors, so that the spy might cut Casanova's beard, which, like the angel's, had grown in captivity,

Soradici ceased to have any illusions on the score of Balbi's celestial nature. Although still intrigued - since he could not guess at the secret correspondence that had passed between Casanova and Balbi - he perceived quite clearly that he had been fooled.

Leaving Soradici in the monk's care, Casanova hoisted himself through the broken ceiling and gained Balbi's cell, where the sight of Count Asquino dismayed him. He found a middle-aged man of a corpulence which must render it impossible for him to face the athletic difficulties that lay before them; of this the Count himself seemed already persuaded.

"If you think, " was his greeting, as he shook Casanova's hand, "to break through the roof and find a way down from the leads, I don't see how you are to succeed without wings. I have not the courage to accompany you, " he added, "I shall remain and pray for you. "

Attempting no persuasions where they must have been idle, Casanova passed out of the cell again, and approaching as nearly as possible to the edge of the attic, he sat down where he could touch the roof as it sloped immediately above his head. With his spontoon he tested the timbers, and found them so decayed that they almost crumbled at the touch. Assured thereby that the cutting of a hole would be an easy matter, he at once returned to his cell, and there he spent the ensuing four hours in preparing ropes. He cut up sheets, blankets, coverlets, and the very cover of his mattress, knotting the strips together with the utmost care. In the end he found himself equipped with some two hundred yards of rope, which should be ample for any purpose.

Having made a bundle of the fine taffeta suit in which he had been arrested, his gay cloak of floss silk, some stockings, shirts, and handkerchiefs, he and Balbi passed up to the other cell, compelling Soradici to go with them. Leaving the monk to make a parcel of his belongings, Casanova went to tackle the roof. By dusk he had made a hole twice as large as was necessary, and had laid bare the lead sheeting with which the roof was covered. Unable, single-handed, to raise one of the sheets, he called Balbi to his aid, and between them, assisted by the spontoon, which Casanova inserted between the edge of the sheet and the gutter, they at last succeeded in tearing away the rivets. Then by putting their shoulders to the lead they bent it upwards until there was room to emerge, and a view of the sky flooded by the vivid light of the crescent moon.

Not daring in that light to venture upon the roof, where they would be seen, they must wait with what patience they could until midnight, when the moon would have set. So they returned to the cell where they had left Soradici with Count Asquino.

From Balbi, Casanova had learnt that Asquino, though well supplied with money, was of an avaricious nature. Nevertheless, since money would be necessary, Casanova asked the Count for the loan of thirty gold sequins. Asquino answered him gently that, in the first place, they would not need money to escape; that, in the second, he had a numerous family; that, in the third, if Casanova perished the money would be lost; and that, in the fourth, he had no money.

"My reply, " writes Casanova, "lasted half an hour. "

"Let me remind you, " he said in concluding his exhortation, "of your promise to pray for us, and let me ask you what sense there can be in praying for the success of an enterprise to which you refuse to contribute the most necessary means. "

The old man was so far conquered by Casanova's eloquence that he offered him two sequins, which Casanova accepted, since he was not in case to refuse anything.

Thereafter, as they sat waiting for the moon to set, Casanova found his earlier estimate of the monk's character confirmed. Balbi now broke into abusive reproaches. He found that Casanova had acted in bad faith by assuring him that he had formed a complete plan of escape. Had he suspected that this was a mere gambler's throw on Casanova's part, he would never have laboured to get him out of his cell. The Count added his advice that they should abandon an attempt foredoomed to failure, and, being concerned for the two sequins with which he had so reluctantly parted, he argued the case at great length. Stifling his disgust, Casanova assured them that, although it was impossible for him to afford them details of how he intended to proceed, he was perfectly confident of success.

At half-past ten he sent Soradici -who had remained silent throughout - to report upon the night. The spy brought word that in another hour or so the moon would have set, but that a thick mist was rising, which must render the leads very dangerous.

"So long as the mist isn't made of oil, I am content, " said Casanova. "Come, make a bundle of your cloak. It is time we were moving. "

But at this Soradici fell on his knees in the dark, seized Casanova's hands, and begged to be left behind to pray for their safety, since he would be sure to meet his death if he attempted to go with them.

Casanova assented readily, delighted to be rid of the fellow. Then in the dark he wrote as best he could a quite characteristic letter to the Inquisitors of State, in which he took his leave of them, telling them that since he had been fetched into the prison without his wishes being consulted, they could not complain that he should depart without consulting theirs.

The bundle containing Balbi's clothes, and another made up of half the rope, he slung from the monk's neck, thereafter doing the same in his own case. Then, in their shirt-sleeves, their hats on their heads, the pair of them started on their perilous journey, leaving Count Asquino and Soradici to pray for them.

Casanova went first, on all fours, and thrusting the point of his spontoon between the joints of the lead sheeting so as to obtain a hold, he crawled slowly upwards. To follow, Balbi took a grip of Casanova's belt with his right hand, so that, in addition to making his own way, Casanova was compelled to drag the weight of his companion after him, and this up the sharp gradient of a roof rendered slippery by the mist.

Midway in that laborious ascent, the monk called to him to stop. He had dropped the bundle containing the clothes, and he hoped that it had not rolled beyond the gutter, though he did not mention which of them should retrieve it. After the unreasonableness already endured from this man, Casanova's exasperation was such in that moment that, he confesses, he was tempted to kick him after this bundle. Controlling himself, however, he answered patiently that the matter could not now be helped, and kept steadily amain.

At last the apex of the roof was reached, and they got astride of it to breathe and to take a survey of their surroundings. They faced the several cupolas of the Church of Saint Mark, which is connected with the ducal palace, being, in fact, no more than the private chapel of the Doge.

They set down their bundles, and, of course, in the act of doing so the wretched Balbi must lose his hat, and send it rolling down the roof after the bundle he had already lost. He cried out that it was an evil omen.

"On the contrary, " Casanova assured him patiently, "it is a sign of divine protection; for if your bundle or your hat had happened to roll to the left instead of the right it would have fallen into the courtyard, where it would be seen by the guards, who must conclude that some one is moving on the roof, and so, no doubt, would have discovered us. As it is your hat has followed your bundle into the canal, where it can do no harm. "

Thereupon, bidding the monk await his return, Casanova set off alone on a voyage of discovery, keeping for the present astride of the roof in his progress. He spent a full hour wandering along the vast roof, going to right and to left in his quest, but failing completely to make any helpful discovery, or to find anything to which he could attach a rope. In the end it began to look as if, after all, he must choose between returning to prison and flinging himself from the roof into the canal. He was almost in despair, when in his wanderings his attention was caught by a dormer window on the canal side, about two-thirds of the way down the slope of the roof. With infinite precaution he lowered himself down the steep, slippery incline until he was astride of the little dormer roof. Leaning well forward, he discovered that a slender grating barred the leaded panes of the window itself, and for a moment this grating gave him pause.

Midnight boomed just then from the Church of Saint Mark, like a reminder that but seven hours remained in which to conquer this and further difficulties that might confront him, and in which to win clear of that place, or else submit to a resumption of his imprisonment under conditions, no doubt, a hundredfold more rigorous.

Lying flat on his stomach, and hanging far over, so as to see what he was doing, he worked one point of his spontoon into the sash of the grating, and, levering outwards, he strained until at last it came away completely in his hands. After that it was an easy matter to shatter the little latticed window.

Having accomplished so much, he turned, and, using his spontoon as before, he crawled back to the summit of the roof, and made his way rapidly along this to the spot where he had left Balbi. The monk, reduced by now to a state of blending despair, terror, and rage, greeted Casanova in terms of the grossest abuse for having left him there so long.

"I was waiting only for daylight, " he concluded, "to return to prison. "

"What did you think had become of me? " asked Casanova.

"I imagined that you had tumbled off the roof. "

"And is this abuse the expression of your joy at finding yourself mistaken? "

"Where have you been all this time? " the monk counter-questioned sullenly.

"Come with me and you shall see. "

And taking up his bundle again, Casanova led his companion forward until they were in line with the dormer. There Casanova showed him what he had done, and consulted him as to the means to be adopted to enter the attic. It would be too risky for them to allow themselves to drop from the sill, since the height of the window from the floor was unknown to them, and might be considerable. It would be easy for one of them to lower the other by means of the rope. But it was not apparent how, hereafter, the other was to follow. Thus reasoned Casanova.

"You had better lower me, anyhow, " said Balbi, without hesitation; for no doubt he was very tired of that slippery roof, on which a single false step might have sent him to his account. "Once I am inside you can consider ways of following me. "

That cold-blooded expression of the fellow's egoism put Casanova in a rage for the second time since they had left their prison. But, as before, he conquered it, and without uttering a word he proceeded to unfasten the coil of rope. Making one end of it secure under Balbi's arms, he bade the monk lie prone upon the roof, his feet pointing downwards, and then, paying out rope, he lowered him to the dormer. He then bade him get through the window as far as the level of his waist, and wait thus, hanging over and supporting himself upon the sill. When he had obeyed, Casanova followed, sliding carefully down to the roof of the dormer. Planting himself firmly, and taking the rope once more, he bade Balbi to let himself go without fear, and so lowered him to the floor - a height from the window, as it proved, of some fifty feet. This extinguished all Casanova's hopes of being able to follow by allowing himself to drop from the sill. He was dismayed. But the monk, happy to find himself at last off that accursed roof, and out of all danger of breaking his neck, called foolishly to Casanova to throw him the rope so that he might take care of it.

"As may be imagined, " says Casanova, "I was careful not to take this idiotic advice. "

Not knowing now what was to become of him unless he could discover some other means than those at his command, he climbed back again to the summit of the roof, and started off desperately upon another voyage of discovery. This time he succeeded better than before. He found about a cupola a terrace which he had not earlier noticed, and on this terrace a hod of plaster, a trowel, and a ladder some seventy feet long. He saw his difficulties solved. He passed an end of rope about one of the rungs, laid the ladder flat along the slope of the roof, and then, still astride of the apex, he worked his way back, dragging the ladder with him, until he was once more on a level with the dormer.

But now the difficulty was how to get the ladder through the window, and he had cause to repent having so hastily deprived himself of his companion's assistance. He had got the ladder into position, and lowered it until one of its ends rested upon the dormer, whilst the other projected some twenty feet beyond the edge of the roof. He slid down to the dormer, and placing the ladder beside him, drew it up so that he could reach the eighth rung. To this rung he made fast his rope, then lowered the ladder again until the upper end of it was in line with the window through which he sought to introduce it. But he found it impossible to do so beyond the fifth rung, for at this point the end of the ladder came in contact with the roof inside, and could be pushed no farther until it was inclined downward. Now, the only possible way to accomplish this was by raising the other end.

It occurred to him that he might, by so attaching the rope as to bring the ladder across the window frame, lower himself hand over hand to the floor of the attic. But in so doing he must have left the ladder there to show their pursuers in the morning, not merely the way they had gone, but for all he knew at this stage, the place where they might then be still in hiding. Having come so far, at so much risk and labour, he was determined to leave nothing to chance. To accomplish his object then, he made his way down to the very edge of the roof, sliding carefully on his stomach until his feet found support against the marble gutter, the ladder meanwhile remaining hooked by one of its rungs to the sill of the dormer.

In that perilous position he lifted his end of the ladder a few inches, and so contrived to thrust it another foot or so through the window, whereby its weight was considerably diminished. If he could but get it another couple of feet farther in he was sure that by returning to the dormer he would have been able to complete the job. In his anxiety to do this and to obtain the necessary elevation, he raised himself upon his knees.

But in the very act of making the thrust he slipped, and, clutching wildly as he went, he shot over the edge of the roof. He found himself hanging there, suspended above that terrific abyss by his hands and his elbows, which had convulsively hooked themselves on to the edge of the gutter, so that he had it on a level with his breast.

It was a moment of dread the like of which he was never likely to endure again in a life that was to know many perils and many hairbreadth escapes. He could not write of it nearly half a century later without shuddering and growing sick with horror.

A moment he hung there gasping, then almost mechanically, guided by the sheer instinct of self-preservation, he not merely attempted, but actually succeeded in raising himself so as to bring his side against the gutter. Then continuing gradually to raise himself until his waist was on a level with the edge, he threw the weight of his trunk forward upon the roof, and slowly brought his right leg up until he had obtained with his knee a further grip of the gutter. The rest was easy, and you may conceive him as he lay there on the roof's edge, panting and shuddering for a moment to regain his breath and nerve.

Meanwhile, the ladder, driven forward by the thrust that had so nearly cost him his life, had penetrated another three feet through the window, and hung there immovable. Recovered, he took up his spontoon, which he had placed in the gutter, and, assisted by it, he climbed back to the dormer. Almost without further difficulty, he succeeded now in introducing the ladder until, of its own weight, it swung down into position.

A moment later he had joined Balbi in the attic, and together they groped about in it the dark, until finding presently a door, they passed into another chamber, where they discovered furniture by hurtling against it. Guided by a faint glimmer of light, Casanova made his way to one of the windows and opened it. He looked out upon a black abyss, and, having no knowledge of the locality, and no inclination to adventure himself into unknown regions, he immediately abandoned all idea of attempting to climb down. He closed the window again, and going back to the other room, he lay down on the floor, with the bundle of ropes for a pillow, to wait for dawn.

And so exhausted was he, not only by the efforts of the past hours, and the terrible experience in which they had culminated, but also because in the last two days he had scarcely eaten or slept, that straightway, and greatly to Balbi's indignation and disgust, he fell into a profound sleep.

He was aroused three and a half hours later by the clamours and shakings of the exasperated monk. Protesting that such a sleep at such a time was a thing inconceivable, Balbi informed him that it had just struck five.

It was still dark, but already there was a dim grey glimmer of dawn by which objects could be faintly discerned. Searching, Casanova found another door opposite that of the chamber which they had entered earlier. It was locked, but the lock was a poor one that yielded to half a dozen blows of the spontoon, and they passed into a little room beyond which by an open door they came into a long gallery lined with pigeon-holes stuffed with parchments, which they conceived to be the archives. At the end of this gallery they found a short flight of stairs, and below that yet another, which brought them to a glass door. Opening this, they entered a room which Casanova immediately identified as the ducal chancellery. Descent from one of its windows would have been easy, but they would have found themselves in the labyrinth of courts and alleys behind Saint Mark's, which would not have suited them at all.

On a table Casanova found a stout bodkin with a long wooden handle, the implement used by the secretaries for piercing parchments that were to be joined by a cord bearing the leaden seals of the Republic. He opened a desk, and rummaging in it, found a letter addressed to the Proveditor of Corfu, advising a remittance of three thousand sequins for the repair of the fortress. He rummaged further, seeking the three thousand sequins, which he would have appropriated without the least scruple. Unfortunately they were not there.

Quitting the desk, he crossed to the door, not merely to find it locked, but to discover that it was not the kind of lock that would yield to blows. There was no way out but by battering away one of the panels, and to this he addressed himself without hesitation, assisted by Balbi, who had armed himself with the bodkin, but who trembled fearfully at the noise of Casanova's blows. There was danger in this, but the danger must be braved, for time was slipping away. In half an hour they had broken down all the panel it was possible to remove without the help of a saw. The opening they had made was at a height of five feet from the ground, and the splintered woodwork armed it with a fearful array of jagged teeth.

They dragged a couple of stools to the door, and getting on to these, Casanova bade Balbi go first. The long, lean monk folded his arms, and thrust head and shoulders through the hole; then Casanova lifted him, first by the waist, then by the legs, and so helped him through into the room beyond. Casanova threw their bundles after him, and then placing a third stool on top of the other two, climbed on to it, and, being almost on a level with the opening, was able to get through as far as his waist, when Balbi took him in his arms and proceeded to drag him out. But it was done at the cost of torn breeches and lacerated legs, and when he stood up in the room beyond he was bleeding freely from the wounds which the jagged edges of the wood had dealt him.

After that they went down two staircases, and came out at last in the gallery leading to the great doors at the head of that magnificent flight of steps known as the Giant's Staircase. But these doors - the main entrance of the palace - were locked, and, at a glance, Casanova saw that nothing short of a hatchet would serve to open them. There was no more to be done.

With a resignation that seemed to Balbi entirely cynical, Casanova sat down on the floor.

"My task is ended, " he announced. "It is now for Heaven or Chance to do the rest. I don't know whether the palace cleaners will come here to-day as it is All Saints', or to-morrow, which will be All Souls'. Should any one come, I shall run for it the moment the door is opened, and you had best follow me. If no one comes, I shall not move from here, and if I die of hunger, so much the worse. "

It was a speech that flung the monk into a passion. In burning terms he reviled Casanova, calling him a madman, a seducer, a deceiver, a liar. Casanova let him rave. It was just striking six. Precisely an hour had elapsed since they had left the attic.

Balbi, in his red flannel waistcoat and his puce-coloured leather breeches, might have passed for a peasant; but Casanova, in torn garments that were soaked in blood, presented an appearance that was terrifying and suspicious. This he proceeded to repair. Tearing a handkerchief, he made shift to bandage his wounds, and then from his bundle he took his fine taffeta summer suit, which on a winter's day must render him ridiculous.

He dressed his thick, dark brown hair as best he could, drew on a pair of white stockings, and donned three lace shirts one over another. His fine cloak of floss silk he gave to Balbi, who looked for all the world as if he had stolen it.

Thus dressed, his fine hat laced with point of Spain on his head, Casanova opened a window and looked out. At once he was seen by some idlers in the courtyard, who, amazed at his appearance there, and conceiving that he must have been locked in by mistake on the previous day, went off at once to advise the porter. Meanwhile, Casanova, vexed at having shown himself where he had not expected any one, and little guessing how excellently this was to serve his ends, left the window and went to sit beside the angry friar, who greeted him with fresh revilings.

A sound of steps and a rattle of keys stemmed Balbi's reproaches in full flow. The lock groaned.

"Not a word, " said Casanova to the monk, "but follow me. "

Holding his spontoon ready., but concealed under his coat, he stepped to the side of the door. It opened, and the porter, who had come alone and bareheaded, stared in stupefaction at the strange apparition of Casanova.

Casanova took advantage of that paralyzing amazement. Without uttering a word, he stepped quickly across the threshold, and with Balbi close upon his heels, he went down the Giant's Staircase in a flash, crossed the little square, reached the canal, bundled Balbi into the first gondola he found there, and jumped in after him.

"I want to go to Fusine, and quickly, " he announced. "Call another oarsman. "

All was ready, and in a moment the gondola was skimming the canal. Dressed in his unseasonable suit, and accompanied by the still more ridiculous figure of Balbi in his gaudy cloak and without a hat, he imagined he would be taken for a charlatan or an astrologer.

The gondola slipped past the custom-house, and took the canal of the Giudecca. Halfway down this, Casanova put his head out of the little cabin to address the gondolier in the poop.

"Do you think we shall reach Mestre in an hour? "

"Mestre? " quoth the gondolier. "But you said Fusine. "

"No, no, I said Mestre - at least, I intended to say Mestre. "

And so the gondola was headed for Mestre by a gondolier who professed himself ready to convey his excellency to England if he desired it.

The sun was rising, and the water assumed an opalescent hue. It was a delicious morning, Casanova tells us, and I suspect that never had any morning seemed to that audacious, amiable rascal as delicious as this upon which he regained his liberty, which no man ever valued more highly.

In spirit he was already safely over the frontiers of the Most Serene Republic, impatient to transfer his body thither, as he shortly did, through vicissitudes that are a narrative in themselves, and no part of this story of his escape from the Piombi and the Venetian Inquisitors of State.

XIII. THE NIGHT OF MASQUERADE

The Assassination of Gustavus III of Sweden

Baron Bjelke sprang from his carriage almost before it had come to a standstill and without waiting for the footman to let down the steps. With a haste entirely foreign to a person of his station and importance, he swept into the great vestibule of the palace, and in a quivering voice flung a question at the first lackey he encountered:

"Has His Majesty started yet? "

"Not yet, my lord. "

The answer lessened his haste, but not his agitation. He cast off the heavy wolfskin pelisse in which he had been wrapped, and, leaving it in the hands of the servant, went briskly up the grand staircase, a tall, youthful figure, very graceful in the suit of black he wore.

As he passed through a succession of ante-rooms on his way to the private apartments of the King, those present observed the pallor of his clean-cut face under the auburn tie-wig he affected, and the feverish glow of eyes that took account of no one. They could not guess that Baron Bjelke, the King's secretary and favourite, carried in his hands the life of his royal master, or its equivalent in the shape of the secret of the plot to assassinate him.

In many ways Bjelke was no better than the other profligate minions of the profligate Gustavus of Sweden. But he had this advantage over them, that his intellect was above their average. He had detected the first signs of the approach of that storm which the King himself had so heedlessly provoked. He knew, as much by reason as by intuition, that, in these days when the neighbouring State of France writhed in the throes of a terrific revolution against monarchic and aristocratic tyranny, it was not safe for a king to persist in the abuse of his parasitic power. New ideas of socialism were in the air. They were spreading through Europe, and it was not only in France that men accounted it an infamous anachronism that the great mass of a community should toil and sweat and suffer for the benefit of an insolent minority.

Already had there been trouble with the peasantry in Sweden, and Bjelke had endangered his position as a royal favourite by presuming to warn his master. Gustavus III desired amusement, not wisdom, from those about him. He could not be brought to realize the responsibilities which kingship imposes upon a man. It has been pretended that he was endowed with great gifts of mind. He may have been, though the thing has been pretended of so many princes that one may be sceptical where evidence is lacking. If he possessed those gifts, he succeeded wonderfully in concealing them under a nature that was frivolously gay, dissolute, and extravagant.

His extravagance forced him into monstrous extortions when only a madman would have wasted in profligacy the wealth so cruelly wrung from long-suffering subjects. From extortion he was driven by his desperate need of money into flagrant dishonesty. At a stroke of the pen he had reduced the value of the paper currency by one-third - a reduction so violent and sudden that, whilst it impoverished many, it involved some in absolute ruin - and this that he might gratify his appetite for magnificence and enrich the rapacious favourites who shared his profligacy.

The unrest in the kingdom spread. It was no longer a question of the resentment of a more or less docile peasantry whose first stirrings of revolt were easily quelled. The lesser nobility of Sweden were angered by a measure - following upon so many others - that bore peculiarly heavily upon themselves; and out of that anger, fanned by one man - John Jacob Ankarstrom - who had felt the vindictive spirit of royal injustice, flamed in secret the conspiracy against the King's life which Bjelke had discovered.

He had discovered it by the perilous course of joining the conspirators. He had won their confidence, and they recognized that his collaboration was rendered invaluable by the position he held so near the King. And in his subtle wisdom, at considerable danger to himself, Bjelke had kept his counsel. He had waited until now, until the moment when the blow was about to fall, before making the disclosure which should not only save Gustavus, but enable him to cast a net in which all the plotters must be caught. And he hoped that when Gustavus perceived the narrowness of his escape, and the reality of the dangers amid which he walked, he would consider the wisdom of taking another course in future.

He had reached the door of the last ante-chamber, when a detaining hand was laid upon his arm. He found himself accosted by a page - the offspring of one of the noblest families in Sweden, and the son of one of Bjelke's closest friends, a fair-haired, impudent boy to whom the secretary permitted a certain familiarity.

"Are you on your way to the King, Baron? " the lad inquired.

"I am, Carl. What is it? "

"A letter for His Majesty - a note fragrant as a midsummer rose - which a servant has just delivered to me. Will you take it? "

"Give it to me, impudence, " said Bjelke, the ghost of a smile lighting for a moment his white face.

He took the letter and passed on into the last antechamber, which was empty of all but a single chamberlain-in-waiting. This chamberlain bowed respectfully to the Baron.

"His Majesty? " said Bjelke.

"He is dressing. Shall I announce Your Excellency? "

"Pray do. "

The chamberlain vanished, and Bjelke was left alone. Waiting, he stood there, idly fingering the scented note he had received from the page. As he turned it in his fingers the superscription came uppermost, and he turned it no more. His eyes lost their absorbed look, their glance quickened into attention, a frown shaped itself between them like a scar; his breathing, suspended a moment, was renewed with a gasp. He stepped aside to a table bearing a score of candles clustered in a massive silver branch, and held the note so that the light fell full upon the writing.

Standing thus, he passed a hand over his eyes and stared again, two hectic spots burning now in his white cheeks. Abruptly, disregarding the superscription, his trembling fingers snapped the blank seal and unfolded the letter addressed to his royal master. He was still reading when the chamberlain returned to announce that the King was pleased to see the Baron at once. He did not seem to hear the announcement. His attention was all upon the letter, his lips drawn back from his teeth in a grin, and beads of perspiration glistening upon his brow.

"His Majesty - " the chamberlain was beginning to repeat, when he broke off suddenly. "Your Excellency is ill? "

"Ill? "

Bjelke stared at him with glassy eyes. He crumpled the letter in his hand and stuffed one and the other into the pocket of his black satin coat. He attempted to laugh to reassure the startled chamberlain, and achieved a ghastly grimace.

"I must not keep His Majesty waiting, " he said thickly, and stumbled on, leaving in the chamberlain's mind a suspicion that His Majesty's secretary was not quite sober.

But Bjelke so far conquered his emotion that he was almost his usual imperturbable self when he reached the royal dressing-room; indeed, he no longer displayed even the agitation that had possessed him when first he entered the palace.

Gustavus, a slight, handsome man of a good height, was standing before a cheval-glass when Bjelke came in. Francois, the priceless valet His Majesty had brought back from his last pleasure-seeking visit to pre-revolutionary Paris some five years ago, was standing back judicially to consider the domino he had just placed upon the royal shoulders. Baron Armfelt whom the conspirators accused of wielding the most sinister of all the sinister influences that perverted the King's mind - dressed from head to foot in shimmering white satin, lounged on a divan with all the easy familiarity permitted to this most intimate of courtiers, the associate of all royal follies.

Gustavus looked over his shoulder as he entered.

"Why, Bjelke, " he exclaimed, "I thought you had gone into the country! "

"I am at a loss, " replied Bjelke, "to imagine what should have given Your Majesty so mistaken an impression. " And he might have smiled inwardly to observe how his words seemed to put Gustavus out of countenance.

The King laughed, nevertheless, with an affectation of ease.

"I inferred it from your absence from Court on such a night. What has been keeping you? " But, without waiting for an answer, he fired another question. "What do you say to my domino, Bjelke? "

It was a garment embroidered upon a black satin ground with tongues of flame so cunningly wrought in mingling threads of scarlet and gold that as he turned about now they flashed in the candlelight, and seemed to leap like tongues of living fire.

"Your Majesty will have a great success, " said Bjelke, and to himself relished the full grimness of his joke. For a terrible joke it was, seeing that he no longer intended to discharge the errand which had brought him in such haste to the palace.

"Faith, I deserve it! " was the flippant answer, and he turned again to the mirror to adjust a patch on the left side of his chin. "There is genius in this domino, and it is not the genius of Francois, for the scheme of flames is my very own, the fruit of a deal of thought and study. "

There Gustavus uttered his whole character. As a master of the revels, or an opera impresario, this royal rake would have been a complete success in life. The pity of it was that the accident of birth should have robed him in the royal purple. Like many another prince who has come to a violent end, he was born to the wrong metier.

"I derived the notion, " he continued, "from a sanbenito in a Goya picture. "

"An ominous garb, " said Bjelke, smiling curiously. "The garment of the sinner on his way to penitential doom. "

Armfelt cried out in a protest of mock horror, but Gustavus laughed cynically.

"Oh, I confess that it would be most apt. I had not thought of it. "

His fingers sought a pomatum box, and in doing so displaced a toilet-case of red morocco. An oblong paper package fell from the top of this and arrested the King's attention.

"Why, what is this? " He took it up - a letter bearing the superscription:

To His MAJESTY THE KING
SECRET AND IMPORTANT

"What is this, Francois? " The royal voice was suddenly sharp.

The valet glided forward, whilst Armfelt rose from the divan and, like Bjelke, attracted by the sudden change in the King's tone and manner, drew near his master.

"How comes this letter here? "

The valet's face expressed complete amazement. It must have been placed there in his absence an hour ago, after he had made all preparations for the royal toilette. It was certainly not there at the time, or he must have seen it.

With impatient fingers Gustavus snapped the seal and unfolded the letter. Awhile he stood reading, very still, his brows knit.

Then, with a contemptuous "Poof! " he handed it to his secretary.

At a glance Bjelke recognized the hand for that of Colonel Lillehorn, one of the conspirators, whose courage had evidently failed him in the eleventh hour. He read:

SIRE, - Deign to heed the warning of one who, not being in your service, nor solicitous of your favours, flatters not your crimes, and yet desires to avert the danger threatening you. There is a plot to assassinate you which would by now have been executed but for the countermanding of the ball at the opera last week. What was not done then will certainly be done to-night if you afford the opportunity. Remain at home and avoid balls and public gatherings for the rest of the year; thus the fanaticism which aims at your life will evaporate.

"Do you know the writing? " Gustavus asked.

Bjelke shrugged. "The hand will be disguised, no doubt, " he evaded.

277

"But you will heed the warning, Sire? " exclaimed, Armfelt, who had read over the secretary's shoulder, and whose face had paled in reading.

Gustavus laughed contemptuously. "Faith, if I were to heed every scaremonger, I should get but little amusement out of life. "

Yet he was angry, as his shifting colour showed. The disrespectful tone of the anonymous communication moved him more deeply than its actual message. He toyed a moment with a hair-ribbon, his nether lip thrust out in thought. At last he rapped out an oath of vexation, and proffered the ribbon to his valet.

"My hair, Francois, " said he, "and then we will be going. "

"Going! "

It was an ejaculation of horror from Armfelt, whose face was now as white as the ivory-coloured suit he wore.

"What else? Am I to be intimidated out of my pleasures? " Yet that his heart was less stout than his words his very next question showed. "Apropos, Bjelke, what was the reason why you countermanded the ball last week? "

"The councillors from Gefle claimed Your Majesty's immediate attention, " Bjelke reminded him.

"So you said at the time. But the business seemed none so urgent when we came to it. There was no other reason in your mind - no suspicion? "

His keen, dark blue eyes were fixed upon the pale masklike face of the secretary.

That grave, almost stern countenance relaxed into a smile.

"I suspected no more than I suspect now, " was his easy equivocation. "And all that I suspect now is that some petty enemy is attempting to scare Your Majesty. "

"To scare me? " Gustavus flushed to the temples. "Am I a man to be scared? "

"Ah, but consider, Sire, and you, Bjelke, " Armfelt was bleating. "This may be a friendly warning. In all humility, Sire, let me suggest that you incur no risk; that you countermand the masquerade. "

"And permit the insolent writer to boast that he frightened the King? " sneered Bjelke.

"Faith, Baron, you are right. The thing is written with intent to make a mock of me. "

"But if it were not so, Sire? " persisted the distressed Armfelt. And volubly he argued now to impose caution, reminding the King of his enemies, who might, indeed, be tempted to go the lengths of which the anonymous writer spoke. Gustavus listened, and was impressed.

"If I took heed of every admonition, " he said, "I might as well become a monk at once. And yet - " He took his chin in his hand, and stood thoughtful, obviously hesitating, his head bowed, his straight, graceful figure motionless.

Thus until Bjelke, who now desired above all else the very thing he had come hot-foot to avert, broke the silence to undo what Armfelt had done.

"Sire, " he said, "you may avoid both mockery and danger, and yet attend the masquerade. Be sure, if there is indeed a plot, the assassins will be informed of the disguise you are to wear. Give me your flame-studded domino, and take a plain black one for yourself. "

Armfelt gasped at the audacity of the proposal,

but Gustavus gave no sign that he had heard. He continued standing in that tense attitude, his eyes vague and dreamy. And as if to show along what roads of thought his mind was travelling, he uttered a single word a name - in a questioning voice scarce louder than a whisper.

Ankarstrom?

Later again he was to think of Ankarstrom, to make inquiries concerning him, which justifies us here in attempting to follow those thoughts of his. They took the road down which his conscience pointed. Above all Swedes he had cause to fear John Jacobi

Ankarstrom, for, foully as he had wronged many men in his time, he had wronged none more deeply than that proud, high-minded nobleman. He hated Ankarstrom as we must always hate those whom we have wronged, and he hated him the more because he knew himself despised by Ankarstrom with a cold and deadly contempt that at every turn proclaimed itself.

That hatred was more than twenty years old. It dated back to the time when Gustavus had been a vicious youth, and Ankarstrom himself a boy. They were much of an age. Gustavus had put upon his young companion an infamous insult, which had been answered by a blow. His youth and the admitted provocation alone had saved Ankarstrom from the dread consequence of striking a Prince of the Royal Blood. But they had not saved him from the vindictiveness of Gustavus. He had kept his lust of vengeance warm, and very patiently had he watched and waited for his opportunity to destroy the man, who had struck him.

That chance had come four years ago - in 1788 - during the war with Russia. Ankarstrom commanded the forces defending the island of Gothland. These forces were inadequate for the task, nor was the island in a proper state of defence, being destitute of forts. To have persevered in resistance might have been heroic, but it would have been worse than futile, for not only would it have entailed the massacre of the garrison, but it must have further subjected the inhabitants to all the horrors of sack and pillage.

In the circumstances, Ankarstrom had conceived it his duty to surrender to the superior force of Russia, thereby securing immunity for the persons and property of the inhabitants. In this the King perceived his chance to indulge his hatred. He caused Ankarstrom to be arrested and accused of high treason, it being alleged against him that he had advised the people of Gothland not to take up arms against the Russians. The royal agents found witnesses to bear false evidence against Ankarstrom, with the result that he was sentenced to twenty years' imprisonment in a fortress. But the sentence was never carried out. Gustavus had gone too far, as he was soon made aware. The feelings against him which hitherto had smouldered flamed out at this crowning act of injustice, and to repair his error Gustavus made haste, not, indeed, to exonerate Ankarstrom from the charges brought against him, but to pardon him for his alleged offences.

When the Swedish nobleman was brought to Court to receive this pardon, he used it as a weapon against the King whom he despised.

"My unjust judges, " he announced in a ringing voice, the echoes of which were carried to the ends of Sweden, "have never doubted in their hearts my innocence of the charges brought against me, and established by means of false witnesses. The judgment pronounced against me was unrighteous. This exemption from it is my proper due. Yet I would rather perish through the enmity of the King than live dishonoured by his clemency. "

Gustavus had set his teeth in rage when those fierce words were reported to him, and his rage had been increased when he was informed of the cordial reception which everywhere awaited Ankarstrom on his release. He perceived how far he had overshot his mark, and how, in seeking treacherously to hurt Ankarstrom, he had succeeded only in hurting himself. Nor had he appeased the general indignation by his pardon. True, the flame of revolt had been quelled. But he had no lack of evidence that the fire continued to burn steadily in secret, and to eat its way further and further into the ranks of noble and simple alike.

It is little wonder, then, that in this moment, with that warning lying there before him, the name of Ankarstrom should be on his lips, the thought of Ankarstrom, the fear of Ankarstrom, looming big in his mind. It was big enough to make him heed the warning. He dropped into a chair.

"I will not go, " he said, and Bjelke saw that his face was white, his hands shaking.

But when the secretary had repeated the proposal which had earlier gone unheard, Gustavus caught at it with sudden avidity, and with but little concern for the danger that Bjelke might be running. He sprang up, applauding it. If a conspiracy there was, the conspirators would thus be trapped; if there were no conspiracy, then this attempt to frighten him should come to nothing; thus he would be as safe from the mockery of his enemies as from their knives. Nor did Armfelt protest or make further attempts to dissuade him from going. In the circumstances proposed by Bjelke, the risk would be Bjelke's, a matter which troubled Armfelt not at all; indeed, he had no cause to love Bjelke, in whom he beheld a formidable rival, and it would be to him no cause for tears if the knife intended for the royal vitals should find its way into Bjelke's instead.

So Baron Bjelke, arrayed in the domino copied from the penitential sack, departed for the Opera House, leaving Gustavus to follow. Yet, despite the measure of precaution, no sooner had the masked King himself entered the crowded theatre, leaning upon the arm of the Count of Essen, than he conceived that he beheld confirmation of the warning, and regretted that he had not heeded it to the extent of remaining absent. For one of the first faces he beheld, one of the few unmasked faces in that brilliantly lit salon, was the face of Ankarstrom, and Ankarstrom appeared to be watching the entrance.

Gustavus checked in his stride, a tremor ran through him, and he stiffened in his sudden apprehension, for the sight of the tall figure and haughty, resolute face of the nobleman he had wronged was of more significance than at first might seem. Ever since his infamous trial Ankarstrom had been at pains to seize every occasion of marking his contempt for his Prince. Never did he fail upon the King's appearance in any gathering of which he was a member to withdraw immediately; and never once had he been known deliberately to attend any function which was to be graced by the presence of Gustavus. How, then, came he here to this ball given by the King's own command unless he came for the fell purpose of which the letter had given warning?

The King's impulse was to withdraw immediately. He was taken by a curious, an almost unreasoning, fear that was quite foreign to him, who, for all his faults, had never yet lacked courage. But, even as he hesitated, a figure swept past him in a domino flecked with flames, surrounded by revellers of both sexes, and he remembered that if Ankarstrom were bent on evil his attention would be held by that figure before which the crowd fell back, and opened out respectfully, believing it to be the King's. Yet none the less it was Gustavus himself that Ankarstrom continued to regard in such a ay that the King had a feeling that his mask was made of glass.

And then quite suddenly, even as he was on the point of turning, another wave of revellers swept frantically up, and in a moment Gustavus and the Count of Essen were surrounded. Another moment and the buffeting crowd had separated him from his grand equerry. He found himself alone in the centre of this knot of wild fellows who, seeming to mistake him for one of themselves, forced him onward with them in their career. For a moment he attempted to resist. But as well might he have resisted a torrent. Their rush was not to be stemmed. It almost swept him from his feet, and to save himself he must perforce abandon himself to the impetus. Thus he was swirled away across the floor of the amphitheatre, helpless as a swimmer in strong waters, and with the fear of the drowning clutching now at his heart.

He had an impulse to unmask, proclaim himself, and compel the respect that was his due. But to do so might be to expose himself to the very danger of whose presence he was now convinced. His only hope must lie in allowing himself to be borne passively along until a chance opening allowed him to escape from these madmen.

The stage had been connected with the floor of the theatre by a broad flight of wooden steps. Up this flight he was carried by that human wave. But on the stage itself he found an anchorage at last against one of the wings. Breathing hard, he set his back to it, waiting for the wave to sweep on and leave him. Instead, it paused and came to rest with him, and in that moment some one touched him on the shoulder. He turned his head, and looked into the set face of Ankarstrom, who was close behind him. Then a burning, rending pain took him in his side, and he grew sick and dizzy. The uproar of voices became muffled; the lights were merged into a luminous billow that swelled and shrank and then went out altogether.

The report of the pistol had been lost in the general din to all but those who stood near the spot where it had been fired. And these found themselves suddenly borne backwards by the little crowd of maskers that fell away from the figure lying prone and bleeding on the stage.

Voices were raised, shouting "Fire! Fire! " Thus the conspirators sought to create confusion, that they might disperse and lose themselves in the general crowd. That confusion, however, was very brief. It was stemmed almost immediately by the Count of Essen, who leapt up the steps to the stage with a premonition of what had happened. He stooped to rip away the mask from the face of the victim, and, beholding, as he had feared, the livid countenance of his King, he stood up, himself almost as pale.

"Murder has been done! " he roared. "Let the doors be closed and guarded, and let no one leave the theatre. " Instantly was his bidding done by the officers of the guard.

Those of the King's household who were in attendance came forward now to raise Gustavus, and help to bear him to a couch. There presently he recovered consciousness, whilst a physician was seeing to his hurt, and as soon as he realized his condition his manner became so calm that, himself, he took command of the situation. He issued orders that the gates of the city should be closed against everybody, whilst himself apologizing to the Prussian minister who was near him for issuing that inconvenient but necessary order.

"The gates shall remain closed for three days, sir, " he announced. "During that time you will not be able to correspond with your Court; but your intelligence, when it goes, will be more certain, since by that time it should be known whether I can survive or not. "

His next order, delivered in a voice that was broken by his intense suffering, was to the chamberlain Benzelstjerna, commanding that all present should unmask and sign their names in a book before being suffered to depart. That done, he bade them bear him home on the couch on which he had been placed that he might be spared the agony of more movement than was necessary.

Thus his grenadiers bore him on their shoulders, lighted by torches, through the streets that were now thronged, for the rumour had now gone forth that the King was dead, and troops had been called out to keep order. Beside him walked Armfelt in his suit of shimmering white satin, weeping at once for his King and for himself, for he knew that he was of those who must fall with Gustavus. And, knowing this, there was bitter rage in his heart against the men who had wrought this havoc, a rage that sharpened his wits to an unusual acuteness.

At last the King was once more in his apartments awaiting the physicians who were to pronounce his fate, and Armfelt kept him company among others, revolving in his mind the terrible suspicion he had formed.

Presently came Duke Charles, the King's brother, and Benzelstjerna with the list of those who had been present at the ball.

"Tell me, " he asked, before the list was read to him, "is the name of Ankarstrom included in it? "

"He was the last to sign, Sire, " replied the chamberlain.

The King smiled grimly. "Tell Lillesparre to have him arrested and questioned. "

Armfelt flung forward. "There is another who should be arrested, too! " he cried fiercely. And added, "Bjelke! "

"Bjelke? "

The King echoed the name almost in anger at the imputation. Armfelt spoke torrentially. "It was he persuaded you to go against your own judgment when you had the warning, and at last induced you to it by offering to assume your own domino. If the assassins sought the King, how came they to pass over one who wore the King's domino, and to penetrate your own disguise that was like a dozen others? Because they were informed of the change. But by whom - by whom? Who was it knew? "

"My God! " groaned the unfortunate King, who had in his time broken faith with so many, and was now to suffer the knowledge of this broken faith in one whom he had trusted above all others.

Baron Bjelke was arrested an hour later, arrested in the very act of entering his own home. The men of Lillesparre's police had preceded him thither to await his return. He was quite calm when they surged suddenly about him, laid hands upon him, and formally pronounced him their prisoner.

"I suppose, " he said, "it was to have been inferred. Allow me to take my leave of the Baroness, and I shall be at your disposal. "

"My orders, Baron, are explicit, " he was answered by the officer in charge. "I am not to suffer you out of my sight. "

"How? Am I to be denied so ordinary a boon? " His voice quivered with sudden anger and something else.

"Such are my orders, Baron. "

Bjelke pleaded for five minutes' grace for that leavetaking. But the officer had his orders. He was no more than a machine. The Baron raised his clenched hands in mute protest to the heavens, then let them fall heavily.

"Very well, " he said, and suffered them to thrust him back into his carriage and carry him away to the waiting Lillesparre.

He found Armfelt in the office of the chief of the police, haranguing Ankarstrom, who was already there under arrest. The favourite broke off as Bjelke was brought in.

"You were privy to this infamy, Bjelke, " he cried. "If the King does not recover - "

"He will not recover. " It was the cold, passionless voice of Ankarstrom that spoke. "My pistol was loaded with rusty nails. I intended to make quite sure of ridding my country of that perjured tyrant. "

Armfelt stared at the prisoner a moment with furious, bloodshot eyes. Then he broke into imprecations, stemmed only when Lillesparre ordered Ankarstrom to be removed. When he was gone, the chief of police turned to Bjelke.

"It grieves me, Baron, that we should meet thus, and it is with difficulty that I can believe what is alleged against you. Baron Armfelt is perhaps rendered hasty by his grief and righteous anger. But I hope that you will be able to explain - at least to deny your concern in this horrible deed. "

Very tense and white stood Bjelke.

"I have an explanation that should satisfy you as a man of honour, " he said quietly, "but not as chief of the police. I joined this conspiracy that I might master its scope and learn the intentions of the plotters. It was a desperate thing I did out of love and loyalty to the King, and I succeeded. I came to-night to the palace with information which should not only have saved the King's life, but would have enabled him to smother the conspiracy for all time. On the threshold of his room this letter for the King was delivered into my hands. Read it, Lillesparre, that you may know precisely what manner of master you serve, that you may understand how

Gustavus of Sweden recompenses love and loyalty. Read it, and tell me how you would have acted in my place! "

And he flung the letter on to the writing-table at which sat Lillesparre.

The chief of police took it up, began to read, turned back to the superscription, then resumed his reading, a dull flush overspreading his face. Over his shoulder Armfelt, too, was reading. But Bjelke cared not. Let all the world behold that advertisement of royal infamy, that incriminating love-letter from Bjelke's wife to the King who had dishonoured him.

Lillesparre was stricken dumb. He dared not raise his eyes to meet the glance of the prisoner. But the shameless Armfelt sucked in a breath of understanding.

"You admit your guilt, then? " he snarled.

"That I sent the monster to the masquerade, knowing that there the blessed hand of Ankarstrom would give him his passport out of a world he had befouled - yes. "

"The rack shall make you yield the name of every one of the conspirators. "

"The rack! " Bjelke smiled disdainfully, and shrugged. "Your men, Lillesparre, were very prompt and very obdurate. They would not allow me to take leave of the Baroness, so that she has escaped me. But I am not sure that it is not a fitter vengeance to let her live and remember. That letter may now be delivered to the King, for whom it is intended. Its fond messages may lighten the misery of his remaining hours. "

His face was contorted, with rage, thought Armfelt, who watched him, but in reality with pain caused by the poison that was corroding his vitals. He had drained a little phial just before stepping into the presence of Lillesparre, as they discovered upon inquiries made after he had collapsed dead at their feet.

This caused them to bring back Ankarstrom, that he might be searched, lest he, too, should take some similar way of escaping them. When he search was done, having discovered nothing,

Lillesparre commanded that he should not have knife or fork or metal comb, or anything with which he might take his life.

"You need not fear that I shall seek to evade the sacrifice, " he assured them, his demeanour haughty, his eyes aglow with fanatic zeal. "It is the price I pay for having rid Nature of a monster and my country of a false, perjured tyrant, and I pay it gladly. " As he ceased he smiled, and drew from the gold lace of his sleeve a surgeon's lancet. "This was supplied me against my need to open a vein. But the laws of God and man may require my death upon the scaffold. "

And, smiling, he placed the lancet on Lillesparre's table.

Upon his conviction execution followed, and it lasted three days - from April 19th to 21 st - being attended by all the horrible and gradual torturings reserved for regicides. Yet possibly he did not suffer more than his victim, whose agony had lasted for thirteen days, and who perished miserably in the consciousness that he deserved his fate, whilst Ankarstrom was uplifted and fortified by his fanaticism.

The scaffold was erected on the Stora Torget, facing the Opera House of Stockholm, where the assassination had taken place. Thence the dismembered remains of Ankarstrom were conveyed to the ordinary gallows in the suburb of Sodermalm to be exhibited, the right hand being nailed below the head. Under this hand on the morrow was found a tablet bearing the legend:

Blessed the hand That saved the Fatherland.

Printed in the United States
99525LV00002B/68/A

9 781406 542622